Young Lions Hunt

Andrew Mackay

Published by New Generation Publishing in 2013

www.newgeneration-publishing.com

 New Generation Publishing

Young Lions Hunt is dedicated to
Herbert Blake who served in the
Royal Air Force during World War Two.

Chapter One

"It's falling as thick as a snow storm out there, sir," Alan Mitchell said with a despondent shake of his head.

"I know, Alan, but we can't go over it and we can't go under it; we'll just have to go through it,"Captain John Baldwin said grimly.

"Yes, sir." Alan gulped with difficulty. His throat felt as dry as a desert.

"Remember what I told you, men: I want you to run for your lives across that bridge. Don't stop for anything or for anyone. Clear?"

"Clear, sir," the Blackshirts chorused.

"Good." Baldwin bared his teeth like a wolf. "Then I'll see you on the other side. Strength and honour, gentlemen."

"Strength and honour, sir."

"Lieutenant, we have had absolutely no reports of the Tommies penetrating our defensive perimeter. You are spreading panic and alarm; calm down and pull yourself together!"

"But we must retreat! We must cross over the bridge! The Reds will kill us if they catch us!" The Blackshirt officer's claw like fingers dug into the shirt of the German Military Policeman with the desperate strength of a drowning man.

"Let go of me at once, young man, or I warn you …!"

"What's going on here, Hauptwachtmeister Bratge?"An angry voice demanded.

"Hauptmann Schiffler," Bratge came to a position of attention and saluted. "This Blackshirt officer says that the Tommies have broken through and are on their way here …"

"They'll be here any minute!" The young Blackshirt officer interrupted with a hysterical high-pitched voice. "They've killed the rest of my men! We're all that's left!" He pointed to his three remaining soldiers. "The Reds will hang me and my men as traitors if they catch us! I must get my boys over the bridge to safety."

"And you are?" Schiffler asked.

Schiffler's dulcet tones seemed to have a calming effect on the young Blackshirt officer's frayed nerves. He recovered his composure, came to a position of attention and gave the Fascist salute, "Hail Joyce! Second-Lieutenant Colin Tyndall, 1st Battalion, Griffiths Brigade, British Union of Fascists Militia, at your service, sir."

"Tyndall?"Bratge repeated with raised eyebrows. "You are not, by any chance, related to Arthur Tyndall, the Deputy Prime Minister?"

"He's my father, Sergeant-Major," Tyndall puffed out his chest with pride as he answered. His breathing was gradually slowing down and his face was returning to its normal colour.

"So you are a bona fide Fascist? Like Prime Minster Joyce himself?" Schiffler said with a raised eyebrow of amusement.

"Yes, sir. I fought alongside my father and the prime minister against the Reds and the Jews in the streets of London before the war." Tyndall seemed to grow an extra inch in his jackboots.

"So you were a street fighter, young Tyndall?" Schiffler asked with interest.

"Yes, sir," Tyndall grinned. "This isn't the first time that I've shed Bolshevik blood for the cause."

5

"I see." Schiffler turned to face the M.P. sergeant major and switched to speaking German. "Hauptwachtmeister Bratge?"

"Yes, sir?"

"Shoot him."

"Sir?"

"Shoot him."Schiffler pointed at Tyndall. "Right here, right now in front of everyone. We're not going to argue with these people. Shoot him on my command with my authority."

Bratge was momentarily lost for words. "But, sir … I've seen this sort of thing before, during the last war," he reasoned. "Young Tyndall has temporarily lost his nerves, sir. He just needs a bit of time away from the front line. He'll recover his courage soon enough, sir, you'll see."

"Time is a luxury that we do not have, Hauptwachtmeister …"

"Tyndall is the son of a powerful Fascist, sir!"

"Then he should have known better!" Schiffler snarled. "Tyndall is a defeatist, a coward and a deserter and the penalty for desertion is death!"

"But, sir …!"

"I'm sure that I don't have to remind you of the penalty for disobeying the orders of a superior officer, Hauptwachtmeister Bratge." Schiffler's voice dripped with venom.

"No, sir. You don't have to warn me." Bratge's shoulders slumped with despair and defeat. He breathed out a heavy sigh of resignation, cocked his Schmessier, flicked off the safety catch and turned to face Tyndall.

"What the-!" Tyndall's eyes bulged as he raised his hands in shock and confusion.

"I'm sorry, son," Bratge said as he shook his head. "I told you to calm down."

"But I was only protecting my men! I was only doing my job!"

"And I'm only doing mine," Schiffler said.

Tyndall looked like a cornered animal as he searched for a means of escape. At last he realised that resistance was futile and his shoulders slumped with resignation. As he recognized and accepted his fate he seemed to recover some of his pride and self-control. Tyndall took a deep breath and straightened his shoulders to a position of attention. "It will take more than this to win the war," Tyndall said defiantly.

"Yes, you're probably right," Schiffler replied. "Hauptwachtmeister?"

Bratge fired a three second burst of bullets at the helpless Blackshirt and Tyndall collapsed to the ground where he lay in a bloody heap. Bratge flicked on his safety catch and slung his weapon on his shoulder. He withdrew his Luger from his holster and shot the young Fascist in the back of the head. "Se acabó, amigo."

"The rest of you men are free to go," Schiffler said. "Return to your positions and nothing more will be mentioned of this matter. I give you my word as an officer and a gentleman."

The three surviving Blackshirts looked at the German captain with disbelief at their lucky escape and tripped over themselves in their haste and hurry to get away. "Thank you … thank you, sir." One of the young Fascists managed to blurt out as he stumbled over the broken bricks and rubble.

Bratge looked at the rapidly disappearing Blackshirts with a heavy heart. As far as he was concerned, he had just committed murder.

A sudden burst of machine gun fire cut down the running Fascists. Bratge turned around with a look of complete shock and horror on his face.

Schiffler was calmly changing his empty Schmessier magazine for a full one. "We can't leave any witnesses alive to whinge and whine to daddy, can we?"

"But … but you promised …?" Bratge protested with wide-eyed disbelief.

"I lied."

"I say, that was a bit harsh," Alan commented as he watched the execution of the four Blackshirt deserters.

"Harsh?" Baldwin guffawed. "That was nothing compared to what I saw in Spain. Anyway, what does it matter whether we kill the Blackshirts or the Nazis do the job for us? The only good Fascist is a dead Fascist and it doesn't matter whether British or German bullets do the job. Good riddance to bad rubbish, I say."

"Hear, hear, sir," Corporal Trevor Rees said. "And you must admit that there is a certain irony in the fact that German Nazis are killing British Fascists. It seems that Fate is not without a sense of humour." Rees and O' Brien had served together in the Royal Engineers during the First World War and they had joined the British Union of Fascists shortly after it had been formed with the express purpose of infiltrating and destroying the party from the inside. They had volunteered their services to MI5 at the start of the Spanish Civil War in 1936 and had been spying on the BUF ever since.

"I'm glad that the execution appeals to your somewhat twisted sense of humour, Sergeant, although I must admit that it tickled my funny bone as well," Baldwin conceded. "However, I had hoped to get across the bridge with the minimum of fuss and bother. These jobs worthy policemen have well and truly thrown a spanner in the works. I very much doubt if

Sherlock Holmes and his faithful Watson are simply going to let us waltz across."

"Sir, if I may," Sergeant Terry O'Brien said with a smile on his face, "I have a cunning plan …"

Bratge grimaced and wrinkled his nose with distaste as he lifted up the blood soaked great coat. The intestines lay curled and coiled up on the stomach of the young Blackshirt like a string of bloody sausages. The wounded Fascist's face was deathly pale and his hair was matted together in a disgusting mixture of blood, sweat and general grime.

"I don't think that he's going to make it, Captain," Bratge said.

"I've got to try …"the Blackshirt captain replied. "He's my brother."

"All right, sir." Bratge put his hand on the Fascist's shoulder. "Over you go."

"Thank you, Sergeant- Major."

"Good Luck." Bratge watched as the three Blackshirts picked up the stretcher carrying their wounded comrade and started to cross the bridge. God only knew that he hated Fascists, and especially turn coat Fascists, but he could not help but feel pity for the wounded young Blackshirt who should have been safely studying at school not bleeding his life away with his guts hanging out on a battlefield. He would surely die before the break of dawn and would soon be good for nothing more than food for the crows.

"Easy, boys! I'm not a sack of potatoes!"

"Simmer down, Alan me lad: You're supposed to be dying!" O'Brien chuckled.

"And I'll soon be dead if you don't stop shaking me around like a cocktail shaker!" Alan protested only half-jokingly.

9

"Listen to you," O'Brien said, "being carried around like the Maharajah of Jodhpur! Honestly, some people don't know that they're living! Mister Baldwin, what do you-?"

A massive explosion suddenly covered the stretcher party with a shower of water. It was as if someone had tipped the contents of an entire bath of cold water over them. They were all completely soaked to the skin.

"What the-?" Alan said as one corner of the stretcher suddenly dropped and he tumbled out onto the shrapnel pitted and explosion scarred deck of the bridge.

"Where's Trev?" Baldwin asked as he slowly got to his feet.

"He's gone," O'Brien answered with a blank stare as he knelt on his knees.

"Gone?"

"He must've been blown into the river ..." O'Brien mumbled in a dazed and confused monotone.

"Christ," Baldwin swore. "He was running right beside me ..."

"Trev always said that when he found the time he would like to learn how to swim. And when he finally did find the time the war came along. That's Sod's law for you." O'Brien shook his head sadly.

"Trev would probably still have drowned with that massive radio on his back, Terry. He would've had a hard time getting it off in the middle of a fast flowing river without anyone to help him." Baldwin walked up to O'Brien and draped his arm across the Irishman's massive shoulders and gave him a comforting squeeze. "Come on, Terry," Baldwin said. "Let's get going." He pulled O'Brien to his feet.

"Yes, sir," O'Brien said as he wiped a filthy battledress sleeve across his tear stained eyes. "Alan, give me a hand loading that wounded Fascist onto this

10

stretcher will you? It's time to get some pay back for Trev."

"What have you got in mind, Sergeant?"

"I want to pour fuel on their fire," O'Brien said with a wicked glint in his eye.

"What have we got here?"

"A wounded Militiaman, Doctor," the nurse answered. "The Blackshirt captain insisted that we treated him as a matter of urgency. He said that this boy was his brother. I thought that in the interests of German-British relations that we …"

The doctor smiled kindly. "It's all right, Sister, I understand." He put a reassuring hand on her shoulder. "You did the right thing. Now, let's inspect the damage…"He lifted up the bloody greatcoat that covered the wounded Fascist. "Hmmnnn … nasty wound, Sister, it looks like he's been shot in the stomach."

"Yes, Doctor."

"Help me roll him onto his side so that we can see if there's an exit wound in his back."

"Certainly, Doctor." The young nurse slid an arm under the wounded Blackshirt's neck and carefully began to roll him onto his side. Her eyes suddenly bulged wide with horror. " Grenade-!"

The three grenades blew up and completely shredded the wounded Fascist, the nurse and the doctor. They had been booby-trapped to explode if the Militiaman was moved. The explosion started a fire that soon burned and raged out of control and led to the frantic evacuation of the recently wounded patients. The Mobile Army Surgical Hospital was burnt to the ground in a fiery inferno and so much vital lifesaving equipment was destroyed or damaged and so many doctors and nurses were killed or wounded that the M.A.S.H. unit was declared inoperative.

The ambulance came to a halt and the driver opened the door and slowly climbed down. His companion climbed down from the passenger seat.

"What are we supposed to do with all of the wounded?" The passenger asked as he pointed at the raging inferno that used to be a hospital.

"I don't know, Walter," the driver shrugged his shoulders, "but we can't leave the wounded in the ambulance. We need to go back to the Front to pick up some more."

"We can unload them all and leave them here, Erich," Walter suggested. "After all, it's our job to deliver them, not to treat them. That's not our responsibility."

Erich seemed to struggle with this idea for a moment before he reluctantly agreed. "We'll unload the wounded, but before we drive off we need to hand over responsibility to someone in authority. Agreed?"

Walter smiled. "Whatever you say, boss."

It took the two men ten minutes to unload the six stretcher cases from the ambulance.

"Look sharp," Erich warned. "Officer approaching."

The two men braced their shoulders and came to a position of attention as the small group of men approached.

"It's all right, Erich," Walter said, "They're not Germans: they're Askaris."

The three Blackshirts emerged from the shadows.

"Ev'nin', gents," O'Brien said genially.

"Good evening, Sergeant-Major." Erich smiled as he recognized the Blackshirt's rank insignia. He was keen to develop his English in order to improve his chances of chatting up the English bar maids. "By the way, I meant no offense by calling you 'Askaris.' It is just the term that the old Africa hands use to describe Tommies who fight on our side. It's become a popular phrase throughout the army."

O'Brien smiled and held up his hands. "No offense taken, Corporal. I've been called far worse."

I bet, Erich thought to himself. Fascist, collaborator, traitor and worse I'll wager. The German kept his thoughts to himself.

"Full tank?" O'Brien asked.

"Excuse me?" Erich said with a puzzled expression on his face.

"Full tank. Of petrol?"

"Ah, no. Half," Erich answered. He noticed for the first time the young Blackshirt captain who was busy inspecting the ambulance and who had so far remained silent.

"I like your ambulance," the Fascist officer said with a full-toothed smile.

Hauptsturmführer Manfred von Stein lowered his binoculars and spoke in a hushed voice to the small group of men who were huddled about him. "Listen in, men: there's the target, Beattie Bridge. However, it looks as if our mission to capture it has failed. The Tommies are still in control." Von Stein stopped talking and gave his men time to absorb the disappointing news. The sound of excited voices talking in English drifted over from the bridge one hundred metres away. The S.S. paratroopers could hear the distinctive sound of caterpillar tracks turning as British tanks crossed the bridge.

"So what now, sir?" Rottenführer Karl Barbie asked. "The Tommies control the bridge."

"Surely we have no option but to surrender, sir?" A young S.S. trooper asked.

13

"Surrender, Hans?" Von Stein spat out the word with distaste. "Never say die!"

Colonel Juan Mendoza took off his helmet and wiped his dirt and sweat encrusted brow as he waited for his second in command to catch up with him. The Legiónaries who formed his bodyguard lay down in a formation of all round defence with their bodies positioned like the spokes of a wheel with Mendoza in the centre. Major Alfredo Astray soon caught up with his commanding officer.

"What now, Colonel?" Astray asked.

"Do you remember at the Academy when we were asked to research the 'Hinge Factor?'"

"No, Colonel," Astray replied with a puzzled frown.

"How chance and stupidity can snatch defeat from the jaws of victory?"

"No, Colonel. I must have missed that lesson." Astray stifled an imaginary yawn.

Mendoza chuckled. "You always were a bad student, Alfredo," Mendoza teased his friend mockingly.

"Studying is for women, Colonel," Astray sneered with derision. "I'm a fighter, not a student."

"Well, my Philistine friend, we are going to teach the Germans the lesson to be learned from the Battle of Karansebes."

"The Battle of what?"

"The Battle of Karansebes that was fought in 1788 between the Austrians and the Austrians."

"Between the Austrians and the Austrians?" Astray looked at Mendoza as if he was mad. "What on earth are you talking about, Jefe?"

Mendoza grinned mischievously. "It's a long story, Alfredo, but I'll make a scholar of you yet …"

Von Stein emerged soaking wet and completely and utterly exhausted from his swim across the river. He lay panting like a dog on the riverbank as he waited for the rest of his motley crew to arrive. He could see the dim and distant outline of Beattie Bridge four hundred metres to his left.

"Thank you, sir," the young storm trooper lying beside him gasped between breaths. "Thank you for rescuing me."

Von Stein shrugged off the S.S. soldier's word of thanks. "Don't mention it, Bruno; I couldn't very well leave you behind. You're one of my men and I'm responsible for you. I would be as likely to leave behind my younger brother! Besides, the Tommies would eat you alive!" Von Stein cuffed Bruno playfully on the shoulder. "You would have done the same for me. Just one word of advice, Bruno."

"Yes, sir?"

"Promise me that when we return to Hereward you'll sign up for swimming lessons?"

"I promise, sir," Bruno said with a smile.

"Good lad," von Stein said as he ruffled Bruno's hair. He counted heads as his men gradually arrived and collapsed beside him. One, two, three, four... fifteen. "Where's Hans?"

"I'm sorry, sir..." Barbie began, "I tried to hold onto him, but I couldn't...He's gone, sir."

"You what!" Von Stein exploded. "You let him go? I was going to look after Bruno, you were going to look after Hans; that was the deal that we made!"

"I'm sorry, sir, the current was too strong and I …"

Von Stein cut him dead. "You can write the letter home to his mother." He suddenly raised his head like a Golden Retriever. "Rottenführer Barbie, you and Bruno search that body that's lying over there," he pointed. "If he's dead and one of our men then collect his dog tags.

15

If he's alive and one of ours then bring him back. Understood?"

"Yes, sir!" Barbie answered as he and Bruno began to cautiously approach the body.

"Men: all round defence!" Von Stein ordered.

Barbie and Bruno soon returned with their arms supporting an unconscious figure around his waist.

"Is it Hans?" Von Stein asked hopefully.

"No, sir," Barbie shook his head. "It's Obersturmbannführer Ulrich."

"There's something wrong, sir, but I can't quite put my finger on it."

"What do you mean, Hauptwachtmeister?" Hauptmann Schiffler asked.

"Well, since we crossed to the northern bank of the river there has been a steady stream of wounded being carried across to the southern bank of the river …" Bratge replied.

"Yes, go on."

"In the beginning it was our boys, the Army; then it was the Spanish with a sprinkling of S.S. paratroopers who had somehow managed to straggle through to our lines… followed by Blackshirts. Basically, casualties have crossed the bridge to the German side in the order that they crossed the bridge to the British side in the first place."

"Yes, that all makes sense," Schiffler said. "What's your point?"

"Well recently, sir, virtually all of the casualties crossing the bridge are Blackshirts and what had been a steady stream of mixed Wehrmacht, Spanish, S.S. and Blackshirt wounded has become a Fascist flood," Bratge explained.

Schiffler snorted derisively. "Hauptwachtmeister Bratge, surely that should come as no surprise to you?

The Blackshirts are scraped from the bottom of the barrel and are the lowest of the low. Most of the 'volunteers' are murderers, rapists and child molesters who were only released on condition that they joined the Fascist Militia! Surely it should not come as a shock to you that they are cowards as well? They will try every ruse and trick in the book to escape from battle! And if that involves drawing lots in order to decide who amongst them suffers from a self-inflicted wound which results in them being evacuated from the field of battle then so be it. These Militiamen are the scum of the earth and they know all too well that they will be executed as traitors if the British capture them. And rightly so, I might add. I have no time for turncoats. These Blackshirts are all untermenschen scum as far as I am concerned."

"Perhaps you're right, sir, and there's nothing to worry about. But have you noticed how each group consists of either four of five Blackshirts? There are never fewer than four or more than five. Also there is always a junior officer in command, a second – lieutenant or perhaps as high as a captain, never an N.C.O. or an ordinary soldier."

"Well, I don't think …" Schiffler began.

"We never see a group of walking wounded trying to get across or a pair helping each other along or even a lone wounded soldier trying to make it across the bridge on his own." Bratge was thinking aloud. "The wounded are always being carried on stretchers by three or four men."

"I think that you might be getting paranoid, Hauptwachtmeister. I don't think that there's anything to be worried about."

"I hope so, sir; I hope so for all of our sakes…"

"What the hell are the Spanish doing coming back this way? They should be heading north towards the S.S. paras at the bridges," Oberleutnant Nicholas Alfonin said with a confused expression on his face as he watched three green flares explode in the sky. He saw a long column of soldiers approaching his position with their weapons held above their heads. "Halt!" Alfonin shouted. "Friend or foe?"

"Friend!" A voice shouted back.

"Advance one and be recognized!"

A lone figure advanced with his weapon held above his head until he reached a point ten metres from Alfonin's position. "Colonel Mendoza, 1st L.V.E. Infantry Regiment."

"Oberleutnant Alfonin, 1st Battalion, Potsdam Grenadiers," Alfonin came to a position of attention and saluted. "How many men do you have, Colonel?"

"About one hundred."

"All right," Alfonin nodded his head. "You and your men may enter the position, Colonel." Mendoza returned the salute, climbed over the sand bag barrier and shook Alfonin's hand.

"Sitrep, Oberleutnant?" Mendoza asked.

"We are holding the northern perimeter of Berwick-Upon-Tweed with a weak battalion of Grenadiers and Jaegers, sir ..."

"A weak battalion? I thought that two battalions crossed last night," Mendoza interrupted.

"That's correct, sir. Two battalions attempted to cross the river, but at least half of the Potsdam Grenadiers and half of the Oberschutzen Jaegers were killed before they even reached the other side. Since then more of our men have been killed or wounded clearing the town of fanatical ultra-die hard Tommies, sir. They simply refuse to give up. We are winkling them out street-by-street, house-by-house, and brick by

18

brick. We may well have to destroy Berwick- upon-Tweed in order to capture it, sir."

"I see," Mendoza said grimly. "Present friendly strength?"

"About five hundred Grenadiers and Jaegers able bodied and walking wounded who are just about able to hold a weapon at a push. There are perhaps the same number of Blackshirts who are responsible for defending the southern perimeter of the town including the bridgehead."

"Understood." Mendoza watched as his last few Legiónaries passed safely through the perimeter lines. All of his men were now positioned behind the backs of the German soldiers who continued to look to their fronts north towards the British.

Alfonin coughed. "Pardon me, Colonel Mendoza, correct me if I'm wrong, but it was my understanding that your mission was to relieve the S.S. paras at the bridges."

"It was."

Alfonin coughed again. "So ... why are you here, sir?"

"Because by the time that we got to the bridges all of the S.S. paras were dead," Mendoza answered coldly. "They had failed in their mission. The British were in control of the bridge."

"I see ..." Alfonin slowly digested the significance of the defeat. If the Germans did not control the bridges then it would be impossible to capture the road leading up to Edinburgh. The eastern part of Operation Thor had failed. "Where are the British now, sir?"

"They are hot on our heels, Oberleutnant. If you listen closely you may be able to hear the sound of their tanks."

Alfonin was completely unfazed by the unwelcome news that the British were so near with tanks. "If we act quickly we may be able to get hold of the Artillery and ask them to supply us with some anti-tank cannons," Alfonin said with fire in his eyes. "They can get them across the river on some rafts or via one of the bridges. With a little bit of luck and if the gods are smiling we may be able to keep the enemy out of Berwick yet!"

Mendoza casually glanced towards his men and collected eyes. He nodded at Astray who nodded back. Mendoza dropped his Cuban cigar on the ground and ground out the flame with the heel of his boot. He shook his head sadly. "I'm afraid that you're fresh out of luck, Oberleutnant …"

"What? What do you mean, Col-?"

Mendoza opened fire with his Schmessier machine gun and cut down Alfonin and the half a dozen soldiers standing next to him. Astray and the rest of the Legiónaries opened fire at the same time and slaughtered the unsuspecting German soldiers who died without having the chance to return fire. The soldiers were killed standing up at their posts with bullets in their backs or in their foxholes with hand grenades. German soldiers who heard the sudden burst of gunfire and rushed from their positions to aid their friends and comrades were knocked off their stride by the Spanish Legiónaries who wore almost identical uniforms as the Germans. That split second of surprise, confusion and hesitation gave the Legiónaries the edge and gave them the chance to shoot first as if in a Western show down. No reinforcements reached the scene of the massacre.

When the screaming and crying had gradually subsided into moaning and groaning Mendoza blew a long whistle blast. "Cease fire!" He shouted. "Major Astray?"

"Yes, sir?" Astray appeared at Mendoza's side and saluted.

"Reorg: distribute arms and ammo and liberate anything useful from the Germans; finish off any German wounded-I don't want any survivors. The dead don't tell tales. Pass the word: we will cut through the German and Blackshirt lines like a lightning bolt. Kill anyone and anything that gets in our way, fly over the bridge like a bat out of hell and we'll all meet together at the rendezvous point which I designated earlier. Understood?"

"Yes, sir."

"Forward on my command."

"Yes, Jefe!" Astray saluted and ran off to pass on his commanding officer's orders.

Mendoza waited until the German wounded were finished off with single shots. "Viva La Legión! Viva España!"Mendoza shouted.

"Viva La Legión! Viva España!" A hundred voices echoed.

"Forward over the bridge!"

The Legiónaries cheered in unison and surged forward like an unstoppable avalanche.

"What the hell is that noise?" Hauptwachtmeister Bratge asked with furrowed brows.

"Tanks?" Hauptmann Schiffler proposed.

Bratge shook his head. "I don't think so, sir. I think that it sounds more like a herd of stampeding wildebeest."

"You were right!"

Bratge remained rooted to the spot with shock and awe as a mob of Fascist Militiamen came running down the street as if the Devil himself was chasing them. They were tearing towards the bridge and they did not look as if they intended to stop and ask for permission to cross.

"Hauptwachtmeister, fire one burst above their heads!"

Bratge obeyed the order without question but the burst failed to halt or even slow down the herd of Blackshirts.

"Fire at the front rank!"

Bratge fired a short burst at the front rank and half a dozen Fascists fell to the ground. The Militiamen in the second rank didn't even break stride and hurdled over their fallen comrades without a moment's concern or hesitation. The following ranks grinded the dead and dying Blackshirts into the cobblestones without shame or pity.

"Hauptwachtmeister, fire a second-!"

Half a dozen German soldiers dropped as the Blackshirts returned fire. The fleeing Fascists hit the M.P.s like a bulldozing rugby scrum and rolled right over the top of them. The German soldiers who survived the initial volley of fire soon disappeared under a barrage of bullets, bayonets and rifle butts. The Militiamen surged onto the three pontoon bridges like a tsunami wave and completely overwhelmed the German reinforcements who were crossing two of the bridges in the opposite direction. The Blackshirts swarmed over the two bridges like an army of red ants attacking an elephant. Panzers, lorries and soldiers alike toppled into the Tweed and disappeared into the murky depths of the fast flowing river. The Fascists left a trail of death and destruction in their wake like a horde of marauding locusts. Dead and dying German soldiers and Militiamen lay on the bridge moaning and groaning. Lorries and panzers lay abandoned, hanging half on and half off the bridges completely blocking the way, causing a massive traffic jam.

The Legiónaries followed hot on the heels of the fleeing Fascists and hurried them on their way like wolves snapping at the heels of sheep with hysterical shouts of "The British are coming! The British are coming!" Blackshirts who tripped and stumbled onto the cobblestones were left where they fell. The Spaniards chose the path of least resistance and ran onto the bridge that the Germans had been using to transport the wounded back to the southern side of the Tweed. There were so many casualties that the Legiónaries were able to cross the river on a carpet of dead and dying Germans and Fascists without touching the wooden planking of the bridge.

When the Spaniards crossed the bridge they found a scene of utter chaos and carnage. The Blackshirts and the Germans were engaged in a Battle Royale. The Fascists were desperately trying to commandeer whatever form of transport that they could lay their hands on in order to escape from their vengeful fellow countrymen and the Germans were trying their utmost to prevent them from doing so.

"What now, Jefe?" Major Astray asked.

Colonel Mendoza looked at the murder and mayhem that surrounded him. The Legiónaries were grouped together in a tight position of all round defence. Their bayonet tipped weapons faced outwards like a bristles of a giant porcupine. Germans or Militiamen who strayed too close were dispatched without ceremony or discrimination. A barricade of dead and dying began to build up around the Spanish perimeter like a British square at the Battle of Waterloo.

"There's no way that we can steal enough lorries to transport all of us south to Hereward, Alfredo," Mendoza said. "The Blackshirts are busy stealing anything with wheels." Mendoza watched as a group of Militiamen pulled an ambulance driver and his passenger from his lorry. Their howls of protest were abruptly cut off when the fleeing Fascists silenced them with a burst of their Schmessier machine guns. " We need to get our hands on at least a dozen lorries ..." Mendoza said as he thought aloud.

"And how are we going to do that, Colonel?"

"I don't know, Alfredo, but I know one thing for sure-we're not going to find them here." Mendoza stood up. "Pass the word along, we're moving south out of the town. Forward on my command!"

"Where...where am I?" Obersturmbannführer Norbert Ulrich asked groggily.

"You're safe, sir. You're amongst friends."

"Who are you?"

"Hauptsturmführer von Stein, sir."

Ulrich launched himself at von Stein like a Jack in the Box and grabbed him around the neck with both hands. Von Stein gripped Ulrich's wrists and tried to prise them away from his throat.

"Get ... him ... off ... me!" Von Stein managed to say as Ulrich's claw like fingers started to cut off his air supply.

Barbie stood up and hit Ulrich on the back of the head with his rifle butt. Ulrich collapsed like a sack of potatoes as his lights went out and Barbie rolled him off von Stein. Von Stein lay panting on the riverbank like a fish out of water, gasping for breath through his bruised throat.

"What the hell was all that about, sir?" Barbie asked.

"Damned if I know, Karl. Maybe it was something I said."

"But you only told him your name, sir."

"I know. That's what I'm afraid of."

"What shall with do with Obersturmbannführer Ulrich, sir?" Bruno asked as he knelt beside the unconscious man.

Von Stein stood up. "Bring him along, Bruno. I'd like to find out why the Obersturmbannführer has taken such a sudden dislike to my company."

Chapter Two

"We're running out of petrol, sir," Sergeant O'Brien explained. "We'll need to fill up at the next petrol station."

"All right, Terry," Captain Baldwin said. "We're approaching the outskirts of Durham. We should be able to fill up with petrol there."

"Look, sir!" Alan pointed ahead. "A petrol station."

"Well spotted, Alan!" O'Brien said with a smile.

The lorry pulled in as dawn was breaking over the horizon. The broken spire of war-damaged Durham Cathedral was silhouetted in the distance.

"Fill her up, Sergeant," Baldwin said. The three Blackshirts climbed down from the cab and stretched their backs and their legs.

"I'm desperate for a shit," Alan announced with a pained expression on his face. "Do you think that they have a loo here?"

"Rather more information than I needed to know, Alan," Baldwin replied with a smile, "but if you do find a sit down toilet with a pull chain, toilet paper and running water be sure to let me know."

"Yes, sir!" Alan saluted and walked away gingerly.

O'Brien unscrewed the petrol tank cap and picked up the nozzle from the sole petrol pump. It took less than a minute to fill up the petrol tank.

"Hands up!" A voice shouted. "If any of you bastards move, I'll execute every one of you!"

O'Brien and Baldwin turned around and were confronted by a middle aged man wearing an old

British Army great coat. He was holding a double-barrelled shotgun in his hands.

"Take it easy, sir," O'Brien said with both hands raised high in the sky. "We only want some petrol and then we'll be on our way …"

"You were going to go on your way without paying, you thieving Blackshirt bastard!" The man accused angrily.

O'Brien turned beetroot red. The man had hit the nail on the head. He had had no intention of paying.

"Look, Mister … Stark," Baldwin read the peeling paint lettering above the garage, "we can pay you for the petrol. My wallet is in my trouser pocket."

"All right, Adolf. Take it out."

Baldwin slowly lowered his right hand to his right hip trouser pocket.

Stark watched him like a hawk. "Slowly, Adolf. Nice and easy does it."

Baldwin slowly withdrew his wallet from his pocket.

"Now, throw it over here," Stark ordered.

Baldwin did as he was told.

"Clumsy bastard," Stark snorted derisively. "You throw like a girl. My grandmother can throw farther than that." Stark bent down to pick it up from a thick clump of tangled up weeds.

"Drop your weapon!"

Stark slowly stood up and found himself staring into the face of O'Brien's Luger pistol.

"Slowly put your shotgun on the floor and take three steps backwards," O'Brien ordered.

Stark did as he was told and stood with his hands in the air. "Now what?" He asked.

"Now we pay you for the petrol and we'll be on our way," Baldwin explained.

27

There were two loud shots and O'Brien crumpled to the ground. Stark turned around as a young man burst out from the petrol station shop. He was frantically trying to reload his shotgun with cartridges from his dressing gown pocket. Baldwin ran to O'Brien, grabbed him by his webbing straps and desperately tried to turn the big Irishman over so that he could pick up the dropped pistol. The young man finished loading his shotgun and swung the weapon around to face Baldwin. There were two loud shots and the young man's knees buckled as he collapsed to the ground.

"Harry!" Stark shouted. He dropped his shotgun and ran over to the young man.

Alan ran over to Baldwin. "Sir, are you all right?" He continued to cover Stark with his Luger as he spoke to Baldwin.

"Yes, I'm all right, Alan," Baldwin answered in a daze.

O'Brien groaned. Baldwin seemed to snap out of his temporary stupor and bent down to examine the sergeant. He tenderly turned him over onto his back. O'Brien's hands tried in vain to stem the flow of blood which pumped out of his body with a regular pulse. The Irishman's face was as white as a sheet.

"Hold on, Terry, we'll get you to a hospital," Baldwin urged desperately.

O'Brien smiled weakly as a thin stream of blood trickled out of the corner of his mouth. "It's no use, Captain, I'm finished." He shook his head sadly. "I saw this type of wound many times during the War."

Baldwin nodded slowly. He'd seem similar wounds in Spain. Stomach wounds were usually fatal.

"Captain, please do one thing for me ...?"

"Yes, Terry- anything."

"Don't … don't hurt the boy. He was only defending his father. An Englishman's castle and all that …"

"Of course, Terry." Baldwin looked over at Stark. He was cradling his son's head in his lap and rocking backwards and forwards on his heels like a rocking horse. A river of tears streamed down his unwashed face. His son's unseeing eyes stared up blankly at the sky. Baldwin looked at Alan who shook his head sadly. "Terry, I'm afraid-."Baldwin stopped abruptly. O'Brien was already dead.

Hauptsturmführer Von Stein lowered the binoculars to his chest and shook his head in confusion. "I don't understand. Our panzers are going the wrong way."

"May I, sir?" Rottenführer Barbie asked.

"Certainly." Von Stein passed the binoculars over.

"The panzers are going the right way, sir."

"How's that?" Von Stein's brows furrowed with confusion.

"The problem is that they're not our panzers, sir," Barbie said grimly as he passed the binoculars back to Von Stein.

Von Stein slowly lowered the binoculars. "You're right: they're British panzers," he said with disbelief. "How did this happen?"

"We've lost control of the bridgehead, sir." Barbie answered matter of factly. "We're cut off and marooned on the wrong side of the river."

"This disaster will make the retreat from Moscow look like a Sunday stroll in the park!" Von Stein said with disgust. He looked at his motley crew of a dozen men. Von Stein sighed despondently; he had lost another three men since they had found Ulrich. None of his cold, wet and exhausted soldiers commented on the disappointing situation. They were too tired to think and too tired to care. Half of his young stormtroopers had fallen asleep in the five minutes that they had spent at the riverbank. All that his men wanted was a hot meal, a hot shower and eight hours uninterrupted sleep. And if truth be told, they were not particularly concerned about whether they enjoyed these luxuries in a German barracks or in a British prisoner of war camp. Von Stein turned back to observe the British flooding across the bridges with his binoculars.

"What now, sir?" Barbie asked.

"We cross the river," von Stein said firmly.

"How?"

Von Stein shrugged his shoulders. "I don't know yet, but where there's a will, there's a way. Vorsprung durch technik."He squeezed Barbie's shoulder. "I'll be damned if I'm going to spend the rest of this war rotting in a P.O.W. camp." He turned towards Barbie with a glint in his eyes. "Are you with me, Rottenführer?"

"To the death, Hauptsturmführer!"

Alice Roberts tore off her headphones and grinned like a cat that had got the cream.

"What is it? What are our orders?" Sam Roberts demanded impatiently. Alice passed the carefully decoded message to her brother.

Sam read the orders from Edinburgh with trembling fingers and read it again just to make sure that he had understood it correctly the first time:

ENEMY FORCES IN FULL RETREAT STOP HINDER HARASS AND HURT RETREATING ENEMY FORCES AND ENEMY REINFORCEMENTS STOP NO GENERAL UPRISING STOP SAY AGAIN STOP NO GENERAL UPRISING STOP ACKNOWLEDGE STOP

"I've acknowledged the order, Sam," Alice confirmed.

Sam nodded his head in acknowledgement. "The question is: when, where and what should be our first target?"

"I don't know what the answer is, but I think that I know someone who does."

The ambush team positioned themselves at the top of a steep hill called "The Knock" where there was a U bend in a narrow single lane road. The Knock was near Archie Leon's deserted farm on the outskirts of Hereward. Alice and Aurora positioned themselves so that they were able to look north down the hill towards Ely and Sam and Greg (Ramón Mendoza) positioned themselves so that they were able to look south down the hill towards Hereward. Each pair was armed with a MG 42 machine gun and lay down in a well-camouflaged shell scrape that provided cover from view and also cover from fire.

"Lorry approaching," Sam announced.

"Enemy or friendly?" Alice asked.

"Definitely enemy," Sam answered as he lowered his binoculars. "It's a McCarthy's fruit and veg lorry covered in camouflage paint."

"Remember the plan, comrades," Greg said. "We open fire as soon as the lorry reaches the U bend where it will be travelling at its slowest …"

"Si, Uncle Ramón," Alice and Aurora answered in unison.

"Only open fire at my command and fire in short controlled bursts," Greg continued. "I'll signal the cease fire and then Sam will check the enemy. Clear?"

"Clear!" The three youngsters chorused.

Sam rolled his eyes and shook his head. Alice and Aurora laughed. As far as the Three Musketeers were concerned Greg teaching them how to ambush the enemy was a complete waste of time and effort. Greg might as well have tried teaching them how to suck eggs.

"Do you think that this is funny? Perhaps you'd care to share the joke?" Greg asked with a schoolteacher like tone.

"I don't mean to be rude, Greg, but between the three of us, we've probably killed more Huns than you've had hot dinners," Sam replied with a cheeky chuckle.

"Well I don't mean to be rude, Sam, but the first and the last time that I took part in an ambush with you resulted in Bob, Archie and Zack being killed, so please forgive me if I am hardly overcome with confidence at the prospect of taking part in another ambush with you."

Sam thought for a moment before he replied. "Touché."

Greg nodded his head. "So let's just do this right so that we can walk away from here with our heads held high at a job well done and more importantly let's walk away from here alive. Agreed?"

"Agreed."

The lorry slowly laboured its way up the long and twisting road until it reached the U bend in the road where it slowed down even more as it changed gear.

Greg tapped Sam on his left shoulder. He immediately opened fire with a controlled three second burst. The rounds ripped through the air and tore through the open window into the cabin where they cut into the lorry commander and the driver. Alice opened fire a split second after her brother and stitched a line of bullets alongside the length of the lorry from front to rear. The rounds punched their way through the plywood bodywork as if it was made of paper. There were screams of pain and shouts of alarm as Alice and Sam continued to fire an entire belt of bullets into the lorry that had now burst into flames. They continued to rake the lorry with bullets from left to right and back again until Greg blew a whistle to cease-fire.

"Sam, check the enemy; Alice, cover him!" Greg ordered.

Sam rolled to his right away from his machine gun and picked up a Schmessier. Greg took his place behind the MG 42 with his finger resting lightly alongside the trigger guard ready to fire at a moment's notice. Sam tucked the butt of his Schmessier into his shoulder and cautiously approached the back of the lorry at a crouch. He fired a three second burst of bullets into the back of the open lorry, took a grenade out of his webbing pocket, pulled out the safety pin and threw it into the back of the vehicle. "Grenade!" He shouted as he ducked. Sam fired another half a dozen rounds into the back of the lorry and then carefully raised his machine gun to shoulder height and looked inside. "Clear!"

"Who have we killed, Sam? Army? S.S? Blackshirts?"Aurora asked excitedly as she advanced towards the smoking and smouldering lorry.

Sam hesitated before he answered. He shook his head slowly. "No, Aurora. Spaniards."

"Spaniards?" Aurora's face drained of colour as she ran to the back of the lorry. "Madre dios … they're Legiónaries … I recognize these men-they're my bodyguard." Aurora's hand went up to her mouth in horror and tears started to flow freely down her cheeks.

Alice walked up to her and wrapped an arm around her shoulders. "I'm so sorry, Aurora …"

"I murdered the men who my father ordered to protect me …"Aurora said through her sobs. "May God have mercy on my soul …" she crossed herself automatically.

"You did not murder them, Aurora," Greg said sternly. "You killed them."

"Murder? Kill?" Aurora said as she wiped away her tears. "Words are cheap- what's the difference?"

"The difference is that these men are the enemy. You don't murder the enemy, you kill them. Murdering is what these dirty Fascists do; they murdered innocent civilians at Guernica and these bastards and their Nazi friends have been doing the same ever since: - Warsaw; Rotterdam; London; the list goes on."

"So, Uncle Ramón, anyone who wears the uniform of the Fascists is the enemy, whether they are Legiónaries, Blackshirts or S.S?"

"Yes, Aurora."

"What about papa? What about your own brother? Is he your enemy?"

Greg hesitated momentarily before he answered. "Yes, Aurora, I'm afraid so: he wears the uniform of the Spanish Fascists and so unfortunately, I must treat him as the enemy," Greg replied grimly.

"What about Alan, Uncle Ramón? He wears a Blackshirt uniform, is he your enemy?"

"Alan joined the Blackshirts under orders, Aurora; he had no choice," Alice answered for Greg with an irritated edge to her voice.

"Sam was also ordered to join the Blackshirts, but he refused, didn't you Sam?" Aurora asked. Sam snorted in disgust at the very idea of joining the Fascist Militia. "Alan had a choice whether to join or not," Aurora continued. "You could argue that Alan chose to join the ranks of the enemy …"

"But not of his own free will!" Alice interrupted angrily. "He was following orders …!"

"Which Sam chose to ignore," Aurora interrupted abruptly. "And what of Norbert, Alice? He chose to join the S.S. No one forced him to. Is your boyfriend your enemy too?"

"Now, that's not fair, Aurora, and you know it," Sam jumped to the defence of his sister. "Alice was ordered to become his girlfriend. Alice has never considered him to be anything other than the enemy, isn't that right, sis?"

"Yet she is proud of his progress and his promotions, are you not, Alice? Were you ordered to feel those emotions as well? Pride? Affection, perhaps more?"

"I …" Alice had turned bright red with shame and embarrassment. She dreaded what Aurora might ask her next.

"Enough!" Greg slapped the side of the lorry angrily. "All of this is getting us nowhere! We are fighting a war against the greatest enemy that mankind has ever faced! We cannot afford to deal with legal technicalities such as whether someone was forced to join the Fascists or did so voluntarily! You're either with us or against us and that's all there is to it! All those who wear the uniform of the Fascist enemy whether Legiónary, Blackshirt, Army or S.S. are considered guilty until proven innocent. Agreed?"

"Agreed," Sam and Alice answered in unison.

"Aurora?" Greg asked.

"Agreed," Aurora answered in a soft almost inaudible voice.

"Say it!" Greg ordered with venom in his voice.

"I agree that all Fascists are to be treated as the enemy unless they have proved that they are our friends."

"Good." Greg looked into the back of the blood, guts and gore soaked lorry. "Now, let's bury all doubts about why and against whom we are fighting once and for all."

"Talking about burying, what are we going to do about all of this lot?" Sam pointed with his head at the dead Legiónaries.

"Partisans have got to fight; pigs have got to eat." Greg smiled wickedly.

Chapter Three

The wretched remnants of the routed German invasion force took the best part of a week to finally straggle their way home to their barracks. Blackshirts were the first to arrive in dribs and drabs and threes and fours on a mixture of hijacked military and civilian vehicles that were abandoned haphazardly within the grounds of the Fascist Militia barracks in Hereward. The exhausted Blackshirts collapsed onto their beds and slept the sleep of the damned for a full twelve hours, still wearing their uniforms. Their black battledresses were so deeply engrained with blood and filth that they were scarcely better than a collection of rags. Units of the von Schnakenberg Brigade arrived next in more or less complete squads or platoons mostly on Army transport. Most of the soldiers spent the first hot meal that they had eaten in nearly a week plotting and conspiring over their dining tables to produce a plan to wreak furious vengeance on the treacherous Blackshirts whom they blamed for sabotaging the invasion. Colonel Mendoza's Legiónaries won the top prize for arriving in style. They confiscated half a dozen lorries from a Blackshirt convoy that was travelling north as reinforcements en route to the Front and drove south to Newcastle where they ran out of petrol. Mendoza then commandeered a train and travelled together with his men to Hereward in the First Class cabins. When they reached Hereward they disembarked, formed up into column of three platoons and marched down Hereward High Street singing "La Cancion del Legiónario,"the Legiónary's

Song, at the top of their voices all the way to their barracks.

"Where … where am I?"

"You're safe, Norbert. You're in hospital in Hereward."

Ulrich slowly opened his eyes and looked at the figure sitting in front of him. His head hurt and he was finding it difficult to focus.

"How do you feel?" Ulrich's heart skipped a beat and he smiled as he recognized his girlfriend's voice. Alice had swapped her Schmessier for a stethoscope and was on a pre-university familiarization visit to Hereward Hospital as she was due to start studying Medicine at Girton College, Cambridge in September.

"Like I've been kicked in the chest by a bull," Ulrich smiled weakly. "What happened to me?"

"You were shot twice in the chest at point blank range."

"Then why am I still alive?"

"Do you recognise this?" Alice handed him a small shiny object.

Ulrich smiled as he turned it over in his hand. "My father's hip flask. He carried it in his breast pocket during the last war. It saved his life more than once." His fingers ran over the shrapnel scarred surface with affection. "My great grandfather carried this in his pocket during the Franco - Prussian war." Ulrich showed Alice the coat of Arms of the Hohenzollern family, the ex-German Royal family, which was engraved on the pock marked front of the flask. "My grandfather carried it during the Herero Rebellion in German South West Africa and then he gave it to my father at the beginning of the last war. My father gave it to me when I joined the S.S."

"And now the same hip flask saved your life. The Cat survives to fight another day. Your great grandfather would be proud."

Ulrich turned the flask over. There were two jagged holes on the back of the flask.

"The flask absorbed most of the force of the bullets," Alice explained. "I don't think that it's any good for holding Schnapps anymore," she chuckled.

Ulrich laughed and smiled in awe and wonder at the miracle of his escape from certain death. "How did I end up here?"

"You were evacuated from the hospital in Newcastle when the British liberated the city," Alice answered. "Your convoy was leaving the city as the British tanks were rolling in."

"The Tommies have captured Newcastle?" Ulrich sat bolt upwards in his bed in shock and winced as a sharp pain lanced across his bruised and bandaged chest.

"Yes, we launched a counter attack hot on the heels of your retreating invasion force and they have advanced as far as Morecombe Bay on the west coast and Middlesborough on the east coast. That's the new front line," Alice announced proudly.

"What are they ... what are people saying about the Invasion?" Ulrich asked sheepishly.

"The Invasion? People can't get enough of it! It's all that they talk about!" Alice snorted derisively, "It's been the front page news all week!"

"Front page news?" Ulrich's eyebrows arched with surprise. "I'm surprised that Goebbels has allowed any news to be released about such a terrible defeat."

"Terrible defeat?" Alice's brows furrowed with confusion. "What on earth are you talking about? Have those bullets damaged your brain as well as your chest? The newspapers claim that your mob have killed and captured hundreds of thousands of enemy soldiers and have captured thousands of square miles of territory."

"Hundreds of thousands of enemy soldiers?" Ulrich's head felt as if it was about to explode, "thousands of square miles of territory - we barely got over the border!"

"Well, that's not what the newspapers are saying. According to them your lot will have captured Moscow well before winter starts-."

"'Moscow?' Has everyone gone crazy? What on earth has Moscow got to do with the Invasion of Scotland?"

Alice's face lit up with understanding. She smiled as she squeezed Ulrich's hand. "I forgot! How would you know? You've been drifting in and out of consciousness for the past week. Your mob invaded Russia on June 22nd!"

"June 22nd?"

"Yes! Operation Barbarossa- the invasion of Russia!"

" But that's when we invaded Scotland!"

Alice nodded her head sympathetically. "I'm afraid that there's been no mention of the Invasion of Scotland in the papers. Most people probably don't even know that such an invasion has taken place, never mind that it has failed."

"But how have they explained away the fact that they have lost all of the land between Morecombe Bay and Middlesborough and the Scottish Border?"

Alice shrugged her shoulders. "The papers have said that it is yet another example of that war mongering gangster Churchill and his Jewish Bolshevik gang stabbing Germany in the back whilst they are trying to defend Europe against their common Communist enemy, the Soviet Union. Your lot are promising that after they've defeated Stalin they will deal with Churchill once and for all. "

"My God. I don't believe it." Ulrich held his throbbing head in his hands. "That would explain why my Brigade has been steadily weakened in the last few months with my best units being redeployed to Poland. Half of the Scottish invasion force was made up of ill equipped, under strength and unmotivated foreign units. No wonder that the Tommies gave us such a thumping. It didn't matter if we succeeded or failed as long as we acted as a diversion. The purpose of the Scottish invasion was to distract Stalin so that he was not paying attention to the invasion preparations that were taking place over the border in German occupied Poland."

"By all accounts your diversion seems to have worked: it appears as if Stalin was caught completely by surprise. The newspapers are saying that he didn't appear in public at the Kremlin and speak to the people for several days. It looks like he was in a state of shock and denial and couldn't believe that Hitler had betrayed him."

"I know exactly how he feels," Ulrich said bitterly. He shrugged his shoulders in resignation. "And in the meantime my Brigade has been virtually destroyed and the Tommies have recaptured a third of England!"

"I'd pack my bags if I was you, Norbert," Alice said with a predatory full toothed smile. "There'll soon be a new sheriff in town."

"There's no need to sound so smug about it," Ulrich huffed.

"How do you expect me to sound?" Alice asked with amusement. "I am British."

"Things will not go well for you if the British drive us out of England, Alice."

"Things are hardly going well for me at the moment, Norbert, and they can scarcely be going any worse. Let me worry about what will happen when Liberation Day comes."

"What do you mean by that? 'Things are not going well for you at the moment?' Did something happen whilst I was away?" Ulrich asked with a furrowed brow.

Alice looked away for a moment and her eyes filled up with tears. She hesitated and bit her lip before she replied. "Something did happen to me when you were away, Norbert …"

"What? What happened, Alice?" Ulrich squeezed her hand gently.

"I … we, Aurora and I were kidnapped …" Alice began with a small voice.

"What?"

"The kidnappers murdered Aurora's bodyguard and took us to Frampton-on-the -Ouse where they held us for three days. We were only freed because a Blackshirt unit was carrying out an exercise in the area."

"Mein Gott!" Ulrich's hand went up to his face.

"The Blackshirts lost sixty men trying to free us…"

"Those Partisan bastards! I swear that they will pay for their lives for this outrage!" Ulrich drove a furious fist into the palm of his hand. "Do you know how many of them there were, Alice?"

"There were at least four, maybe more. And there's something else, Norbert …" Alice grabbed his hand. "They weren't British, they were German …"

"What?" Ulrich's eyes bulged wide with shock, "Why would Germans-? Surely, you've made a mistake, Alice; how do you know that they were Germans?"

"I know that they were German, Norbert, because they spoke German all of the time and because I could

42

smell their rancid Garlic sausage and sauerkraut breath!" Alice exclaimed furiously.

Ulrich let go of Alice's hand as if it had suddenly burnt him. " ' Smell their breaths?' You don't mean-?"

Alice nodded her head as the tears flowed freely down her cheeks. "Yes, Norbert - they raped us."

"My God." Ulrich covered his mouth with his hand in horror. "I had no idea."

"I ... I was going to tell you after you got better, but now's as good a time as any ..."Alice's voice trailed off.

"Could you recognize them if you saw them?" Ulrich gently cradled Alice's hand in his own.

"No," Alice shook her head "Our heads were covered by a filthy pillow case for most of the time."

" Did they use any names?"

"Yes, they called each other Tom, Dick and Harry." Alice shrugged her shoulders. "I guess that they thought it was funny because I was English."

"I can check the list of names of everyone who deployed north to take part in the invasion and of everyone who was left behind."

"Why would anyone be left behind?"

"If they were a patient in the Brigade Sick Bay or in the hospital in Hereward, for example ..."

"Oh yes!" Alice interrupted excitedly, "I forgot, there is one name that they mentioned -."

"What was that?"

"Von Stein. Do you know him?"

"I'm glad to hear that Alan is alive and well, Aurora."

"So am I, papa!" Aurora's face lit up at the mention of her boyfriend. "When Alan phoned to tell me that he was all right I burst out crying!"

Mendoza smiled and patted his daughter's hand as Aurora's eyes filled up with tears. "I remember your

43

mother crying with relief when I phoned her after a big battle in Morocco."

"I miss her, papa."

"So do I, my little butterfly." Mendoza kissed his daughter on her forehead. "Did Alan tell you how he managed to escape?" He asked the question as casually as he could.

"Alan said that his commanding officer, Major Mason, explained that the Tommies had broken through the defensive perimeter and gave the order for a general retreat. Alan said that he and Captain Baldwin were one of the first Blackshirts to cross the bridge. He explained that if the Tommies caught any Blackshirts then they would be strung up from the nearest lamp post by their short and curlies."

" Short and curlies? " Mendoza's brow furrowed in confusion. "I'm not familiar with that particular English expression."

Aurora laughed and raised her fingers to her lips. "Oh, papa, the Tommies would hang them by their -," she pointed south with her hand.

"Ah, I see," Mendoza laughed. "How eloquent! Now I understand why Alan was so keen to escape so quickly."

"Anyway, he's safe and sound and that's what's important."

"Yes, I agree. And what have you been up to since I've been away?"

"Oh, this and that, keeping busy," Aurora answered off handedly.

"I bet." Mendoza smiled knowingly. "And Sam as well I can imagine. I have no doubt that you, Sam and Alice have been up to mischief since the invasion of Scotland began."

"I could tell you but then I'd have to kill you, papa," Aurora said with a mock serious voice.

Mendoza held up both of his hands, "I understand: on a need to know basis I don't need to know and I don't want to know either," he chuckled.

"Let's just say that we've been keeping the Germans on their toes." Aurora smiled wickedly.

"I would not expect anything less! And how is Alice, your partner in crime?"

"I haven't seen a lot of her lately, papa. She's spent a lot of time in hospital."

"In hospital?" Mendoza's eyebrows rose in alarm and concern. "Is something wrong? Is she ill? Is she sick? Is it because of what those evil S.S. swine-?"

"No, papa, it's nothing to do with that," Aurora interrupted. "She's been visiting Norbert."

"Who?"

"Norbert Ulrich. Her boyfriend."

Mendoza's face turned as white as a sheet.

Aurora reached over and grabbed his hand. "Papa, are you all right? You look like you've seen a ghost."

"I ... I got a bit of a surprise, that's all. I didn't know that he had survived. I didn't know that any S.S. paratroopers had escaped across the Border."

"Well, Ulrich escaped. He's not called The Cat for nothing."

Mendoza thought for a moment before he asked the next question. "Aurora, can you do me a favour?"

"Yes, papa. Of course."

"Next time that you see Alice, could you ask her if she can tell you the story of how Ulrich survived?"

"In fact, I'm going to meet Alice now. I'll ask her today."

"Thank you, my little butterfly." Mendoza had recovered his composure and his complexion had returned to normal. "Incidentally, do you know what happened to your bodyguard?"

Aurora shrugged her shoulders. "Manuel told me that they were leaving for the Front one day and then they left."

"Did he give you any reason?"

"No," Aurora shook her head. "Nothing. They just packed up all of their gear and left one day in a hurry."

Mendoza nodded his head sombrely. "No one has seen them since. They were probably ambushed and killed by Partisans on their way up north to the Front."

"I'm sorry, papa."

"So am I, Aurora. They were good men." Mendoza shrugged his shoulders dismissively. "But they were Legiónaries and they knew the risks and they took their chances. I will have to arrange a new bodyguard as a matter of urgency. Having said that, there are so few S.S. in Hereward that at the moment they do not pose a significant threat."

Aurora nodded her head in agreement. "I will tell you what Alice says, papa. Goodbye!"

"Goodbye, my butterfly." Mendoza kissed his daughter. He waited until she had left the house before he went into his study. Mendoza picked up the phone and dialled a number. "Alfredo. We have a problem."

Chapter Four

The S.S. officer marched into the office, halted, clicked his heels together and thrust out his right arm. "Heil Hitler!"

"Heil Hitler, Hauptsturmführer." Ulrich stood up, walked out from behind his desk and shook von Stein's hand. "Please sit down."

"Thank you, sir." Von Stein took off his cap, smoothed back his hair and sat down.

"Whiskey?"

"Yes please, sir." Von Stein watched as Ulrich poured a glass of Whyte and Mackay single malt into a heavy crystal tumbler. Von Stein took a sip of the amber nectar. "My God, sir, it's a relief to see that you're alive and kicking. The boys will be pleased to hear that you're in good health."

Ulrich smiled. "I don't know if I'm kicking, but I'm alive and that's what counts."

"I must admit, sir, that when we left you in Newcastle we didn't know if you would make it."

"You were the one who found me in Scotland and took me to Newcastle?" Ulrich's eyes bulged wide with shock.

"Yes, sir." Von Stein's brows furrowed with surprise. "Did nobody tell you?"

Ulrich shook his head. "I woke up in hospital here in Hereward and nobody has told me anything. All I know is that I left in the last convoy to leave Newcastle before it was captured."

"We found you on the river bank by Beattie Bridge with two bullets in your chest more dead than alive."

"We?"

"Yes, sir." Von Stein nodded. "Myself, Rottenführer Barbie and about a dozen men. We were the sole survivors of our company."

"Mein Gott."

"We took it in turns to carry you to the Tweed where we managed to salvage and cannibalise enough equipment to build a raft. We swam and floated ourselves across the river in the middle of the night."

Ulrich took a sip of whiskey. "What was the situation like on the south side?"

"Complete carnage, sir. The Tommies had already crossed the Tweed in force and were in hot pursuit of our retreating forces. The only Germans on the southern side of the river were dead ones…"von Stein's voice trailed off as he remembered the scenes of complete and utter death and destruction which greeted him and his men when they swam across the river.

"How did you get to Newcastle?"

"We had to fight a platoon of Blackshirts for ownership of two lorries and we used these to travel to Newcastle. We delivered you to the hospital and then continued to follow in the wake of the advancing British Army. We slept during the day and at night we drove our lorries south. It took us about three or four days to reach Hereward, sir."

"How many of you made it in the end?"

Von Stein held up the fingers of one hand. "Five, sir. Including myself."

"I'm sorry to hear that, Manfred," Ulrich said sombrely.

Von Stein drew himself up so that he was sitting straighter in the chair. "The important thing is that you survived, sir. Nothing else matters. As long as you survive then the Brigade survives." Von Stein picked up the tumbler "To the Triple S Brigade!" He toasted.

"The Triple S!" Ulrich took a sip. "Talking of the Triple S, Manfred, what is our sitrep?"

Von Stein shook his head in despair. "The Brigade is in a terrible state, sir. As far as the 4th and 5th S.S. are concerned we can barely muster two companies of two hundred and fifty men between us, sir. Roughly three quarters of the two battalions were either killed, wounded, captured or missing and the two battalions are to all intents and purposes combat ineffective."

"My God," Ulrich put his hand up to his mouth. "I had no idea that the situation is so terrible."

"I'm afraid that it is, sir," von Stein agreed sadly. "We are in urgent need of reinforcements. At the moment the Partisans are running rings around us. We have lost effective control of Hereward and the surrounding area. We simply do not have enough men to patrol our territory effectively."

"I've asked Berlin to send reinforcements as a matter of urgency. Manfred, I'm sure that you well-understand that the war against Russia has top priority as far as reinforcements are concerned. Berlin has assured me that they are aware of our situation and that reinforcements are on the way. However, I'm not holding my breath."

"Yes, sir."

Ulrich looked directly at von Stein. "How is Colonel Mendoza?"

Von Stein was caught off guard by the mention of his archenemy. "Colonel ... Colonel Mendoza, sir? I'm afraid that I don't know what you mean."

"What's the state of his Battalion? The Legiónaries are still part of my Brigade, are they not?"

"I've absolutely no idea, sir. However, if they were as badly mauled as we were then they probably have no more than one hundred men." Von Stein was thinking aloud as he spoke.

"You mentioned a combined S.S. strength here in Hereward of about two hundred and fifty men, is that correct?"

"Yes, sir," Von Stein nodded, "but that really is scraping the bottom of the barrel. That figure includes all of those who were left behind in Sick Bay and all of the rear echelon Brigade H.Q. personnel: - cooks, clerks and stores men. Every cook and office clerk will have to pick up a rifle and start earning their combat pay."

"You seem to have the matter well in hand, Manfred; well done."

"Thank you, sir." Von Stein bowed his head.

Ulrich took a sip of whiskey and swirled the contents around in his glass. "The unfortunate events of the last week have led to several sudden vacancies in the Brigade command structure, Manfred." He paused for dramatic effect. "It's my pleasure to promote you to Sturmbannführer."

Von Stein was caught by surprise and was momentarily speechless.

Ulrich stood up and walked around his desk to face von Stein. Von Stein saluted and Ulrich returned the salute and shook von Stein's hand. "Congratulations, Sturmbannführer von Stein."

"Thank you, sir." Von Stein was grinning like a cat that had got the cream.

"Sit down please, Sturmbannführer." Ulrich gestured with his hand as von Stein sat down.

"Your first task will be to rebuild the 4th S.S. from scratch. I want you to make a list of all present members of the Battalion and I want you to indicate who took part in and who did not take part in the invasion of Scotland. Clear?"

"Clear, sir."

"Good," Ulrich nodded. "Then we can begin the process of rebuilding the Battalion step by step from the bottom up."

"I will get the names to you by the end of the day, sir," von Stein promised. "With your permission, Obersturmbannführer?"

"Very good, Sturmbannführer von Stein. Carry on, dismissed"

Von Stein stood up, saluted and left the office.

Ulrich looked through the window as von Stein met up with one of his N.C.O.s. What was his name again? He couldn't remember. Never mind. Ulrich rubbed his hands with satisfaction at a job well done. What was the phrase? Keep your friends close and your enemies closer? Well, he had certainly achieved that goal by binding von Stein closer to him. Now, as soon as he gave him the list of all of the base personnel he could begin his mission of hunting and striking down with great vengeance and furious anger the beasts who had kidnapped and raped Alice and Aurora.

Greg looked down at the body of the despatch rider and shook his head sadly.

"Are you all right, Greg?" Sam asked. "You seem a wee bit upset."

"I'm not upset, Sam, it's just … the Nazis are sending children to do a man's job. Look at him, he's barely older than you or Alan."

Sam looked down at the torn and twisted body of the young S.S. storm trooper. He looked like a broken toy. Sam shrugged his shoulders dismissively. "If he's old enough to kill, then he's old enough to die. He's not the first teenage Nazi that I've killed and he certainly won't be the last."

"I know that, Sam, it's just that he should be working in a nine to five job or studying at university, not lying here with a broken neck on an English country road …"

"You're not going all touchy feely on us, are you, Greg?" Alan asked with a sardonically raised eyebrow.

" I've been fighting and killing them since '36! I've killed more Fascists and Nazis than you've had hot dinners!" Greg ranted. "But every time that I've killed one of them, two more spring up to take their place - they're like Hydra's teeth! I fought against them in Spain with the International Brigade; I fought against them in France with the Foreign Legion and here I am fighting against them in England with the Resistance. What difference has it made? I'll tell you- absolutely none! And yet I have all of this blood on my hands! Blood that I'll never be able to wash off!" Greg's face was covered with sweat and his chest was heaving. As his breathing slowly returned to normal he seemed to physically shrink like a deflating balloon.

Sam and Alan looked at each other with concern. Was this the same Greg who had made his hell fire and brimstone 'all those who wear the uniform of the enemy are to be treated as the enemy unless proven otherwise speech' only a few days ago?

Aurora walked up and tenderly kissed her uncle on his unshaven cheek. "Uncle Ramón, you're just tired, that's all …"

"Yes, I am, Aurora," Greg nodded his head wearily. "I am tired of all the fighting and the killing to no avail …"

"You just need a rest, that's all …"

"Yes, I do."

"Perhaps we could stand down for a few days?" Aurora asked the group.

"Stand down?" Sam positively bristled with disbelief and indignation. "Maybe your uncle has lost his nerve and is sick and tired of killing Nazis, but I'm not. I'm just getting started!"

"My uncle has not lost his nerve, Sam, and if I was a man and this was Spain then I would challenge you to a duel for daring to question my uncle's courage!" Aurora said with fire in her eyes. She looked at her uncle but Greg would not look at her. Aurora looked at Alan for support with an imploring look in her eyes.

Alan chose his words carefully before he spoke. "Aurora, it's not possible for us to 'stand down' unilaterally. We are a military unit and we follow orders from Headquarters in Edinburgh. We have been ordered to 'hinder, harass and hurt the enemy' and we will continue to do that until we are told otherwise or until we are all dead. We swore an oath to defeat the King's enemies and until that day is won and we stake the Union Jack through Hitler's evil heart, we fight on."

"Alice?" Aurora asked her friend with tears in her eyes.

"Your uncle joined our Resistance Unit, Aurora. It existed before him and it will continue to exist without him. However, your uncle is under no obligation to remain a member; he can have a rest for as long as he wants and then he can re-join us when he's recovered his … composure."

"Uncle Ramón?" Aurora asked tenderly.

Greg nodded slowly. He seemed to be in a daze.

"Agreed." Aurora nodded her head slowly.

"Greg can rest at the farm and look after the pigs. He should be safe there," Alice suggested.

"Bingo!" Sam shouted excitedly as he held in the air the dead despatch rider's satchel. "It looks as if we've hit the jack pot!"

"What is it, Sam?" Alan asked excitedly.

"I don't know, Al, it's in German, but it looks important. Sis, can you translate?" Sam handed over a

53

torn open brown manila envelope to Alice who swiftly skim read the letter.

"What's the news, Alice?" Alan asked.

"S.S. reinforcements are arriving in Hereward soon …"

"Shit!"

"… A full company of stormtroopers …"

"Bloody hell!"

"Well. At least they're sitting up and beginning to take notice of us," Sam said haughtily. "There's only one thing that I hate more than being taken for granted and that's being ignored." He watched as Alice furrowed her brows. "What is it, sis?"

"These soldiers are not simply reinforcements for Ulrich's Brigade," Alice replied as she continued to read. "They're special. They are to act independently from the Brigade and don't fall under Ulrich's command. They are called Einsatzgruppe Großbritannien and they are to be based in Hereward under the command of a Sturmbannführer von Horn."

"What on earth is an Einsatzgruppe?" Aurora asked.

"An Einsatzgruppe is a task force, Aurora."

"The question is: what is the task of Einsatzgruppe Great Britain?" Alan asked.

"Thank you for compiling this list so promptly, Manfred," Ulrich said warmly.

"My pleasure, Obersturmbannführer." Von Stein smiled as he clicked his heels together and gave a slight bow.

"Please sit down, Sturmbannführer."

"Thank you, sir." Von Stein sat down and removed his peaked officer's cap.

"Would you care for a whiskey, Manfred?"

"Yes please, sir."

"And a cigar? Finest Cuban from Brigadeführer Schuster's private and personal collection?"

Von Stein's eyes opened wide with pleasant surprise. He had never been treated with so much attention, care and hospitality by a superior officer before. "Yes please, sir."

Ulrich opened up a box on his desk and offered a cigar to von Stein.

Von Stein ran his nose along its length and sucked in the cigar's strong scent. "Thank you, sir."

"My pleasure, Manfred." Ulrich handed over the glass of whiskey to von Stein who sniffed the aroma of the amber liquid with the appreciative nose of a practised connoisseur.

"Whyte and Mackay single malt, sir?"

Ulrich nodded his head. "I'm impressed, Sturmbannführer. You have a good nose." He passed over a cigar cutter and a box of matches.

"Thank you, sir." Von Stein cut off the end of the cigar and took a sip from the crystal tumbler.

"I've only had time to skim read the list, Manfred. Perhaps you would care to fill me in with the details?"

"Certainly, sir." Von Stein put down his drink. "About twenty men from the 4th S.S. were left behind when we invaded Scotland, sir. The majority remained in Hereward either because of wounds and injuries that they had suffered as a result of anti- Partisan operations or parachute training. Those with major injuries stayed in Hereward Hospital and those with minor injuries stayed in the Sick Bay here at Brigade HQ."

"How many of those men will be returning to active duty?"

"About a dozen, sir. However, the earliest ones will not be ready for two weeks and the latest ones will not be ready for six weeks and even then they will have to be restricted to light duties. None of them will be combat effective until three months from now, sir."

"October at the earliest … what happens to those who will never be combat effective?"

"They will be returned to Germany together with the casualties that we suffered in the recent invasion, sir."

"I see." Ulrich took another sip of whiskey. "I notice that there's another list, Manfred."

"Yes, sir." Von Stein nodded. "That's the list of the able bodied men who remained at H.Q. during the invasion. They're all rear echelon personnel. Office clerks and the men who worked in the Armoury and Quartermaster Stores. About a dozen men in total, sir."

"I see." Ulrich started to read the list of names.

Von Stein took the opportunity to light his cigar. He took a long deep breath and blew out a perfect smoke ring that floated gently away from him. He took a sip of whiskey and gazed out of the double door French windows that led out to Ulrich's balcony. Yes, life was good at the moment. He had been promoted to the rank of sturmbannführer and he was acting commander of his old regiment, the 4th S.S. The vendetta with Mendoza seemed to have simmered down for the moment and he had the support and confidence of the new Brigade commander, Obersturmbannführer Ulrich. Von Stein took another sip of whiskey. Yes, you had to be grateful for the little pleasures of life. He took another puff of his cigar. "I haven't had one of these since Spain…" von Stein said wistfully.

Ulrich's ears pricked up like a Golden Retriever. "I understand that the Regimental Quartermaster Sergeant, Hauptscharführer Ernst Kumm is an old comrade of yours, Manfred," he said as casually as he could.

"Hauptscharführer Kumm, sir?" Von Stein's eyebrows were raised with surprise and confusion. "I'm afraid that I don't understand, sir."

"Ernst is an old Spanish hand. According to his service record he served in the Condor Legión during the Spanish Civil War and he fought alongside you during the Battle of the Ebro River in '38. Is this not true?"

Ulrich watched von Stein's reaction like a hawk.

Von Stein clicked his fingers as realization finally dawned. "Yes, sir. I was confused there for a second. Ernst was an unterscharführer then, sir and he was my platoon sergeant. I was the platoon commander. He was seriously wounded in the leg at the beginning of the battle and he was evacuated back home." He shook his head as his mind drifted back to the battle. "It was a real shame, sir, as Ernst was a bed rock in the platoon, a real character and he was sorely missed. I had forgotten all about him until he was called up from the Reserves to serve as RQMS here in Hereward." Von Stein smiled warmly as he remembered the emotional reunion. "It was a hell of a shock to see him again, sir, a real blast from the past, but a welcome surprise never the less. And although he can no longer fight as a result of his leg wound he has performed sterling service in charge of the Quartermaster stores." Von Stein took another sip of whiskey.

"Yes, I've heard nothing but praise for the service that he has performed."

Von Stein suddenly laughed aloud. "Ernst was best mates with one of my squad commanders, Rottenführer Kophamel, sir. The jokes that those two used to play on each other and on the platoon, sir. It would make your hair stand on end! They used to drive the Spaniards crazy!"

"I'm sure that they did." Ulrich smiled paternally as if listening to an oft-repeated story told by a favourite nephew.

"It's a small world, sir." Von Stein shook his head in wonder as he took another sip of whiskey.

"It certainly is, Manfred, and I'm afraid that the big world is about to intrude. I'd like you to continue to build up at least one full company in your regiment, Sturmbannführer. We will base the rest of the regiment around your complete company when the reinforcements arrive from home."

Von Stein felt a warm glow of pride spread through his body at Ulrich's mention of 'his' regiment. "Yes, sir. Do we have any idea when the reinforcements will arrive, sir?"

Ulrich shook his head. "Unfortunately not, Manfred. As you know, Russia has top priority."

"Very well, sir. Is there anything else that you would like to know about the state of the Regiment, sir?"

"No, Sturmbannführer. You've told me everything that I want to know. Dismissed!"

Von Stein stood up, put on his hat and clicked his heels together, "Heil Hitler!"

Ulrich returned the salute and steepled his fingers on his desk as von Stein marched out of his office. He smiled with satisfaction at his amateur detective work. Sherlock Holmes, eat your heart out. He nodded to himself as he planned his next course of action. First step: deal with Kumm and his fellow rapists; second step: deal with von Stein, the spider at the centre of the web. Yes, the whiskey and the cigar had worked its magic far more effectively than torture or any truth drug: Von Stein had indeed told him everything that he wanted to know.

Chapter Five

"Percy has informed us about the imminent arrival of Einsatzgruppe Great Britain," Major Peter Ansett announced. He was reading a message that had only been recently deciphered. "What I'd like to know is: what on earth is an Einsatzgruppe?"

"Pass the message to me, please Pete," Brigadier John Daylesford asked. He read the message and thought for a moment before he replied. "I won't tell you what an Einsatzgruppe is-I'll show you what an Einsatzgruppe does. Follow me." Daylesford stood up and put on his peaked cap. He opened the door and gestured for Ansett to follow him. The two men walked along a series of long corridors and then descended down a flight of stairs that led to the basement.

"My God, it's enormous," Ansett exclaimed with awe. "It's as big downstairs as it is upstairs."

"Well, Redford Barracks was built in order to accommodate an entire cavalry regiment of one thousand men plus their horses and families. It was the regimental headquarters of the Royal Scots Greys before it became Special Operations Executive headquarters. It housed the garrison for Edinburgh Castle." Daylesford stopped in front of a door guarded by two Military Police sentries. "Here we are."

"Identification please, gentlemen," the sentry asked. Daylesford and Ansett both showed the guard their I.D. badges and signed a logbook recording their time of entry. The second sentry unlocked the door and stood aside. Daylesford and Ansett both entered the room.

"What is this place, sir?" Ansett looked at row upon row of filing cabinets that filled the room and which stretched into the distance. He noticed that another two M.P.s guarded the inside.

"This is where we keep our secrets," Daylesford revealed.

A woman wearing the uniform of the First Aid Nursing Yeomanry (F.A.N.Y.) walked up to them. "How can I help, gentlemen?"

"I'd like you to give me all of the information that you have on the Einsatzgruppen please, Lieutenant," Daylesford asked.

"Certainly, sir. Please take a seat." The officer gestured towards a table with a library lamp and four chairs. The two men sat down.

The Lieutenant soon returned with a bulky string bound file. "Write your autograph here please, sir." Daylesford signed the form on the Lieutenant's clipboard and another form glued to the inside of the file. "Please tell me when you have finished with the file. I am obliged by the Official Secrets Act to inform you that you are not authorised to remove any of the contents of the file from this room. Do you understand?"

"Yes, Lieutenant, we understand," the two men answered in unison.

"Thank you, gentlemen." The Lieutenant flashed a Hollywood starlet smile and walked away.

"Pete, is it just me or did this encounter involving a young attractive female junior officer giving us orders send a delicious shiver up your spine?" Daylesford asked with a mischievous twinkle in his eye.

"It's not just you, sir. She had exactly the same effect on me. We're just getting old."

Daylesford laughed and clapped a hand on his companion's shoulder. "There's life in these old dogs yet! Now, to the matter in hand. I want you to take a long hard look at these photos which were smuggled out of Poland, Pete."

Ansett looked at the two photographs. "These photos show executions of partisans?"

Daylesford shook his head.

"They must be hostages, then?" Ansett was not particularly shocked. After all, the Germans had executed hostages in Belgium during the last War and the Austro-Hungarians had done the same thing in Serbia.

Daylesford shook his head again. "I'm afraid not, Pete. The first photograph shows the execution of all of the male teachers at a primary school in Warsaw and the second one shows the execution of the entire male medical staff at a hospital in Cracow."

Ansett's brow furrowed in confusion. "The teachers and doctors were executed as hostages in retaliation for a partisan attack on German forces?"

"No, Pete." Daylesford shook his head sadly. "The truth is worse than that: Einsatzgruppen murdered those men simply because they were primary school teachers and doctors ..."

"What?"Ansett's eyes bulged wide with disbelief. "I don't understand ..."

"The Einsatzgruppen are trying to wipe out the entire Polish middle class: - doctors, lawyers, teachers, politicians, university professors, anyone with a university degree, and anyone with a higher education."

"For God's sake, why?"

"The Nazis don't want the Poles to be able to count to more than fifty. They want to turn the Poles into slaves and they want to kill anyone who might be capable of leading a slave revolt."

Ansett put his hand to his mouth in horror. "My God, it's monstrous ..."

Daylesford nodded his head. "We think that there are eight separate task forces currently operating in Poland and we estimate that the Einsatzgruppen have murdered over sixty thousand members of the intelligentsia so far and that number is rising daily. Einsatzgruppen have also followed the invading forces into the U.S.S.R. and they have been busy murdering Jews, partisans and political commissars. There are also disturbing reports that many of the locals in Estonia, Latvia, Lithuania and the Ukraine have joined the Germans in murdering their Jewish neighbours, friends and colleagues."

Ansett shook his head slowly in disbelief. "It's sounds as bad as the massacres that were carried out by the Black Hundreds in the bad old days of the Tsars."

"I would like to think that the Einsatzgruppen would find it more difficult to recruit people here to help them carry out their dirty work, but I'm not so sure," Daylesford said sadly. "Maybe I'm just being pessimistic."

"Unfortunately, I don't think that you are being overly pessimistic, sir; I think that you're being realistic. People are people the world over regardless of race or religion. There's good and bad in all of us and wars bring out the best in some people and the worst in others. I'm sure that the Nazis would have no difficulty recruiting scum bags and riff raff to help them murder their fellow citizens here. Look how many turncoats have joined the Fascist Militia, look how many traitors have joined the S.S. Legion of Saint George to fight against the Soviets. Are we certain that the Einsatzgruppen are coming here, sir?"

"I'm afraid so," Daylesford said grimly. "Although Percy has not yet discovered a date I think that we can safely assume that Einsatzgruppe Great Britain will arrive sooner rather than later."

"What are we going to do about them?"

"We are going to kill every dirty Nazi one of them and send them home to their mothers in a coffin."

Alice finished deciphering the message and handed the piece of paper to Alan.

FIND OUT EGB MISSION STOP CONTINUE TO HARASS ENEMY FORCES STOP KEEP ON BACK FOOT AND DO NOT ALLOW TO RECOVER STOP AWAIT FURTHER INSTRUCTIONS REGARDING EGB STOP

"That's that then," Alan said grimly. "We find out what the Einsatzgruppe are up to and report back. Otherwise, it's business as usual."

Alice did not respond and she seemed to be preoccupied.

"What's up, sis?" Sam asked with concern. "You seem worried. Is something bothering you?"

"It's just … it's probably nothing …" Alice began.

"Come on, sis. What is it?" Sam pressed.

Alice thought for a moment before she replied. "Do you remember Lucy and Sophie Cobb, the two little girls whom I used to baby sit?"

"Yes, of course I do," Sam nodded. "They used to live across the road. Those murdering Nazi bastards killed their parents in May."

"When their parents were murdered the authorities tried to get in contact with their closest relatives, but their grandparents were dead and it wasn't possible to find their uncles and aunties."

"Their uncles and aunties may well have been killed during the invasion, sis," Sam said sadly.

"Or they might have fled to Scotland," Alan added optimistically.

"Anyway, the authorities found room for them in the Hereward Home for Orphan Children," Alice explained. "As you know, Sophie has Downs Syndrome so they found a place for her in the wing for handicapped children and they found a place for Lucy in the wing for able bodied children."

"That was lucky, Alice," Alan said. "I bet that there's a shortage of spaces in orphanages. There must be thousands of new orphans whose parents have been killed in the recent fighting."

"Ourselves, for example," Sam said grimly.

"Sorry, Sam," Alan put his hand on his friend's arm. "I didn't mean to bring up such painful memories."

"It's all right, Al. It's the memories which give me the motivation to keep fighting."

"I walked to the orphanage this morning and I found it all boarded up," Alice continued. "It's closed. I asked a lady who lived next door what's happened and she told me that the orphans have all been transferred to an orphanage in Cambridge. Apparently, it's bigger than this one. The Hereward Orphanage is going to be transformed into a hospice for fatally injured Blackshirts …"

"Fascist scum!" Sam spat the words out. "The only good Blackshirt is a dead Blackshirt!"

"That would seem to make sense, Alice. The Hereward Orphanage was only a small operation. The authorities probably want to pool their resources. I'm sure that the facilities in Cambridge will be far better than they are here in Hereward. Maybe the government has finally decided to do something that would benefit the people for a change." Alan shrugged his shoulders.

"It sounds too good to be true."

"That's exactly what I'm afraid of," Alice said.

"So he's alive then," Major Astray said grimly. "That's damned bad luck."

Mendoza shook his head in disbelief. "I can't believe it, Alfredo. I shot him twice at point blank range in the chest and he still didn't die. He's more difficult to kill than Rasputin."

"I guess that they don't call him the Cat for nothing, sir. What do we do now, Jefe? Kill Ulrich?"

"First things first, Alfredo. Pleasure before business. We find out who kidnapped Aurora and Alice and we kill them, then we kill von Stein and then we kill Ulrich. We can't afford to let word get out that we deliberately and successfully sabotaged the invasion of Scotland."

"As you command, Jefe." Astray grinned like a wolf.

"I'm sorry, Mrs Stratton; I must have misunderstood you: did you say that the orphans have not arrived yet?"

"That's correct, Miss Roberts."

"But I don't understand; the orphans left Hereward yesterday and the orphanage is now closed," Alice said with mounting anxiety.

"I'm sorry, Miss Roberts. No orphans arrived yesterday and there are no plans for any large groups of orphans to arrive today or at any time in the future," Mrs Stratton said apologetically. "I'm sorry that I can't help you, Miss Roberts."

Alice was completely speechless. She looked at the phone that she held in her hand like she had never seen one before.

"I have your phone number, Miss Roberts and I will phone you as soon as I hear any news. Miss Roberts? Miss Roberts?"

"What's the matter, sis?" Sam asked with concern. "You look as white as a ghost."

"Lucy and Sophie …" Alice spoke as if she was in a daze, "something's happened to them …" her voice trailed off as she placed the phone on its cradle.

"What do you mean, Alice?" Alan walked up and carefully placed his hand on her shoulder.

"The girls aren't at the Cambridge orphanage, they never arrived," Alice explained as if in a trance, "and I don't think that they're ever going to arrive. Something terrible has happened to them. I just know it, I can feel it my heart." Alice pressed her hand against her chest.

"Maybe the lady whom you spoke to made a mistake," Sam suggested earnestly. "Maybe she misheard. Perhaps the girls were transferred to another orphanage."

"Where?" Alice asked.

"I don't know," Sam shrugged his shoulders, "Maybe Peterborough, maybe Norwich …"

"That makes no sense," Alice interrupted, "Cambridge is only fifteen minutes away from here. It makes no sense to transfer them to Peterborough or Norwich, they're miles away."

"Then where are they?" Alan asked.

"I don't know, but there is only one road that runs through Hereward and that's the King's Lynn to Cambridge road," Alice answered. "The girls were either taken north towards King's Lynn or south towards Cambridge and onto London."

"Maybe this transfer is not a one off," Alan suggested. "Maybe Hereward is not the only orphanage that has been closed down …"

"Where's the nearest orphanage to Hereward? Does Ely have one?" Alice asked.

"I don't think so, sis," Sam answered with a shake of his head. "Ely is even smaller than Hereward. I don't think that they have one."

"Then what about King's Lynn?" Alice asked.

"I'll phone them, Alice," Alan volunteered.

"How many orphans are there, sis?" Sam asked.

"About thirty. Ten disabled children and about twenty able bodied children. We'll have to search the roads all the way north from here to King's Lynn and all the way south from here to Cambridge for any clues …" Alice thought aloud.

"And how are we going to do that?"

"We'll have to use one of the lorries that we've hidden at the Farm."

"But none of us can drive."

"I know. We'll have to ask Greg to drive or failing him, Mr Baldwin."

"Captain Baldwin?" Sam was horrified. "I don't know, sis," Sam said as he shook his head with doubt. "I mean Captain Baldwin is a deep cover sleeper agent, I don't know if Edinburgh will authorise him risking his cover like this-"

"Bugger Edinburgh!" Alice bared her teeth in a sudden burst of anger. "The Nazis are stealing our children! If that's not worth risking your cover for that then what is?"

"Well, I … Al! What news?"

Alan shook his head. "Bad news, I'm afraid. I spoke to Mrs Colvin who is the manager at the King's Lynn Orphanage. She was in floods of tears and she could barely talk. The children were transferred this morning-"

"Did she say where to?" Alice interrupted.

"To Norwich, she said."

"Damn! We're too late," Sam said.

"And there's one more thing; the orphanage was not shut down by the Nazis, it was shut down by Blackshirts."

"Dirty Fascist bastards!" Sam swore through clenched teeth. "Trust the Fascist Militia to do the Hun's dirty work for them-!"

The sound of the phone ringing made them all jump. Alan picked up the phone, spoke for a few moments and then he put it down. "That was Mrs Stratton, Alice, the manager at the orphanage in Cambridge. She seems to be in a state of shock. The Blackshirts are coming to shut down and transfer the children to London tomorrow morning at nine o'clock."

"Shut down Cambridge?" Sam said incredulously. "Why on earth are they going to take all of the children to in London? Cambridge has the biggest orphanage in the whole of Cambridgeshire!"

"Well, we're going to find out tomorrow, Sam."

The S.S. lorry was parked down a side street, which lay at right angles to the main street that the Cambridge Orphanage was positioned on. Sam and Alan sat on a low wall where they could watch the front of the orphanage less than a hundred yards away. They were wearing their black Fascist Militia uniforms and they were each cradling a Schmessier machine gun in their experienced hands. They each took a perverse pleasure in the way that the good citizens of Cambridge crossed over to the other side of the street rather than walk on the same side of the pavement as them.

"My God, they treat us as if we are lepers," Alan said.

Sam nodded his head, "and so they should, Al. All Blackshirts are cursed by God." Sam shivered. " Even wearing this uniform makes me feel dirty and unclean."

"Welcome to the dark side," Alan said with a wicked smile.

"Oh, here's movement," Sam said. "Let's go!"

Sam and Alan both quickly walked the dozen yards to the lorry and climbed into the cab.

"They're moving, sir," Alan said.

"Well done, lads," Baldwin replied. "Ramón! We're moving!" He shouted into the back of the lorry.

"Bueno! Vamos!" Ramón replied.

Baldwin started the engine and turned the corner. He slowly drew nearer to the two lorries in front of him and carefully followed them as they drove out of the town. However, when the two lorries reached the main King's Lynn to London road the first lorry turned right heading north and the second lorry turned left heading south.

"Which way?" Baldwin asked frantically.

Alan hesitated for a split second before he replied. "Turn right towards King's Lynn. The disabled children are in the front lorry." Alan could hear curses coming from the back as Alice swore that they had now lost one of the lorries.

Baldwin continued to follow at a discrete distance as the lorry travelled north towards Hereward on the King's Lynn road. His eyebrows furrowed in confusion as the lorry turned left following a sign towards One Hundred Acre Wood, a popular recreation park and nature reserve. Baldwin noticed an 'Achtung! Minen!' sign warning that this area was now out of bounds and trespassers risked being blown up if they ignored the warning. Baldwin brought the lorry to a stop by the side of the road. He knew that the single track road only extended into the park for about four hundred yards and he knew that the Blackshirts would park their lorry at the end of it.

"What the hell are the Blackshirts doing here, sir?" Sam asked. "There's nothing here but trees."

"I have absolutely no idea what the Fascists are doing here, Sam, but we're going to find out. Everyone ready?"

"I was born ready, sir!" Alan replied with a grin.

Baldwin smiled. "All right, people, you know the drill: two fire teams: - Sam, Alice and myself, Charlie fire team; Alan, Aurora and Ramón, Delta fire Team. Clear?"

"Clear, sir," everyone chorused.

"Everyone tooled up with plenty of personal ammo and grenades?"

Everyone nodded.

"Sam, have you got the ammo box for the MG 42?"

"Yes, sir," Sam replied as he lifted up the ammunition box for the machine gun.

"Good. Make ready!" Baldwin ordered.

The partisans all cocked their weapons and sent a round up the spout of their weapons.

"From here on in we are tactical. Shake out into extended line: Charlie to my left and Delta to my right."

The partisans carried out the manoeuvre quickly and quietly. When Baldwin was satisfied with their positions he gave the hand signal to advance. The two fire teams began to carefully walk through the wood with their weapons in the ready position pulled tightly into their shoulders ready to open fire at a moment's notice. Baldwin and Ramón both carried a MG 42 machine gun at the hip with a belt of ammunition draped across both of their shoulders. As they slowly neared the end of the road they could see the Blackshirt lorry. Baldwin gave the hand signal to take cover and the partisans did as they were ordered. Each soldier crawled into a good firing position and aimed towards three Fascists whom they could see standing less than two hundred yards away. Baldwin took out his binoculars and observed the Blackshirts for a full five minutes before he gave the hand signal for Ramón to join him. His second in command used the trees as cover to join his leader.

"What's the sit rep, Jefe?" Ramón asked.

"I can see three Fascists, Ramón, but I can't see any of the children. You take a look, but it doesn't look good." Baldwin handed over the binoculars to Ramón.

The Spaniard observed the scene for a few minutes and handed back the binos. He shook his head. "I can't see the children either, John. That's not a good sign."

"Well, we need to find out where they are. Here's what we're going to do …"

The MG 42 cut down the two Blackshirts like so many sheaves of wheat and the surviving Fascist emptied his bowels in absolute terror.

"Hands up!" A voice shouted and the Blackshirt obeyed immediately dropping his rifle to the ground beside him. "Put your hands straight up in the air where I can see them!"

The Fascist was shaking with fear as Baldwin walked up to him.

"Is there anybody else?"

"N-no. just the three of us-"

"Where are the children?" Alice demanded.

"The-the children?"

Alice rushed up to him and pushed him hard in the chest sending him sprawling over to land in a heap on the dusty ground.

"Where are the children, you Blackshirt bastard? I swear if I have to ask you again I will shoot you in your bloody face!"

"They're-they're over there."

"Where?"

"Over there," the Blackshirt pointed.

Alice's brow furrowed with confusion. There was nothing over there but a slight rise in the ground, a ridge. But then it hit her. There were no birds singing. It was deathly silent. And then the smell…

"Alice, wait!" Alan shouted.

Alice ran up to the top of the ridge and stopped as if she had run into a brick wall.

The ditch was full of bodies. Bodies as far as the eye could see. Little bodies. The bodies of children. The missing children from the orphanages. And with a sinking feeling of despair Alice knew in her heart that she would find Lucy and Sophie lying amongst the murdered children.

"Why? Why? You evil Nazi bastard?" Sam demanded as he hauled the Fascist to his feet with clawed fingers of fury.

"We-we were ordered to kill the disabled children-"

"But why?"

"Because they were not fit for life; that's what we were told. They were a drain on our limited resources-"

"And that's why you murdered them?"

"If we had refused to do it they would have found someone else and we would have been-!"

The single shot shattered the silence. The Blackshirt toppled over onto his back. Alice walked up to him and shot him twice more in the forehead making a messy modern art masterpiece of his face. She spat between his eyes. "I told you that I would shoot you in your bloody face, you dirty Blackshirt bastard."

Chapter Six

Major Ansett and Brigadier Daylesford read the deciphered message together:

ENEMY ARE MURDERING DISABLED ORPHAN CHILDREN STOP SUSPECT ALL DISABLED CHILDREN WILL BE MURDERED NEXT STOP ABLE BODIED ORPHAN CHILDREN HAVE BEEN KIDNAPPED STOP PRESENT LOCATION UNKNOWN STOP DESPERATELY REQUEST HELP TO PREVENT MASSACRE OF INNOCENTS STOP

"It's far worse than we first feared, Pete," Daylesford said grimly. "It's not an isolated incident; the enemy are closing down orphanages and murdering disabled children up and down the entire country. They are turning the Occupied South into a slaughterhouse. And to add insult to injury, it's not the Germans who are doing it; it's our own people, it's the Blackshirts."

"Except they're not our own people, sir," Ansett said. "As soon as you put on a black shirt you become one of them, you cross over to their side, you become the enemy. There'll be a hell of a reckoning when we liberate the South. We'll be hanging turn coats and traitors on lamp posts and trees all the way from Middlesborough south east to Dover and south west to Land's End. What I don't understand is why the Fascists are doing it. What possible threat do disabled children represent to Joyce's Government of National Unity?"

"I'm afraid that it's a classic copycat action, Pete," Daylesford answered sadly. "Hitler enacted the Law for the Prevention of Genetically Diseased Offspring back in '33. We reckon that he's sterilized over two hundred thousand people with hereditary mental or physical disabilities in Germany so far. Intelligence reports indicate that Hitler started murdering disabled orphan children first in the summer of '39 before he started murdering all disabled children. We estimate that he's murdered about five thousand disabled children in Germany so far. Latest intelligence reports indicate that he's started murdering all disabled adults as well."

"My God, it's absolutely monstrous!" Ansett rubbed his head in despair. "First we hear news of the Einsatzgruppen, then this? Are there no depths to which the Nazis will not sink?"

"We think that Joyce is merely following in the footsteps of his master. There are also reports that Petain is also carrying out a similar copycat Euthanasia program in France."

"Holy Mary, mother of God!"

"And that's not the worst of it, Pete," Daylesford continued. "We are starting to get unconfirmed reports that the able bodied orphan children are being offered up for adoption to childless couples in the British Union of Fascists and that some of our children have even been shipped abroad to Germany to be offered up for adoption to childless couples in the Nazi Party."

"What?" Ansett held his head in his hands in despair. "But the Germans will be able to indoctrinate and brain wash our own children and turn them against us! The next time that they might come to Britain may be with a rifle in their hands with a swastika armband on their arm!"

"I'm afraid so, Pete," Daylesford said grimly.

"What happens to the rest of the children who are not chosen for adoption?"

"There are rumours that the Fascists are setting up their own orphanages where the boys will be trained from the age of seven to become soldiers and the girls will be trained to become nurses and domestic servants. The orphanages for boys are being called Spartan Academies.

"We have to stop them, sir." Ansett drove a fist into the palm of his hand.

Daylesford nodded his head in agreement. "The way I see it our mission has three components: - one: destroy the Blackshirt units carrying out the operation; two: force Joyce to halt the entire operation; three: rescue the disabled orphan children," Daylesford explained.

"Component number one should be relatively straight forward, sir," Ansett stated confidently. "We simply order each Resistance cell to find out if there is an orphanage in their particular town or city. If there is they need to find out if the Blackshirts have already removed the orphans. If they have then I' m afraid to say it, sir, but it's too late."

"Agreed. And if it's not too late?"

"Then the Resistance unit asks the orphanage to contact them as soon as the Blackshirts tell them when they are going to arrive and collect the children."

"The Resistance unit will then ambush the Blackshirts when they arrive."

"That may be tricky, sir," Ansett said. "The partisans may not have the necessary numbers or expertise to carry out the mission. Once the first Blackshirt units have been ambushed I have no doubt that Joyce will order that they be reinforced. Instead of dealing with a section of eight or ten men the Partisans may have to deal with a platoon of thirty or more Fascists. They might even dragoon in St. George Legionaires or even S.S. stormtroopers. The local

Resistance cells might not be able to cope, sir. Might this be the time to activate selected Jedburgh teams, sir?"

Daylesford thought for a moment before he replied. "Not yet, Pete. I strongly feel that activating the Jedburgh teams at this time would be premature and would be a waste of their potential."

"But we would not need to activate all of the Jedburgh teams, sir. Only the teams in the areas where they would have a chance to save the children."

"No can do, Pete," Daylesford shook his head forcefully. "The Jedburgh teams were established to link up with the Resistance so that they could carry out sabotage operations and guerrilla warfare behind enemy lines after our invasion of the Occupied South on L-Day. I hate to say it, Pete, but this issue of the Fascists murdering the disabled orphan children, horrific though it may be, is not important enough to jeopardise and risk the lives of the Jedburgh teams."

Ansett did not reply.

"You disagree, Pete? You think that I'm being cold hearted?"

Ansett still hesitated. "Permission to speak freely, sir?"

"Oh for Christ's sake, Pete," Daylesford was exasperated by his old friend's unnecessary formality. "We've known each other for thirty years! Permission granted. Come on, speak your mind and say your piece."

"If we're not willing to risk the lives of the Jedburgh teams to save our children then what are we willing to risk their lives for?"

"Well I-"

"Would it make any difference if the children were able bodied? Or if they weren't orphans? Or if they were Jewish or Gypsies? They're still children! Caring

76

for and protecting our children is precisely what separates us from the Nazis!"

"Now, Pete, that's not fair-"

"What's not fair is that you want the Resistance to carry out the mission, but you're not willing to give them the tools to finish the job."

"I will not give you the Jedburghs," Dayelford said defiantly. "They're far too important to risk."

"Then who will you give me?"

"What? I'm afraid that I don't understand-"

"If you won't give me the Jedburghs then who will you give me? Do you agree that the Resistance units need trained support?"

"Yes, I do," Daylesford conceded. "But both you and I know that this will be a very difficult mission. If we are to succeed then we will have transport in dozens if not hundreds of men. It will be far easier to get these men into the Occupied South them it will be to get them out. Many of them will not be coming back again."

"Then give me men who will not be missed."

"Not be missed? What do you mean?"

"Men who are expendable. Men who are desperate with nothing to lose. Men who are to all intents and purposes already dead."

"You know of such men?" Daylesford was absolutely flummoxed.

Ansett nodded. "Yes I do, sir. In fact I know of at least one hundred such men and they are currently residing in this very building at His Majesty's pleasure, sir."

Daylesford face lit up like a light bulb. "Set a thief to catch a thief?"

"My thoughts exactly, sir," Ansett smiled.

"And if they don't volunteer for this suicide mission, what then?"

Ansett's face suddenly darkened. "Then they'll join the rest of their treacherous friends in front of the firing squad. This will be their last chance of redemption, their last chance to wipe the slate clean, to begin again with a fresh start."

"Make sure that they understand that, Pete. Just having those treacherous swine in the same building as me makes my skin crawl." Daylesford shivered. "You have my permission to send them as reinforcements to support the Resistance cells. However, you must make this clear to them: If any of them betray us we will hunt them down to the ends of the earth and follow them to hell if necessary," Daylesford said coldly.

"Yes, sir. I will make your threat crystal clear to them."

"I want your teams ready to go within the week, Pete."

"Very good, sir. What shall we call them?"

"Call who?"

"The turncoats, sir."

Daylesford thought carefully for a moment before he replied. "Call them Redemption Teams, Pete. I want the bastards to be reminded why they volunteered for this mission."

"Very good, sir." Ansett grinned mischievously. The name appealed to his dark and twisted sense of humour. "Permission to carry on, sir?"

"Permission granted, Pete. You have one week to get them ready."

Ansett nodded as Daylesford left the room. The traitors would be ready by the end of the week all right, or they would be dead.

"Why did you join the Blackshirts, Tommy?" Ansett asked.

"I joined them because the terrorists killed my sister," Second Lieutenant Ball of the 1st British Union of Fascists Militia answered.

"Rachel's dead?" Ansett asked with his hand on his mouth with horror. "I'm sorry, Tommy; I had no idea. I'm sorry for your loss." Ansett paused for a moment as he digested the terrible news. Ansett had taught Ball's younger sister, Rachel at St. John's Academy and he had also taught Tommy Ball. "How did she die?"

"Arsonists fire bombed our house."

"Rachel was sleeping with the enemy?" Ansett asked with eyebrows raised with surprise.

Ball shook his head vigorously. "No, the arsonists got the wrong address. A simple case of mistaken identity."

Ansett dreaded asking the next question, but he knew that he had to. "And … and your parents, did they-?"

"My parents were burnt alive in their beds, as was Rachel. Now do you understand why I joined the Blackshirts?" Ball hissed through teeth clenched tightly shut with anger.

"Yes, Tommy: I do understand. I am truly sorry for your loss. Your father and I served together in the Fusiliers in the last war. He was a good friend of mine."

Ball acknowledged the friendship with a nod. "I was up at Cambridge at the time studying Mechanical Engineering, so I escaped."

"And you wanted to track down and kill the arsonists who had murdered your family," Ansett suggested.

"Yes, I did," Ball nodded. "The Specials had been disbanded following the execution of Kaiser Eddie and so I had no option but to join the Blackshirts if I wanted to avenge my family's death."

Ansett noticed that Ball said the 'execution of Kaiser Eddie' as opposed to the 'murder of King Edward.' He wondered if Ball's choice of words indicated where the young man's political loyalties truly lay.

"And were you successful in your quest?"

Ball bared his teeth with a wide mouthed wolfish grin. "I had the pleasure of watching the arsonists beg on bended knee for mercy, the same mercy which they had not extended to my family. They begged for their lives and cried for their mothers." Ball's eyes glazed over as he remembered the scene. "I executed them with a single shot to the forehead and I left them lying bleeding in a pool of their own blood."

"How did you feel afterwards?"

Ball looked at Ansett with a dazed expression on his face. "How did I feel? I felt … nothing. I felt empty. I thought that I would feel satisfied, but I didn't. After I had executed them, the blood lust passed and I felt completely drained. I somehow made it back to the barracks. I collapsed on my bed and I slept for a full twenty four hours. I woke up the next day still wearing my blood splattered Blackshirt uniform. Blood from the four boys whom I had executed. Yes, they were school boys from St. John's."

"My God, did you recognize them?"

"Yes, I did, unfortunately. They were the younger brothers of boys who were in my own year at St. John's."

"My God, how terrible. You must have felt awful. What made you desert and come over to our side?"

"We were ambushed by S.S. stormtroopers whilst we were driving through Frampton-on-the-Ouse."

"Why on earth did they do that? I thought you lot and the S.S. were supposed to be on the same side?" Ansett asked with surprise.

Ball visibly winced when Ansett said "you lot" and the "same side." "The S.S. opened fire on us because we had accidentally stumbled upon their hide out where they were keeping two girls whom they had kidnapped."

"Kidnapped?"

"Yes, the S.S. had kidnapped them and were raping them."

"My God!" Ansett covered his mouth with horror. "Did you manage to rescue them before … before-?"

"Before they killed the girls? Yes, we did. Thank God. Although it cost the lives of over sixty of my men."

"How … how terrible." Ansett sounded his best to sound sympathetic. "Did you recognize the girls?"

"Yes, I did. One of them was Alice Roberts, my old friend Angus's younger sister, and the other girl was Aurora Mendoza, Colonel Mendoza of the Spanish Volunteer Legión's daughter."

"Lucky…lucky for the girls that you turned up. Talk about saved by the cavalry. Do you or Colonel Mendoza have any idea why the stormtroopers kidnapped the girls? Was it on purpose or was it sheer bad luck that the girls happened to be in the wrong place at the wrong time?"

Ball shook his head. "It was not bad luck-it was on purpose. Colonel Mendoza and an officer in the S.S., Manfred von Stein, are engaged in a vendetta that started three years ago during the Spanish Civil War."

"I see. And Alice Roberts as Aurora's best friend somehow got herself caught up in it …" Ansett's voice trailed off as he thought aloud.

Ball watched Ansett as the older man ran through the sequence of events in his head. How did Ansett know that Aurora and Alice were best friends? Ball knew that Ansett had disappeared around about the time of the St. George's Day Massacre. His father had assumed that his old friend had been killed in the cross fire which was a fate that many an unlucky civilian had suffered on that fateful and fatal day. Aurora had only arrived in Hereward at the beginning of the Easter school term AFTER Ansett had already left. Ansett had been in Scotland since the Massacre so how would he know that Alice and Aurora were best buddies unless…

"So why did you desert and come over to our side during the Invasion?" Ansett's question rudely interrupted Ball's train of thought.

"Because I finally realized that I'd been fighting on the wrong side. There was simply no way that I could fight on the same side as those S.S. animals who kidnapped and raped defenseless school girls no matter what wrongs my family had suffered at the hands of those … terrorists, those … school boys. I spoke to someone who suggested that the only way that I could make amends for my sins, the only way that I could wipe the slate clean and start again was to desert at the earliest opportunity."

"Do you seek forgiveness, Tommy?"

Ball shook his head as tears at last began to flow down his face. "No, Mr. Ansett, I seek redemption."

"I'll see what I can do." Ansett wrote the word 'GREY' at the top of Ball's file and left the captured Blackshirt officer crying on the hard backed chair.

British Intelligence estimated that the British Union of Fascist Militia consisted of approximately 25,000 full time and part time members. About half of the Fascist Militia had taken part in the invasion of Scotland and about four thousand Blackshirts had been captured, four thousand had been killed and four thousand had escaped by the skin of their teeth back to the Occupied South. Approximately 2,500 prisoners had been interrogated so far in order to separate the fair weather Fascists from the fanatical Fascists. Those Blackshirts who were identified as having less strong Far Right views and those who had had other extenuating circumstance such as having suffered as a result of Resistance actions were dealt with more leniently with the long term aim that these men might eventually be rehabilitated and rescued rather than executed as traitors. British intelligence designated the fanatical Fascists as Black; fair weather Fascists as Grey and those who were pressured into joining the Blackshirts or joined the Blackshirts as a means to fight back against the Fascists from within the organization as White. All Blacks were executed; all Greys were closely scrutinized in order to determine their suitability for eventual rehabilitation and all Whites were recruited into the Armed forces where a suitable cover story was concocted in order to explain their sudden appearance.

"Aurora, my little butterfly, what is the matter? Why are you crying?" Mendoza asked with fatherly concern. He had returned home from another hard day's work at the barracks to find his daughter sobbing uncontrollably on the sofa.

"Oh, papa!" Aurora replied. "It's absolutely terrible." She then proceeded to tell her father about the horrific discovery that the Blackshirts were murdering disabled orphan children and were kidnapping able-bodied orphan children.

Mendoza was positively seething with anger and barely suppressed rage at the evil injustice of the slaughter of the innocents. He had been a professional soldier for all of his adult life and he had witnessed many terrible scenes but he had never heard of anything as morally reprehensible as the deliberate massacre of children. However, despite his heated emotion, Mendoza possessed sufficient discipline and self-control to resist the urge to ask his daughter how she had discovered this information. He knew very well that Aurora was buried up to her neck in Resistance business. Although he knew that it was risky, she was safer under the protective wing of Alan, Sam and Alice as an active member of a well-armed partisan unit than she would be under his own. Mendoza knew that they would fight to the death to protect her. He was painfully aware that he did not have enough Legiónaries to assign Aurora a dedicated bodyguard and it was extremely unlikely that he would have any soldiers to spare in the future. The Russian Front was the main destination for all Spanish reinforcements and would remain so for the foreseeable future or at least until Stalin surrendered. The British Front had been relegated to the status of a provincial backwater and was even further down the pecking order for reinforcements than Spanish Morocco. Mendoza was barely managing to field enough men to guard the Legiónary Barracks and had been only paying lip service to German requests to mount anti partisan patrols in the Cambridgeshire countryside.

"The way I see it we have two tasks: - number one: stop the Blackshirts killing the disabled orphans; number two: evacuate all of the children to a place of safety."

"Why do we need to evacuate all of the children, papa?"

"Because there is no guarantee that if we stop the Fascists murdering the children any halt to the slaughter will be permanent," Mendoza explained. He was too preoccupied thinking aloud to notice Aurora smile at her father's use of the word 'we.' "We must assume that any stop to the operation will be temporary

84

and could resume at any time. Therefore, we must rescue the children and get them out of harm's way to a guaranteed and permanent place of safety."

"And how are we going to do that, papa?"

"You concentrate on stopping the Blackshirts, Aurora, and I'll concentrate on arranging the evacuation of all of the children." Mendoza did not ask Aurora about how she and her motley crew were going to go about stopping the Fascists. The less he knew about Aurora's involvement with the partisans the less he would be able to reveal if he was ever arrested and tortured.

"Oh, papa! I'm so proud of you!" Aurora jumped on her father, wrapped her arms around his neck and gave him a ferocious bear hug. "I'm so glad that we are finally fighting on the same side!"

"So...so am I, my little butterfly," Mendoza managed to pries his daughter's arms away from their vice like grip around his neck before he passed out.

"I will go and tell my comrades!" Aurora announced excitedly as she flew out of the room with the good news. She was too preoccupied to notice her father wince involuntarily at his daughter's use of such a blatantly Red term. "I'm so happy that you've finally decided to renounce the dark side." Aurora's words floated in from the hallway before she disappeared with a dramatic slam of the front door.

Mendoza shook his head with amusement and chuckled good-naturedly to himself. Aurora had an uncanny knack of cutting through the chaff and hitting the nail on the head. She was right: it did feel good to finally renounce the dark side. To do something good for a change, to do something pure and true which was not tainted and corrupted with dark and sinister motives of revenge or vendetta. To do something right. And what could be more right than saving children from being murdered by Fascist thugs? Mendoza picked up the telephone. Truth be told, he had turned his back on the dark side a long time ago. He was sure that Aurora would be amused to discover that.

Chapter Seven

"Two weeks? Two weeks?" Alice's eyes were wide open with horror, "the orphans won't last two days at this rate." She dropped the decoded message with disgust as if it was diseased and dirty.

Alan reached down and picked up the message. "Edinburgh has ordered us to stand down and await reinforcements," he read aloud with a voice dazed with disbelief.

"We can't wait for two weeks and we certainly can't wait for reinforcements," Sam snarled with derision. "The Blackshirts have already murdered the disabled children from the orphanages in Hereward, King's Lynn and Cambridge and that's just the orphanages that we know about. By the end of two weeks the Fascists could have killed all of the disabled children in the whole of the Occupied South. Edinburgh obviously does not realize how serious the situation is down here and has their head up their arse."

"Or perhaps they do recognize that we are in dire straits, but they are simply not able or willing to deal with the problem," Alice suggested.

"What do you mean, sis?" Sam asked.

"What I mean is that whether or not Edinburgh saves or doesn't save a bunch of disabled children will not bring us any closer to achieving final victory over the Huns, will it?"

"Crikey, Alice, that's rather cynical, isn't it?" Alan said with distaste. "I mean we are supposed to be the good guys. Surely Edinburgh would not stand idly by and allow tens or perhaps hundreds of thousands of disabled children to be slaughtered?"

Alice shrugged her shoulders. "I'm not saying that Edinburgh will do nothing; they will try to do something, but they may not be able to do it in time. If all of the disabled children are killed by the end of August, Edinburgh will be able to hold their hands up and say with a clear conscience: 'sorry chaps, we were organizing reinforcements but we weren't able to train and transport them down south to you in such a short space of time, but at least we tried. Awfully sorry, chaps. Better luck next time.' "

"In other words, a complete cop out," Alan said with disgust.

"I'm afraid so, Al."

"My God, sis. That's really dark and depressing. I'd like to think that our side is not as cold and calculating as that. After all, we are supposed to be fighting on the side of truth, justice and the British way of life."

"Perhaps I'm merely playing Devil's advocate, Sam. Perhaps I'm being overly pessimistic. But I am certain of one thing: regardless of Edinburgh's orders, we cannot afford to wait two weeks before we take further action."

"What do you propose?" Alan asked.

"I propose that we strike hard, we strike fast and we strike without mercy! Agreed?"

"Agreed!" The boys answered in uniform.

"Strength and honour, boys!"

"Strength and honour, Alice!"

The partisan leader slowly lowered his binoculars to his chest. He looked to his left and gave a thumbs down hand signal indicating that the enemy had been sighted. The two guerrillas acknowledged with a nod that they had understood the signal. The commander then repeated the signal to the two fighters to his right.

He raised the binoculars to his eyes and continued to watch as the two lorries slowly crawled up the steep, long and windy single-track road to the top of the hill. The five minutes that the enemy lorries took to reach the ambush point seemed to stretch into hours and the partisan was unaware that he was impatiently drumming his fingertips on the butt of his Schmessier machine gun.

The first lorry reached the sharp curve of the hairpin bend. The commander tapped the shoulder of his MG 42 machine gunner. "Rapid fire!" He ordered. The machine gunner squeezed the trigger and fired twenty rounds per second into the cab of the first lorry punching holes through the right hand side door as if it was made of matchwood. Another burst of bullets shattered the front wind screen as the right hand cut off team opened fire with their MG 42 catching the first lorry in a deadly cross fire. The leader watched as the driver tumbled out of the broken and buckled door like a bloody rag doll. "Switch fire!" He ordered curtly. The machine gunner swiftly repositioned his weapon and opened fire on the front windscreen of the second lorry. However, the commander quickly realized that the left hand cut off team had already taken care of business and his own machine gunner was simply wasting bullets. He tapped his companion twice on the shoulder.

"Cease fire!" He ordered. He repeated the order to the left and right cut off teams. "Check the enemy!"

One guerrilla from the left hand cut off team emerged from the forest and carefully approached the rear lorry with the butt of her Schmessier machine gun pulled tightly into her shoulder and her right forefinger resting lightly on the trigger. Another partisan approached the front lorry as the remaining members of the Resistance unit covered their comrades with their automatic weapons. The left hand guerrilla reached the bullet peppered cab door and pulled it open. The driver toppled out and lay in a bloody heap on the road. The partisan carefully looked into the cab and was puzzled to discover that there were no other passengers sitting with the driver.

"There's no one else in here!" She shouted.

"Check the back!"

The guerrilla walked to the back of the lorry and pulled open the rear door. "There's no one in the back either!"

"There's no one in the front lorry cab either!" The right hand guerrilla shouted.

The leader furrowed his brow in confusion. The Fascists usually travelled with at least three Blackshirts per lorry, not one. They could not possibly kill and bury a lorry load of children with only one man per vehicle. Perhaps the Fascists were merely delivering the lorries from one place to another and were not intending to use them for their murderous purposes that morning. Perhaps the information that he had received that morning had been wrong.

"Boss, come and have a look at this," the left hand guerrilla said urgently.

"Yes, what is it?" The partisan commander walked over to the back of the lorry and looked in.

"It's a completely normal lorry, boss," the left hand guerrilla explained. "It's not a mobile gas killing lorry."

"Neither is this one, boss," the right hand guerrilla added. "This one is a completely normal lorry as well."

The leader's face suddenly drained of colour as comprehension finally dawned.

"What is it, boss?" The left hand guerrilla grabbed her commander's arm with concern, "What's the matter? You look as if you've seen a-"

A sudden burst of bullets cut down the guerrilla like a felled tree.

"Take cover! "The leader shouted.

"What the-?"A second fusillade of fire knocked down the second guerrilla.

The commander looked on with horror as two lorries loaded with Blackshirts drove up the hill from the left and another two lorry loads of Militiamen approached from the right."Fifty yards to the left and right rapid fire!"

The two machine gunners opened fire and each cut down about half a dozen Blackshirts as they piled out of the lorries but there were simply too many of them and the remainder made it to the safety of the forest where the thickly dense trees gave them cover from fire as well as cover from view.

"Both of you bug out to the RV point. I'll cover you!"

"What about the girls?"

"They're both dead!"

"They might only be wounded! I'm going back to get them!"

"No! Stand down! Bug out to the RV point! That's an order!"

"Bugger your order!" The left hand machine gunner dumped his MG 42, drew his Luger pistol and broke cover from the forest. He was cut down as soon as he emerged from the tree line.

"Hands up!"

The leader turned around and faced his rear to see at least twenty fully armed and dangerous Blackshirts running towards him.

"Put your hands up, you Jew loving Red bastard, I won't ask you again!" A Blackshirt captain snarled angrily.

The commander looked to his left and to his right. There were Fascist Militiamen as far as the eye could see. The partisans were completely surrounded. It was over. Surrender was the only option if they wanted to survive. The leader carefully placed his Schmessier on the ground and stood up with his hands in the air. He didn't see the rifle butt that smashed into the back of his skull and knocked him unconscious.

"Pick him up," the Blackshirt captain ordered tersely.

Two militiamen hauled the semi-conscious guerrilla to his feet. The partisan slowly opened his eyes and realized that the other two surviving members of his Resistance unit were also being held with their arms handcuffed behind their back.

"What's your name, Shylock?" the Blackshirt captain asked.

"Well, it's not Shylock, Adolf."

The Blackshirt casually shot one of the other guerrillas in the stomach. He turned to face the partisan leader. "That was for trying to be funny. Imagine what I would do if you were trying not to be funny. What is your name, you Bolshevik Jew lover? I won't ask you again." He swung his revolver around to point at the other surviving guerrilla.

"Smith … John Smith."

"Very funny …"

"No! Really, it is John Smith," the partisan protested.

"It better be, John boy, because if I find out that you're lying, I will let my boot boys loose on you and they will beat you so badly that your own mother wouldn't recognize you."

The partisan nodded in abject defeat.

"Who told you that we were coming this morning to clean out all of the retards from the orphanage, was it the manager?"

The partisan said nothing.

"Was it the manager?" The Blackshirt aimed his weapon at the other guerrilla.

The partisan leader gave the barest detectable nod.

"Just as I thought," the Blackshirt smiled with grim satisfaction. "I knew that we couldn't trust that bitch. I knew that she would contact the local branch of the Jews and Retards Appreciation Society."

"Sir, one of the Red bitches is still alive," a militiaman announced triumphantly.

The partisan's ears pricked up with concern.

"How badly wounded is she, sergeant?"

"She's been shot in the legs but that's about it, sir. What should we do with her?"

The Blackshirt shrugged his shoulders without concern or interest. "Do what you want with her and then string her up with the rest of them."

"You … you cold hearted bastard!" The partisan spat with poison.

"Pick a number and get in line, John boy."

The Blackshirts hung the three captured partisans from a tree with the words 'Jew lover' written on a cardboard sign around their necks. The convoy then travelled on to Portsmouth where they emptied the orphanage of the children. The able bodied children were taken to London where they were processed for either adoption or entrance to one of the new Spartan training academies. The disabled children were murdered in the mobile gas killing truck and their

93

bodies were unceremoniously dumped in a mass grave dug deep in the Forest of Bere. The manager of the orphanage was hung from a lamppost outside the closed building with the word 'traitor' written on a sign around her neck.

"Are you absolutely sure that this is your final decision?" Mendoza asked through gritted teeth.

"I'm afraid so, Colonel Mendoza," Ambassador Antonio Diaz answered. "As a result of the Civil War there are tens of thousands of orphans in Spain. We are finding it extremely difficult to find adoptive parents for Spanish orphans and until we successfully place these children we will not be in a position to allow any foreign orphans to enter the country."

"But your Excellency, these children will be slaughtered ..."

"I'm aware of that, Colonel, but can you imagine what the Caudillo would say if I asked him if it would be possible to accept tens of thousands of British orphans, many thousands of whom are disabled? He would think that I was mad."

"But it's cold blooded murder. There must be something that we can do to help, your Excellency?" Mendoza persisted, "Perhaps a diplomatic protest? From one Christian nation to another?"

There was a pause on the other side of the phone before Diaz responded. "Colonel Mendoza, I am sure that as a serving officer and a patriot you are aware of the Caudillo's passionate desire to restore Gibraltar to the welcome bosom of Mother Spain?"

"Yes, of course, your Excellency. It is the desire that beats within the heart of every true Spaniard." Mendoza sat straighter in his chair as he spoke.

"The Caudillo is determined to recover it through fair means or foul; through peace or war. However, as a result of the recent unpleasantness we are not in a position to take Gibraltar through force; it will take decades to recover from the devastation and damage caused by the Civil War. So we have no option but to strive to recover it through peaceful means. To that end, we are helping Prime Minister Joyce and his Government of National Unity to maintain law and order throughout England and Wales. Once the Leader has built up his forces he will launch a second invasion of Scotland and we will support him. After he has conquered Scotland he will turn Gibraltar over to us as a token of his gratitude."

"And you know this for a fact, your Excellency?"

Diaz laughed over the phone. "Who do you think helped to negotiate the Treaty over at this end? It is my signature on the paper."

"So Spain will not be making any diplomatic protests?"

"No, I'm afraid not, Colonel," Diaz replied heavily. He seemed to hesitate before he continued the conversation. "Although as the Spanish Ambassador I have no official position over this matter; personally I find this massacre of the innocents to be completely and utterly morally reprehensible. I wish you every luck and success in your effort to protect the children and put a stop to this repugnant practice and I'm sorry that I have not been able to be help you any further."

"Thank you for your time and for your advice, your Excellency."

"You're very welcome, Colonel Mendoza. Please do not hesitate to contact me if I can be of any further assistance."

Mendoza put the phone down and his shoulders sagged as he slumped into his chair in abject defeat. He felt physically and emotionally drained. Mendoza had spent the best part of a day calling the military attaches of the various embassies based in London: - the Portuguese; the Finns; the Vichy French; the Italians and the Croatians amongst others, but alas, to no avail. All of his contacts had replied that none of their governments were prepared to accept British orphans and certainly not disabled ones. Some of them had said that they strongly suspected that their own governments, as fellow Fascists or German allies, were strongly considering the possibility of introducing similar programs in their own countries. They were gearing up to follow in the footsteps of their Nazi brethren and start the extermination of those they considered to be 'unfit for life.' Phoning the Spanish ambassador had been his last and only hope. What was he going to tell Aurora?

"We can't wait two weeks, sir," Ansett announced as he showed Daylesford the deciphered message. "Partisans are attacking the Fascist extermination squads up and down the length of the entire Occupied South …"

"The disobedient swine! I explicitly ordered the undisciplined fools to stand down and await reinforcements and further orders!" Daylesford positively fumed with anger.

Ansett shrugged his shoulders. "I guess that they got fed up with waiting for the cavalry and decided to take matters into their own hands."

"But we need them!" Daylesford protested. "We need the partisans to stay undercover and to keep a low profile. We gave them express instructions not to rise up until Liberation Day, L-Day. Do we have any idea of casualties?" Daylesford dreaded the answer.

"Intelligence estimates that between a quarter and a third of all Resistance units have been destroyed in the last week or so trying to stop the slaughter."

"My God, Pete. It's far worse than I thought. We simply can't afford to wait two weeks. How are your Redemption Teams doing?"

"The training is proceeding as planned, sir ..."

"Can we send them south after only one week's worth of training?" Daylesford interrupted impatiently.

Ansett shook his head. "If we send them in after only one week's training then we might as well throw them out of an airplane without a parachute because the end result will be the same: death. You cannot train a wireless operator to use Morse code and perform the role of a signaler overnight, sir. It takes time and practice. Quite frankly, sir, If we manage to train any of the signalers to a level that is anything above adequate in the two weeks that we have given them it will be a miracle and I will eat my hat."

"If we don't send the Redemption Teams south now it will be too late," Daylesford maintained.

"But if we send in the Redemption Teams now before they're ready then they will be massacred ..."

"If we don't send them in now then the children will continue to be massacred until every single disabled child in England and Wales has been murdered," Daylesford interrupted angrily.

"And the partisans will continue to be massacred trying to save them until they are completely and utterly wiped out. If we don't send reinforcements to them soon there will no Resistance movement left. And there is another situation to consider: so far the Jedburgh Teams have obeyed their orders not to take part in any attacks against the Blackshirt Extermination Squads. They fully understand that they are not to activate until L-Day. However, how long will they be prepared to stand idly by and watch innocent children be murdered and their partisan comrades be slaughtered? It is only a matter of time before they decide to say 'to hell with the orders' and activate themselves. If that happens then many of the Jedburgh Teams will be destroyed well before Liberation Day and all of our careful planning and preparation will be for nothing."

"Point taken, sir," Ansett admitted grudgingly.

"Anyway, wasn't that the whole point of forming the Redemption Teams in the first place? To make use of men who will not be missed? The purpose of the Redemption Teams is to act as expendable assets to be used where and when we see fit and I think that now is the time to use them whether they are fully trained or not. I'm sorry, Pete, but time is a luxury that we simply do not have."

"I agree, sir. When do you want them to be ready to deploy south?"

"Let's see, today's Thursday," Daylesford thought aloud. "Can you give them a warning order this morning so that you can brief them today after lunch? Can you make sure they're ready to leave tomorrow night?"

Ansett nodded "Yes, sir. I can have thirty teams of three men each ready to deploy south on Friday night."

"Excellent, Pete." Daylesford squeezed his shoulder. "And there's one more thing to consider, Pete. With the best will in the world I don't think that the combined might of the partisans and the Redemption Teams will be strong enough to physically stop the Fascist murder squads. We need to force Joyce and the Government of National Unity to call a halt to their entire Eugenics extermination program."

"And just how are we going to do that, sir?"

"I don't know, Pete, but I know a man who does."

"Are you absolutely sure about this, Ben?"

"Yes I am, Brigadier. I've never been more sure about something in my life."

"And you're aware that although we'll probably be able to get you in we may not be able to get you out?" Daylesford asked.

"I'm aware of the risks and I'm prepared to take my chances, sir. Anyway, I've spent the last four months since the assassination of Kaiser Eddie training with the S.O.E. at the taxpayer's expense. It's about time that the great British public found out what their hard earned pounds have been spent on. What's the point of creating a lean, mean fighting machine if the machine doesn't get the chance to fight?"

"Brave words, Ben." Daylesford smiled and squeezed the man's shoulder. "I knew that I had picked the right man for the job. Anyway, I'll leave you to it. You've got a lot of work to do. You've only got a day and a half to write the sermon that will force Joyce to stop his Eugenics Extermination program. Good luck, Ben and God speed." He shook the man's hand.

"Thank you, Brigadier. Strength and honour!"

"Strength and honour, Ben!"

Ben and his friend, Peter Ansett, had been evacuated from Hereward after the St. George's Day Massacre and he had spent the past four months training as an SOE secret agent. Although he had thoroughly enjoyed his training, and he had embraced his new role with gusto and enthusiasm, he had not been able to shake off an over powering sense of guilt and shame that he had abandoned his flock to their fate. He woke up every night dreaming the same nightmare, with his sheets soaking wet, shouting "No! No! No!" as images of the massacre of his congregation flashed across his eyes. The tortured souls of hundreds of his parishioners cried out for revenge and retribution and so it was with profound relief, and a determined sense of purpose that he looked forward to returning to Hereward. Bishop Ben Rathdowne was going back to war.

Chapter Eight

"Contact, wait out!" Von Stein shouted into his radio as his lorry raced around the corner on two wheels. "Come on, Honecker! Step on it or we'll be too late!"

Von Stein's patrol drove towards the sound of the firing as fast as the two furniture removal lorries could travel. However, five minutes was a long time in a gunfight and by the time that they reached the scene of the ambush it was all over. Two Blackshirt lorries were on fire and half a dozen dead and dying Fascists lay scattered around the burning vehicles together with their weapons and spent cartridges.

"Stop!" Von Stein shouted. "Everybody out! All round defense!" The patrol of twenty stromtroopers piled out of the back of the lorries and immediately took up a position pointing their weapons out in all directions like the spokes of a wheel. "Patrol, one hundred metres, twelve o' clock, ambush site, seen?"

"Seen!" The patrol chorused.

"Rottenführer Barbie?"

"Yes, sir?"

"Position your squad in extended line on the left hand side of the road and I'll position my squad in extended line on the right hand side of the road. We'll then advance to contact. Clear?"

"Clear!" The patrol answered in unison.

"Go!"

The patrol swiftly divided into two squads and positioned themselves as von Stein had ordered. Von Stein gave the hand signal to advance and the patrol began to move through the trees towards the ambush site. However, the two squads reached the ambush site without incident and the only sound was the noise of the Blackshirt lorries burning.

"Rottenführer Barbie?"

"Yes, sir?"

"Take up a position of all round defense with your squad taking up position from twelve o' clock through to six o' clock. My squad will take up position from six o' clock through to twelve o'clock with the road leading towards Cambridge as twelve o'clock. Detail two of your men to search through the woods for any sign of the enemy for one hundred metres on the left hand side of the road and order two of my men to do the same on the right hand side of the road. Clear?"

"Clear, sir!"

"Go! Signaler, on me!" Von Stein crouched down behind a thick tree that provided him with cover from fire and also cover from view from a potential enemy hiding in the trees. His signaler soon joined him, "Contact Headquarters." Von Stein ordered.

"Headquarters, sir," the Signaler said as he passed over the telephone handle.

"Hello Tiger One, this is Tiger Two, message over," Von Stein announced.

"Hello Tiger Two, this is Tiger One, what is your sitrep, over?"

"Tiger One, Contact at …" von Stein looked at his watch, "fourteen thirty hours, ambush of Blackshirt patrol at map reference …" he looked at his map, "271191."

"Tiger Two, what are friendly and enemy casualties, over?"

"Tiger One, six Blackshirts killed and …" He saw Barbie hold up four fingers with one hand and give a thumbs down with the other hand, "four Partisans killed, over." They must have killed each other in the firefight, von Stein thought to himself.

"Tiger Two, confirm six friendlies and four enemy KIA, over."

"Tiger One, ambush took place between the villages of Oxhead and Leatherted. Request permission to execute hostages from nearest population centre as per standard operating procedures, over?"

"Tiger Two, are there any German casualties, over?"

"Tiger One, negative, over."

"Tiger Two, no German casualties suffered, Blackshirt responsibility to decide response. Request to execute hostages denied, I say again, request to execute hostages denied. Acknowledge order, over?"

"Tiger One, confirm request to execute hostages denied, over."

"Tiger Two, return to HQ immediately with all dead bodies, acknowledge over."

"Tiger One, confirm order to return to HQ with dead bodies, over. Tiger One, out."

Barbie had been patiently waiting for the radio conversation to finish. "Orders, sir?"

"We've been ordered to collect all of the bodies and return to headquarters, Klaus."

Barbie's eyebrows were raised with surprise. "What about executing hostages, sir?"

"It's Blackshirt business, Klaus. I imagine that the Brigadeführer feels that if the British want to go about slaughtering each other then it's their prerogative. He doesn't want the S.S. to get involved in their bloody civil war. So I'm afraid that they'll be no raping and pillaging today."

"The boys will be disappointed, sir. They were looking forward to getting to know the English girls better …"

"Ours not to reason why, Klaus," von Stein said with his hands in the air indicating that it was not his fault.

"What the British need is an iron fist, sir, not a velvet glove. The Brits will interpret this lack of retribution as a sign of weakness."

"You have your orders, Rottenführer," von Stein said with a cold face, warning Barbie to drop the subject before he said something that he would come to regret. "Rottenführer Barbie, load the bodies and the men back onto the lorries. We're leaving."

"Yes, sir." Barbie saluted and started bellowing orders.

Von Stein watched as the man who had saved his life in Scotland walked away. He regretted being rude to him, but he could not allow a junior N.C.O. to think that it was acceptable to criticize the orders of a superior officer. Privately, von Stein also wondered if Ulrich was using the fact that the partisans had attacked Blackshirts rather than Germans as an excuse not to execute hostages. Perhaps he had gone native. With such a beautiful girl friend, it was no surprise. But if Ulrich's personal feelings were beginning to influence, cloud and confuse his professional judgment then he was in danger of jeopardizing the war effort. Despite the fact that Ulrich was his patron, as a serving S.S. officer, von Stein could not allow that situation to continue.

Alice looked up at the sky as the four parachutes slowly floated to the ground. She ran over to the nearest parachutist with her heart beating with excitement. This was the first time that Alice had been part of a reception committee for welcome guests from the Free North. She suddenly stopped in her tracks as if she had run into an invisible force field. Alice's eyes widened with shock and surprise.

"Alice?" The camouflaged parachutist asked.

Alice flung herself at the figure and wrapped her arms around his neck. She gave him an enormous bear hug.

"Easy, tiger!"

"Bishop Rathdowne! What on earth are you doing here? Have you come to help us take our revenge on the Blackshirts?"

Rathdowne placed a hand on Alice's shoulder. "Beloved, never avenge yourselves, but leave it to the wrath of God, for it is written, 'Vengeance is mine, I will repay, says the Lord.' "

The Blackshirt captain walked up to the door and tore down the tape that had been stretched across it blocking the entrance. He unhooked a huge set of keys from his belt, selected the largest one and opened the door. He swung open the other massive twin door as well and rubbed his hands together with satisfaction. A curious crowd of onlookers was starting to gather. Hereward Cathedral had been closed since the Bloody Sunday massacre had taken place in March five months before when the entire congregation had been slaughtered by the S.S. in retaliation for a partisan attack.

"Open for business as usual, ladies and gentlemen," the Fascist officer announced with a smile. "Please feel free to enter."

"Will this work?" Another Blackshirt asked.

"It better," the Captain answered grimly, "or this will be the most unsuccessful resurrection from the dead in history. Come on; let's get out of the way. Our uniforms are putting people off and scaring them away."

The small section of Fascist Militiamen moved out of sight around the corner and divided into two teams. Each team mounted a half-track armoured personnel carrier.

Townspeople were attracted to the open doors of the cathedral like bees to honey, They could hear the organ playing at full blast and as the clock on the Town Hall struck eleven the cathedral bells started to peal for the first time in five months. As people walked through the main entrance they instinctively took a seat in the pews as if what they were doing was perfectly normal and was part of their run of the mill Sunday routine. They seemed to forget the fact that the cathedral had been shut for almost half a year and that the last people to sit in the same seats on a March Sunday morning had all been killed in cold blood.

There was a sudden gasp as the people sitting at the front of the cathedral spotted a familiar figure weaving his way through the milling crowd greeting parishioners with a warm handshake, a kiss, a bear hug or for the particularly privileged, all three.

Bishop Ben Rathdowne.

But … wasn't he supposed to be dead?

The Second- Lieutenant stood with his back to the stairs leading up to the pulpit cradling his Schmessier machine gun in his arms. He watched the congregation like a hawk looking for any sign of a possible threat against the Bishop. Two more members of his team guarded the main entrance to the Cathedral allowing people to enter but not allowing them to leave. The two soldiers stood in the shadows and made sure that they could not be seen from the Town Square outside. They watched the two entrances at the northwest and northeast corners of the Square for any sign that the alarm had been raised. The soldiers felt more confident knowing that the partisans were guarding the southwest and southeast entrances to the Square. Never the less, they felt butterflies in their stomachs: the soldiers knew that it was only a matter of time before either a Police, Blackshirt or German patrol came to investigate why the Cathedral bells were ringing.

The young officer swept his eyes over the congregation again. As expected, most of the people were watching and listening to Bishop Rathdowne deliver his sermon. However, many of the young boys and several of the young ladies were watching him with interest and admiration. They appreciated the risks that he was taking appearing as he was undisguised in his true form. An older man's piercing blue eyes met his own and he snapped his right arm up into a parade ground salute, "Strength and Honour,"the old soldier mimed.

The young officer nodded with a glowing smile and mimed the same words in reply. He felt a wave of emotion sweep over him like a tsunami and a single tear slowly found its way down his right cheek. He felt pride and something else: love. Love for the people that he had sworn the oath to his King to protect. There was no more doubt or hesitation in his heart concerning where his true loyalties or his true duty lay: it lay with his King and his people. Second-Lieutenant Thomas Ball had come home.

"What the-?" Ulrich furrowed his brow with confusion as he heard church bells begin to peal. He stood up from his desk and walked through the French windows that led onto his balcony. Yes, he was correct: it was the Hereward Cathedral bells ringing. Ulrich wondered who had given permission for the Cathedral to be reopened, because he certainly hadn't. Mayor Keeler? Ulrich shook his head, the Mayor was a real brown noser and would not have dared to have opened the Cathedral without first having been granted permission by the German occupation authorities i.e. himself. Superintendent Branson? Branson was a career Police officer who had recently been transferred from London to command the Hereward Police Force. This could possibly be an example of him trying to flex his muscles and demonstrate his independence. Captain Baldwin? Following the disastrous failure that was the invasion of Scotland, Baldwin was the highest-ranking Blackshirt in the whole of Cambridgeshire and his total forces in the whole of East Anglia barely consisted of a company of Fascist Militia. It was perfectly understandable that he might try to build bridges and curry favour with the local community by reopening the Cathedral. In fact…Ulrich trained his binoculars on the two half-tracks that were positioned in front of the Cathedral. Yes, it was just as he suspected. He picked up the telephone on his desk. "Hello, Sturmbannführer von Stein? Yes, it's Ulrich. Would you be so kind as to find out why Captain Baldwin has taken it upon himself to reopen Hereward Cathedral without first seeking my permission to do so? Thank you."

"Uh-oh. Here comes trouble,"

Baldwin shrugged his shoulders. "We knew that it was only a matter of time, Ramón, before the Nazis came to investigate. Go and tell Ball and his men to prepare for visitors."

"Si, Jefe."Ramón walked inside the Cathedral to warn Ball, Rathdowne and his two companions.

Baldwin turned around to face his remaining four Blackshirts. "Man your battle stations and make ready," he ordered.

Sam and Aurora climbed into the back of one half track and Alan and Alice climbed into the back of the other. Both of the boys cocked their MG 42 machine guns and checked that the safety catch was on. They didn't want to prematurely open fire.

"Are you ready?" Baldwin asked.

"We were born ready!" The boys answered in unison.

"Bueno."Baldwin nodded his head with satisfaction as he looked at his two young Spartan warriors. "Strength and honour, Comrades!"

"Strength and honour, Captain!" The four partisans chorused.

"Pull in over there, Honecker," von Stein ordered.

The lorry stopped at the side of the pavement and the second lorry pulled in behind the first. Von Stein got out of the lorry and walked back to the first lorry. "Klaus, I'm going to speak to the Blackshirt captain and find out what why he reopened the Cathedral without our approval."

"Very good, sir. Shall I get the men out of the lorry?"

Von Stein shook his head. "There' s no need, Rottenführer. I'm sure that it's just a bureaucratic mix up. Jumbled lines of communication. That sort of thing. I'll get this all cleared up and then perhaps we'll be able to get back to barracks in time to finish our breakfasts. It's pork sausages from a local farm butcher, my favourite."

"Mine as well, sir. As you command." Barbie gave a short bow and clicked his heels together. He walked to the back of each of the lorries in turn and told the men to relax.

Von Stein straightened his tunic, adjusted his hat at a jaunty angle and started to walk towards the Blackshirts.

Baldwin's heart skipped a beat as he watched the S.S. officer rapidly approaching. He forced himself to take slow measured breaths in an effort to calm himself down and stop his teeth from chattering.

The German seemed to falter momentarily and lose his rhythm as he walked towards the half-track. Or was Baldwin simply imaging things?

"Good morning, Sturmbannführer," Baldwin said with a welcome smile. "Have you come to attend the service, sir?"

"Good morning, Captain," von Stein answered. "No, I haven't come to attend the service. Perhaps another time. Would you be so kind to tell me who gave you permission to reopen the Cathedral?"

Baldwin's eyes narrowed with confusion. "Why certainly, sir. Superintendent Branson ordered me to reopen the Cathedral. I thought that S.S. Headquarters had given him the necessary permission to do so, sir."

"I'm sure that you're right, Captain; I'm certain that it's all a simple misunderstanding. I'll just pop over to Headquarters and ask for confirmation that Superintendent Branson requested permission to reopen the Cathedral and that permission was given."

"Very good, sir." Baldwin clicked his heels and bowed like a true Prussian.

Something about the gesture gave von Stein a curious tingling feeling in his stomach. "May I congratulate you on your German, Captain. It is completely fluent with hardly any trace of an English accent."

Baldwin smiled. "I studied German at Cambridge before the War and in fact I teach it here at St. John's. "

"And Spanish as well, unless I'm mistaken?" Von Stein asked casually.

"Spanish?" Baldwin was flustered and he was thrown completely off guard.

110

"I understand that you also speak Spanish as well. I heard you talking to one of your men. Or is it perfectly normal and common place for Blackshirt officers to speak Spanish to their men, Captain?"

"I … Ramón is from Gibraltar, sir. Virtually all Gibraltarians speak Spanish." A trickle of sweat ran down his cheek. "My father was based in Gibraltar with the Royal Navy for most of his career and I learned to speak it like a native."

"Ah … a life on the ocean wave."

"Yes, sir."

"And have you ever been to Spain, Captain?" von Stein asked conversationally.

"Living in Gibraltar? Of course, sir, many times. Before the war."

"I have also spent a lot of time in Spain. Before the War. Perhaps we could meet sometime and reminisce about our time in Spain over a pint of San Miguel beer and a plate of tapas?"

"Definitely, sir. I would enjoy that very much."

Von Stein chuckled good-naturedly. "Forgive me, Captain; much as I would like to continue this conversation with a fellow old Spanish hand I'm afraid that duty calls. I must confer with H.Q. concerning Superintendent Branson's request to reopen the Cathedral. Excuse me, Captain."

"Certainly, Hail Joyce!" Baldwin flung out his right arm in the Fascist salute.

"Heil Hitler!" Von Stein replied.

"Did you recognize him, Jefe?"

"Of course I recognized him, Ramón! I was close enough to kiss him!" Baldwin exclaimed.

"It's von Stein! It's the cold-hearted bastard that killed our boys in Spain! It was almost inevitable that we would bump into him at some point in Hereward."

"Did he buy your story?"

Baldwin shook his head. "Did he hell. I doubt that he bought a single word of it. He's on to us. We are well and truly rumbled. He's off to tell his boys to prepare for action and we must do the same." He watched as von Stein quickly walked towards his two lorries. "Comrades! Fifty metres! Two S.S. lorries! Rapid fire on my command!"

"Is everything all right, sir?" Barbie asked.

"I think so, Karl." Von Stein nodded his head slowly as he spoke. "I've no reason to think otherwise. However…I'm getting a distinct feeling of déjà vu. I'm pretty sure that I've met that Blackshirt Captain before, but I can't for the life of me remember where …"

"Perhaps at a pre- invasion briefing before we attacked Scotland, sir?" Barbie suggested.

Von Stein shrugged his shoulders. "Perhaps, Karl. God knows I attended enough of them." He clapped Barbie on the shoulder. "I'm probably worrying about nothing. I'm sure that everything is kosher and above board. I'm just going to check with Headquarters that Superintendent Branson was given permission to open the Cathedral as the Blackshirt Captain said. It's probably nothing more than the usual break down in communications and a simple misunderstanding. I'll be back in five minutes."

"Very good, sir."

"All the same, get the boys out of the lorries and get them formed up in two squads ready for action. Just in case."

"As you command, sir." Barbie clicked his heels together.

"Oh, Klaus. Do it casually. I don't want the Blackshirts to think that anything's up."

"Yes, sir." Barbie grinned. He was sick and tired of continually carrying out unsuccessful anti-partisan patrols and chasing shadows through the Fens countryside. He was looking forward with excited anticipation to what promised to be a straightforward stand up fight.

"Ramón, tell the Bishop to wrap it up," Baldwin ordered. "As soon as von Stein discovers that Branson did not ask for permission to reopen the Cathedral all hell will break loose. I want Ball to start evacuating the congregation through the side entrance into Waterloo Street immediately. I want the evacuation to be completed within five minutes. Clear?"

"Clear, Jefe!"Ramón swiftly walked away to pass on the order.

"Those Askaris are up to something …" Barbie said to himself. "Platoon! Make ready!" He bellowed. There was a metallic clang as the twenty stormtroopers cocked their weapons sending a round up the spout and flicked off their safety catches.

"… I call upon the great British public to defend our children against the Blackshirt murderers and the treacherous and evil regime of Joyce and his Fascist turncoats and traitors," Rathdowne thundered ferociously with the passion of Martin Luther. "We are talking about the cold blooded killing of disabled children, babies, toddlers and teenagers, our sons and daughters. They might be disabled, but they are human beings and they have not lost their right to live."

"Bishop Rathdowne, you have to stop immediately. The Germans are about to attack," Ramón interrupted. "Lieutenant Ball, you need to evacuate the congregation through the side entrance immediately."

"Walters, Porter! Bring up the rear and start shepherding the congregation towards the side entrance," Ball ordered. "Bishop Rathdowne, if you'd like to lead the way?"

"Certainly, Lieutenant."Rathdowne climbed down from the pulpit. "Everybody follow me!"

"I'm sure, sir," The signaling captain said. "I've checked the communication log book twice. There is no record of a phone call from Hereward Police station requesting permission to reopen Hereward Cathedral."

"Thank you, Sturmhauptführer," von Stein said.

The signals captain clicked his heels together and bowed. "My pleasure, sir."

Von Stein slapped his leather gloves together in his palm as he quickly descended the steps leading to the exit. His sixth sense had not failed him. He was right to suspect that there was something rotten in the state of Denmark.

"Rapid fire!" Baldwin ordered. Sam and Alan squeezed the triggers of their MG 42 machine guns sending a torrent of rounds at the rate of one thousand two hundred bullets per minute tearing into the assembled stormtroopers who were mown down before they had a chance to return fire.

Von Stein quickly ran down the stairs and took cover behind the rear wheel of the second lorry. He drew his Luger, cocked the pistol, flicked off his safety catch and caught his breath.

"Alan, switch fire to the ground floor door and windows!" Baldwin ordered. "Sam, switch fire to the first floor windows!" The boys did as they were told and started to systematically sweep their machine guns across the rows of windows sending cascades of shattered glass falling in a shower to the ground.

Von Stein carefully peered around the wheel and looked through the space underneath the lorry at the mangled bodies of his massacred men. He looked behind him and saw a squad of stormtroopers taking shelter within the main entrance to the Headquarters. The young sturmführer in charge caught von Stein's eyes and shouted, "We're coming!"

"No! It's not safe! They'll cut you down!"

`The sturmführer braced himself and then charged out of the entrance with the rest of his squad hot on his heels. They were cut down before they had covered half a dozen metres and lay sprawled all over the stairs.

"Oh, the bloody fools!" Von Stein punched his thigh with frustration.

However, slowly but surely the Germans were beginning to recover and rifles and machine guns were starting to poke out of the ravaged windows and return fire.

Ulrich lay flat on the floor and looked at the body that lay sprawled next to his desk. Rottenführer Lammers had been handing him a cup of coffee when a fusillade of machine gun bullets had smashed through the window and had caught the young soldier in the chest. Lammers lay with a look of complete shock and incomprehension on his face as if he was surprised to discover that he was dead. Ulrich had only survived because he had been sitting down. There but for the grace of God go I, he thought to himself. He stretched out his right arm and grabbed hold of the Schmessier machine gun that he always kept underneath his desk to be used in case of an emergency. Well, this definitely counted as an emergency. "It's time that I got back into this war," he said aloud.

"Ramón!" Baldwin shouted. "We're leaving! I'll go first and you follow! We'll rally back at the RV point! Clear?"

"Clear!"

"Sam! Cover me!" Baldwin ordered. He stopped firing his MG 42, slipped on the safety catch, climbed into the cab of the half-track and started the engine. Sam kept firing the other machine gun from the back and Alice continued to feed him ammunition belts of bullets.

"Alan! Aurora!"Ramón shouted. "We're leaving! Cover me!" He abandoned his MG 42, climbed into the driver's seat and turned the ignition key.

Baldwin's half-track started to drive and headed for Blenheim Road, which led out of the Town Square with Ramón closely following behind him.

"Think you can get away with this, you Blackshirt bastards?" Ulrich shouted through his shattered French windows. "Over my dead body!"

Ulrich took careful aim at the spot where the second half-track would turn right into Blenheim Road. He knew that would be the place where the vehicle would slow down so that it could maneuver around the corner. Ulrich pulled the Schmessier tightly into his shoulder and aimed carefully through the fore and rear sights. As the half-track slowed down Ulrich gently squeezed the trigger and fired in short sharp controlled bursts through the driver's door and window.

The half-track suddenly accelerated and crashed straight through the front window of a tobacconist shop. Alan and Aurora were thrown off their feet and

116

fell to the floor. Alan was the quickest to recover and looked into the driver's cab. "Ramón, are you all right?" There was no reply. Ramón lay slumped over his wheel, his back was smoking and he was sitting in a pool of blood.

"Uncle … Uncle Ramón, are you all right?" Aurora asked anxiously.

Alan shook his head frantically. "No, Aurora. He's dead."

"No!" Aurora shouted. "He can't be!"

"He is Aurora, and we will be as well if we don't get out of here!" He looked over the side of the half-track and saw a horde of stormtroopers charging out of S.S. Headquarters in hot pursuit.

"Come on, we've got to go. There's nothing that we can do for him."

"All right," Aurora said numbly as if she was in a trance.

Alan opened fire with the machine gun and grinned with satisfaction as he saw half a dozen Nazis fall dead and dying to the ground. "I'll give covering fire whilst you run to the other half track," Alan pointed ahead to Baldwin's vehicle that had stopped fifty metres away.

"No, Alan! We must stick together!"

"We don't have time to argue, Aurora! I can't hold them off forever. The Huns will be here any minute. When you get to the halftrack give me covering fire and I'll run to you!"

"Do you promise that you'll come? I can't lose you!"

"Cross my heart and hope to die. Now go!"

Aurora squeezed his hand and quickly climbed over the side of the half-track. She ran the fifty metres to the other vehicle and climbed into the back. She looked back towards her boyfriend.

"Come on, Alan!" But he suddenly stopped firing. Aurora watched helplessly as Alan frantically tried to clear the jammed weapon. There was a cheer of victory as the stormtroopers charged towards the half-track. Alan abandoned the MG 42 and picked up his Schmessier, but it was too late. A potato masher grenade flew through the air and landed in the vehicle. There was an explosion and Alan disappeared in a cloud of smoke. "Alan!" Aurora shouted. She started to climb out of the half-track but Alice grabbed her arm and pulled her back in.

"We're leaving!" Alice shouted. "Alan is gone! There's nothing that we can do."

"Sam?" Aurora begged desperately for support.

Sam said nothing. He shook his head as rivers of tears ran down his dirt-encrusted cheeks. He continued to fire his machine gun like a man possessed at the Germans who were swarming like ants around the captured vehicle.

"Where's Alan?" Baldwin shouted over his shoulder.

"Alan's … dead, sir," Alice answered.

Baldwin hesitated for a second before he spoke. "He gave his life to save ours. Let's make sure that his sacrifice was not in vain." He gunned the engine and drove away into the distance.

Chapter Nine

Von Stein pulled the door open so forcefully that he almost wrenched it off its battered and broken hinges. He fired twice at the body that lay sprawled over the driver's seat and gear stick.

"This one's dead," he announced. "Pull him out." A soldier standing behind him grabbed the corpse by its webbing straps and pulled the body out of the cab where it flopped lifeless to the ground.

"We've got another one here." Von Stein pointed his pistol at the second body. He was shocked to find out that the partisan was considerably younger than he had expected. The guerilla's chest was slowly rising up and down. "This one's alive." He spoke over his shoulder. "Open the other door and lift him out. Check how badly wounded he is. If he's alive then we can question him."

Two stormtroopers lifted the partisan out of the cab and laid him on the bloody cobblestones. They quickly checked his breathing and the rest of his body for breaks and burns. "He seems to be all right, sir. I can't find any obvious external injuries."

"Good," Von Stein said. "Carry him downstairs to the interrogation cells. I've got a few questions to ask this naughty school boy."

Alan woke up to the sound of screaming. The agonized shriek pierced his eardrums and made the hair on the back of his neck stand on end. Simultaneously he felt a sharp pain on his chest and smelt the stomach turning stench of burnt flesh. Alan slowly opened his eyes and looked up. There was a constant pounding in his head. He remembered that he had felt this way before when he had woken up after the disastrous battle at Fairfax. Alan raised his head. Someone was standing in front of him but it was difficult to see his face. But Alan could see what he was holding, a lighted cigar. Now Alan knew who had been screaming. The figure leaned forward and casually ground the lighted cigar into Alan's right nipple. Alan screamed in agony and rocked backwards and forwards in his chair. He couldn't move his arms or his legs and he realized that his wrists and his ankles were securely tied with rope to the chair. The pain came in waves but eventually subsided to the point where the twin points of agony from his burnt nipples blurred to become a constant ache. Alan's breathing gradually slowed down to something approaching normal and he stopped rocking. He looked down at his bare thighs that were covered in a mix of blood, sweat and saliva. Alan realized with a sudden feeling of horror that he was completely naked.

"Have you finished?" The voice asked him conversationally. He spoke as if he was asking Alan if he had finished eating his dinner.

Alan nodded heavily.

"Because I've hardly started," the voice continued. "And the pain that you've felt? That's only the beginning. That's about as good as it's going to get. There's far worse to come, I promise you, unless you tell me exactly what I want to know."

Alan nodded.

"What's your name, boy?"

"Alan Heyburn, private, 24860147." Not my real name, but a fake name, because my real name will lead them to Cromwell House, Davie and then Sam and Alice.

"How old are you, Alan?"

"16." Captain Baldwin would be able to get Davie away to a place of safety.

"You're a brave boy, Alan. I'll give you that." The German took a puff of his cigar and tapped the ash onto the floor of the cell. "Where are you from?"

"Hereward." The Lysander would arrive that night at midnight to evacuate Rathdowne. Alan knew that he had to hold out for twelve hours in order to allow the bishop to escape to Scotland.

"Ah, so you're a local," the German said jovially. "Do you go to school at St. John's?"

"Yes." Twelve hours would also give Baldwin, Sam, Davie, Alice and Aurora a head start to escape north to Scotland.

"Who's your favourite teacher?" The German asked conversationally like a father asking his son.

"Mr. Mason." Alan guessed that the German might have known that a Major Mason had been the acting commanding officer of the East Anglia Blackshirt Battalion and had also been the deputy rector of St. John's before he was killed in the ill-fated invasion of Scotland. Alan guessed that the German did not know that it had been Alan that had killed him.

"Why did you reopen the Cathedral?"

Alan shook his head and spat a globule of blood onto the floor. The German immediately thrust the cigar into the centre of Alan's stomach and ground it into his belly button as the boy screamed. The German grabbed Alan by the hair and brutally wrenched his head back. "Listen, boy! I'm not going to play any games with you! You and your friends killed a lot of my men today! You killed the man who saved my life in Scotland, so I'm not exactly in the best of moods. The only reason that you are still alive is because you have information that I want in that stupid and foolish head of yours! You are going to die today, make no

121

mistake about it, but you can choose whether you die quickly in front of a firing squad or you die slowly in indescribable agony in this torture chamber! It's up to you!"

Twelve hours. Alan shook his head and spat a globule of blood that landed on the front of the German's tunic. He smiled like a deranged lunatic.

The German's face blazed with uncontrollable anger. He yelled and he struck Alan with a vicious backhand right across his face. Alan toppled sideways and his head hit the rough concrete floor with an ominous crack that echoed throughout the torture cells.

"But we've got to save him! We've got to! We can't just leave him to die!"

"Aurora, listen! There are only four of us left! Ramón is dead and Alan probably is too. There's nothing that we can do!" Baldwin answered.

"But what about Lieutenant Ball and his men? They can help!"

Baldwin shook his head. "No, they can't, Aurora. Their mission is to protect Ben and make sure that he is safely evacuated to Scotland."

"But what about after that? They can help after that, can't they? When their mission has been accomplished?"

Baldwin looked at Alice for support. She could not trust herself to speak. Sam refused to meet his eyes and was chewing on his lip as tears ran down his face.

"Aurora. By then it will be too late," Baldwin said gently as he placed his hand on her arm.

"What do you mean?" Aurora asked with wide-eyed terror. She pulled her arm from under Baldwin's hand as if he had touched her with a red-hot poker.

"The time is now twelve o' clock. Ben leaves at midnight twelve hours from now. If Alan is alive; if he is alive, he will try to hold out for twelve hours …"

"You don't think that he will last that long?" She stood up with horror. "You think that the Germans will have…tortured and killed him?" It caused Aurora physical pain to imagine the agonies that the Germans would inflict on him in order to extract the important information that they wanted. She clenched her fist against her heart, which was beating madly.

Baldwin nodded.

"So then … what's the plan? What's your solution to the problem? That we do nothing? We let Alan, your best friend," she looked accusingly at Sam, "your adopted brother, Alice, be …be tortured to death in an S.S. prison?" She demanded furiously.

"Aurora, I-"

"No! No! No! I refuse to accept that! I swear on my mother's grave that I will not let Alan die alone and in agony in a Nazi torture chamber! And although I have not loved him as long as you have," she looked with barely concealed contempt and loathing at Sam and Alice, "my love will not allow him to die! I will rescue him alone if necessary or die in the attempt!" Aurora grabbed her Schmessier and stormed out of the farmhouse without looking back.

"Aurora, wait!" Alice shouted. She quickly looked back at Baldwin, shrugged her shoulders, grabbed her machine gun and chased after her friend.

"Alice, come back!" Baldwin shouted.

Sam wiped away his tears and made to follow his sister.

"And where do you think you're going?"

"I'm going to free my friend," Sam answered matter of factly.

"Sam, don't go: that's an order."

"Alan would do the same for me."

"But it's a suicide mission."

Sam posed the question in his mind before he answered. "Look sir, Ramón is dead and I'm sorry because he was a good man and I liked him. He was a good friend of yours and his death has understandably knocked you for six and taken the wind out of your sails. However, imagine that you knew that he was alive and was being held in an S.S. torture chamber. Would you not bend over backwards and willingly risk life and limb to rescue him even if you knew that there was only the slightest chance of saving him?"

"Yes, but-"

"And would Ramón not do the same for you?"

Baldwin slowly smiled and nodded his head. He picked up his Schmessier, "For Ramón."

"For Ramón."Sam smiled. "Strength and honour, sir!"

"Strength and honour!"

Alan slowly opened an eye a fraction of an inch. His head was throbbing as if someone had hit it with a sledgehammer. There was an S.S. stormtrooper sitting on a chair by the open door reading a newspaper. He had not noticed that the prisoner had regained consciousness. Alan tried to figure out how long he had been unconscious for. An hour? Two hours? Three? He had absolutely no idea. He imagined that the cell was underground in the basement where the Town Hall records used to be kept. There was no outside window so it was impossible to tell whether it was light or dark outside. The German yawned. Perhaps that was a good sign. Perhaps it was late at night or early in the morning- perhaps Ben had already gotten away! Or perhaps the Nazi was simply bored out of his skull having to guard this unconscious schoolboy.

Alan tried to run through his cover story to make sure that he correctly remembered the details. Alan Heyburn was a real person and had been a student at St. John's and a fellow boarder in Cromwell House. He was also sixteen and his birthday was only a few days before Alan's. His father was in the Royal Navy and served with the South China Fleet based in Hong Kong. Alan Mitchell's father served with the Hong Kong Police Force so the two Alans had a common background. Heyburn had also served with the RRiFFs at the beginning of the war but had been wounded at the Battle of Wake and had been evacuated back to Hereward. Heyburn had also joined the Fascist Militia and had unsuccessfully tried to recruit Alan to a Resistance group known as The Moles who had joined the Blackshirts in order to acquire weapons and infiltrate and destroy the organization from within. Alan had politely declined the offer to join the secret group and Heyburn had treated him with hostility and suspicion ever since. Alan knew that it would be only a matter of time before Heyburn decided that the safest thing to do in order to preserve security was to kill him. Fortunately for Alan, Heyburn had disappeared during the invasion of Scotland and had since been officially posted as Missing. He was probably lying at the bottom of the Tweed or had been buried under tons of rubble at Berwick.

"Has he recovered consciousness yet?" A voice asked.

"I … I don't know, sir," newspaperman answered nervously.

"Well, don't just stand there, Merkel! Wake him up!" The S.S. officer ordered angrily.

Merkel kicked Alan hard in the buttocks and the boy groaned in pain. "Wake up, Tommy!"

Alan was suddenly covered in a bucket full of freezing cold water. "Wakey, wakey, rise and shine! Pick him up!" Two stormtroopers picked Alan up and dumped him roughly on the torture chair. "Tie him up." The Nazis tied Alan's wrists and ankles to the chair. His wrists and ankles had already been rubbed raw and had scabbed over. Alan winced when the rough rope bit deeply into the wounds and reopened the scabs, which began to bleed profusely. The S.S. officer pulled up a chair and sat in front of him.

"Now Alan, I warned you that I wasn't going to play any games with you, didn't I? I have neither the time, the inclination or the patience to do so." The German blew out a series of smoke rings from the end of his cigar. "I'll ask you again: Why did you reopen the Cathedral?"

Alan said nothing. Twelve hours. Less by now.

"I thought so."

Alan mentally braced himself to be burnt by the cigar.

"You're a brave young man, Alan, I'll give you that."

Alan remained silent.

"I ordered my men to round up all of the people who live in Hereward with the surname ' Heyburn.'"

Alan felt an alarm bell go off in his head. He had forgotten something.

"We found out that your Uncle Albert and your Auntie Carolyn, your mother's big sister, live in Hereward …"

"How did you-?"

A vicious jab to the face broke Alan's nose. "I'll ask the questions here, Alan. You answer them."

Alan's nose was bleeding furiously and sharp pain was stabbing like a pulse from his nose into his brain. I don't know how much more of this I can take. Twelve hours. Twelve hours. I don't know if I can last another twelve minutes. Tears streamed from Alan's eyes down his dirty face and saliva ran like a river from his split and bloody lip.

"How did we find out that Albert and Carolyn were your uncle and aunt? Through a process of elimination of course."

"No-!"

"We eliminated three entire families, fifteen people in total, men, women and children ..."

"You bloody bastard!"

The S.S. officer smiled. "I've been called worse. And all because you wouldn't cooperate, Alan. All because you wouldn't answer a simple question. I hope that you can live with their deaths on your conscience, Alan, the deaths of three entire innocent families, because I don't know if I could."

Alan's burnt chest heaved with hate and anger.

"Ah, but I've saved the best for last. I have brought you some visitors ... Merkel, show our guests into the room, please."

Merkel herded Uncle Albert, Auntie Carolyn and Alan's two cousins Ruth and Janet into the room.

Carolyn's hand went up to her mouth in horror. "Alan ... what ... what have they done to you?" she started to walk towards her tortured nephew. Merkel forced her back with his rifle. "You ... you monsters! He's just a child!"

"Your beloved nephew is a terrorist who has killed many of my men!" The S.S. officer snarled. "If he wants to fight like a man then he must be prepared to die like a man! War is a man's game with man's rules.

127

Your nephew understood that when he picked up a rifle! Merkel, get them out of here!"

The S.S. officer waited until Merkel had ushered them out before he continued. "Alan, if you do not tell me exactly what I want to know then I will execute your uncle by shooting him in the face right in front of you and his family. After that, I will turn your auntie and her beautiful two young daughters over to my men. How old are the girls? If they're both a day over fourteen then I'm a Dutchman! But what lookers, eh? You're a man of the world, I'm sure that I don't have to spell it out to you what my young soldiers, who have lost friends and comrades today, will do to Carolyn, Ruth and Janet before they kill them. So I will ask you for the last and final time: why did you reopen the Cathedral?"

"We can't ask your father to help us, Aurora!" Baldwin's eyes bulged wide with disbelief at the suggestion.

"Why not?"

"'Why not?' Why not? Because he's a colonel in the Spanish Foreign Legión, Aurora! Because he's the enemy!"

"He may be the enemy, Captain, but he's also my father and more importantly than that, he is a Spanish father," Aurora said with pride. "He will not refuse a request to come to his daughter's aid and rescue."

"Your father would be willing to risk his life in order to save a school boy partisan?"

"Alan saved his life, Captain. In fact, he saved both of our lives when we were held captive by the S.S. My father owes Alan a debt of honour and he would consider it to be his duty to attempt to rescue him whatever the odds of succeeding."

Baldwin looked at Sam who nodded in confirmation.

"Although your father may be willing to risk his life to save Alan," Baldwin conceded, "I doubt that he would be willing to risk the life of his soldiers. He will not be able to rescue Alan by himself."

Aurora shook her head and smiled. "You do not know the Legión, Captain. As Alexander Dumas said, it is very much the case of 'one for all and all for one.'"

"Never the less, as the commander of this Resistance unit I consider it to be too much of a security risk to involve your father in any rescue mission," Baldwin said with an air of finality.

"Very well, Captain," Aurora said stiffly. "Then how do you propose to rescue Alan?"

"We will collect Ben, Lieutenant Ball and his team from the rendezvous point and we will use the German reputation of respect for authority against them," Baldwin announced triumphantly.

Sergeant Robbie Keeler's brows furrowed in confusion as he heard the lorry driving up the street. "That's strange. They're early. It's only six o' clock. I thought Captain Baldwin said that they would get here at ten." Keeler stood up and headed for the front door.

"Sergeant, wait!" Ball warned. "We must stand to and wait until they give us the pass-!"

Keeler opened the door and was immediately cut down by a burst of machine gun fire that almost sawed him in half.

"Take cover!" Ball shouted as he knocked over the table smashing the lamp and putting the light out. The living room was suddenly plunged into darkness. "Walters, take up position at the bedroom window upstairs! Ben, take up position in the kitchen facing the rear! Only open fire when you can see the enemy!

Conserve your ammo! We need to hold out until reinforcements get here!" in four hours' time, Ball thought to himself.

"It looks like Hepburn was right," von Stein said. "The four Partisans are hiding in this house. Correction: three Partisans now." He smiled with grim black humour. The farmhouse was situated on the edge of the deserted village of Frampton-on-the-Ouse. "That's where the Lysander will land at mid night." Von Stein pointed at the field that lay beside the house. Von Stein assembled the three sergeants who were his squad leaders. "Listen in, we've scouted around the farm house and we've established that there are only two ways in: through the front door into the living room at the front of the house and through the back door into the kitchen at the rear of the house. Scharführer Bedurftig, your squad will provide covering fire at the front of the house. Your mission will be to divert their attention and keep the enemy occupied. Scharführer Friedemann, your mission will be to provide covering fire at the rear of the house whilst Scharfurher Zenter's squad assaults the position. Clear?"

"Clear, sir!" The three sergeants answered in unison.

"Scharführer Berturftig, if the enemy switches his attention to the rear of the house then I want you to use your own judgment as to whether or not it would be practical to carry out a simultaneous assault at the front of the house."

"Yes, sir,"Berturftig answered.

"One more thing: we want to capture at least one partisan alive if possible. Clear?"

"Clear, sir!" The sergeants answered.

Von Stein felt an electric shock of excitement shoot up his spine. He was delighted to see the fire of battle burning in the eyes of his three scharführers. "Sieg heil!"

"Sieg heil!" The three sergeants chorused enthusiastically.

"They're attacking at the rear!" Rathdowne shouted. He fired a short burst from his Schmessier and saw a stormtrooper drop to the ground, but there were too many of them. The other Nazis didn't hesitate or falter but kept on coming. Rathdowne dropped as a burst of machine gun bullets raced through his open window and stitched a line of holes in the back wall. He wiped broken glass from his head and fired another short burst at the advancing stromtroopers. Rathdowne didn't know if he hit anyone. The Germans continued to advance towards the farmhouse in two fire teams, leap frogging each other towards their target. Rathdowne fired another burst and watched another stromtrooper fall into the field of wheat. He felt a sudden sting in his right arm and he involuntarily dropped his weapon. Rathdowne looked down at his arm, dripping blood and hanging uselessly at his side. "I'm hit!" He shouted.

"Ben! I'm coming! Chris! Are you able to switch fire to the rear of the house?" Baldwin shouted upstairs.

But there no answer.

"Shit!" Baldwin fired a final burst through a window at the front before he ran through the house to the kitchen at the rear. "Ben!" he rushed over to the bishop who lay with his back against the cooker.

"My arm…" he said weakly, "I think it's broken …" Rathdowne's face was deathly pale. He had lost a lot of blood.

"It's all right, Ben. You're going to be all right. Here, take this and press it against your wound." Ball handed Rathdowne a dishtowel.

"Chris?"

Ball shook his head slowly. "He's dead. I'm afraid it's just you and me now, Ben."

"Partisans! Surrender! You are completely surrounded! Come out with your hands up! You have thirty seconds to comply before we come in and get you!" A guttural German voice shouted.

"Tommy!" Rathdowne grabbed Ball's arm with a vice like grip. "They mustn't take us alive! We know too much!" He rasped as his life's blood slowly seeped out of him. Ball looked with alarm at the pool of blood that was rapidly growing and spreading over the kitchen floor. Rathdowne must have suffered a more serious wound that he was not aware of. "They will torture us. I don't think that I would have the strength or the courage to withstand it. The mind is willing, but the flesh is weak … the children …"

"Here we come! Ready or not!" There was a furious fusillade of fire as the Nazis simultaneously opened fire at both the front and the rear of the house. Von Stein watched with admiration and pride as his stromtroopers carried out a textbook fire and maneuver towards the target. Two soldiers reached the back door, kicked it open and fired a burst of machine gun bullets inside. "Grenade!" One of them shouted and threw a potato masher grenade into the kitchen. The pair waited for the grenade to explode and then fired another short burst inside. The stromtroopers entered the room with their Schmessiers pulled tightly into their shoulders. They both spotted the two bodies lying beside the cooker. The grenadier started to squeeze the trigger when his partner pushed the barrel of his weapon to the side. "Wait. They might be alive. Prisoners." The grenadier nodded in understanding and lowered his machine gun. "Room clear!" He shouted.

"Room clear!" Scharführer Berturftig shouted as he and his squad entered through the front door and checked the living room. "Rottenführer Maurice, take your fire team upstairs and check the first floor."

"Yes, Scharführer," Maurice replied as he led his men upstairs.

"Kohl and Ulbright, check the partisans in the kitchen," Berturftig ordered.

"Yes, Scharführer." The two Nazis walked towards the partisans.

"The partisan upstairs is as dead as a dodo, Scharführer," Maurice shouted downstairs.

"All right, Rottenführer. Bring the body downstairs and dump him outside."

"Yes, Schar-"

There was a massive explosion as the two grenades that lay underneath Rathdowne's body detonated. The blast shredded Kohl and the unlucky Ulbright who had set off the booby trap when he had rolled Rathdowne's body over. The explosion also killed Berturftig and injured half of his squad.

Baldwin and the rest of his team stopped in their tracks as they heard the double explosion. They had stopped their lorry when they had heard the firing begin and had continued the rest of their journey towards Frampton on foot.

"What ... what does this mean?" Aurora asked.

"That we're too late and Alan talked," Sam answered grimly.

"I'm afraid That Sam's right, Aurora," Baldwin said. "How else would the Huns find out that Ben and the rest of the team are hiding here? That's the only logical explanation."

Aurora said nothing. What could she say?

Chapter Ten

Von Stein ran towards the farmhouse as fast as his legs could carry him. However, before he reached the house there was another massive explosion and he was knocked over onto his back as if he had been pushed over by a giant invisible hand. A wave of hot air swept over his body and he felt as if his face was on fire. He slowly raised himself up from his back onto his elbows. "My God …" he said to himself, "the explosion must have ignited the gas mains …"There was a sudden blood-curdling scream that made von Stein's hair stand on end. He watched with open-mouthed horror as one of his men ran out of the kitchen with his entire body on fire like a human torch. He collapsed onto the ground and died with a final agonizing groan.

Von Stein felt as if his heart was going to explode with hate and anger. "That little partisan bastard is going to pay for this," he threatened through gritted teeth. "As God is my witness, Hepburn, you are going to rue the day that you were born."

Baldwin waited until the two lorries had just turned the tight corner where the village road met the main road before he gave the order to spring the ambush. The two MG 42 s opened fire at point blank range and killed the two stormtroopers sitting in each of the drivers' cabs instantly. The lorries juddered to a stuttering stop.

"Hande hoch!" Baldwin shouted as he fired a quick burst of his Schmessier into the sides of each lorry.

"Kamerad! Kamerad!" Frantic voices yelled.

"Hande hoch! Come out with your hands up!"

Two soldiers climbed out of each of the lorries with their hands held high above their heads. Baldwin looked at each of them in turn. They kept their eyes looking down at the floor and desperately tried to avoid eye contact.

"Who's in charge here?" Baldwin demanded in German.

"Scharführer Zenter, sir," an anonymous voice answered.

"Where is he?"

"He was sitting beside the driver in the front lorry, sir."

Dead. Excellent, Baldwin thought to himself. The young stormtroopers were leaderless.

"What's in the back of the lorries?"

"Our wounded, sir."

"How many?"

"Six seriously wounded men."

"Any dead?"

"Nine killed, sir. Three of the bodies are in the back. The other six bodies were too badly burnt to be moved."

"How many partisan casualties?" Baldwin used all of his self -discipline to control the tremor in his voice.

"Four killed, sir."

Baldwin swore under his breath.

"That's settled it then," Sam said coldly. "I say that we kill them all." He raised his machine gun up to his hip and pointed it at the prisoners.

The prisoners raised their hands higher up in terror. "Bitte, bitte, kamerad!" They begged.

"Wait a minute, Sam." Baldwin pushed the barrel to the side. "We need to find out if Alan is still alive and discover how they found out about the hide out."

"All right." Sam reluctantly lowered his MG 42. "But after that, we kill them."

Baldwin nodded. "You captured a partisan earlier. Is he still alive?"

"The School boy?"

"Yes."

"He is still alive." But in a bad way, the German was tempted to add, but stopped himself in the nick of time.

"Thank God." Alice was overcome by a tidal wave of emotion as a feeling of relief surged through her body. Aurora unsuccessfully tried to wipe away the tears of joy which flowed down her face with the back of her dirty hand and Sam smiled for the first time since Alan's capture.

"How did you find out about the partisan hideout?" Baldwin asked.

There was a sudden burst of machine gun fire. Baldwin and the German that he was talking to crumpled to the ground.

"Take cover!" Sam shouted as he let rip with his machine gun in the general direction of the enemy fire.

Alice and Aurora each grabbed one of Baldwin's arms and dragged him to cover behind one of the lorries.

"It's no use, girls ... I'm finished," Baldwin groaned.

"No!" Aurora said through tear filled eyes.

"Save yourselves ... and save Alan ..."

"We can save you as well!" Alice protested.

"No, you can't ... leave me, I'm dying, that's an order!"

"Whatever you're going to do, do it fast!" Sam shouted. "I can't hold them off forever! They're almost on top of me!"

"Sam!" Baldwin shouted. "Leave me your machine gun. I'll hold them off whilst you escape!"

"But-!"

"No 'ifs,' no 'buts,' Sam! Just do it! Now!"

Sam looked at Alice who nodded. Alice and Aurora looked at each other for a split second. Aurora nodded her head. "All right." Sam fired another burst whilst the girls moved Baldwin into position and made him as comfortable as possible.

"Thank you, girls. Alice … leave me a grenade. I won't let them take me alive …"

Alice handed Baldwin a potato masher.

"Now go!"

Alice squeezed his hand for the last time. "God bless you, sir!"

Baldwin smiled through teeth gritted tight with pain. "Strength and honour, Comrades!"

"Strength and honour!"

Von Stein approached the partisan with his Schmessier pulled tightly into his shoulder and with his forefinger applying first pressure on the trigger.

The guerrilla groaned.

"Turn him over," von Stein ordered as he aimed his weapon at the wounded man. A soldier did as he was ordered. "Clear!" No grenade. Von Stein flicked on his safety catch and lowered his Schmessier. He cautiously approached the partisan. "For you the war is over, Tommy…and your life too by the looks of it."

Much to von Stein's surprise, the fatally wounded man laughed, coughing up blood that seeped out of his mouth in a constant stream. "Hello, von Stein. Remember me?"

Von Stein looked at the guerrilla with confusion. "Hereward Cathedral?"

Baldwin shook his head. "No, we go further back than that, Manfred. May I call you Manfred? I've known you for so long. Since 1938, to be precise."

"1938?" Where was I in '38, von Stein asked himself? I was in Spain. The Civil War. Baldwin spoke Spanish. The Battle of …? The penny dropped. "You were at Ebro River."

Baldwin smiled. "I was the commanding officer of the British Battalion …"

"I captured you," von Stein nodded his head in recognition and pointed.

"And you tortured and murdered one of my men," accused Baldwin coldly.

"No, not me-"

"But it was one of your stormtroopers," Baldwin interrupted angrily, "that cut the ears off one of my men and slit his throat like a pig. You were in charge, von Stein and you allowed it to happen. You encouraged it and gave him the green light."

Von Stein thought for a moment before he replied. "Yes, I admit that it was my fault. It was my responsibility. But I was young and foolish back in those days, three years ago. I would not allow it now. I have seen too much horror …"

Baldwin smiled in the darkness. He had achieved his purpose. He had kept von Stein talking and he had stalled, slowed down and delayed the pursuit of Sam and the girls. Now it was time to draw the affair to a close. "Von Stein. I have a final favour to ask of you. I have something to give you."

"Certainly." Von Stein knelt down beside the dying guerrilla.

Baldwin took something out of his dirty and disheveled battledress and handed it to von Stein. "This is from Aurora."

Von Stein looked at it. It was a grenade.

"The wheel turns full circle …"

"Oh shit."

The retreating partisans stopped running and came to an abrupt stop.

"Was that-?" Aurora asked.

"Yes," Sam answered. "Baldwin's dead. It's over. What now?"

"We must reach the farm and regroup and recover …" Alice answered.

"And then we must rescue Alan," Aurora interrupted.

"But how?" Alice asked.

"By asking my father to help." Aurora held her head up defiantly.

Ulrich recoiled in horror when he saw the naked prisoner lying in a pool of his own piss, blood and vomit on the cold concrete floor. "Who is responsible for…for this?" He demanded furiously.

The soldier guarding Alan looked up in confusion. "Stur … Sturmbannführer von Stein, sir. I assumed that you knew …"

"You assumed that I would permit the torture of a child?"

"He … he is a terrorist, sir."

"He is a child! Look at him; he can't be more than fifteen! Is this what we've been reduced to? Torturing children?" Ulrich ranted and raved, "We're the S.S., not the bloody Gestapo and we're not those wretched cowards who guard the camps either! I return from visiting our wounded in hospital and find out that Headquarters has been turned into a bloody torture chamber?" Ulrich exclaimed incredulously. "We are the fighting S.S.! I don't call this fighting, do you? Stubbing out cigarettes on the stomach of school children! This isn't what I signed up for! Is this what you signed up for?"

"No ... no, sir." The stormtrooper looked at his commanding officer with fear and incomprehension in his eyes. Steam was virtually coming out of Ulrich's ears.

"Get a medic team in here at the double and get this boy's wounds treated!" Ulrich ordered. "You better hope and pray that any injuries that this boy has suffered are not permanent or life threatening or they'll be hell to pay!"

The soldier drew himself up to a position of attention. "But sir," he began to protest, "We carried out the tor-, the interrogation under Sturmbannführer von Stein's orders-."

"I don't give a damn who gave you the orders!" Ulrich exploded. "We will not torture children whilst I am in command of the Brigade! Is that clear?"

"Yes, sir," the stromtrooper clicked his heels together.

"It better be or else you will find yourself on the next train to the Russian Front! Now get out of my sight and find me a medical team!"

"Yes, sir!" The soldier saluted and left with his tail between his legs.

Ulrich waited until the stormtrooper had left and then he knelt down beside the injured prisoner. "Alan, Alan," he said in his ear. "You need to hold on. I'll get you out of here."

"Who ... who are you?" Alan asked through his broken and bloody lips.

"A friend."

"Alan Mitchell is my daughter Aurora's boyfriend. He is also a partisan and a British patriot. Alan has been captured and he is currently suffering under terrible torture in S.S. headquarters. He is being held captive by the same S.S. who took me and Aurora prisoner and

140

who tortured me and who ... who raped and defiled her." Mendoza stopped speaking as the words caught in his throat. He could barely carry on as a sudden pain pierced through his heart. "Alan Mitchell rescued me and Aurora and he saved our lives. The S.S. attempted the same tactic again and captured Aurora and this time her friend, Alice, as well. They murdered many of our comrades who served as my daughter's bodyguard." At this the assembled Legiónaries grumbled and growled like wild animals.

"And again the S.S. savages, they ... they ..." Mendoza's words trailed off. "I owe a debt of honour to Alan Mitchell. It is my duty to rescue him, but I cannot do it alone. I need your help. But I cannot order you to do it. What I am asking you to do is highly illegal. If we take up arms against our allies and we are caught then we will be shot as traitors." Mendoza swept his eyes slowly over the ranks of the assembled Legiónaries. "If any off you do not wish to take part in this mission then take one step backwards and nothing more will be said ..."

The platoon of Legiónaries took one step forward as one unit. "We are with you, Colonel! For Spain, for the Legión, to the death!"

Mendoza stepped forwards and placed his hand on the shoulder of the Legiónary who had spoken on behalf of his comrades. Mendoza was lost for words and was too choked with emotion to speak. A solitary tear ran down his cheek. He smiled as he regained his composure. "I have never felt more proud to be a Legiónary. Viva España! Viva la Legión!"

"Viva España! Viva la Legión!"

Merkel was still replaying the episode in his head as he paced around the ramparts that surrounded the cobbled courtyard at the rear of the Town Hall. He was convinced that he was the victim of a heinous and horrendous miscarriage of justice. Furthermore, Merkel felt hurt that he had been treated with such terrible contempt and with such a complete and utter disregard for his personal feelings by a commander whom he admired and respected. As far as he was concerned, he had been guilty of nothing more than dutifully carrying out the lawfully given orders of a superior order. Merkel felt furiously indignant that Ulrich had seemed to hold him personally responsible for the torture of the prisoner even though he had done nothing more than tie his wrists and ankles to the chair. Strumbannführer von Stein was the one who had used the boy as a human ashtray, not him. However, Merkel knew the way that the world worked. It was common knowledge that von Stein had saved Ulrich's life in Scotland. All that Ulrich would say to von Stein was: "You've been a naughty boy. Don't do it again." Merkel knew bitterly that if there was any fall out from this torture of a child incident none of it would stick to von Stein; Ulrich would protect his rescuer. Instead, someone from the rank and file would be found responsible-someone like him. Merkel shook his head with despair and resignation. What was it that Shakespeare had said? "I am a man more sinned against than sinning." That quote seemed to sum up his situation perfectly.

"Hello, what's this?" Merkel watched as two lorries slowly pulled in against the pavement on his side of the road. Merkel instantly stopped feeling sorry for himself and became a professional soldier again. He cocked the bolt of his rifle and sent a round up the spout of his barrel making his weapon ready to fire. Merkel's thumb hovered over his safety catch and he rested his forefinger against the trigger guard. He watched like a hawk as a soldier jumped down from the passenger cab.

"Morgen!" The soldier shouted up at Merkel.

"Morgen!" Merkel shouted down from the top of the five metre high wall. "Was ist hier los?"

The soldier walked to the rear left hand wheel and kicked it with disgust. "Punctured tyre."

"Bad luck!" Merkel replied. The soldier laughed and shrugged his shoulders. Merkel watched as the driver appeared and talked to the soldier. Merkel's brows furrowed with confusion as he looked at the soldier's unfamiliar uniform. They weren't German: French? Spanish? Italian perhaps? Merkel peered over the parapet and listened more closely to the soldiers talking. Were they speaking Spanish? Or perhaps it was Italian? Merkel also realised that the soldier that he had been speaking to was not an ordinary soldier but was an officer of some sort. In the poor, pre-dawn light he could not recognize the rank insignia on the officers' shoulders.

The officer walked to the rear of his lorry and gave orders to the soldiers sitting in the back. There was a chorus of moans and groans as the soldiers protested good-naturedly. They had probably been on their way back to their barracks from yet another unsuccessful anti-partisan operation in the flat and monotonous Fens countryside when the lorry had suffered a puncture. They were no doubt looking forward to collapsing in their beds for a few hours well-deserved shuteye. Merkel smiled. He knew exactly how they felt. The officer walked to the second lorry and spoke to the officer in charge of that lorry. The second officer saluted and repeated the order to his own men who responded with a similar symphony of sighs and huffing and puffing. The soldiers in the first lorry all climbed out and formed a chain between the lorry and the wall directly below Merkel. He watched as the soldiers began to pass out crates of equipment that they piled up against the wall. Merkel understood that the

143

soldiers were emptying the lorry so that it would be easier for the driver to jack up the lorry and change the tyre.

Merkel turned around and faced the courtyard. A Firing squad made up of ten men commanded by an officer was lined up facing the execution post that was situated directly opposite Merkel at the other side of the courtyard. At exactly ten minutes to six Alan Hepburn appeared flanked by two guards. The prisoner slowly walked towards the execution post with his hands tied behind his back but with his head held high. Hepburn stared resolutely straight ahead of him at the firing squad as he refused the offer of a blindfold and a last cigarette. Merkel nodded his head with respect. That's the spirit, my boy: don't show the bastards that you're scared. That was the last thought that passed through Merkel's head.

There was a massive explosion as the wall collapsed underneath Merkel. The force of the explosion sent a shower of shrapnel and bricks and mortar flying towards the firing squad and cut them down instantly. At the same time the stormtroopers guarding the prisoner were picked off by precision shots fired by a pair of snipers located in an a block of flats which overlooked the courtyard. A squad of soldiers hurdled over the fallen masonry and took up a position inside the walls. They immediately started to open fire on all of the doors and windows that looked down on the courtyard. A second squad passed through the ranks of the first squad and snatched the dazed and confused prisoner and carried him out through the ruined wall. They passed through a third squad who had formed a protective perimeter of all round defense around the second lorry. Hepburn was lifted into the rear of the second lorry and the snatch squad followed him. The first squad then withdrew through the wrecked wall and ran towards the second lorry. As the last man ran passed he threw two grenades into the back of the first lorry that exploded and ignited a jerry can of petrol. The fire soon spread throughout the lorry incinerating any incriminating evidence that might identify the attackers. The second squad also mounted the rear lorry and was quickly followed by the third squad.

"Are we all here?" Mendoza asked.

"All present and correct, Jefe!" Astray answered with a smile.

"¡Excelente! Vámonos!"

The entire prison break had taken less than five minutes and was over before a single German had managed to return fire.

Daylesford read the message in silence and handed the piece of paper over to Ansett.

OPERATION BARNADO ACCOMPLISHED STOP BISHOP AND TEMPLARS KILLED STOP FAWKES AND PICASSO KILLED STOP ROBIN WOUNDED STOP URGENTLY REQUEST IMMEDIATE CASUALTY EVACUATION SAY AGAIN URGENTLY REQUEST IMMEDIATE CASUALTY EVACUATION STOP LOCATION PAPUA FOXTROT STOP

Ansett translated the decoded message in his head as he read the piece of paper: the operation to alert the public to the existence of Action T2, the Joyce Government plan to terminate all those with hereditary mental or physical disabilities within two years, had been successfully accomplished. However, in the process Ben Rathdowne, all three members of the Redemption Team, Captain Baldwin and Ramón Mendoza had all been killed. Ansett shook his head in sorrow. He had known Rathdowne for more than twenty five years since they had served together in the

Fusiliers during the Great War where Rathdowne had been a stretcher-bearer and Ansett had been an infantryman. Ansett would find time to grieve for his old friend later and he knew that Daylesford would as well. He recognized that the Redemption Team was established as an expendable asset to be used if and when necessary. However, he still felt guilty that they had more or less been thrown away before they were fully trained. Ansett knew that John Baldwin and Ramón Mendoza had been fighting the Fascists for longer than anyone else in S.O.E. since the Spanish Civil War began in 1936. It was a tragedy that the pair of them would not be able to witness the final defeat of the Fascists and the victory of the democracies. Ansett straightened his back and braced his shoulders; Rathdowne, the Redemption Team, Baldwin and Mendoza had all been soldiers: they knew the risks and they took their chances. Alan, on the other hand, was a completely different kettle of fish. He was only a child and was barely sixteen. Alan was a boy fighting in a man's war. He should have been holding a pencil in a classroom, not holding a machine gun in a half-track. But Britain was in dire straits and had summoned all of her sons and daughters to answer the call and play their part in what might prove to be Albion's final Act. And Alan had certainly played his part and paid the price. Sam and Alice had demanded that he be evacuated immediately from Archie Leon's pig farm indicating that Alan's injuries were serious. The thought that Alan might be seriously wounded hit Ansett harder than the death of his old friend.

Ansett turned to look at Daylesford. He was so angry that his whole body was shaking with barely controlled rage. "I hope that it was worth it," he managed to force out through gritted teeth.

"So do I, Pete," Daylesford answered grimly. "So do I."

Chapter Eleven

The Lysander landed at midnight and delivered a resupply of arms, ammunition and medical supplies to the waiting partisans. Sam, Alice and Aurora carefully strapped their unconscious friend into the small seat at the back of the airplane and watched with trepidation as the Lysander took off and flew back to Scotland.

Ansett, Daylesford and a small reception committee of medical staff greeted Alan when he arrived in the wee small hours of the following morning. He was carried on a stretcher into the back of an ambulance which sped off with an armed escort towards Craiglockhart Hospital in Edinburgh.

The doctors discovered that the most serious injury that Alan was suffering from was moderate concussion. Following his removal from the torture chamber, his burns had been expertly treated by S.S. doctors and following his prison break; he had been cared for by Legión doctors. The doctors manipulated Alan's broken nose back into position whilst he was unconscious. They were confident that as long as their patient was allowed to rest and recuperate he would be back on his feet and ready to start exercising in one week's time.

Identical sermons were delivered throughout Occupied Britain from York to Bournemouth and from Plymouth to Dover. The horrific revelation that the Joyce Government was carrying out a systematic policy of murdering disabled orphan children spread like wild fire up and down the length of England and Wales. A general strike was called and shops, businesses and factories shut down all across the Occupied South.

Millions of ordinary people came out onto the streets and marched, protested and demonstrated against the Fascist government's plan to carry out its murderous eugenics policy by carrying placards that read ' Save the children!' and by chanting 'Smash the G.N.U.!'. Protestors carried out candlelit vigils outside orphanages that had already been closed down and demonstrators formed a human chain outside orphanages that were still open in order to prevent Fascist Death Squads from removing the children. Protestors picketed Blackshirt barracks and bases and chased away any Fascists who were foolish enough to try to force their way through the cordon. A handful of Blackshirts who did try to penetrate the human barricade in Southampton were chased through the streets until their pursuers caught them. They were unceremoniously lynched from the nearest lamppost whilst a mob of onlookers jeered and cheered. The Police lacked both the means and the motivation to intervene and so did nothing. When Blackshirt barracks were set alight the Fire Brigade only took action when there was a risk that the fire would spread to adjoining buildings. Otherwise the firemen were content to do nothing and enjoy the bonfires together with the arsonists.

The German Occupation Authority did not lift a finger to crush the General Strike and restricted itself to carrying out anti - partisan operations in the countryside. As far as Reichkommissar Schenk was concerned, as long as the strike was not directed against the German Occupation Authority and no Germans were killed or injured it would remain an internal political affair. The Government of National Unity bore the sole responsibility for dealing with the situation as it saw fit. However, if the G.N.U. asked their fellow

Fascists for help then the German Occupation Authority would of course be only too willing to render military assistance to the civil authority. On the other hand, it was understood that if Joyce asked for help then this would be a tacit admission that he could not handle the situation and was not up to the job. The Germans would be left with no alternative but to find someone who was.

Joyce was not going to allow that to happen. After five days of strikes the G.N.U. caved in and cancelled the Action T2 program. Of course Joyce did not admit that the euthanasia campaign had been his idea and placed the blame for the whole program on the narrow shoulders of half a dozen fanatical eugenic zealots with high and influential positions within the British Union of Fascists. After a televised show trial, which was shown in cinemas across the Occupied South, the six accused were found guilty by a kangaroo court and were summarily executed by firing squad.

Reichkommissar Schenk breathed a sigh of relief that Joyce had not asked him to help the G.N.U. to crush the General Strike and had managed to solve the crisis by himself. Schenk had barely enough combat troops to defend what used to be known as the Scottish Front that now ran from Morecombe Bay on the west coast across England to Middlesborough on the east coast. He had scraped the bottom of the barrel to round up enough clerks, cooks and other rear echelon base personnel to keep a lid on the simmering partisan problem and he simply did not have enough bodies to carry out the two former tasks and also help the Blackshirts to crush a general strike and force people to go back to work. Schenk had not received any reinforcements from Germany since the disastrous invasion of Scotland had failed and far from being given fresh new blood,

Occupied Britain was bleeding the blood that she already had. Russia had been sucking men and material from Britain like a leech ever since the launch of Operation Barbarossa. Schenk had been absolutely horrified by the Top Secret report he had read indicating that Germany had lost an average of 60,000 men killed per month on the Eastern Front since the invasion of the U.S.S.R. began in June 1941.As a direct result, Britain had slipped far down the league table of reinforcement destinations. More reinforcements were being sent to North Africa than to Britain. Schenk was painfully aware that his defensive position in Britain was starting to resemble that of an egg: hard on the outside, but soft on the inside.

As soon as Joyce announced that he was terminating the Action T2 program Schenk authorized all German military units to resume carrying out their normal duties in the towns and cities. The first action that the 4th S.S. Infantry Regiment took was to avenge the death of their popular and well-respected commanding officer, Sturmbannführer von Stein and the killing and wounding of approximately sixty fellow stormtroopers by partisans and British commandos. Soldiers from von Stein's old company, led by their new C.O, the recently promoted Sturmbannführer Ernst Zimmer, rounded up worshippers and tourists from Hereward Cathedral and herded them outside into the Town Square at the point of the bayonet. The stormtroopers surrounded the petrified townspeople and at Zimmer's command, opened fire at point blank range into the crowd of screaming and crying civilians. Zimmer eventually gave the order to cease firing when the last man standing had been cut down. He wandered with his soldiers amongst the dead and dying men, women and children personally administering the coup de grace, a double tap to the head, to at least half a dozen victims who had managed to survive the initial fusillade. When the murderous deed was done and Zimmer was finally satisfied that no one was left alive he made safe his Luger pistol, returned it to his holster and calmly ordered his men to climb aboard their lorries and return to their barracks. Zimmer led his stormtroopers in singing the ' Horst Wessel' the S.S. marching song, at the top of their voices as they drove back to their base. The soldiers did so with great enthusiasm and gusto and fired their weapons in the air, at unlucky passersby who happened to be in the wrong place at the wrong time and also at any windows where the occupants were foolish enough to try to satisfy their curiousity as to the source of the singing. When the Police and ambulance crews arrived at the scene they discovered that the S.S. had murdered over one hundred men, women and children.

However, the Nazis had not satisfied their thirst for blood and after a hearty lunch the same company ventured out once more in their quest for revenge. They returned to the scene of von Stein's death and consulted their maps. Zimmer knew that Frampton-on-the-Ouse was a deserted village: its occupants had been massacred in a previous anti-partisan operation, so he simply selected the nearest village as the target of his terror and the recipient of his revenge.

Zimmer's stormtroopers completely surrounded the sleepy village of Trumpton with a blood tight blockade and made sure that no one could either enter or escape. When the quarantine was complete the soldiers started to move the shocked and startled villagers onto the village green like Alsatians shepherding sheep. When the vicar assured Zimmer that all of the villagers were present and correct the sturmbannführer ordered all of the women and children to enter the church whilst the men remained outside. As soon as the church was full, Zimmer ordered it to be locked shut. The men were then summarily executed in groups of ten by an S.S. firing squad. The last men to be executed lived long enough to hear a handful of grenades explode as the stormtroopers set fire to the church and the villagers' loved ones were burnt alive and died in indescribable pain and agony.

When Hereward's two fire engines arrived they were too late: the village church, which had stood undisturbed for a thousand years, was a raging inferno. Miraculously, two small boys appeared who had been skiving off school and so had survived when their schoolmates and teachers had been massacred. They had hidden themselves up a tree when the shooting had started and had witnessed the whole murderous event. The boys had only felt that it was safe to climb down when they heard the bells of the fire engines approaching. The boys estimated that the Germans had killed virtually the entire population of Trumpton: approximately four hundred and fifty people.

Sturmbannführer Ernst Zimmer drove back to barracks with a smile on his face and a warm glow in his heart with the feeling of a job well done. He grinned as he listened to his boys singing a rude and ribald rhyming song about the obvious attractions of English girls. His boys. His men. He smiled with paternal pride as he remembered the cool, calm and collected manner in which the soldiers of his company had carried out their duties that morning. It was not easy to execute men, women and children in cold blood at point blank range where you were so close that you could see the whites of their eyes and smell their sweat. Smell their fear. Of course, it was far easier to kill Jews, or even Poles and Russians. But they were untermenschen scum and were barely human, if at all. Executing Englishmen, women and children was different because they were fellow Aryans. Not as good as Germans, of course, but at least near the same level on the evolutionary ladder. No, killing fellow Aryans was not for the faint hearted. Not everyone was up to it. Not everyone was capable of summoning the strength of character and conviction that was necessary to carry out what would strike most people to be an inhumane and barbaric task. But his soldiers were not ' most people.' They were the best. They were the elite and they were his. His company. No, correction- they were his regiment! The 4th S.S. belonged to him. Zimmer sat up ramrod straight with pride. He was confident that they would not let him down.

"ROBIN MADE FULL RECOVERY STOP STAND DOWN ALL RESISTANCE OFFENSIVE ACTIVITIES STOP REARM RECOVER RECRUIT SAY AGAIN STAND DOWN ALL RESISTANCE OFFENSIVE ACTIVITIES STOP"

Alice breathed out a massive sigh of relief as she held the piece of paper to her chest. "Alan's all right. Thank God." She handed the message over to Aurora.

Aurora skim read the decoded message as fast as her eyes could travel across the paper and then read it a second time more slowly to make sure that she her understood the message correctly. "Thank God that he's safe," Aurora said as tears flowed freely down her face.

Sam took the paper from Aurora and read it with a massive smile on his face. "No doubt he's living it up in Edinburgh as we speak, stuffing his face with haggis, neaps and tatties-"

"And I don't blame him either," Alice interrupted. " That's what I'd be doing."

"Breathing free air in a free country," Aurora shook her head wistfully. "I haven't lived in a free country since the Civil War started in '36. I've almost forgotten what it's like."

"The Huns haven't even been here for a year yet and I HAVE forgotten what it's like to live in a free country," Sam said bitterly. "I'd give all the tea in China for the chance to spend just one day not constantly looking over my shoulder to make sure that the Gestapo, the S.S. or one of those dirty Blackshirt bastards wasn't following me."

"Maybe Edinburgh will be able to transfer us up north to Scotland one at a time for a week or two's rest and recuperation," Alice suggested hopefully.

Sam shrugged his shoulders. "Perhaps," he nodded his head. "But I very much doubt that organizing a holiday for us in the highlands features particularly highly in their list of priorities. In the meantime, what are we supposed to do whilst Al is enjoying himself in Edinburgh with all of those bonnie Scottish lassies?" Sam smiled wickedly at Aurora.

"Well, the 'bonnie Scottish lassies' have been pretty clear with their orders, Sam," Aurora refused to rise to the bait. "We are to stand down and rearm, recover and recruit more members …"

"Recruit more members?" Sam guffawed with disbelief. "From where? Everyone we know is either too old for the Home Guard or too young! I'm certainly not going to ask my grandfather to join us! He can barely hold a walking stick never mind a rifle! He runs out of breath walking from the kitchen to the living room."

"What about school children then?" Aurora suggested. "What about the boys in Alan's boarding house? I'm sure that Alan's little brother Davie hates the Germans as much as we-"

"Davie?" Sam exclaimed incredulously. "He's thirteen years old! I'm sure that Alan would have more than a few harsh words to say if I told him that I had recruited his little brother to the Resistance!"

Aurora opened her mouth to reply but then thought better of it and closed it again.

"It will take a significant amount of time to recover from this bloody disaster and recruit new members. We lost Ramón, Al, Ben, his three bodyguards and Captain Baldwin all in one day. We won't be able to rebuild our unit overnight," Sam said somberly.

"Tiocfaidh ár lá, Sam," Alice said confidently as she squeezed her brother's shoulder. "Our day will come."

"I hope so, sis," Sam said grimly. "I really do. I'd just like to be alive when it does, that's all."

Alan did indeed spend a week in Edinburgh, as Sam had predicted with eyes green with envy. However, even Sam would be forced to grudgingly admit that what Alan spent his time doing six days per week from dawn to dusk and for many hours beyond for the whole of August could hardly be described as ' living it up.' Alan spent his first week in Scotland in Craiglockhart Hospital recovering from his horrific session in the S.S. Headquarters torture chambers. He then travelled up to the S.O.E. Headquarters at the Alligin Hotel on the shores of Loch Torridon, on the west coast of Scotland opposite the Isle of Skye.

Alan trained with fellow S.O.E. agents on an extremely physically and mentally demanding course that was designed to prepare agents to survive and operate on their own in enemy occupied territory. He woke up at dawn every day and ran three miles before breakfast in physical training kit and once a week he carried out an eight mile combat fitness test in full battle dress complete with rifle and weighted webbing over rough country roads with a platoon of fellow S.O.E. male and female trainee agents. Alan learned how to use a dozen different types of homemade and manufactured explosives on a dozen different objects ranging from buildings to bridges and he learned how to strip and assemble a dozen friendly and enemy weapons ranging from revolvers to machine guns. He learned how to parachute and how to kill a man with a knife, his bare hands and every day household objects ranging from a pen or pencil to a plastic bag. Alan learned how to operate a radio and how to send a message using a wireless code and ciphers and how to disguise his appearance and deceive the enemy and friends as well if necessary.

At the end of August Alan's trainers declared that he was ready to be returned to the field. He passed through the course with flying colours and he graduated with a manly handshake and a few carefully chosen words of advice. There was no certificate or coloured beret, no wings, promotion or parade to celebrate his achievement. Alan was a secret agent and so his achievements would also remain secret. Ansett had suggested that it would be a good idea if Alan was reinserted to the South in time for the new school term so that no one would ask awkward questions concerning his where abouts. Daylesford had agreed and the reinsertion date was set for the start of September.

"Sir, there's a Sturmbannführer von Horn here to see you," a smartly dressed officer announced as he entered the office and clicked his heels together.

"A sturmbannführer who?" Ulrich asked as he raised his head from examining the paperwork on his desk.

"Sturmbannführer von Horn, sir," Ulrich's adjutant replied.

"Are we expecting a Sturmbannführer von Horn to arrive today, Albert?"

Hauptsturmführer Mackensen consulted his clipboard before he replied. "No, sir." He shrugged his shoulders. "However, that does not necessarily mean that he is not supposed to arrive today, sir."

Ulrich sighed with resignation. "Please be so kind as to show him in, Albert."

"Very good, sir."

Ulrich used the opportunity to straighten his tunic and make himself appear more presentable.

An S.S. officer marched into Ulrich's office, came to a halt and thrust out his right arm.

"Heil Hitler!"

Ulrich responded with the same salute but with rather less gusto and enthusiasm. He had never been a big fan of what he regarded as unnecessary 'yes sir, no sir, three bags full sir' parade square bashing.

"Sturmbannführer Georg von Horn reporting for duty as ordered, sir!"

"Please take a seat, Sturmbannführer." Ulrich gestured to a chair with a friendly smile.

"Thank you, sir." Von Horn took off his peaked cap, ran his fingers through his hair and sat down.

"Would you care for a drink? A shot of whiskey perhaps? I have a bottle of the finest Whyte and Mackay single malt."

Von Horn grimaced as if he had been offered a glass of Ulrich's warm urine to drink. "No thank you, sir. I'd prefer a glass of something German if you don't mind. Perhaps schnapps or a glass of wine. I've been drinking filthy foreign muck for so long that I've forgotten what a good, clean glass of German alcohol tastes like."

"Have you been in Russia?" Ulrich asked as he poured himself a glass of the water of life.

Von Horn nodded. "Yes, sir. I've spent the last two months since the invasion began working in Russia and before that I was in Poland for ten months. I'll be quite happy if I never set eyes on another bottle of vodka again. Or on another dirty unwashed Slav for that matter."

Ulrich laughed.

"Perhaps now you can understand why I would like to drink something German, sir," von Horn said with a smile.

"Certainly, Sturmbannführer." Ulrich gave the necessary instructions to a clerk sitting outside his office. "Now tell me, Sturmbannführer: to what do I owe the pleasure of this visit? Have you brought a regiment of reinforcements to assist my anti-partisan operations?"

Von Horn reacted as if Ulrich had thrown a bucket of freezing cold water over him. "Sir? I don't understand ..."

"Why have you come to Hereward?"

"Surely you know, sir? Berlin sent a courier many months ago with a briefcase containing detailed top secret information concerning what my mission was to be here ..."

"By courier?" Ulrich guffawed with disbelief at the obvious foolishness of that decision. "I presume that for the last part of the journey the briefcase was carried by a motorcycle dispatch rider?"

Von Horn shrugged his shoulders. "I don't know, sir. I'm not familiar with the procedure that we use for conveying top secret information in England ..."

"Well, I can assure you that that type of information is carried in England by motorcycle," Ulrich said sharply. "I can also assure you that your dispatch rider did not reach me."

"Do you mean-?"

"Yes, Sturmbannführer von Horn," Ulrich nodded his head grimly. "Partisans must have ambushed your dispatch rider. I have no doubt that your unfortunate motorcyclist is lying rotting in some unmarked grave somewhere in some God forsaken corner of the waterlogged Fens countryside and I also have no doubt that Edinburgh is fully aware and familiar with the purpose of your mission here in England. Which is more than can be said for me as I haven't the foggiest idea about the purpose of your mission …"

Von Horn sat in stunned silence and reacted as if Ulrich had told him that his mother had died. The colour drained from his face and he turned as white as a sheet. It was several seconds before he was able to speak. "Then my mission here may have failed before it has even began …"

"What do you mean?"

"I mean that the birds may well have already flown the coop …"

"I'm afraid that I don't understand, Sturmbannführer. You will have to enlighten me." Ulrich leaned forward in his chair with anticipation.

Von Horn hesitated for a moment before he spoke. "Are you familiar with the activities of the Einsatzgruppen in Poland and Russia, sir?

Ulrich nodded. "Of course. The Einsatzgruppen have been carrying out vital work behind the lines dealing with continuing opposition to our rule, fighting partisans and so on," he stated confidently.

Von Horn did not look Ulrich in the eye as he continued. "Ah, yes…in a manner of speaking. We have been dealing with actual and potential opposition behind the lines and of course this does include partisans and also other groups as well …" von Horn left his final words hanging in the air.

Ulrich looked puzzled and perplexed. "I'm sorry, Sturmbannführer. I don't quite follow you. What do you mean by 'potential threats?' "

"I mean people who might not represent a threat now but could very well pose a threat in the future."

"Such as?"

Von Horn coughed into his hand to clear his throat before he answered. "Our plans for Poland and the other occupied territories focus on the elimination and suppression of political, religious and intellectual leaders. Our policy has two aims: firstly, to prevent Slav elites from organizing resistance or from ever regrouping into a governing class; and secondly, to exploit the great unwashed masses, the less educated majority of peasants and workers as unskilled slave laborers in agriculture and industry." Von Horn explained the plan to Ulrich in exactly the same way that he had first explained it to his soldiers.

"Poets, priests and politicians have much to say for their positions, Sturmbannführer, but surely they do not pose as much of a clear and present threat to our rule as partisans? Why are we wasting our precious and rapidly diminishing resources on killing these intellectuals? I mean, we're losing 60,000 men per month on the Russian Front. Surely we should be concentrating on defeating the partisans, not murdering teachers, doctors and lawyers?"

"With all due respect, Brigadeführer, I disagree and so does the Führer. He considers the middle class in the towns and cities to be as much of a threat to our rule as partisans in the countryside. The Führer has also widened the net to include not just intellectuals, but also in the case of Russia, Communist Party political commissars as well and of course the eternal enemy, the Jews."

"But why are you here?"

"We are establishing a regional task force to be based in Cambridgeshire which is to be comprised of one battalion of S.S. stormtroopers. One company of approximately one hundred men, commanded by yours truly, is to be based in Hereward."

"And what is your mission?" Ulrich asked with an increasing sense of dread and foreboding.

Von Horn looked at Ulrich as if he was speaking to the village idiot. "Begging your pardon, sir, but I thought that the purpose of my mission would be obvious by now: We are going to carry out the same mission in England and Wales as we have carried out with so much success in the East," von Horn's eyes glowed with the burning intensity of a religious fanatic. "We will cleanse and purify this land of the Jewish vermin by using bullets, bombs and bayonets."

Chapter Twelve

"Mr. Coward? Mr. Noël Coward?"

"Yes, that's me, for my sins. And who the devil might you be?"

The S.S. officer smiled with amusement at the man's bravado. He had been looking forward to this meeting and he was glad that Noël Coward had lived up to his reputation as a fiery and feisty character. "My name is Sturmbannführer Georg von Horn and I'm sorry to disturb your breakfast, Mr. Coward, but I'm afraid that I've been ordered to take you into Protective Custody."

"Protective Custody?" Coward guffawed, "against whom, might I ask?"

"Against terrorists, Mr. Coward."

"The only terrorists around here have either a crooked cross or a lightning bolt on their armbands," Coward answered defiantly. "Asking a German to protect an Englishman is like asking a cat to protect a canary."

"How very eloquent and expressive, Mr. Coward. But then again I would have expected no less from such a famous and distinguished actor and playwright such as yourself." Von Horn bowed mockingly. "You are, of course, not entitled to your opinion. After all, this is not a free country."

Coward opened his mouth to deliver a witty reply, but shut it again when he realized that he might say something that he might come to regret. "So, what happens now?"

"I will give you five minutes to pack a toothbrush, a pair of pajamas and a spare pair of clothes. And then you will come with us."

"And if I refuse?" Coward crossed his arms.

"Then my men and I will remove you by force from your home and take you with us anyway, but this time without your toothbrush. We will also remove anyone else who is living here with you and we will burn your house to the ground," von Horn responded using exactly the same answer that he had given countless times before in exactly the same situation.

"I see. Then you leave me with little choice."

"That's the general idea." Von Horn gestured with his hands held wide apart. Coward was faced with a fate accompli.

"Where will you take me?"

"To Hereward Town Hall."

"I heard that the Town Hall was in drastic need of repair, renovation and redecoration following the recent partisan attack," Coward said with a mischievous twinkle in his eye.

"Ah, you have been sadly misinformed, Mr. Coward. The damage was not as extensive as we had first been led to believe and it is a case of business as usual as far as my comrades at S.S. Headquarters are concerned. You are surprised?"

"No. Only disappointed."

"The hole in the wall has been repaired and the walls are twice as thick and as high as they used to be. Also new protective crash barriers have been built so that vehicles will no longer be able to come so close to the walls. Plus, we will have your good self, amongst others as … how can I put it? An extra insurance policy to deter a possible terrorist attack."

" 'Terrorists?' don't you mean 'patriots?' " Coward said provocatively.

164

Von Horn shrugged his shoulders dismissively. "You say tomato, I say tomato. One man's terrorist is another man's freedom fighter. Words are cheap. What matters is power and who wields it."

"May I inquire as to the identity of my fellow hostages?"

"You will not be a 'hostage,' Mr. Coward," von Horn protested with surprising sincerity. "You will merely be a guest at the Führer's pleasure ..."

"And for long will it please your Führer to hold me?" Coward interrupted.

"For as long as the Führer deems it necessary to protect you."

"I see ..."

"I'm sure that you will not be held for very long. After all, the war can't go on forever. I'm sure that it is only a matter of time before the politicians see sense and make peace. Then we can all go back to doing what we used to do before the war."

Coward shook his head heavily. "I disagree. Churchill and the King will continue to fight until Germany has surrendered and Hitler is safely behind bars or swinging at the end of a hangman's noose as he so richly and rightly deserves," Coward said provocatively. He smiled with gratification as he saw von Horn wince with discomfort. Coward was certain that it had been many years since the German had heard the Führer being described in such a derogatory and derisive manner and it gave him a wicked thrill of pleasure to twist the Nazi's tail feathers . "This infernal war will become even more cruel and violent," he continued. "We are living through dark times and there are more dark times just around the corner. There are black clouds travelling through the sky and it's no good hoping for a silver lining. For we know from

165

experience they won't roll by. We will continue to fight this war for some time yet, I'm afraid."

"I had never thought of you as a pessimist, Mr Coward."

"I prefer to think myself as a realist."

Von Horn tried to lighten Coward's dark mood. "For your information, Mr. Coward, the other guests include such esteemed individuals as H.G. Wells and E.M. Forster and these are just a few of the guests who will be staying in Hereward. There will be no shortage of fellow guests with whom you will be able to engage in witty conversations."

"I'll talk to anyone as long as they amuse me, or move me. If they don't do either I shall want to go home."

"You will be able to discuss, criticise and reflect on each other's work."

"I love criticism just so long as it's unqualified praise."

Von Horn smiled. He seemed to have succeeded in shaking off Coward's depressing mood.

"You may even be able to take long walks in the Cambridgeshire countryside. With an armed escort to protect you from the terrorist threat, of course," he added hurriedly.

"I like long walks, especially when they are taken by people who annoy me."

Von Horn chose to ignore Coward's caustic remark. "You will have no shortage of talented and interesting people to spend the day with."

"Thousands of people have talent. I might as well congratulate you for having eyes in your head. The one and only thing that counts is: Do you have staying power? Will I be able to entertain and amuse my fellow guests on these long walks that you envisage or will we all have decided to bump each other off out of sheer boredom and so cheat the Reaper? Oh, Sturmbannführer, the people I should be seen dead with."

Von Horn was put out and genuinely tried to reassure the Englishman. "Mr. Coward, I urge you to dismiss such macabre thoughts from your mind. There is no reason why your life and the life of your fellow countrymen should be at risk as long as-"

"As long as the Resistance does not carry out any attacks?" Coward interrupted.

Von Horn thought for a moment before he answered. "Just so."

Coward smiled with amusement at the German's naivety. "I'm afraid that you have rather overestimated the extent of my influence and also the extent of my fellow countrymen's appreciation for the Arts, Sturmbannführer," Coward laughed with self deprecation. "Some might see it as an incentive to attack the Germans rather than a deterrent if they thought that I would be executed in reprisal."

"Surely not, Mr. Coward!" Von Horn recoiled in shock and horror. "Surely not a man of your position and reputation! You are a national treasure!"

Coward shook his head. "My importance to the world is relatively small. On the other hand, my importance to myself is tremendous." He looked at the German's confused expression. Coward laughed again and patted the S.S. officer on the shoulder. "I'm only pulling your leg, Sturmbannführer."

Von Horn was visibly relieved.

"I'm afraid to inform you that I don't think that Hitler's cunning plan to convince the partisans not to carry out acts of resistance by threatening to execute hostages is going to work. I fully expect that you will have murdered me by October."

"I … we …" von Horn stumbled and tripped to find the right words.

"It's discouraging to think how many people are shocked by honesty and how few by deceit. I'm merely calling a spade a spade." Coward thought for a moment before he spoke. "Five minutes, you said?"

"Make it ten, Mr. Coward."

"Thank you, Sturmbannführer von Horn. You're an officer and a gentleman." Coward took a long look outside at his front garden before he retreated inside his house.

After fifteen minutes had passed von Horn entered the house to hurry Coward along. He found the actor hanging from the rafters. Despite desperate attempts to revive him it was all to no avail. The S.S. medic who arrived shortly pronounced him dead. Von Horn removed the elegantly written note that the playwright had left on the dining room table. It read in the actor's own script:

'By name, but not by nature.'

"It's started. The Einsatzgruppen have started to arrest V.I.P.s and they are holding them hostage as a deterrent against partisan attacks," Daylesford announced grimly.

"The question is: what are we going to do about it?" Ansett asked.

"The problem is that this is a German operation whereas Action T2 was a Blackshirt operation. The Germans will not give a damn about public reaction. We will not be able to organize protest marches and demonstrations because the Jerries will not care about the extent of public support or opposition. If we organize another general strike the Huns will interpret it as an act of defiance expressly directed against them and will react accordingly with a massive and overwhelming display of force and power. There will be a massacre. In fact, most members of the public probably do not even know about the arrest of the V.I.P.s and some of them probably couldn't care less if they did know. I mean, who cares if a bunch of toffs and big wigs get arrested and held hostage? And if they get executed as revenge for a Resistance attack, well, so what? Ordinary people are executed every day of the week as punishment for partisan attacks." Daylesford paused for thought. "I didn't know that Noël Coward lived in Cambridge, did you, Pete?"

"No, sir, and I bet that most of the good citizens of Cambridge did not know either. And neither do they care."

"Precisely. Another problem is that we don't know how many V.I.P.s the Germans plan to arrest and who they are."

"You said that the Einsatzgruppen have so far murdered more than sixty thousand people in Poland, sir. Our population is approximately twice that of Poland so we're talking about a potential target figure of around about one hundred and twenty thousand!" Ansett exclaimed in horror.

Daylesford shook his head. "I think that you're being overly pessimistic, Pete. Remember that the Germans lump the Poles and the Russians together in the same basket as untermenschen Slav scum. They want to turn those poor people into slaves. However, they regard the British as fellow Aryans only one rung below them on the evolutionary ladder. They want to turn us into fellow masters not slaves. Whereas the Germans will always regard the Slavs as enemies to be destroyed they want us to become their friends and allies. The Germans regard the S.S. Legion of Saint George as only the beginning. Once they have conquered the whole of the U.K. they want to transfer the remnants of the entire British Army to the Eastern Front to join their Holy Crusade against the Communists. The Germans won't be able to do that if they've exterminated our entire officer class. They need officers and generals to command the troops. It doesn't make sense to murder all of our intellectuals if the Germans want to see us fighting side by side, shoulder to shoulder with them against the Soviets."

"Since when have the Germans started to make sense? This whole war doesn't make sense."

"I think that we can reduce the size of the target list."

"How many Einsatzgruppen have been identified, sir?"

"Four groups, so far. There's a headquarters einsatzkommando based in London and three regional ones. They're based in Cambridge, Birmingham and Liverpool."

"There were eight Einsatzgruppen operating in Poland and they killed sixty thousand people. Therefore four Einsatzgruppenn are capable of killing at least thirty thousand people. Do we have any idea who might be on the target list, sir?"

"No we don't, Pete," Daylesford shook his head grimly. "But Huns being Huns I'm sure that with their usual Teutonic thoroughness they will have compiled a list. I refuse to believe that the Nazis are murdering people simply because they speak like the King, look like little Lord Fauntleroy and behave like Bertie Wooster."

"The question is simple: how do we get our hands on a list?"

"The answer is equally simple, Pete," Daylesford smiled like a cut throat pirate, "we steal one."

"How old did you say he is, sir?" The young corporal asked.

"He's eighty four years old, Scharführer," von Horn answered. "But don't underestimate him. Don't be fooled by first impressions."

"Are you absolutely sure that it's strictly necessary to accompany him at all times, sir? I don't mean to boast, but if he decides to try to escape I'm fairly confident that I'll be able to catch him."

"Scharführer Becker, I don't want you to let him out of your sight," von Horn said sternly. "I want you to stick to him like glue. I don't want any repeat of the Coward incident. Is that absolutely clear?"

"Crystal clear, sir." Becker turned to his squad. "All right, lads. Let's get into character. Make ready."

Becker's soldiers cocked their weapons and pulled their weapons tightly into their shoulders. They ran their forefingers along the trigger guard and lightly rested their thumbs on the safety catch.

"Let's go and arrest grandpa." Becker's men laughed and followed their leader up the gravelly garden path towards the front door of the house. Becker stopped in front of the door and knocked. He heard someone put down a cup and saucer in the kitchen and shuffle slowly towards the door.

The door opened. "Yes?"

"I've been ordered to take you into protective custody," Becker announced. "You have five minutes to gather your things," he said brusquely.

"I was wondering when you vultures might appear," the old man said matter of factly. "It's been like waiting for the Grim Reaper to turn up. I'll just go to the bathroom, get my toothbrush and pay a quick visit to the thunder box."

"Thunder box?" Becker asked with a brow furrowed with confusion.

"The W.C. the toilet, the crapper," the old man spat the words out like bullets from a machine gun.

Becker followed the old man up the narrow staircase to the first floor landing. The man reached the toilet door and turned around. "Young man, unless you want to come in and help me to wipe my arse, I suggest that you stand outside."

Becker was knocked off his stride by the man's rude remark. He slung his rifle on his shoulder and stood outside the door with his back to the bannister, drumming his fingers impatiently on the wood.

"Tell me, Corporal," the man asked through the closed door, "were you ever a scout in your misspent youth?"

"Ah, no," Becker shook his head. "Hitler Youth. The Führer banned the Scouts."

"So you are not familiar with the Scout motto?" A sapphire bright blue eye peered through a cunningly disguised and camouflaged hole in the door.

"No, what might that be?"

"Be prepared." The old man kicked the door wide and opened fire with a single barrel of his .577 Nitro Express rifle. The elephant gun bullet blasted a saucer shaped hole in Becker's stomach and he collapsed to the floor in a bloody heap. The man stepped over the dead German and opened fire with the second barrel at another stormtrooper who was charging up the stairs. The force of the blast ripped his chest open and threw him down the stairs where he lay in a crumpled heap at the bottom. The man dropped the empty elephant gun and drew a revolver from the small of his back. He flew down to the ground floor and turned right into his living room. He fired three shots at the Germans who had been busy admiring his hunting trophies and souvenirs scattered around the room. They didn't even have time to unsling their weapons. He felt a sudden sting in his left arm and as he spun around to his rear he managed to snap off two more shots. Another stormtrooper collapsed to the ground with two gaping wounds in his chest. The man felt two massive punches to the chest and fell to the floor where he lay on his back. The soldier who had shot him walked up to him and aimed his rifle at his chest as the man's life rapidly ebbed away with every last tortured breath.

Von Horn walked into the house with a drawn Luger pistol. He knelt down carefully next to the dying man, picked up his weapon and gave a long, slow whistle of appreciation. "A Wembley Mark IV Revolver. Just as deadly as the day that it was manufactured forty years ago."

"Forty years ago, sir?" The soldier with the rifle asked.

"Yes, Schmitt. Standard issue for British Army officers during the Boer War. This will be a welcome addition to my collection."

"You mean that this old man used to be an Army officer?"

"This 'old man', Schmitt, as you so eloquently describe him, was one of the most famous British soldiers who ever lived. I take it that you were never a Scout?"

Schmitt shook his head. "No, sir. Hitler Youth."

"Well, I was a scout. This is the man who started the whole movement. Lord Robert Baden-Powell, the hero of the Siege of Mafeking."

Schmitt shrugged his shoulders. "I thought that he was just a harmless old man-"

"Who killed six of our comrades," von Horn interrupted.

"Becker and the others are all dead, sir." Another stormtrooper reported.

Von Horn shook his head sadly as he gently closed Baden-Powell's eyes with his fingertips.

"Ah, the folly of youth. I warned Becker not to underestimate him."

The partisans watched with mounting excitement as the two parachutes slowly floated down to the ground. Sam ran up as the first man landed and struggled to his feet. He rugby tackled the parachutist and knocked him to the ground. Sam wrestled with him, ignoring the parachutist's shouts to get off him, until the man used a Judo move to throw Sam off. Sam stood up and pulled the parachutist to his feet. "Welcome back to England, you skiving Scotch swine!"

"Glad to be back, Sam. Thanks for the warm welcome," Alan answered sarcastically. "I was getting tired of eating Scottish beef and drinking whiskey all the time."

Sam responded with a playful punch that gave his friend a dead arm. As Alan was busy rubbing his sore arm he was suddenly jumped on from behind and knocked to the ground once more. His unknown assailant rolled off him and stood up.

"I've missed you, Alan. Have you missed me or have you been busy enjoying the company of all the bonnie red haired Scottish lassies?" Aurora asked.

Alan smiled and held a handful of Aurora's raven coloured hair. "You know what they say, Aurora: the darker the berry, the sweeter the juice. Nothing compares to you."

Sam smiled. "I'll leave you two love birds to get reacquainted." He walked away to greet the other new arrival.

Alice walked arm in arm with the second parachutist towards her brother.

"Major Ansett, I presume?" Sam saluted.

Ansett returned the salute. "The very same." Ansett shook his young apprentice's hand. "Your sister tells me that you've all been up to mischief since I left."

"That's rather an understatement, Mr. Ansett," Alice said. "We've been raising merry hell since you left in April."

Sam smiled like a hungry jackal. "In the last five months we've killed more Huns than you've had hot dinners, sir."

"I'm glad to hear it, Sam." Ansett clamped a hand on his shoulder. "I knew that you wouldn't disappoint me. "

"Why are you here, sir?" Sam asked.

"My mission is twofold: firstly to disrupt Einsatzgruppen operations in Cambridgeshire; secondly to lay the ground work for L-Day."

"So it's coming?" Sam asked excitedly.

"Liberation is coming as assuredly as Christmas," Ansett answered with a smile.

"But not necessarily this Christmas?" Alice asked.

Ansett turned to face her. "Unfortunately, you're correct, Alice."

Alice's face fell.

"But it is coming," Ansett placed a reassuring hand on her arm.

Alan arrived with his arm wrapped around Aurora. The two starstruck lovers were smiling as if Christmas had come early.

Sam walked up to his friend and wrapped an arm around his shoulder. "The boys are back in town."

Ansett smiled with warmth and affection at his happy few, his band of warriors. "Good. Then let's go to work."

"How are things going, Georg?" Ulrich asked.

"Slowly, sir," von Horn answered with a shake of his head. "It's like looking for a needle in a haystack. In Poland we would simply arrest all the teachers at a primary school or all of the doctors and nurses at a hospital, march them outside into the playground or the street and shoot the lot of them in batches of ten with machine guns. Here we have to arrest specific targets and take them to a prison where they are to be held as hostages to be executed in the event of a partisan attack. And all because the British are so called Aryans like us." Von Horn shook his head with frustration. "If the Englanders are Aryans like us then why are they fighting against us so ferociously? And if we are fighting this war in order to gain lebensraum for the German people how does it make sense to preserve the enemy's population?"

"It makes sense to the Führer, Georg, and that is what is important," Ulrich explained patiently as if to a child. "The decision to preserve the British instead of exterminate them is all part of the Führer's master plan."

"But surely it makes more sense to kill as many of the natives as possible so that our settlers can move in?" Von Horn persisted. "That's what we are doing in the East."

"We are seeking to preserve the British instead of kill them precisely because they are fellow Aryans, Georg, and not untermenschen Slav scum," Ulrich explained. "It is possible and desirable for us to become friends and allies with fellow Aryans whereas, as a matter of principle, it is impossible for us to be anything other than enemies with the Slavs."

"But that is not strictly true, sir. We are allies with the Slovakians, the Croatians and the Bulgarians and all of these people do not deny that they are Slavs and neither do we. In fact, these people are as proud to call themselves Slavs, as we are proud to call ourselves Aryans." Von Horn shook his head in bewilderment. "I know that it's hard to believe, sir, but it's true. I've been fighting in the East for ten months and although the Poles and Russians hate each other's guts they are both equally proud to call themselves Slavs."

"That's like a dog being proud to be a mongrel instead of a pure breed," Ulrich interjected.

"I agree, sir, it's absolutely bizarre and beggars belief. Never the less, it is true. As I was saying, sir, according to the Führer, the Slavs are our blood enemies but yet we find ourselves fighting alongside them against the common Communist enemy who happens also to be Slav."

"But the Slovakians, the Croatians and the Bulgarians are all Fascists like us, Georg, so the Führer is prepared to put aside the inconvenient fact that they are Slav for the moment. I am sure he has plans to deal with them in the future after they have served their purpose."

"I see, sir. So we have established that politics is more important than principles and it is possible to make alliances with Fascist Slavs."

"Georg, you are playing with fire," Ulrich warned. "This is the Führer that you are talking about."

Von Horn nodded in acknowledgement of the risks that he was taking. "We have made alliances with the Italians who are Latins and we have made alliances with the Romanians who insist that they are also Latin, although I am rather skeptical of their claim. I think that they are more likely to be Slavs. We have made an alliance with the Hungarians who originally came from east of the Ural Mountains that makes them basically Slavs like the Romanians. We have made alliances with the various Fascist Slav nations such as the Croatians and so on whom I've already mentioned. However, at least they are all European and White. But we have also made an alliance with the Japanese who are definitely not European or White. Where do they stand on the evolutionary ladder and how can the Führer justify this alliance?"

"I … I don't know, Georg. Perhaps they are above Slavs but below Latins? Maybe the Führer has given them the status of Honourary Aryans?"

Von Horn nodded. "Perhaps, sir. But if we take this one stage further …" von Horn looked over his shoulder to make sure that the door to Ulrich's office was firmly shut, "if we take this one step further, sir. If you would permit me to play devil's advocate: what is to stop us making an alliance with a long lost tribe of Fascists whom we find living in the Amazon jungle who happen to be Jewish?"

Ulrich suddenly slammed the top of his table with an open palm and jumped to his feet like a jack in the box. "Enough! That's enough, Sturmbannführer von Horn! I order you to stop this conversation immediately. What you are saying is tantamount to treason and if I reported this conversation to the Gestapo it would be regarded as such!"

Von Horn bowed his head in subjection. "I apologise, sir. I did not intend to cause any offense."

Ulrich's face was absolutely scarlet with barely controlled rage and fury. "Your outrageous outburst has placed me in an impossible situation, Sturmbannführer! It is my duty to report such a treasonous tirade against the honour and integrity of the Führer to the Gestapo!"

Von Horn averted his eyes as Ulrich ranted and raved. A bead of sweat trickled slowly down his cheek. His heart was beating so fast that it threatened to burst through his rib cage.

"However …" Ulrich looked at the firmly closed door, "however, I realize that you have been under a lot of stress and pressure recently and I realize that your question was … hypothetical. So I am willing to forgive your indiscretion on this occasion only."

"Thank you, Brigadeführer Ulrich." Von Horn dared to raise his eyes in hope. "It won't happen again. I won't let you down."

"Good." Ulrich pulled down and straightened his tunic. "Once is an accident, Sturmbannführer, and can be considered as an error of judgment and a momentary lapse of reason. However, twice is something rather more sinister and would be regarded as treason. Is that clear?"

"Crystal clear, sir. It won't happen again, sir."

"Good." Ulrich nodded. "And if I smell the faintest whiff or hear the quietest whisper of any similar expressions of doubt or disagreement about our present policy regarding the treatment of the British, the Slavs, the Jews or anyone else then I will hold you personally responsible for encouraging sedition and mutiny in the ranks. You will be arrested, put on trial and executed so quickly that your feet will not even touch the floor."

"Yes, sir." Von Horn bowed his head once more in acknowledgement.

"Now, is there anything further that you wished to discuss with me, Sturmbannführer?"

"No, sir."

"Very well. Dismissed! Sieg Heil!"

Von Horn leapt to his feet. "Sieg Heil!" He saluted, about turned and marched smartly out of the office.

Ulrich watched as the chastened officer left his room. He then dropped his angry face as if he was taking off a mask. Ulrich smiled to himself and poured a glass of whiskey. He took a sip of the amber nectar. Well, that really set a cat amongst the pigeons, he thought to himself with satisfaction. I rather enjoyed that. I must do it again.

179

Chapter Thirteen

"My God," Aurora covered her mouth with horror. "That's my piano teacher."

Alan took her by the elbow and guided her away from the Wanted poster through the crowd of readers. "Are you sure?"

"I'm absolutely sure, Alan. Ignacy Jan Paderewski: pianist and former prime minister of Poland. It can't be anyone else."

"All right," Alan nodded his head resolutely. "What do you want to do?"

"I'm not the only person who Ignacy teaches piano to. It's only a matter of time before another one of his students sees the poster; they're all over town. One of them, or one of their parents, may be tempted to turn him in to the Nazis. £1000 is a lot of money."

"We can warn him, Aurora, and then he can escape to the North."

Aurora shook her head. "He's eighty one years old, Alan. He's not as quick on his feet as he used to be. He won't be escaping anywhere in a hurry."

"Well, can he hide somewhere? There must be someone who lives nearby who can hide him?"

"Perhaps," Aurora nodded. "But he only arrived in Britain after the fall of Poland less than two years ago. He speaks English with a thick Polish accent and I would imagine that most of his friends are also Polish and they are probably also on the Wanted list. But there IS someone who lives nearby who can hide him …" Aurora turned to look at her boyfriend.

"Who?" Alan looked his girlfriend in the eyes. "You've got that crazy look in your eye that you get when you come up with a mad plan …"

"Not a mad plan, Alan. I prefer to think of it as being an inspired plan," Aurora said with a cheeky grin.

Comprehension dawned. "No! You cannot be serious?" Alan exclaimed with shock.

"But I am, my love." Aurora gave Alan her sunshine smile and wrapped her arms around his waist. "It's perfect. It is secluded and out of the way. The Germans will never suspect anything."

"But I didn't join this man's army in order to be put in charge of running an old folks' home!" Alan protested.

Aurora squeezed her boyfriend tighter around the waist. "Come on, Alan, it's the right thing to do and you know it." She looked up at him and fluttered her eyelashes. "And it would make me happy." She knew exactly what she was doing.

Alan tried to stay strong, but resistance was futile. "Oh, all right." He laughed. "You win." He had always known that he would eventually give in. "By the way. I meant to ask you: how did your father find out when I was going to be executed?"

Aurora shrugged her shoulders nonchalantly. "An anonymous tip off. Someone made a phone call to the Legión Headquarters. It seems that you have a guardian angel, my love."

"I wonder if he's German."

"Are you sure that this is the place, Hans?" The young S.S. corporal looked at his map with a perplexed look on his face. "The place looks deserted."

"This is the address that Sturmbannführer von Horn gave us, Kurt. Frampton-on-the-Ouse. We haven't made a mistake with our map reading. This is the place all right," Rottenführer Hans Krenz assured him.

"Then where the hell are all the people?" Scharführer Kurt Schabowski asked. "I've seen more life in a funeral parlour."

"The S.S. killed all of the villagers in retaliation for a partisan attack about six months ago."

Schabowski shivered. "No wonder that this place gives me goose bumps. There are too many ghosts here."

Krenz laughed. "You're getting soft in your old age, Kurt. Our Einsatzgruppe unit alone must have killed tens of thousands of people in Poland and Russia. I wouldn't have thought that you would become squeamish about this sort of thing."

"I did what I had to do because it was my duty, Hans," Schabowski said stiffly. "It doesn't mean that I enjoyed it." Kurt thought for a moment before he started to speak. "Do you remember what happened at Byelaya Tserkov in August?"

"Yes, Kurt. I remember."

Schabowski nodded his head slowly. "The Jewish children were brought along to the freshly dug grave in a tractor. I remember that I was trembling so much that I could barely hold my rifle still. We took the children down from the tractor. We lined them up along the top of the grave and shot them so that they fell into it. I remember that I didn't aim at any particular part of the body. I fired blindly until my magazine was empty. Automatically, without thinking, like a robot, like a machine." He paused and swallowed hard. "They fell into the grave. The wailing was indescribable. I will never forget the scene throughout my life. I've found it very hard to bear and I have difficulty sleeping at night. I have nightmares …"

"We all have nightmares, Kurt."

"I ... I remember a small fair-haired girl who took me by the hand as if she felt sorry for me. She looked like my niece, Frieda. I ... I murdered her ."

"You didn't murder her, Kurt. You killed her. You executed her under orders. There is a difference." Krenz walked up and put a hand on his friend's shoulder. "Don't blame yourself. It wasn't your fault, Kurt. You were following orders. No one said that it would be easy to carry out our duties."

Schabowski ignored what his friend said and talked as if he was in a trance. "Many children were hit four or five times before they died. I know, because I checked the bodies. Some of them weren't dead, they were only wounded. Some of them were still alive when we buried them."

Krenz placed both of his hands on his friend's shoulders. "Listen, Kurt. I know that it's gloomy work. It is no easy thing to kill woman and children. But we are fighting this war for the survival or non-survival of our people. We are literally fighting for the existence of the German Race. The Jews would do the same to our children if they conquered Germany. The Jews started this war and so they are the first to feel our revenge. We are Crusaders in a Holy War against the Jews and we must make sure that wherever the German soldier goes, no Jew remains."

"I understand what you're saying, Hans, I really do. But it makes no difference. I'm finished, I'm through. I've had enough. I've ... I've killed my last child in cold blood." He turned to look at his friend. "I'm not like you, Hans. I'm not strong enough. This is my last job. As soon as it's over I'm going to request permission to transfer to an S.S. unit which is fighting up north on the Scottish Front."

"Kurt, I think that you're making a big mistake ..."

"The little girl looked like Frieda, Hans." Tears ran freely down Schabowski's face. "And I murdered her."

Krenz looked at his friend with sympathy and understanding. Schabowski was not the first man in the unit to have requested a transfer away from the slaughter. "All right, Kurt. I understand. If that's what you want then I'll help. I won't stand in your way."

"Thanks … thanks, Hans. You're a true friend."

Krenz had a sudden brain wave. "I tell you what, Kurt. To prove what a good friend I am, why don't you sit this one out? Me and the boys can bring the old man out ourselves."

Schabowski's eyes lit up with relief. "Are you sure?"

"Of course, I am." Krenz patted his friend's shoulder.

"Thank you. It's just that I don't really feel up to it at the moment …"

"Certainly. Don't give it a second thought, Kurt. Come on, boys!" Krenz shouted at his half a dozen stormtroopers. "Let's pick up our Polack piano teacher!"

"Be careful, Hans!"

"Be careful?" Krenz guffawed. "You're starting to sound like my grandmother! He's just an old man."

"Famous last words, Hans. That's exactly what Becker said!" Schabowski sat on a wall and watched as Krenz gathered his men around him to issue his orders.

"Now men, the target is Ignacy Jan Paderewski, an eighty one year old-" Krenz's words were abruptly cut off by the chain saw like staccato of two MG 42 firing at the rate of 1,200 rounds per minute. The stormtroopers were cut down in a murderous cross fire and collapsed to the ground where they lay in a crumpled heap.

Schabowski looked at the scene of death and destruction with open-mouthed horror. He felt a warm sensation spread down his leg and he became aware that he had pissed himself.

"Hande hoch, Fritz!" A voice ordered.

Schabowski raised his hands in the air and turned towards the source of the voice. He was shocked to see a very attractive blonde young woman walking towards him dressed in a rag tag mix of British and German uniform.

"Raise those hands higher, Adolf!" Another voice ordered. Schabowski turned towards the second voice and was surprised to see another female partisan walking towards him. This one had jet-black hair and was also wearing a piratical mix of friendly and enemy clothing. Has he been ambushed by an all-female band of guerrillas? Were they a lost tribe of Amazons?

"Hey, Fritz!" The blonde ordered.

As Schabowski turned around the partisan cracked him on the chin with her rifle butt. The German fell to the ground like a felled tree.

"Good night, Vienna," Alice said.

Schabowski slowly opened his eyes. He felt as if he had been kicked in the chin by a donkey and the whole of his face throbbed painfully. "Where … where am I?"

"In hell," an anonymous female voice answered.

Schabowski looked to his left and recoiled with shock. His hands strained and jerked as he struggled to free himself from the handcuffs that chained him to the wall. "My God! Hans … what have you done to him?" His eyes bulged wide with horror as he stared at his friend's body. Krenz's head sagged against his chest. Dried blood had formed a trail from the torn and broken skin on his wrists down to his elbows. The front of Krenz's jacket was saturated and soaked through

185

with blood. Schabowski's eyes travelled further down his friend's body that abruptly ended just below his knees in a bloody mess of bones and tattered shreds of flesh. "What? How …?"

"Although we asked Hans a few simple questions in a very polite and courteous manner, I'm afraid to report that he was less than forth coming with the necessary information." A man wearing the uniform of a British Army major explained. "So we were forced to resort to using more … persuasive methods."

"You … you tortured him? You cut off his legs?"

"I prefer to think that we interrogated him vigorously. 'Torture' is such a medieval term, don't you think? It conjures up images of the rack and cold, dark and damp dungeons and as you can see, we have used neither. And incidentally, we didn't 'cut off' his legs! That would be completely barbaric!" The Major smiled. "Hannibal ate them."

"Hannibal? Who on earth is Hannibal?"

"Sam? Would you be so kind as to introduce Hannibal to our welcome guest?"

Sam smiled like a wolf about to devour its prey and left the shed.

Schabowski's mouth hung open as he found himself looking into the face of the biggest pig that he had ever seen. It was snorting and snuffling noisily and long tendrils of drool hung from its mouth. Shredded rags of uniform stuck to its hairy body that was thickly matted with blood and gore. Schabowski noticed that a necklace made up of German dog tags hung from the pig's studded leather collar.

"Schabowski, meet Hannibal. He'll be having you for dinner," Sam announced with a wide toothed grin.

"No!"

"Hannibal was enjoying eating your friend over there, but then Krenz was inconsiderate enough to die

186

on him. Hannibal prefers to eat his prey when it's alive, rather than dead. I think it's' because the blood is still warm and flows better, so he stopped eating when Krenz died," Sam explained matter of factly. "But I think that he's still hungry, don't you?"

Schabowski's mouth hung open with terror.

"Hans was the starter, Schabowski, and you'll be the main course unless you answer every single question that I ask you. And If I have the slightest suspicion that you are not telling us the truth, the whole truth and nothing but the truth then I will feed you to Hannibal one piece at a time starting with your toes. You have ten toes and you can probably afford to lose a couple of them, Kurt, but Hannibal will work his way up until he eats something that you definitely cannot afford to lose if you want to raise a family in the future. Do I make myself clear?"

Schabowski was too petrified to speak and nodded vigorously instead.

"Good. Then let's begin ..."

"So what have we got?" Ansett asked.

"Schabowski has described some of the events that his unit has taken part in. Between June 23rd and June 27th 1941 in Kaunas, Lithuania, 4,000 Jews were killed on the streets of Kaunas by local people." Alice read from a piece of paper which she held. "He specifically mentioned the 'Death dealer of Kaunas', a young man who murdered Jews with a crow bar before a large crowd who cheered each killing with clapping and shouts of encouragement."

"The Jews were killed by fellow Lithuanians?" Alan asked. "Not by the Germans?"

Alice nodded somberly. "The Jewish victims were killed by their friends and neighbours."

"My God!" Alan raised his hand to his mouth with horror. "It's unbelievable!"

Alice continued to read the sworn testimony. "The young man stopped every now and again to play the Lithuanian national anthem with his accordion before continuing with the killing. He pulled out one man at a time from the group and hit him with the crowbar with one or more strikes to the back of his head. Within forty five minutes he had beaten to death the entire group of forty to fifty people in this manner. After all of the people had been beaten to death, the young man put the crowbar down, picked up an accordion and climbed on top of the pile of victims and played the Lithuanian national anthem. The behaviour of the men, women and children present was absolutely unbelievable. After each man had been killed, they began to clap and when the national anthem started up they stood at attention and joined in with the singing. In the front row there were women with babies and infants in their arms who stayed there right until the end of the whole murderous affair. Some people explained to me that the parents of the young man who had killed the other people had been taken from their beds two days earlier by Lithuanian Communists working for the Soviet Occupation Authorities and had been executed. The mother and father were murdered because they were suspected of being nationalists, and this was the young man's revenge."

"Revenge on between forty and fifty people? He knew, without doubt, that each and every one of those specific people had murdered his parents?" Sam asked incredulously.

"So, Schabowski and his unit did not carry out the killings?" Ignacy Jan Paderewski asked in his heavily accented English.

"No, they didn't," Alice conceded.

"But the arrival of his Einsatzgruppe created the situation which allowed the massacre to take place," Aurora added.

"Look, Ignacy, these are the photos which Schabowski took of the killings." Alice handed the man two photos.

Paderewski looked at the photos with eyes wide with shocked disbelief. "These are ... these are monstrous ..." The first photo showed a young man with rolled up shirtsleeves about to strike another man lying face down on the ground with a giant crow bar. The second photo showed the same man sitting on a mountain of half a dozen corpses playing an accordion with tears streaming down his face. In the background men, women and children were clapping and punching their fists in the air in triumph. "What are you going to do with him?"

"With Schabowski?" Ansett answered with eyebrows raised with surprise. "Why, we're going to kill him, of course."

"Kill him?" Paderewski exclaimed. "But he's a prisoner of war!"

"Listen, grand dad, we're not in the capturing Nazis business, we're in the killing Nazis business," Sam explained.

"And business is good," Alan added.

"But that means that we are no better than the Nazis!" Paderewski protested.

"Listen, Ignacy," Ansett said patiently, "You've got a good heart and I know how you feel, but we're not exactly equipped to look after P.O.W.s. even if we wanted to. I mean, where would we keep them? In the sheds with the pigs? The Nazis execute any partisans that they capture and we do the same to any Jerries that we catch. We need to fight fire with fire," Ansett said.

"Keeping them with the pigs is too good for them. Anyway, the pigs would object," Alan said.

"Maybe we could let him go-?"

"Ignacy, he knows that we are on a farm and that we keep pigs. How long do you think it would take for the Nazis to put two and two together and search all of the pig farms in the area?" Ansett asked.

"What if he gives us his word of honour-?"

" 'His word of honour?' " Sam laughed sarcastically. "From a Nazi? I would rather accept a jackal's word of honour!"

"Ignacy, I'm beginning to regret risking my life to rescue you. Maybe we should have let the Nazis find you," Alan said.

"Maybe we should feed you to the pigs," Sam added.

"There must be a better way …"

"Ignacy, please listen to this letter which we found on one of the Germans," Aurora said.

" 'I helped to execute the Jews. The men, women, children and mothers were pushed into the pits. Children were first beaten to death with rifle butts and then were thrown feet first into the pits. There were a number of filthy sadists in my platoon. For example, pregnant women were shot in the belly for fun and then thrown into the pits, pretty girls were raped and then were shot in the breasts. Before the execution the Jews had to undergo a body search for jewellery and money. Men from my unit used this as an excuse to sexually assault women before they murdered them' … it goes on."

"It sounds as if the German who wrote this letter was expressing remorse …" Paderewski grasped at straws.

"For God's sake! Stop making excuses for them!" Alice exploded. "Are these Nazis 'expressing

190

remorse?' " She thrust a pile of photos into Paderewski's hands. "Schawbowski's unit killing Polish civilians in Leszno and Kórnik in October 1939; killing a Jewish mother trying to protect her child with her own body in the Ukraine, 1941; killing a Jew at a mass grave in the Ukraine, 1941. Look at the back, the Nazi bastard has written 'The last Jew in Vinnitsa.' " Torrents of tears ran down Alice's face. "These baby killers certainly aren't expressing any remorse!"

Paderewski stood up with a face drained of all emotion and handed the photos back to Alice. "Major Ansett, I have a favour to ask you."

"Certainly, Ignacy."

"May I borrow a gun?"

Paderewski returned to the kitchen five minutes later. "I have executed Schabowski, Major Ansett. You were right and I was wrong. We have to win this war by any means necessary if we are to save ourselves from the enemies of Humanity."

"Even if it means killing prisoners?" Ansett asked with a raised eyebrow.

Paderewski nodded. "Even if it means killing prisoners." He returned the revolver to Ansett. "Thank you, Major."

"You're welcome, Ignacy," Ansett replied.

"What will you do with his body?"

"Feed it to the pigs."

Paderewski shrugged his shoulders dismissively. "Pigs have got to eat. However, I'll never be able to eat a bacon sandwich with quite the same gusto and enthusiasm again."

Everyone laughed.

"It disturbs me to think that in the dim and distant past Schabowski's family must have been Polish. We share the same roots yet he has transformed into becoming a German and he has devolved and degenerated into becoming a Nazi." Paderewski shook his head with disappointment. "I have no doubt that Schabowski was personally responsible for murdering hundreds of his fellow countrymen. His Polish ancestors must be turning in their graves. How did this happen?"

"I ask myself the same question when I look at the Blackshirts, Ignacy," Ansett answered sadly. "Intelligence estimates that there may be as many as thirty thousand full and part time members of the Fascist Militia. The S.S. have also recruited about seven thousand British members of the Legion of Saint George to fight on the Russian Front. How can any Briton fight for the Nazis when the Huns continue to butcher our people?" He shook his head with despair and disbelief. "At least you can hold your head up high with the knowledge that the Germans have failed to find enough Poles to serve in a puppet government in Poland. There is no Polish Fascist Militia or S.S. unit. Poland has upheld her honour, Ignacy."

Paderewski stood up straight with pride. "Thank God for small mercies." He crossed himself. "We have not sold our souls to the Devil."

"Would you like to have a look at the list of targets which Schabowski was kind enough to give us?" Ansett held up four pages of type written paper.

"Is it the complete list of all targets in Britain?"

Ansett shook his head. "No, it's just the list of targets which his platoon were ordered to eliminate by the end of the month."

"Well, it's September 14th so Schabowski only had two weeks to go." Paderewski began to read: " 'Sir Norman Angell: Labour MP; Robert Baden-Powell: founder and leader of Scouting …' "

"The Einsatzgruppen killed him last week, but he managed to kill half a dozen Huns first," Ansett interrupted.

"That's the spirit!" Paderewski said with a smile. " 'Edvard Beneš: President of the Czechoslovak government in exile.' I met him a few times when I was the prime minister of Poland. He was a scholar and a gentleman. I heard a rumour that he was living somewhere in East Anglia, but I don't know where."

"Let's hope that the Germans don't know where either," Ansett said seriously.

" 'Violet Bonham Carter, an Encirclement lady politician; Vera Brittain: an Encirclement lady politician.' What on earth is an 'Encirclement lady politician?' "

"An anti-Fascist, I suppose," Ansett answered.

Paderewski shrugged his shoulders with bemusement. "Noël Coward: homosexual. I didn't know that he was queer."

"Noël Coward was a famous playwright, composer, director, actor and singer, a real Renaissance man," Alice said. "It's common knowledge that he was a homosexual and he was accepted as such. It's typical of the Nazis that this was the reason why they should want to kill him," she said angrily. "He committed suicide last week in order to avoid being captured and held as a hostage."

Paderewski nodded his head with respect. "I hope that I will have the courage to die by my own hand in a time and place of my own choosing rather than at the hands of the Nazis." He continued reading. " 'E. M. Forster: author; Sigmund Freud: Jew.' The Nazis are not particularly well informed: Freud died two years ago. Sir Philip Gibbs: author; J. B. S. Haldane: Communist; Ernst Hanfstaengl: German refugee; Aldous Huxley: author ..."

"The Huns should definitely sack whoever wrote this list: Huxley emigrated to America five years ago!"

" 'Harold Laski, political theorist; David Low: cartoonist …' "

"Hitler definitely doesn't have a sense of humour!" Sam said with a smile. "Low's cartoons taking the mickey out of Hitler and Mussolini used to make me laugh out loud! What was the name of his Hitler-Mussolini composite character again?"

"Muzzler!" Alan answered triumphantly.

Both of the boys laughed uproariously.

Ansett smiled with paternal affection. It was good to see the boys smile and laugh again.

"'F. L. Lucas,'" Paderewski continued, "'encirclement politician; Jan Masaryk: foreign minister of the Czechoslovak government in exile.' Surely he would have escaped with Beneš to Scotland?"

Ansett shrugged his shoulders. "He may have been left behind in the withdrawal. The retreat to Scotland was rather chaotic."

Paderewski nodded. "Gilbert Murray: League of Nations activist; Vic Oliver: Jew;" he smiled as he read the next name, "Ignacy Jan Paderewski …"

"Hey! You're famous!" Alice said.

"Congratulations!" Aurora added.

" … Former Prime Minister of Poland," Paderewski continued.

"And world famous concert pianist and composer," Aurora said. "The Germans should give credit where credit is due!"

Paderewski bowed his head in thanks. "Thank you, Aurora. 'J. B. Priestley: anti-Nazi popular broadcaster and author; Hermann Rauschning: German refugee; Paul Robeson: Communist …' "

"Robeson has already returned to America," Ansett interrupted.

"That was a lucky escape," Paderewski replied. "'Bertrand Russell: philosopher, historian and pacifist; C. P. Snow: physicist and author; Stephen Spender: poet and author; Gottfried Reinhold Treviranus: German refugee; Beatrice Webb: socialist; Chaim Weizmann: Jewish leader; H. G. Wells: author and socialist; Rebecca West: English suffragist and writer,' … the list goes on." He glanced over the remaining names.

"How many names are on the list, Ignacy?" Alice asked.

Paderewski looked at the number typed at the bottom of the final page. "There are exactly one hundred names written here …"

"My God! How many people are the Germans planning to arrest?" Alice asked.

"Schabowski said that the Germans planned to arrest two thousand eight hundred and twenty people in the British Isles in total." Ansett answered. "However, since they failed to conquer Scotland, Ulster and Eire they have been forced to reduce their target to around about two thousand five hundred."

"There will be people who were on their list who are now untouchable and out of reach such as the Prime Minster and the King," Alice said.

"Let's hope that Churchill and the King are untouchable," Alan said only half-jokingly. "Do we have a complete list of the targets?"

Ansett shook his head. "Unfortunately not. Schabowski only has the list of targets which his platoon were ordered to capture, his company commander has the target list for the company, and his commanding officer, Sturmbannführer von Horn, has the target list for the complete battalion. The names are written in a book called 'The Black Book.' "

"So, if the target for Schabowski's platoon was one hundred people and there are three platoons in a company then the total target list for the Hereward company is three hundred people," Alan said as he thought aloud.

Sam whistled. "That's quite a wanted list."

"So how are we going to rescue them all?" Alice asked.

Sam reacted as if he had been slapped on the face. "'Rescue them all?' Perhaps I'm missing something here, but why on earth would we want to rescue them?"

"Are you joking, Sam?" Alice asked with a raised eyebrow.

"No, I'm certainly not joking, sis," Sam answered. "I'm perfectly serious." He turned to look at the Pole. "Ignacy, are there any scientists on that list?"

Paderewski skimmed through the list. "Just one: C.P. Snow, a physicist."

"Any engineers, mathematicians, doctors or nurses?"

"No ... not that I can detect at first glance," Paderwski shook his head. "Perhaps if I read through the list more carefully ..."

"They are mostly poets, authors and politicians, aren't they?"

"Yes, they are."

"And I bet that there are no car mechanics, carpenters, builders or farmers in your list either."

Paderwski shook his head.

"What would you say is their average age? Forty? Fifty? Sixty?"

"I know that both Beneš and Masaryk are in their late fifties. I would say that the average age of the rest is about sixty, actually, and that's being generous."

"So, let me get this right, Alice: you want us to risk our lives in order to rescue approximately three hundred old people with no practical skills what so ever?"

"Well, I wouldn't-"

"Three hundred useless mouths?" Sam interrupted his sister. "How is H.G. Wells going to help us? Will he be able to help us to design a space ship or a ray gun to kill Nazis? I don't think so, Alice. These people are too old and lack any practical skills. They are useless."

"I say, that's a bit harsh, Sam!" Alan protested.

"I'm afraid that Sam is telling the truth, Alan," Paderewski agreed. "The only reason that I am still alive is that I am Aurora's piano teacher. I'm eighty one years old and my days of hand to hand combat are over. I don't think I would be much good at running across a field carrying a heavy machine gun."

"Thank you, Ignacy," Sam bowed his head in deference. "And where would we keep people? Here at the farm? We would have to house them, feed them and protect them twenty four hours a day, seven days a week. We simply do not have the necessary facilities or the adequate manpower to look after them even if we wanted to."

"What about the disabled children, Sam?" Alice asked. "You were perfectly willing to risk your life to save them."

"And I'd do it all again at the snap of a finger, without a moment's hesitation, if necessary," Sam said defiantly.

"But there weren't any scientists or engineers amongst their number either. They were also 'useless mouths' as you so eloquently put it."

"Yes, but that was different. They were children and some of the orphans may well still end up as scientists and engineers or make a worthwhile contribution to society. Think of Louise Braille or Helen Keller. They still have the rest of their lives to live. The people on the target list are old people. They've had their chance to shine in the sun and their time is nearly up. They've served their purpose and they've exhausted their usefulness. I don't mean to offend you, Ignacy, but it's true."

"I don't take any offense, Sam, because I happen to agree with you," Ignacy smiled indulgently as if he was listening to a favourite grandson spout forth a familiar and oft repeated line of argument.

"I doubt that many of the disabled children whom you rescued would find it easy to run across a field carrying a heavy machine gun either, Sam," Alice said with her head held high.

Sam opened his mouth to reply but thought better of it and closed it again. He had nothing to say because he knew that Alice was right.

Paderewski stood up and walked to stand beside Sam. "I understand and agree wholeheartedly with what Sam says. In the Sioux tribe, when old people considered that they were more of a hindrance to the tribe than an asset, they would take the long walk into the wilderness to die."

"Now wait a minute, Ignacy; I'm not for a minute suggesting that you take a long walk into the Fens wilderness to die," Sam said with concern.

Paderewski laughed and squeezed Sam's shoulder. "I know, Sam, I'm only teasing you. However, I do agree that it does seem suicidal for you youngsters to risk your lives to save a bunch of old past it has beens like me."

Aurora stood up. "When I studied religious education at home in Spain we discussed Judaism. There is one phrase from the Jewish Talmud which I always remember: 'Whoever saves one life saves the

198

world entire.' I believe that we should save and protect as many people as we can, when we can; whoever they are, young or old, male or female, able bodied or disabled, Jew or Gentile. We have to show the Nazis that we are not like them, that we can defy them and that we can defeat them."

Ansett waited for Aurora's words to sink in before he began to collect eyes around the room. Sam was the last one to signal his agreement with an emphatic nod.

"Then it's decided: we save as many people as we possibly can on the list."

"The problem is: how do we find out where they all live?" Alice asked.

Chapter Fourteen

"Mr. Bruce will see you now, Mr. Smith," the secretary announced. "If you'd like to come this way."

"Thank you," Smith replied. He stood up and followed the secretary to an office at the end of a corridor. The secretary knocked once and announced the name of the visitor.

"Come in, Mr. Smith," Bruce smiled as he stood up from behind his desk. "Please come in and take a seat."

"Thank you." Smith sat down and took off his hat.

"Now, Mr. Smith, how can I help you? I understand that you have some questions to ask about how the rationing system works."

"Yes, I have, Mr. Bruce. I can see that you served in the last War," Smith said as he looked at the row of medals attached to Bruce's jacket.

"Yes, I did. I was a major in the Royal Engineers. I helped to detonate the Hawthorn Ridge mine. I lost my left arm at the Somme." Bruce tapped his empty sleeve which was pinned to his jacket breast pocket. "I like to wear my medals because it annoys the Huns."

Smith smiled at Bruce's bravado. "I also served during the war. I fought as a sergeant major in the Royal Regiment of Fens Fusiliers and I was also at the Somme."

"Ah, a fellow Somme veteran! The RRiFFS, a fine regiment." Bruce exclaimed. "I understand that you suffered heavy casualties on the first day."

"Yes, we did." Smith nodded his head sadly. "Over five hundred out of a total strength of eight hundred men in the regiment were killed. I lost a lot of good friends and colleagues that day."

"I lost many good friends as well, but not as many as you brave men in the poor bloody infantry. If I hadn't joined the Sappers then I would have joined the RRiFFs." Bruce expertly filled the bowl of his pipe with tobacco using his one remaining hand. "But I'm sure that you haven't come here to tell old war stories." He raised a quizzical eyebrow.

Smith stood up, walked to the office door and opened it. He glanced down the corridor, closed the door and sat down again. "Mr. Bruce, the question I want to ask you is: are you ready to serve your king and country again?"

Bruce almost bit through the stem of his pipe with excitement and enthusiasm. "I am always ready to serve, Mr. Smith, if that is indeed your real name, and I have been waiting for this precise moment for a long time. I wasn't able to join the Home Guard for obvious reasons, but I still want to do my bit. Tell me how I can help?"

Smith smiled as he took out four pieces of paper from his jacket pocket. "Mr. Bruce, I need to know the addresses of all the people on this list."

"Why?"

"Because the Germans want to find them and kill them," Smith explained matter of factly. "We want to find them and rescue them."

"Who's 'we?' "

"'We' are the British Resistance," Smith replied.

"How do I know that you're telling the truth, Mr. Smith? I mean, I don't know you from Adam. You could be a Blackshirt spy, for all I know. The Jerries may have sent you here to find out where these people live in order to arrest them. How can you prove to me that you're the real McCoy and not a dirty, stinking Fascist traitor?"

"Easily, Mr. Bruce," Smith answered with a smile. "Do you listen to the B.B.C. broadcasts from Edinburgh?"

"Of course, as does every true and loyal patriot."

"I would like you to choose a memorable phrase or line from a song which will be broadcast one evening before the weekend during the B.B.C.'s 'message to our friends in the Occupied South' program. That will prove that I am who I say I am."

Bruce nodded. He thought for a moment. "I'll choose a line from My Fair Lady: 'the rain in Spain falls mainly on the plain.' If you are who you say you are then come back the next day with the list and I will find out the addresses for you."

"Thank you, Mr. Bruce." Smith stood up and put on his hat.

"No. Thank you, Mr. Smith, for giving an old soldier another opportunity to serve his country. God save the King!"

"God save the King!" Smith shook Bruce's hand and left.

A man named Mr. Brown paid a visit to the main Post Office in Hereward the same day and made a similar request to the manager, Mr. Melville. Melville had served in the Royal Navy in the First World War and he had risked his life using his private yacht to ferry soldiers from the beaches at Dunkirk to the destroyers waiting off shore. Melville's eldest son had been a Hurricane pilot in the R.A.F. and had been killed during the fighting in Greece. Although he was burning with a desire for revenge, Melville was adamant that he would only hand over the addresses after the B.B.C. had confirmed that Brown was a true blue member of the Resistance.

"How many addresses have we got, Mr. Ansett?" Alice asked.

Ansett glanced down at the half a dozen sheets of paper in his hand. "The Rationing Office and the Post Office have managed to gather between them the addresses of about fifty people on Schabowski's target list. About twenty people on the list have never lived in Hereward or in the surrounding area and about another thirty people used to live around here, but have stopped collecting their rations since the Invasion happened one year ago."

"My God, did the Huns invade only year ago?" Sam asked. "It seems like they've been here forever."

"I know exactly how you feel, Sam," Ansett agreed. "Unfortunately, I think that we may have to put up with our unwelcome guests for a wee while longer to come. I don't see how we're going to get rid of them unless the Yanks come into this War."

Sam's eyes lit up with hope. "Do you think that that is likely to happen, sir?"

Ansett shrugged his shoulders. "I certainly hope so, Sam. However, I don't think that they'll come in unless the Huns attack them. Remember what happened in the last war? And since the Jerries stopped their policy of unrestricted U-boat attacks on neutral ships I don't think that's likely to happen any time soon. The Huns are being very careful not to sink American ships."

"That's not to say that the Jerries might not sink an American ship by accident," Alan suggested.

Ansett nodded. "We must hope that the Huns are that careless."

"Or that stupid. But accidents do happen," Alan said.

Alice coughed. "What do you think has happened to the thirty people who used to live here, Mr. Ansett?"

"They probably fled the area when the Huns captured Hereward. The lucky ones will have found a safer place to settle somewhere else and the luckier ones will have made it to the Scotland."

"What about the unlucky ones?" Alice asked.

"The unlucky ones will be lying in some unmarked grave somewhere along with tens of thousands of other refugees who were killed during the retreat north," Ansett answered grimly.

"There but for the grace of God go I," Sam said somberly. "So, what do we do now?"

"We have the names and addresses of fifty people. The Nazis have put up two Wanted posters so far and they are now on their third. Each list names about twenty five people. I think that we need to contact the people on the first list and bring them to the farm before the Huns can find and arrest them. Once we have made contact with those people then we move onto the second list and so on."

"What if they refuse to come with us?" Sam asked.

"Then we leave them," Ansett answered. "We can't force then to come with us."

"Good," Sam said. "This farm is getting crowded enough as it is. It's bad enough sharing my bed room with Alan. He snores like a trooper. I certainly don't want to share my room with a bunch of bed wetting geriatrics. And I don't want the farm to turn into an old folks' home either."

Ansett chose to ignore Sam's deliberately provocative remark. He knew that Sam still had reservations about the wisdom of the rescue operation and he was prepared to allow Sam to blow off steam. "Bruce and Melville both told me that the Jerries have made no attempt to contact either of them in order to find out the addresses of the people on the target list. It is possible that the Huns have access to a different source in Cambridge or even London that is giving them the relevant information."

"However, most of the names that were written on the first Wanted poster have also appeared on the second one and some of the names on the first Wanted poster have even appeared on the third," Alice observed.

"Which means that the Nazis have not been very successful in locating and arresting their targets," Alan added.

"The Jerries are relying on the rewards of £1000 per name to encourage people to inform on their neighbours," Ansett said.

"The sneaky bastards!" Sam snarled. "Although if the same names have appeared on all three posters then it does mean that their tactic of rewarding treachery with money is not proving particularly effective."

"When do we make contact with the targets?" Alice asked.

"Well, you're home from Cambridge for the weekend, Alice," Ansett answered. "Why don't we start tomorrow on Saturday morning?"

Alice nodded enthusiastically. "No rest for the wicked. Let's start tomorrow."

"Lady Violet Bonham Carter?" Alice asked as the door opened.

"Yes. What can I do for you, young lady?" A middle aged lady with fine bone structure asked as she opened the door.

"You can come with me, Lady Violet."

"And why on earth should I do that?" Bonham Carter asked imperiously.

"Because your life is in great danger. Your name is on Wanted posters all over the town. The Germans are searching for you and when they find you, they will arrest you."

"But they don't know where I live. Only a handful of my closest friends and family know that I live in Hereward."

"But we found out and if we found out then the Germans can find out too."

"Who's 'we?'"

"We are the British Resistance," Alice replied in a hushed voice.

"And how do I know that?"

"Lady Violet, we don't exactly go around carrying identification cards! I don't have a membership badge which I can show you!" The young lady was becoming increasingly exasperated.

"How can you prove to me that you are a member of the Resistance? You may be a member of the beastly Blackshirts for all that I know. Prove that you are who you say you are and then I will come with you, but not a moment before." Bonham Carter folded her arms on her chest. It was obvious that her decision was final.

Alice chewed her lip for a second as she thought. "All right. Do you listen to B.B.C. Edinburgh?"

"Of course."

"Good. Choose an easily memorable phrase and listen to the 'messages to our friends in the Occupied South' program over the weekend. The B.B.C. will prove that I am who I say I am. Can you think of a memorable phrase?"

Bonham Carter smiled. "Yes, I believe that I can. There is something that our esteemed prime minister said to me at a dinner party the first time that I met him: 'Of course, we are all worms, but I do believe that I am a glow worm.' When Winston hears that message it will make him chuckle."

"Excellent!" Alice smiled. "Listen out for that message over the weekend. We will come and collect you the afternoon after the message is played. Be prepared to leave with a bag of your belongings, but don't tell anyone that you are leaving."

"All right, that's a deal. I'll see you the afternoon after the message is played."

Over the weekend the partisans split into pairs and managed to visit the addresses of nearly everyone on the list. Some of the people on the list were not at home and Ansett reckoned that some of them had already fled or had been captured by the Nazis. Others were sufficiently alarmed by the Wanted posters to leave with the Partisans without any proof of identity. Still others would only go if their visitors used the B.B.C. to verify that they were members of the Resistance.

Alice and Aurora visited Bonham Carter after the girls had finished their Monday classes. Alice had gone up to Cambridge University and was studying Medicine at Girton College and Aurora had started her fourth year at St. John's. Alice bounced up to the door with a spring in her step until she suddenly stopped dead in her tracks. She signaled for Aurora to stop walking as the front door swung open. "Silencers," Alice ordered.

The two girls quickly looked up and down the street. They reached behind their backs and took out their Lugers which had been hidden beneath the waist band of their skirts. The girls each took out a magazine of rounds from their right hand jacket pockets and inserted it into their pistols. They took out a silencer from their other pocket and screwed it onto the end of the barrel. The girls cocked their weapons sending a round up the spout and flicked off their safety catches.

"Cover me," Alice ordered. Aurora nodded. The two girls entered the house with Alice in the lead. Both girls held their Lugers in their right hands and steadied the weapons under the pistol grip with their left hands. Alice slowly but steadily worked her way through each room with Aurora at her shoulder. They cleared the living room, the dining room and the kitchen and were approaching the back of the ground floor when they heard voices talking and laughing uproariously. Alice cautiously walked towards the staircase leading up to the first floor. She bent down, untied her shoelaces and took off her shoes. Aurora copied her. Alice carefully started to climb the stairs, wincing with every step as she waited for a creaking board to give her away. She reached the top and wiped a bead of sweat from her forehead. Alice looked behind her and saw Aurora smiling at her like a crazed banshee. "We need a prisoner," Alice mouthed the words. Aurora held up one finger and raised her eyebrows. Alice nodded. The girls crept stealthily and silently down a long corridor towards the master bedroom. The door was open. Alice peered through the gap between the door and the door frame and rocked back on her heels with surprise. She looked over her shoulder. "Ready?" She mouthed. Aurora smiled in response. Alice crept through the open door into the bedroom. "Hands up!" She ordered.

The laughter stopped as if it had been cut off with a knife.

"Turn around," Alice ordered.

Two young men turned around with their hands raised as high in the air as their muscles and ligaments would allow. They were shaking and shivering with fear. They were not Blackshirts; they were civilians and were no older than sixteen or seventeen.

"Why are you wearing women's clothes?"

"They … they told us that we could take whatever we wanted as a reward for helping them," one of the young men stammered. "We were collecting the clothing for our mothers."

"Who's 'they?' "

"The … the Germans."

"Be more specific," Alice ordered. "Army? S.S.?"

"S.S.," the older one answered. "Einsatzgruppen."

"How did you help them?" Alice dreaded the answer.

"We helped them to find the addresses of the people on the list."

"Including Lady Violet?"

The older prisoner nodded.

"Where have the Nazis taken the prisoners?"

"I don't know."

"Listen, Adolf: I'm going to put a pencil and a list of names and addresses on the bed. I want you to write an A next to the names of all of the people that you helped the Nazis to arrest over the weekend. If you try to escape then I will shoot you and simply ask the same questions to your friend. Do you understand?"

"Yes."

Alice placed the pencil and paper on the bed and the teenager did as he was told. "Are you sure that the list is complete?"

"Yes, I am."

Alice gave the list a cursory glance, carefully folded it and placed it back in her jacket pocket. She returned her gaze to the two young prisoners. "Why did you help the Nazis to arrest our own people?"

"They gave us £30 to share for each person that they arrested."

"£30 was enough to make you turn Judas and become a traitor?" Aurora asked with disgust. "Is that all that the life of one of your countrymen is worth?"

"They weren't 'our countrymen,'" the younger one interrupted. "And they weren't 'our people' either. They were mostly Jews and dirty foreigners-"

The sudden shot made Alice and the older prisoner jump. The younger prisoner stared at Aurora with a look of complete shock and surprise on his face before he collapsed onto the bed. Aurora stepped forward and shot the younger prisoner once in the back of the head. "You distinctly said 'one prisoner.'" She stepped up to the body and spat on the back of his splintered skull. "I'm a 'dirty foreigner,' Oswald."

"You-you killed my brother, you bitch!" A flood of tears streamed down the older prisoner's face. He launched himself at Aurora. The double tap hit the teenager in the side of his body. He slumped to the floor and lay in a crumpled heap next to his dead brother. He lay moaning and groaning as his life's blood flowed steadily out of him.

Alice knelt down beside him and grabbed him by the scruff of the neck. "How did the Nazis find out the addresses?"

The dying young man smiled through blood smeared teeth.

"How did they find out the addresses?"

"A ... a postie told them," the man gasped painfully. "A postie betrayed them ... for money."

Alice and Aurora looked up and down the street before they crossed the road. They walked down the street opposite Bonham Carter's house towards a parked lorry. Alice opened the door to the cab and climbed in whilst Aurora got in the back.

"Trouble?" Ansett asked.

"Nothing that we couldn't handle," Alice answered matter of factly.

"Where's Lady Violet?"

"The Germans have arrested her and everyone else marked with an A on this list." Alice handed over the half a dozen pieces of paper. "Ten people in total."

Ansett looked at the blood stained paper. "Are you hurt? Is Aurora all right?" He asked with concern.

Alice smiled. "Yes, we're all right. It's not our blood."

"Whose blood is it? Were any other people hurt?"

Aurora shook her head. "No other people. Just two teenage traitors," Alice answered matter of factly.

"Blackshirts?"

"No. Opportunists who betrayed Lady Violet and the others for thirty pieces of silver: Nazi blood money. We killed them."

"Good." Ansett nodded. "We must send a clear message to all those who are thinking about working for the enemy that treachery doesn't pay."

"So what do we do now?" Alice asked.

"Did the traitors indicate that anyone else on the list had been arrested?"

"No." Alice shook her head. "He gave me the impression that only ten people had been betrayed and arrested."

"Who's the traitor?"

"A postman."

Ansett swore under his breath. "We need to collect all of the people on the list that were waiting for confirmation of our identities from the B.B.C. and we also need to dispose of the bodies of the two traitors."

"Good, because they are bleeding all over Lady Violet's bedroom at the moment."

"And then we need to capture this treacherous postman and send a message to the Germans and the Blackshirt traitors that they will not forget."

Ansett collected about fifteen people on the list and transported them to Leon's Pig Farm. He had expected to pick up a few more but many of the people decided that they would be safer and were less likely to be discovered if they stayed where they were. Ansett warned them that ten people had been arrested by the Germans that very morning and that they would be safer if they accompanied him. Although some of the waverers decided to jump ship at the last moment and join Ansett, the majority stuck to their guns. They were aware of the risks but were prepared to take their chances. They would remain at home or make their own arrangements to protect themselves.

The farmhouse had four bedrooms and the new arrivals were able to fit in with a squash and a squeeze. Whilst the guests were sorting themselves out the partisans gathered in the kitchen in order to plan how to find out the identity of the treacherous postman. Alice marked the addresses of all of the arrested people on a street map of Hereward and discovered that they were all located in an area of the city called Brunswick. The entire area could be covered by one postman in a few hours walk.

"Are we sure that we're in the right place?" Ansett asked as he spotted the target approaching in the distance.

Sam looked at the map that lay on his lap and nodded his head. "Yes. According to Alice's map this is the street where three of the arrested people lived. Fitzroy Street."

"It's just that we need to be sure that this is the postie who betrayed our people ..." Ansett's voice trailed off.

Alan noticed the hesitation in Ansett's voice and raised a quizzical eyebrow. "Might I suggest that we watch what happens when the target reaches one of the arrested people's houses?"

"What do you mean, Alan?" Ansett asked.

"Does the target change walking pace and speed up or slow down or look at the house or not look at the house? Anything unusual or out of the ordinary? Then we will have a better idea that this is the right postie."

"Good idea." Ansett raised his binoculars and watched carefully as the target approached the first house. The postie suddenly looked down at the ground and speeded up walking. When the postie had passed the house she resumed her normal walking pace. Ansett nodded his head emphatically. "We haven't made a mistake: she's the traitor." Ansett opened the car door with a heavy heart and started walking towards the target.

"Hello, Diana," Ansett said. "How are you?"

The postie stopped dead in her tracks. Diana Miller did a double take as she looked at the man standing in front of her. "Pete ... Pete Ansett? Is ... is it really you?"

"Yes, it is."

Miller rushed over and gave him a kiss on the cheek and an enormous bear hug. "I thought that you were dead. Nobody has seen you for months."

"Well, I'm very much alive," Ansett smiled. He released her and looked at her uniform. "I didn't know that you were a post woman."

"And I didn't know that you were a Blackshirt major." Miller touched the crowns on the epaulettes of his black battledress.

"Yes, I joined the Militia after the terrorists murdered the King and Queen in April."

"Oh ..." Miller was caught off guard. She was more used to people referring to Edward and Wallis as Kaiser

213

Eddie and the Wicked Queen. At least she knew which side Ansett's bread was buttered on.

"I was sorry to hear about Will's death, Diana. We served together in the RRiFFs during the War. He was a brave man and a loyal friend."

"He certainly was a loyal friend, Pete," Miller said. "When Will joined the Home Guard and you didn't, he bent over backwards to defend your reputation against old comrades who called you a coward."

"I ... I didn't know that."

"Well, you know now," Miller nodded her head. "Will told everyone that you had your reasons." She looked at Ansett's lightning flash armband with disbelief. "I always wondered why you didn't join the Home Guard like Will and now I know."

"I'm not a Fascist, Diana," Ansett protested. "But I'm not a Communist either. And I certainly am not prepared to allow chaos and anarchy to take over which is exactly what will happen if we don't have law and order. We can't allow Jewish Bolshevik terrorists to rule the streets and do whatever the hell they want to. At the moment, Joyce's Government of National Unity represents the best guarantor of law and order."

Miller said nothing.

"I've had to make ... difficult decisions. We've got to survive as best as we can," Ansett continued. "We've all had to make ... compromises."

Miller thought for a moment before she answered. "Yes, we have. We've all been faced with hard choices. Some ... compromises have been more difficult to make than others. Anyway, I'm sure that us meeting up like this isn't a coincidence. Why are you here?"

Ansett came to a position of attention. "My orders are to escort you to Blackshirt headquarters in Cambridge so that you can collect your reward."

Miller looked at the ground and couldn't look Ansett in the face. "You … you know what the reward is for? You know what I've done?"

Ansett nodded.

"I didn't want to do it, but I've also had to make difficult decisions, Pete. I also need to survive. And not just me, my two boys as well. It's been really tough since Will died. The boys really miss their father and so do I. It became impossible to survive on Will's pension and even with my job it's virtually impossible to make ends meet. The reward will set us up for life. £10,000 is a lot of money. The reward will give us financial security for the future. I'm not proud of what I've done, but I did what I did for my boys." Miller's words rushed out in an unstoppable torrent. Her chest was heaving heavily with relief that she had finally told someone. A great weight had been lifted from her chest.

"How old are your boys?"

"Bert is seventeen and Ernie is fifteen. They're like two peas in a pod," Miller said happily.

Ansett smiled. "I would imagine that they're still tucked up in bed at this time in the morning."

Miller smiled. "They usually would be, but they didn't come home yesterday. They were probably out on the town last night spending the reward money that the Jerries gave them."

"Reward money?"

"Yes, the boys helped to guide them to the houses of the people that the Jerries wanted to arrest. The Jerries gave them £30 for each person that the boys helped them to find. Bert and Ernie probably slept over at one of their friend's houses last night."

A cold sweat suddenly broke out on Ansett's forehead and he felt physically sick.

Miller noticed that all of the colour had drained from Ansett's face. "I made sure that I only gave them the names of foreigners; they all had German and Eastern European names, none of the ten people were British. Pete, are you all right? You look as white as a ghost." Miller put her hand on Ansett's sleeve with concern.

Ansett gently lifted Miller's hand from his sleeve and kissed her on the forehead. He extracted his revolver from his holster, cocked it, flicked off the safety catch and pointed it at Miller's face. "Diana Miller, I accuse you of betraying your countrymen to the Germans. How do you plead?"

"What is this? Some sort of joke? Put the gun away, Pete. You're scaring me." Miller laughed uneasily.

Ansett shook his head sadly. "I'm afraid that I'm not joking, Diana: I'm deadly serious. I'm not a Blackshirt, I lied to you. I'm a member of the British Resistance. How do you plead to the charge of treason?"

"No, this is all wrong! This isn't right!" Miller protested with horror. "They weren't British! They were foreigners!" Miller sank to her knees. "Please don't kill me!"

"I pronounce you guilty of treason."

"No! Don't kill me! I beg you! The boys! My boys!"

"The punishment is death and the sentence is to be carried out immediately."

"Please let me go, I'm begging you! I won't do it again! I'm … I'm sorry!" Miller sobbed.

"So am I, Diana. May God have mercy on your soul."

"No-!"

Ansett shot her twice in the head and walked away leaving his friend lying in a pool of her own blood.

"What are we going to do with the bodies, sir?" Sam asked when Ansett returned to the car.

Ansett's brow furrowed with confusion. "What do you mean, Sam?"

"Are we going to bury them or are we going to feed them to the pigs?"

"Feed them to the pigs?" Ansett's eyes bulged wide with horror. "I knew this woman, Sam! I served with her husband in the last war." He shook his head. "No, we are certainly not going to feed Diana Miller and her two boys to the pigs. We only feed Germans to the pigs, not British people."

"But they're not British people, sir," Sam maintained. "They ceased to be British when they betrayed the people on the poster to the Germans. I'm sure that you would have no hesitation in feeding the bodies of dead Blackshirts to the pigs or live Blackshirts for that matter."

"Diana Miller was not a Blackshirt and neither were her sons," Ansett said stubbornly. "She was a widow whose sole concern was to look after her boys. She made an error of judgement that's all-"

"Well, her error of judgement got her and her two sons killed," Sam said coldly. "She and her boys were traitors, plain and simple. Did they capture the people on the list themselves? No. Will they be the ones who pull the triggers in the firing squad? No. But their actions allowed that to happen and that makes them no better or worse than the many dirty Blackshirt bastards whom we've killed and executed as traitors."

Ansett didn't answer as he chewed over Sam's words in his head.

Alan coughed discreetly. "I hate to say it, but Sam's got a point you know, sir."

Ansett nodded his head grimly. "I know he has, damn his eyes. But I still don't want to feed Diana and

217

her two sons to the pigs. I owe Will that much at least, God rest his soul."

"So what do you suggest, sir?" Alan asked.

"I suggest that we make the most of this tragic incident," Ansett answered sombrely. "We can send a message to all those who are thinking of betraying the people on the list to the Germans that treachery does not pay."

The next morning the Town Square was busy as usual as the good citizens of Hereward walked to work or to school or went shopping in the weekly Monday market. No one paid any attention as a Fascist Militia lorry drove through the crowded Square at a walking pace. There was a loud clang as the tailgate was dropped and three heavy bundles were rolled out of the back and landed on the cobblestones with ominous thuds. There were gasps of shock and horror as the people nearest the discarded loads recognized them as bodies. People formed a wide circle around the corpses as if they thought that the bodies carried an infectious disease. There was a sudden burst of machine gun fire and people screamed in panic and alarm as they ducked to the ground. A balaclava clad figure appeared at the back of the lorry wearing the rag tag uniform of a partisan and holding a Schmessier in his hand.

"These three traitors betrayed the people written on the Wanted poster to the Germans. However, they have not been able to collect their Nazi silver. Their only reward has been death. Such is the fate reserved for traitors. For those of you who may be thinking of following in their treacherous footsteps-you have been warned. God save the King!"

Several people in the crowd repeated the same familiar words without thinking.

The partisan smiled through his balaclava, fired another burst in the air and raised the tailgate as the lorry drove away.

By the time that the Police and German soldiers arrived the crowd had already dispersed and no one claimed to see, hear or know anything about the dumping of the bodies.

Chapter Sixteen

Over the course of the next few days Ansett seemed to recover and become himself again. He could not help but become infected with the contagious optimism and good cheer of the recent arrivals. Ansett shook off the cloak of deep depression and guilt that he had been wearing since he had executed Diana Miller and he resolved to make a fresh start and put the past behind him. He was pleasantly surprised to discover that the new comers did not require any babysitting and did not need to be looked after. On the contrary, it soon became clear that the recent arrivals were determined to look after him. The new arrivals immediately began to organise themselves and identified three main areas of responsibilities: - the house, the farm and the defence of the base. The visitors divided themselves into three groups of about five people each made up of a more or less equal mix of men and women. Group A was in charge of household chores for one day e.g. preparing three meals a day, washing dishes and laundry etc.; group B was in charge of looking after the farm e.g. feeding the animals and carrying out maintenance work such as repairing broken fences etc.; group C was in charge of military operations e.g. defending the farm and weapons training etc. Each group performed their respective responsibilities for one day and then moved onto the next duty in rotation. Ansett was so impressed by the new partisans' boundless energy and enthusiasm that he began to turn his thoughts towards mounting a rescue operation to free the captured hostages. He started to daydream about establishing a haven for the persecuted and the dispossessed at the farm, an oasis in the wilderness, and began to toy with the idea of building a private army. However, Ansett's plans were abruptly interrupted by a new message from Scotland.

CEASE ALL PRESENT OPERATIONS STOP PREPARE FOR ARRIVAL OF NEW VISITORS FROM THE NORTH STOP PREPARE FOR NEW OPERATION STOP ARRIVAL DATE TO BE CONFIRMED STOP

A few days later the partisans greeted eight parachutists who landed on and near the farm. They were escorted to the farm and were welcomed with hugs and kisses by the women and manly handshakes and bear hugs by the men. Six of the soldiers were taken to their sleeping quarters by the excited Resistance fighters and were left to settle in. The paratroopers soon fell into an exhausted sleep.

"Now, what's this all about, Captain Smith?" Ansett asked with mounting excitement as he sat with the paratrooper commander at a table in the kitchen.

"As I'm sure that you know, sir, the first anniversary of Operation Sealion is on September 27th, in exactly one week's time."

Ansett nodded. "Yes, I was aware of that unfortunate fact. What of it?"

Smith looked at his second in command, Second-Lieutenant Jones, and gave him a conspiring wink. "Well, sir, Edinburgh has received intelligence that the Huns plan to carry out a victory parade in Hereward on the 28th."

"Why not on the 27th? Why a day later?"

"Because the two guests of honour cannot be in two different places on the same day. They will be attending the official anniversary parade in London on the 27th."

"You mean-?"

"Yes, sir," Smith interrupted, "the two guests of honour will be Prime Minister Joyce and Reichkommissar Schenk. They will attend a parade of S.S. stormtroopers, Wehrmacht soldiers, Spanish Legiónaries, Blackshirts and units of the newly raised Legion of Saint George."

Ansett's face turned scarlet with anger at the mention of the new S.S. unit of British traitors. "That nest of treacherous vipers. Well, they're certainly in good company. Should be quite a party," he hissed through clenched teeth. "I presume that the parade will take place in the Town Square?"

Smith nodded. "Yes, sir."

"And what are your orders, Captain?"

"Our orders are to rain on their parade, Major," Jones replied on behalf of his captain with a bloodthirsty smile.

"That's exactly the answer that I was hoping for," Ansett said. "But how exactly do you intend to achieve that? Security's bound to be tighter than a pauper's purse. The Huns won't be willing to risk a repeat of the St. George's Day massacre."

"I was ordered by Brigadier Daylesford to deliver this letter to you, sir," Smith announced as he handed over an envelope. "I think that this letter will reveal how we can attack the Parade."

Ansett did a double take as he recognized the handwriting. His fingers trembled as he carefully opened the envelope and extracted the letter.

"My old friend,

If you're reading this letter it means that I'm dead and you're alive. I have sent you this message from beyond the grave in the hope that you may use the information on the following page on behalf of the cause against the foe. When I was appointed to my position my predecessor passed on to me a secret that has been handed on down through the generations. Unfortunately, the recent unpleasantness and my untimely death has meant that I have not been able to pass on the secret to my successor. So I now pass on the secret to you. It is your responsibility to use the information as you see fit and also to pass on the secret to my successor when a new one is eventually appointed in happier times.

I will see you again, my friend, of that I have no doubt-but hopefully, not too soon! I will say hello to our mutual friends for you and put in a good word on your behalf to Saint Peter! I miss you already!

Your friend."

Ansett chuckled as he read the letter for the second and the third time. He marvelled at his friend's ingenuity. The message was cryptic enough that it would not make sense to a casual reader if the letter was intercepted. Even the diagram on the second page did not give much away and did not provide many clues. The message would only make sense if the person reading the letter knew who had sent it, what the sender did for a living and where the sender lived.

Sam, Alan and Alice appeared at the door after they had finished settling in the new guests.

"Partisans," Ansett announced with an infectious grin, "Ben Rathdowne has sent us a message from heaven. Gather around. We have God's work to do."

Ansett glanced over at his companion with an amused grin on his face. Captain Smith's forehead was covered in a thin sheet of sweat and he was gripping the stock of his Schmessier so tightly that his knuckles were bone white.

"Are you all right, Captain?" Ansett asked mischievously. "You seem a little tense."

"Actually sir, I'm very far from being 'all right.' " Smith admitted. "I feel as tense and as tight as a coiled spring. How can you live like this? I feel as if we're walking into the lion's den."

Ansett chuckled darkly. "Well, Captain Smith. You know where's the best place to hide a leaf?"

"No, sir," Smith shook his head, "but I have a sneaking suspicion that you're about to tell me."

"In a forest." Ansett drove the Blackshirt lorry into the Town Square and parked it between a Fascist Militia lorry on one side and an S.S. half-track on the other side. Ansett turned off the ignition. "Oh, one more thing, Captain. I may not be Sherlock Holmes, but I don't think that Second-Lieutenant Jones here is from the valleys. He's about as Welsh as I am."

Jones laughed and gave a mock bow. "Ah, Mr Holmes, you are wrong and you are also right: I am from the valleys, but they are not Welsh valleys."

Ansett chuckled. "Well, just remember to try and keep your mouth shut in public: your English might fool the Jerries, but it won't fool the local Fascists. Your accent will definitely give the game away."

"Yes, sir."

Ansett nodded. "Good. Let's go." Ansett opened the door and climbed down from the cab. Smith and Jones did the same and walked around the front of the lorry to meet Ansett. Sam and Alan were already there and were deep in animated conversation. They were full of beans and they could barely contain their excitement at the thought of impending action. The boys greeted the two paratroopers with a hearty smile. They seemed completely comfortable and at ease as if donning Blackshirt uniforms and masquerading as Fascist Militiamen was all in a day's work. Sam and Alan seemed to have nerves of steel. Smith, on the other hand, was painfully aware that he was so scared and nervous that he could barely trust himself to speak. The two boys confidently cradled their sub machineguns in their hands with their fore fingers resting lightly on the trigger guard as if they were professional soldiers and had been handling weapons for half of their lives. Smith shook his head in awe and wonder. He found it hard to believe that these young partisans were barely sixteen and little more than a year ago they had never fired a gun in anger. According to Ansett, in the year since the Invasion, Sam and Alan had killed more Huns than German measles. The boys were natural born killers. Smith didn't know whether he should feel impressed or horrified. One day this war would end. What would become of Sam and Alan and the rest of the world's child soldiers then? How easy would it be for them to put down their guns and pick up a pencil?

Ansett led his fellow Blackshirts out of the Square and around the side of the Cathedral. Smith was surprised to find that the crowd parted in front of Ansett as if he was Moses crossing the Red Sea. Passers-by made a point of avoiding eye contact and crossed the road as the small group of Fascist Militiamen approached. Smith smiled for the first time since they had entered Hereward. He began to think that they might actually get away with it and end up safe and sound back in the kitchen at the farm instead of in the torture chamber at Gestapo headquarters. His heartbeat gradually slowed down to normal as he began to hope that they might successfully complete the reconnaissance mission. Ansett led the Blackshirts down a narrow road that ran down the other side of the Cathedral and stopped in front of an ornately decorated solid wood door.

"The plan seems to have worked," Smith said with relief. "These uniforms appear to have fooled people into believing that we're genuine Blackshirts."

Sam chuckled. "And so these uniforms bloody well should work, sir. Pardon my French. We stripped them off the backs of a squad of dirty Blackshirt bastards barely a month ago before we killed them."

Smith shivered involuntarily as Sam and Alan both laughed at his obvious discomfort. Natural born killers indeed. He was glad that the two boys were on his side. "Where are we, Major?" Smith asked.

"This is the official residence of the Bishop of Hereward, Captain," Ansett answered. He inserted a large metal key into the lock and turned the key. The door swung open silently on well-oiled hinges. "Come on in."

Ansett entered the house and was swiftly followed by Smith and Jones. Alan and Sam took one last look up and down the narrow lane in order to make sure that the coast was clear. When they were satisfied that no one had followed them they followed the two paratroopers into the house.

"This place gives me the creeps," Alan said as he adjusted his eyes to the gloomy interior.

"It's like a haunted house."

"Boo!" Sam jumped out and grabbed Alan's shoulders as his friend followed him around a dark corner.

Alan pushed him off with angry eyes and a thump on the arm. "Quit fooling around!"

Ansett rolled his eyes at Smith and smiled indulgently at Sam's tomfoolery.

"Boys will be boys," Jones said with a paternal grin. "Who used to live here, sir?"

"This is where Ben Rathdowne used to live when he was the Bishop of Hereward. No one has lived here since the St. George's Day Massacre in April."

"So it's been empty for five months?" Smith asked.

"Yes," Ansett nodded.

"What are we looking for?"

Ansett smiled. "I'll show you." The partisans followed Ansett down a long dark corridor that led to a massive room. They stared with open-mouthed awe and admiration at the sheer size and grandeur of what must have been Rathdowne's study. A giant bookcase ran along three walls of the room and gave the impression that the walls were built of books instead of bricks.

"The book case must be four yards high. However do you reach the books on the top shelf?" Alan asked.

"Look, Al, a ladder," Sam pointed to a ladder that was leaning against one of the bookcases.

Smith and Jones walked towards the giant desk that faced the door to the study. Smith ran his fingers lightly across the top of the desk with admiration. "Very nice."

"Solid oak, sir," Jones observed. He sat down in the large leather upholstered chair and let out a contented sigh. "I'd wager that the desk has a professionally French polished surface too. I could get used to this very nicely." He patted the two armrests. " Perhaps I'll become a priest. After the War."

"After the War," Smith smiled at his second-in-command. The likelihood of either of them surviving the war seemed rather slim, but you had to live in hope.

Sam and Alan walked towards the French windows that ran along the entire length of the wall behind the desk.

"Be careful, boys!" Smith warned. "Someone might see you."

"It's all right, sir," Sam answered. "These windows open out onto the bishop's private garden. The courtyard is entirely enclosed by the house. You can't see the garden from the Cathedral.

"Are you sure?"

Sam nodded. "Yes I am, sir. If you want to make sure why don't you ask Mr Ansett? Mr Ansett? Mr Ansett?"

But Ansett was nowhere to be seen. He had completely disappeared. It was as if the books had swallowed him whole.

Ansett stood as still as a statue with all of his senses on high alert. He looked around the room that was the mirror image of the room that he had just left. However, this room was the bishop's public office in the Cathedral whereas the room that he had just left was his private study in his home. Ansett smiled. He knew that he had to get back to the study as soon as possible. The rest of the partisans were probably having kittens.

"Hello, chaps," Ansett said with an impish smile. "Have you missed me?"

"What the-?"

"Where did you come from?" Smith asked with wide-eyed disbelief. "You disappeared a moment ago and now you've reappeared without so much as a puff of smoke. Are you a wizard?"

"No, I'm not a wizard," Ansett laughed, "Although I may be a magician. Look at this." Ansett picked up a book from the shelf and handed it to Smith. The captain looked at the book: "Fly fishing" by J.R. Hartley. The significance of the title and author completely escaped him. Smith shook his head with confusion. "You want me to read a book about fly fishing?"

Ansett chuckled. "No, Captain: forget the book," Ansett ordered. "Look at the bookshelf." The book had concealed a cunningly disguised latch. Ansett gently pulled the latch and opened a door, which swung away from him.

"Well, I'll be damned. A secret door." Smith shook his head with amazement. "Wonders will never cease."

Ansett stepped through the concealed door into Rathdowne's office. Smith and Jones followed him.

"It's like Alice in Wonderland," Alan said excitedly.

"I just hope that we don't bump into the Queen of Hearts," Sam said as he stroked his trigger guard.

"Quiet now, chaps," Ansett ordered. "We're going to search the Cathedral for Huns. The Cathedral is closed and is strictly off limits to civilians and it's unlikely that it's guarded. However, the Jerries are sneaky blighters and you can never take them for granted. They may well have sentries in here."

"Or it might be guarded by Blackshirts, sir," Alan suggested.

Ansett nodded. "Quite right, Alan."

"What are our actions on contact with the enemy, sir?" Smith asked.

"We avoid contact if possible, Captain," Ansett answered. "We are a reconnaissance patrol, not a fighting patrol. Our mission is to find out if we can use the Cathedral in our plans. If we see the enemy and they don't see us then we withdraw as quickly and as quietly as possible. If we have to fight then we have to kill them as swiftly and silently as possible and take them with us back to the farm."

"Take them with us, sir?" Jones asked.

"Yes, Lieutenant. We can't let the Jerries find the bodies here. They would search the Cathedral from head to toe in order to find out who killed their men. They might well find the secret door."

"And they would also take reprisals, sir, if they find the bodies of their men here," Alan added.

"Yes, they would, Alan," Ansett nodded his head grimly. "And unfortunately, they have no shortage of hostages to choose from."

"What's the current rate of exchange?" Smith asked.

"One hundred hostages are executed for every German soldier who is killed, sir," Alan answered.

Smith gave a low whistle.

"Just like Poland," Jones said bitterly.

"Unfortunately so, sir," Alan said grimly.

"What do we do with the bodies back at the farm?" Jones asked.

Ansett looked at the boys and winked.

"Feed them to the pigs!" The boys collapsed in fits of laughter.

Jones shook his head in disbelief. He would never understand the British sense of humour.

The partisans carried out a patient and methodical search of the Cathedral from the bishop's office to the main door of the Cathedral and back again. They did not make any contact with the enemy and did not find any evidence to suggest that the Cathedral was regularly patrolled and guarded by either the Germans or the Fascist Militia. In fact, it appeared unlikely that anyone had visited the Cathedral since Ben Rathdowne had successfully delivered his anti-euthanasia sermon in July.

"Where are we going, sir?" Alan asked excitedly.

"You'll see," Ansett said mysteriously as he continued walking.

Alan stopped dead in his tracks as Ansett halted at the top of a narrow staircase. "No, for the love of God, sir," he protested. "You've got to be joking."

"What? What is it, Alan? What are you so worried about?" Smith could see by the expression on his face that Alan was genuinely alarmed. More than that, the boy was positively petrified.

"The Crypt," Sam answered glumly. "I'm not exactly overjoyed at the idea of going down there either."

Jones said something under his breath in an unidentifiable language and crossed himself.

"Do we have to, sir?" Alan pleaded.

"I'm afraid so, Alan," Ansett said sympathetically. "However, you can sit this one out if you want to. You don't have to come downstairs if you don't feel that you're up to it."

Alan hesitated as he ran through his options in his head. He shook his head. "No, sir. I'll come down stairs with you. I'm getting too old to be scared of the dark."

Ansett smiled. "That's my boy!" He ruffled Alan's hair affectionately. Alan smiled bashfully at his momentary lapse of nerves. "Is everyone ready to descend into the depths of Hell?"

"Just a moment, sir." Alan slung his Schmessier onto his shoulder and reached around to the small of his back. Smith and Jones' eyes widened with surprise as their young companion extracted a Luger pistol.

Ansett sighed. "I've told you before, Alan, the-"

"I know, sir," Alan interrupted and held up his hands in acknowledgement. "The dead can't die twice. It just makes me feel safer, that's all."

"Just make sure that the safety catch is on, Alan," Ansett ordered. "I don't want you tripping over a skeleton in the dark and shooting one of us in the back."

"Yes, sir." Alan smiled queasily as he pictured the scenario in his head. He was more distressed at the thought of tripping over a skeleton than he was at the

231

prospect of accidentally shooting a comrade in the back.

Ansett took off a small rucksack that he had been wearing and placed it on the floor. He unbuckled the strap and took out five torches, which he handed to the members of his group.

"I was afraid that you were going to give each of us a crucifix and a clove of garlic to hang around our necks, sir," Alan laughed nervously.

"I'm sure that won't be necessary, Alan," Ansett answered. "This is Cambridgeshire, not deepest, darkest Transylvania."

"I could sure do with a some water right now."Sam said.

"Why?" Alan asked. "We've just had breakfast. Surely you can't be thirsty already, Sam. Anyway, I don't think drinking a glass of water down here would be a very good idea. You have a bladder the size of a walnut and I don't know about you, but I haven't seen any toilets down here."

"Not a glass of water to drink, Al. I was thinking more about a bottle of Holy Water to carry to ward off evil spirits and the Undead."

"That's not very helpful, Sam," Ansett scolded Sam jokingly.

Alan gave his friend a dirty look and gulped nervously. His throat was bone dry and felt like a badger's bottom. "If we've got to do this, let's get it over with. After you, sir."

"Age before beauty, eh Alan?" Ansett chuckled.

"Something like that, sir."

"Everyone ready?" Ansett asked.

"Yes, sir," the partisans answered in unison.

"Good," Ansett nodded. "Then let's go." Ansett switched on his torch and started to descend the stairs that led down to the Crypt. The others followed suit.

"Into the Valley of Death rode the six hundred..." Sam started. "Corpses to the left of them, corpses to the right of them moaned and groaned..." Sam continued.

"Sam! For the love of God, knock it off!" Alan protested.

"Sorry, Al." Sam chuckled evilly.

The stairs seemed to go on forever and Alan thought that he was descending into the depths of Hell itself. He remembered with a shiver how terrified he had been the first time that Ansett had led him down here nearly a year ago when he had shown him the secret Resistance hide out. Although he had been down to the base in the Crypt at least a dozen times since, he had never lost the feeling of fear and dread that he always felt. He wondered if anyone else was as scared as he was.

Ansett stopped at the bottom of the stairs. "Is every one all right? Are we all here? The ghosts and ghouls haven't managed to kidnap anyone, have they?"

The partisans laughed uneasily.

Ansett shone the torch at the map that he was holding in his hand. "According to this map, the entrance should be over here." Ansett walked over to a large tomb in the nearest right hand corner of the Crypt. He shone the torch on the inscription and read the name. "Robert St. John."

"Who was he, sir?" Sam asked. "The first Baron of Hereward?"

Ansett shook his head. "No, Sam. The first Baron of Hereward was called John. This is the tomb of his younger brother, Robert."

"Oh."

"Except that Robert was killed fighting Anglo-Saxon rebels in Yorkshire and he's buried in the grounds of what later became Fountain Abbey near Ripon."

"So why is his tomb here, sir? Did John build it as a token of brotherly love, perhaps?"

Ansett shook his head. "I'll show you why he built the tomb, Sam." He shone his torch on the map for a few seconds and then knelt down on the stone floor. He carefully felt around the vertical left hand edge of the front of the tomb. "Ah ha! Bingo!" He said with a smile. There was a click and Ansett grabbed hold of the edge of the tomb and pulled towards him. The entire front of the tomb opened like a door and swung away from Ansett on a hinge.

The partisans stopped and stared at the secret opening with amazement.

"You've got to hand it to those Normans. They were clever swine," Sam said with admiration.

"Yes, they were. Shall we, gentlemen?" Ansett asked.

Alan visibly balked at the prospect of entering the tomb.

Ansett placed his hand on Alan's shoulder and gave him a reassuring squeeze. "I'll go first, Alan and you follow immediately afterwards, all right?"

Alan nodded. He was too petrified to speak.

"Sam, you follow next and then Captain Smith and Lieutenant Jones bring up the rear, all right?"

Everyone nodded. A cat had caught their tongues.

Ansett shone his torch into the darkness. "Once more unto the breach, dear friends …" He entered the tomb and the rest of the group followed. In matter of a few seconds they were swallowed up by the darkness.

In 1069 the north of England rose in rebellion against the Norman invaders and Robert St. John was one of the knights who was despatched to Yorkshire to crush the rebels. He marched up north with enthusiastic excitement in the hope that if he fought well, the recently crowned King William I would reward him with a fiefdom of his own. Alas, all of Roberts' ambitious plans came to nought: he was killed by Anglo-Saxon rebels who burned down the wooden castle in which Robert was sleeping in a sudden night attack. What little was left of the young knight's charred remains was buried near Ripon. The horrific death of his younger brother acted as a wakeup call for John St. John. He suddenly realised that he had taken his own safety and security arrangements for granted and had failed to recognize the threat that he faced from his own Anglo-Saxon peasants. St. John hired the best architects and engineers in the kingdom and embarked on a rapid building program replacing his wooden Motte and Bailey castle with a cutting edge concentric castle made of stone. Such was his determination not to suffer the same terrible fate as his brother that he ordered that a secret escape tunnel was to be built that connected the dungeon below the castle keep to the Cathedral Crypt. The tunnel stretched for half a mile and was regarded as a major feat of engineering. However, within a generation, the secret of the tunnel was largely forgotten. The architect who designed the Castle was robbed and killed in a forest whilst travelling from Hereward back to London and the engineer who built the tunnel was killed in a drunken pub brawl. The peasants who dug the tunnel all lived in the same village and were slaughtered when a gang of bandits attacked the village during a particularly harsh winter. Thus, the story of the secret tunnel passed into legend, myth and obscurity until it was lost in the mists of time.

Chapter Seventeen

Obersturmbannführer Ulrich stood with his knuckles leaning on the table as he looked at the map of Hereward Town Square. He had been staring at the map for so long that his eyes had started to ache.

"There must be some way that we can prevent the partisans from attacking the Parade," Oberstleutnant Dahrendorf said as he looked at the map. Dahrendorf had been in charge of escorting the Royal convoy from Cambridge to Hereward and he had successfully defended the convoy against an attack by the Resistance in which all of the guerrillas had been killed. Although Edward VIII and Queen Wallis had subsequently been killed by another group of partisans in the Town Square, Dahrendorf's commanding officer, the late Generalmajor von Schnakenberg, had written a glowing report in which he sang Dahrendorf's praises and gave him credit for fending off the initial Resistance attack. Following von Schnakenberg's untimely death, Dahrendorf had been promoted to fill dead man's shoes. He had skipped the rank of oberst in order to command von Schnakenberg's Brigade during the invasion of Scotland and he had been promoted to the rank of generalmajor. However, Operation Thor was a disastrous failure and Berlin needed scapegoats to explain the debacle. Headquarters selected the recently promoted Dahrendorf to be the Fall Guy and take the blame and accused him of being an inexperienced amateur who had been prematurely promoted beyond his skills and abilities. He was reduced in rank back to oberstleutnant and fully expected to be either sent back to Berlin in disgrace or posted to the Russian Front as a punishment. In fact, he suffered neither as Berlin simply had no one to spare whom they could send to replace him, so he remained as commander of Wehrmacht forces in Hereward. However, Dahrendorf was painfully aware that he was skating on thin ice. It was perfectly clear that the Soviets were on their last legs and had their backs against the wall. Everyone agreed that it was only a matter of time before Stalin realised that the game was up and threw in the towel. The end of the war in the east would release hundreds of thousands of veteran German soldiers and tens of thousands of ambitious officers who would all flock to the west in the hope of securing a 'soft' posting in the fleshpots of Paris and London. Dahrendorf knew that it only had a limited amount of time to prove that he deserved to be left in command of Wehrmacht forces in Hereward.

Ulrich looked at his opposite number and felt a surge of sympathy for the older man. He was aware of the intense pressure that Dahrendorf was under. He, on the other hand, was under no pressure at all. He had saved the Führer's life and he had been promoted to the rank of obersturmbannführer and was the youngest man to hold that position in the entire S.S. Ulrich had been personally promoted and decorated with Germany's highest military medal, the Iron Cross First Class, by the Führer himself and he had been identified as a rising star and a young man who would go far. Indeed, the Führer had said that he would take a personal interest in the young officer's career. Ulrich was the Golden Boy of the S.S. Anyone who was foolish enough to attempt to defy the path of destiny that had been mapped out for the Chosen One would be sure to incur the wrath of the Führer himself. "Are you sure that the Resistance will launch an attack, Oberstleutnant?"

"I would if I was in their position, wouldn't you?"

"Yes," Ulrich conceded. "However, with a little bit of luck they'll hit the convoy before it gets to Hereward and it will not be our problem."

"Unfortunately, we can't take that for granted, Obersturmbannführer. We need to be prepared for the worst case scenario that they will launch an attack on the Parade in the Town Square."

"We could threaten to execute the hostages that we currently hold?" Ulrich suggested.

Dahrendorf shook his head. "I don't think that will work, Norbert. That tactic hasn't had a deterrent effect in the past whether we've threatened to execute twenty hostages or one hundred hostages as a reprisal for the death of a German soldier. It hasn't worked in Russia, Poland, Yugoslavia or any of the Occupied territories and it certainly hasn't worked here. The partisans are ruthless bastards and they operate with a complete disregard for civilian casualties," Dahrendorf spat out the words with disgust without the slightest hint of irony.

Ulrich nearly said 'wasn't that like the pot calling the kettle black,' but bit his tongue in the nick of time. He didn't think that Dahrendorf would see the funny side of such a comment. "The guerrillas also know that we're going to eventually execute all of the hostages that we hold anyway. So they rationalize that it makes no difference whether we kill the prisoners now or later."

"So we've established that the threat to execute hostages has no deterrent effect on the partisans what so ever," Dahrendorf was thinking aloud.

Ulrich nodded. "The Resistance could not care less if we execute captured men and women. They think that we're going to kill them all regardless of whether they attack or not."

Dahrendorf's eyes suddenly lit up. "Eureka! You've hit the nail on the head! The partisans don't care if we execute British MEN and WOMEN, but what about children?"

"I'm sorry, Kurt. I don't quite follow," Ulrich shook his head with confusion.

"What about if we held British children as hostages?"

"What?" Ulrich said with horror. "You cannot be serious!"

Dahrendorf nodded his head vigorously. "I'm deadly serious, Norbert. We could capture British children and threaten to execute them in reprisal for any guerrilla attack on the Parade."

Ulrich stared at Dahrendorf with eyes wide open with shock and surprise. He knew that Dahrendorf was desperate for success, but he had not realised the lengths to which he was prepared to stretch and the depths that he was prepared to sink in order to achieve success.

"I don't think that you've thought this through, Kurt. Where would you find the children?"

"From the schools, I guess."

"And what if your plan to deter the Resistance failed? What if they attacked the Parade anyway? Would your men be prepared to murder innocent and defenceless school children if the partisans carried out their attack?" Ulrich's face was starting to redden with barely controlled rage and anger. "And how old will the children be that you hold hostage? Teenagers? Toddlers? Babies?"

Dahrendorf straightened up to his full height. "They will execute who ever I order them to execute whether they are babies, toddlers or teenagers. They are German soldiers and they will carry out their lawful orders," he said stiffly.

"That's precisely my point- they are German soldiers, not murderers! They are not concentration camp guards! And I'm sure that murdering innocent children does not constitute as a 'lawful order!' "

"Who are you to lecture me on what constitutes a 'lawful order?' " Dahrendorf exploded with frustration. "You're a serving S.S. officer, for Christ sake! Do you not know what your brethren are doing in the East? Do you not know what the Einsatzgruppen are doing in Poland and Russia? They are slaughtering people by the tens of thousands, by the hundreds of thousands! Defenceless people! Innocent people! Men, women and children; young and old; rich and poor. They have murdered mothers holding their babies in their arms! And now the Einsatzgruppen are in Britain! I'm certain that they will have no qualms about executing your precious British children," Dahrendorf sneered with contempt. "I'm sure that they are not as squeamish as you are."

Now Ulrich drew himself to his full height and stood at a position of attention. "Oberstleutnant Dahrendorf, it is my duty to inform you that I will not give unlawful orders to my men to capture and hold British children as hostages and I will not give unlawful orders to my men to murder children as a reprisal action in the event of any partisan attack on the Parade," he announced formally.

"I'm disappointed to hear you say that, Obersturmbannführer Ulrich."

"And I'm disappointed that you have left me with no option but to say it."

Ulrich picked up his officer's cap, put it on his head and adjusted it to a jaunty angle. He saluted Dahrendorf with a conventional German Army salute and Dahrendorf returned the salute. Ulrich turned to walk away but paused when he reached the door leading out of Dahrendorf's office.

"Oh, I almost forgot. One more thing before I leave."

"Yes?"

"I am also going to give orders to my men to prevent any of your men from capturing any children as hostages."

Dahrendorf sat bolt upright in his chair with a shocked impression on his face. "You're going to try to prevent men under my command from carrying out the orders that I have given them? Are you sure that is a wise decision?"

"Yes, I am. In fact, I've never been more sure of anything in my life. Furthermore, I'm going to order my men to open fire on your men if they attempt to harm or murder any children."

"What?" Dahrendorf leapt out of his chair. "Are you crazy?"

"No, I'm perfectly sane."

"You are prepared to order your men to kill fellow German soldiers?"

"If your men murder innocent children in cold blood then they are no longer fit to be called soldiers: they are simply murderers."

"You'd never get away with it," Dahrendorf threatened.

"Oh yes, I would. After all, the dead tell no tales. I will give express orders not to leave any survivors. And if any of your men do survive, whom will Berlin believe? A decorated war hero, the man who saved the Führer, the youngest obersturmbannführer in the S.S. or a broken, busted down Colonel who bungled and botched the invasion of Scotland? If I was a gambling man I know who I'd put my money on," Ulrich said breezily. "Good day to you, Oberleutnant."

Dahrendorf was far too shell shocked to reply and watched impotently as his young nemesis strolled casually and calmly out of his office.

"Sam and Alan, listen carefully," Ansett said seriously. "You're not going to like what I'm about to tell you, but I have to give you these orders never the less and it's vitally important that you obey them."

"Yes, sir," the boys answered in unison.

"You are not to tell Alice and Aurora about the mission, is that clear?"

"In case they compromise it?" Sam asked.

"Yes, Sam," Ansett nodded his head. "Unfortunately, I can't trust either of the girls to keep their mouths shut and not warn the people who might be effected."

"Yes, sir," Alan said.

"It is not a reflection on their character, Alan." Ansett shook his head. "It's just that the girls might be tempted to tip them off. It's perfectly understandable: If I was in their position I might be tempted to do the same thing. So the easiest solution is not to put them in that tricky situation. I don't want either Alice or Aurora to have a crisis of conscience. And I don't want a repeat of the Guy Fawkes debacle."

"It's all right, sir," Alan nodded. "I perfectly understand. We can't afford to be sentimental. Everyone who takes part in the Parade is the enemy and must be treated as such, regardless of any favour that they might have done for us in the past. After all, there's a war on."

"That's my boy, Alan," Ansett smiled. "I knew that you'd understand."

"What will you tell the Alice and Aurora instead, sir?" Sam asked. "They'll want to know what we're up to and why we can't tell them."

"If they ask you why all the hush hush, tell them that you can't spill the beans because of operational security. Loose tongues and all that," Ansett answered. "I will also keep them busy carrying out another part of our mission."

"Which is?"Alan asked with a smile.

Ansett put his finger to his lips. "I can't tell you, Alan. Operational security."

"Touché!" Alan said with a mock bow.

"Very good, sir," Sam said.

"Now." Ansett stood up. "Let's get to work."

Alice and Aurora were glad to be given a mission, as they knew that something was up and they were frustrated that they had not yet been given a role to perform. Ansett had emphasised the need not to appear too earnest or desperate in their quest to gather the necessary information. They were to be interested, but not too interested in the Parade and they were to be cool, calm and collected at all times. He emphasised that they were not to put themselves in danger and if there was even the merest chance that their true purpose might be discovered then they were to abort the mission.

"I don't understand," Aurora said. "How can you take part in the Parade?"

"I have no choice," Mendoza replied. "Ambassador Diaz has given me a direct order from the Caudillo himself: I am to provide one platoon to take part in the Parade."

"But I don't understand why Spain continues to support the Nazis here in Britain after their invasion of Scotland has failed," Aurora argued. "What possible reason could Franco have for allying our country with the Germans?"

"The reason has one word, Aurora: Gibraltar."

"What do you mean, papa?"

"We cannot get the Rock back by ourselves, my little butterfly. It pains me to say it, but we need the Germans to help us. And we're not the only ones either, my sweet. The Italians and the French are also taking part in the Parade."

"Why?"

Mendoza shrugged. "The Germans have something that they want or the Germans have the power to help them to get what they want. The Germans captured the English Channel Islands from the British and the Vichy French wants them back. The Italians want to capture Malta from the British but they need German aid to help them to do that. Hence they are also providing one platoon each to take part in the Parade."

"But where will they all stand, papa?" Aurora asked innocently. "I don't think that the Square is big enough to hold them all."

Mendoza paused thoughtfully for a moment before he answered. "The Square is big enough to hold ten platoons of men, Aurora. Here, I'll show you where they'll stand, my little butterfly." Mendoza stood up and walked through to the kitchen where he took out ten cups from a cupboard. He placed them on a tray and carried them back through to the living room where he put the tray down on the coffee table. "Imagine that the table is the Square, my sweet. Here is the Town Hall and there is the Cathedral directly opposite. In the centre is the War Memorial." He placed an ashtray in the middle. "A German military band will lead the march into the Square and they will enter from the north east corner of the Square via the Ely Road." Mendoza picked up a cup and placed it on the table. "The band will lead platoons of Luftwaffe aircrew, Navy sailors, Army soldiers and S.S. stormtroopers around a complete circuit of the Square and then they will halt here in the front rank." Mendoza placed five cups on the table. The Germans in turn will be followed by platoons of Italian troops, French Legionnaires, Spanish Legiónaries, Blackshirts and Legion of St. George Legionnaires-"

"The British will be taking part in a Parade to celebrate the first anniversary of the invasion of their country?" Aurora asked incredulously.

"You have to remember, Aurora, that although the Blackshirts may include a significant number of opportunists and criminals, the British Legionnaires are all fanatical Fascists. These men were members of the British Union of Fascists before the war. They're not fair weather Fascists like many members of the Militia who've jumped on the bandwagon since the Germans completed the successful occupation of the South. The Legionnaires probably don't think of Operation Sea lion as an invasion, they probably think of it as being liberation from that arch reactionary Churchill and his 'Jewish-Bolshevik clique of war mongering gangsters.' So they will no doubt celebrate the day as enthusiastically as their German overlords."

"Dirty, stinking Fascist traitors!" Aurora sneered with hatred and contempt.

"Aurora, you seem to have forgotten that it was those 'Fascist traitors' who rescued you from the S.S. Blackshirts freed you from the stormtroopers who were … who were … imprisoning you." Mendoza found it too painful to find accurate words to describe his daughter's ordeal.

Aurora shook her head. "No, papa. I haven't forgotten. I did not mean to appear ungrateful. And I remember that over sixty Blackshirts were killed and wounded trying to rescue me. However, despite what they did for me," Aurora sat up straighter, "they remain the enemy. After all, there is a war on."

"Bueno. Spoken like a true Spartan," Mendoza said with admiration. When had his little girl become such a spitfire?

"Where did you say that the other Fascists were going to stand, papa?"

"Oh yes. Here." Mendoza placed the remaining five cups in the second rank directly behind the cups in the front rank. "In this order from the west side of the Square to the east: Italians, Spanish, French, Blackshirts and finally, bringing up the rear, the St. George Legionnaires."

"So you will be directly behind the Luftwaffe platoon?"

"Well, not me personally. Captain Santa Anna will be in command of the platoon."

"And where will you be, papa?" Aurora asked casually.

"On the podium in front of the Town Hall together with the other big wigs …"

"Oh, really?" Aurora's eyes lit up with interest. "Who else will be with you on the podium?"

"Prime minister Joyce, Reichkommissar Schenk, Konteradmiral Dietl of the Kriegsmarine, Generalmajor Carls of the Luftwaffe, Oberstleutnant Dahrendorf of the Wehrmacht, Obersturmbannführer Ulrich of the S.S. The other Fascist national contingents are represented by colonels from their respective units."

Aurora whistled and smiled mischievously. "Quite a rogue's gallery of villains and ne'er do wells."

"Yes," Mendoza nodded. "It should be quite a juicy target for your friends in the Resistance, my sweet."

Aurora reacted as her father had thrown a bucket of freezing cold water over her. "Why did you say that, papa? I don't know what you're talking about," she protested.

Mendoza leaned forward and kissed his daughter on her forehead. "It's all right, my little butterfly, don't worry," he smiled. "Whatever happens, I'll be all right."

"But, papa-!" Aurora grabbed the sleeves of her father's shirt.

"No ifs, no buts, Aurora. We must all perform our roles in the play to the best of our abilities. Whatever will be, will be and there's absolutely nothing that we can do about it."

"Papa, I-!"

"We can't afford to be sentimental, Aurora. After all, there is a war on."

"What's wrong, Norbert? You seem anxious." Alice placed her hand on Ulrich's arm with concern.

"That's because I am anxious, Alice," Ulrich replied with a face pale with worry.

"What are you worried about?" Alice asked as she placed both of her hands on Ulrich's shoulders.

"The Parade." The Parade was hardly a state secret. After all, posters were on display throughout the town encouraging the good citizens of Hereward to attend the Parade and demonstrate their faith and trust in the New Order.

Alice laughed. "Are you worried that not enough people will turn up? I hate to tell you this, Norbert, but most people in Hereward will not consider watching a German victory parade to be their idea of a fun day out."

"No, Alice." Ulrich gently removed Alice's hands from his shoulders. "I'm worried that if the Resistance attack the Parade there will be a bloodbath."

"A Resistance attack? But you told me that the S.S. had smashed a Resistance cell at the beginning of the summer holidays. I wouldn't have thought that there were enough partisans left in Hereward to mount a serious attack on the Parade." Alice tried her best to remain calm but her heart was beating as fast as that of a humming bird. "And if they were foolish enough to try, I'm sure that they wouldn't be able to inflict very many casualties. After all, there will be nine platoons of fully armed soldiers on parade, as well as dozens, if not hundreds of additional troops actually guarding the Parade."

Ulrich nodded his head. "Alice, I'm afraid that you've misunderstood me: I'm not worried about military casualties that we might suffer as the result of a partisan attack. I'm worried about civilian casualties; I'm worried about the hostages that we will have no choice but to execute in retaliation for any attack."

Alice's face darkened with anger. "Norbert, I thought that you and your Nazi friends would have realised this by now: executing hostages does not work. It has no deterrent effect what so ever. The partisans know that you will eventually murder all of the prisoners that you hold anyway whether they attack you or not. Killing innocent men and women merely encourages the Resistance to fight harder."

"Except this time the hostages will be children."

"What?" Alice's voice cracked with disbelief.

"The Army has threatened to specifically execute child prisoners if the partisans carry out an attack on the Parade."

"But that's -, but that's - monstrous!"

Ulrich nodded. "I agree, Alice, and I've ordered my men to take action and intervene if they see the Army attempting to capture children as hostages."

"So they haven't arrested any children yet?"

"Not as far as I know."

Alice looked Ulrich directly in the eyes. "But why are you telling me all of this?"

"Because a deterrent doesn't work unless the enemy knows about it."

Hereward Castle had been under siege during the civil war between the Empress Matilda and King Stephen and had been held by Edward St. John on behalf of the King. In 1143 Geoffrey de Loreto, a supporter of the Empress, captured the Cathedral and the town in a lightning attack, but was unable to capture the castle. The morning after the siege began Loreto and all of his knights were discovered dead in their bloody beds. They had been slaughtered as they slept in the Cathedral during a surprise night attack. There was no sign of any struggle and there was no sign of their attackers either. The sentries who had guarded all of the entrances to the Cathedral had sworn that no one had entered or left the Cathedral during their watch. The leaderless army was spooked by Loreto's mysterious murder and voted with their feet; they abandoned the siege that day and Hereward was soon liberated. Loreto's murder had remained a mystery until now. Ansett, Smith, Jones and the other six paratroopers spent from dawn till dusk from Monday to Friday clearing the tunnel of any booty that Edward's men had dropped that threatened to block the tunnel. By Friday night they had assembled a veritable treasure trove of artefacts that any museum would be proud to put on display. However, the exhibition would have to wait: all of the artefacts were transported to the farm where they were buried underground and where they would be left undisturbed for the duration of the War. Ansett and the paratroopers replaced the booty in the tunnel with booty from the skies that had been dropped by parachute.

"What are we going to do, sir?" Alice asked after she had told Ansett that the German Army was prepared to capture children and murder them if the Resistance attacked the Parade.

Ansett clenched and unclenched his fists as he fought to control his anger. "Ulrich is certain that Dahrendorf has not captured any children yet?"

"Yes, sir."

"So we must stop him from capturing any children in the first place. The question is simple: how do we do that?"

"The answer is also simple, sir: we fight fire with fire: we give Dahrendorf a taste of his own medicine."

"What is this?" Dahrendorf asked as his adjutant handed him a brown paper package wrapped up in string.

"A Blackshirt motorcycle despatch courier delivered it this morning, sir," Hauptmann von Gersdorff answered. "The Askari asked me to deliver it to you personally."

Dahrendorf picked up a pair of scissors, cut the string and opened the package. Ten metal objects spilled out onto his desk. "What the -?"

Von Gersdorff stopped in his tracks as he was walking out of the office and was at his C.O.'s side in an instant. "What is it, sir?"

Dahrendorf picked up one of the rust encrusted and blood covered objects and read the inscription. "Verdamnt!" He swore and handed it over to his adjutant. He picked up the letter that was enclosed in the package and began to read:

Oberstleutnant Dahrendorf,

You have threatened to murder child hostages if partisans attack the Parade. If you do this then we will execute Wehrmacht and S.S. prisoners that we are currently holding. We have sent you and Obersturmbannführer Ulrich the dog tags of ten Army and ten S.S. prisoners that we are currently holding as proof of life. If you capture or kill any child hostages then we will send you the Army and S.S. pay books covered in the blood of your men as proof of death. This is a man's war- fight it like a man! You have been warned.

The Sons of Hereward.

Von Gersdorff looked at the bloody dog tag that he was holding. "Sergeant Kitzinger is reported missing, presumed dead, sir." He picked up another damaged dog tag. "As is Leutnant von Seeckt. He was in command of an anti-partisan patrol that disappeared without a trace last month, sir. Kitzinger was second in command of the patrol." He picked up a handful of I.D. tags. "I can check the records of these men, sir, but I have a sneaking suspicion that I'll discover that the rest of these men were also part of von Seeckt's patrol and are also missing, presumed killed."

"Bloody hell," Dahrendorf was wide eyed with surprise. "So the swine do have our men …"

"And they've also sent a similar package to the S.S." Von Gersdorff looked shocked. "They'll lean on us even more heavily to call off any plan to arrest any children. There will be hell to pay if the Resistance execute any of their men …"

"My God." Dahrendorf put his hand up his mouth with despair. "As the British say: we are truly stuck between a rock and a hard place. But we have to do something. If we don't, the Resistance will attack the Parade and there will be a massacre …"

"But we can still do something, sir," von Gersdorff insisted.

"What?"

"We've already established that the partisans have total disregard for the lives of British men and women. They continue to attack us despite our execution of hostages as retaliation. However, the sentimental affection that the British have for their pets also extends to their children. We can still use the feelings that the British have for their children against them."

"How?"

"If you allow me to use your map, sir, I will show you …"

"So we are definitely going to attack the Parade?" Aurora asked Alice as they sat in the schoolgirl's bedroom.

"Yes, we are."

"Except that we haven't been consulted about it," Aurora protested. "We don't know anything about the plan and we haven't been told anything about the attack. After all that we've done for the cause, the ungrateful swine …"

Alice put a sympathetic hand on her friend's arm. "Now, Aurora, there's a very rational reason why we haven't been briefed about the plan. Don't take it personally; Major Ansett is very grateful for the services that we have performed on behalf of the Resistance -"

"Then why aren't we part of the attack?" Aurora interrupted angrily.

"Because we pose a security risk, Aurora."

"What? A 'security risk?' Does Major Ansett think that I am a traitor?" Aurora bristled with indignation as she launched into a torrent of Spanish oaths and curses.

"No, Aurora," Alice chuckled at her friend's emotional display of furious indignation. "But he does think that our knowledge of the operation may affect the success or failure of the mission."

"Why?"

"Because if the operation is successful it will probably kill your father and my boyfriend."

Ansett and the partisans had spent the week prior to the Parade clearing the tunnel of any dirt and debris that might impede their passage. They had ferried all of the flotsam and jetsam to the farm where the rescued hostages buried it in a deep hole that they had dug behind one of the barns. The partisans had transported the special cargo that had arrived with the commandoes back to the Cathedral on the return trip from the farm.

Captain Smith, Second-Lieutenant Jones and Major Ansett carefully consulted the ancient map that Ben Rathdowne had given them. According to the map, the distance from the secret entrance in the Crypt of the Cathedral to the secret entrance in the dungeon of the Castle was approximately eight hundred yards or half a mile. The problem was that neither the Town Square nor the Town Hall had existed when the secret tunnel was built and the map had been drawn. However, the Cathedral had been built on what later became the south side of the Square and the Town Hall was built on the north side of the Square directly opposite the Cathedral. Rathdowne's map showed that the secret tunnel led directly north from the Crypt to the main entrance to the Cathedral and then veered off at an angle and headed straight off towards the Castle. If one stood on the steps leading to the main entrance of the

Cathedral it was possible to look at the northeast corner of the Square where the Ely Road connected and see the square tower of the Castle keep in the distance. Ansett, Smith and Jones agreed that the route of the secret tunnel probably led from the Cathedral entrance to the northeast corner of the Square and then straight towards the Castle keep. The partisans consulted an Ordinance Survey map of Hereward and compared it with Rathdowne's map. They knew that the Germans had built a rostrum directly in front of the Town Hall for Reichkommissar Schenk, Prime Minister Joyce and the other big wigs to stand on and watch the Parade. Unfortunately, the centre of the stage was a good one hundred yards away from the nearest part of the tunnel.

"Is it close enough?" Ansett asked.

Smith shook his head. "I'm not sure, Major. I don't think the blast will be powerful enough to kill all of the Hun Top Brass. What do you think, Lieutenant?"

"We would need twice as many explosives to make sure, sir," Jones answered with disappointed honesty. "We simply don't have enough. One hundred yards is too far away. However, we may kill or injure some of them with shrapnel and flying debris such as cobblestones …"

"Killing or injuring some of them is not good enough," Ansett hissed through clenched teeth. "I want to kill the whole lot of them, especially that treacherous Blackshirt bastard Joyce."

"There is one way to make sure that we wipe them all out, sir," Jones suggested.

"How's that, Lieutenant?"

"Well, the other lads have been positively chaffing at the bit to have a go at the Huns, sir. You have to understand that they are highly trained commandoes, sir. And they have been frustrated at what they see as their role as glorified bodyguards guarding Captain

Smith, the plastic explosives and myself. They want to see some action and get stuck in."

"Go on," Ansett encouraged.

"When the bomb goes off there will be a lot of confusion, carnage and chaos and the Huns will run around like headless chickens trying to search for survivors. That will present us with the perfect opportunity to kill the Big Wigs. The Jerries guarding the Cathedral will be sure to rush outside and find out what the hell is going on. One of our fire teams can join the Jerries, cunningly disguised in German uniforms, and attack the rostrum whilst the other fire team provides covering fire. Once the assault team has killed the Brass they can rendezvous with us at the getaway vehicle."

"If any of them have managed to survive," Ansett said grimly.

"I agree that it's risky, Major, but the men volunteered to join the commandoes, not the Boy Scouts. I can't think of a better way to increase the chances of us killing the Hun big wigs and successfully completing the mission."

"Nor can I, sir," Smith agreed. "Anyway, I'm sure that the lads will leap at the chance to kill some high ranking officers. The fact that they're Germans is an added bonus!"

Ansett considered his choices for a moment before he spoke. "All right: as soon as the explosion occurs your commandoes will assault the stage in order to make sure that we kill all of the Brass. They will then rendezvous with us at the getaway lorry that will be parked at the rear of the Cathedral. Agreed?"

"Agreed, sir," Smith and Jones answered in unison.

"Good." Ansett nodded. "Then let's tell the others the plan and finish moving and setting up the explosives. I suggest that we all get an early night. We've got a big day ahead of us tomorrow."

Lieutenant - Colonel Mendoza adjusted the straps of his highly polished Sam Browne belt as he read the letter for the third time. An unknown messenger had delivered it anonymously the previous night.

My Lord, out of the love I bear to some of your friends, I have a care of your preservation. Therefore I would advise you, as you tender your life, to devise some excuse to shift your attendance at this parliament; for God and man hath concurred to punish the wickedness of this time. And think not slightly of this advertisement, but retire yourself into your country where you may expect the event in safety. For though there be no appearance of any stir, yet I say they shall receive a terrible blow this Parliament; and yet they shall not see who hurts them. This counsel is not to be condemned because it may do you good and can do you no harm; for the danger is passed as soon as you have burnt the letter. And I hope God will give you the grace to make good use of it, to whose holy protection I commend you.

The page had been roughly ripped out of a book of some kind and the passage had been circled with a red crayon. Mendoza did not have to read the text surrounding the passage in order to discover the context of the source. He had learned about the unsuccessful Spanish Armada at school and he had also studied it at the Military Academy when he was training to become an officer. This had sparked an interest in Anglo - Spanish relations during the Tudor and Stuart period and he had become fascinated by the Gunpowder Plot.

So it was with a little smile of self - satisfaction that he recognized the famous letter that Lord Mounteagle had received which had warned him about Guy Fawkes' plan to blow up the Houses Of Parliament. Someone was trying to warn him to stay away from the Parade. Mendoza's guardian angel had not written on the letter or on the envelope and had probably not left any fingerprints on the paper either. It appeared as if his mysterious benefactor wished to remain unknown. Mendoza chuckled. The ironic thing was that the warning would not make one little difference to his plans whatsoever. He could not change his plans to attend the Parade and even if he had a choice he would choose not to do so either. If he did not turn up, then the Germans would become suspicious and they would soon smell a rat. And he could hardly order Second - Lieutenant Santa Anna to carry on with the Parade if he was not there himself, and if he ordered the young officer to pull out all together then the Germans would definitely decide that there was something rotten in the state of Denmark: they might even decide to pull the plug on the whole Parade. Mendoza was also aware that rumours were beginning to circulate that Spanish Legiónaries were responsible for deliberately sabotaging Operation Thor and were partly, if not wholly, to blame for the disastrous failure of the invasion of Scotland. He did not know where the rumours had come from, possibly from Prisoners of War who had been captured by the British, nor did he particularly care. What was important was that the rumours were out there and they would continue to gather speed and momentum until they eventually reached Hitler and Franco themselves. As the Americans say: that is when the shit would really hit the fan. Mendoza's only hope was to ride out the storm and dismiss the ridiculous rumours as brazen and bare

257

faced British propaganda designed to sow discord and distrust between allies. Once again, Mendoza cursed his failure to insist on his Legiónaries spending more time practising shooting on the rifle range. It appeared as if poor marksmanship had allowed Germans to survive the massacre at Beattie Bridge and also at Berwick – upon - Tweed. Pandora's box had been opened at the Battle of Ebro River in Spain and despite valiant efforts; it did not look as if it was going to be shut any time soon.

Chapter Eighteen

Ansett, Sam, Alan and the commandoes spent the whole of Saturday making plans and preparations to rain on the German's parade the following day. As the partisans settled down for the night in Rathdowne's old house Ansett insisted that Alan return to Cromwell boarding house so that he would not be missed and suspicions would not be aroused. After much huffing and puffing Alan eventually relented and left the Cathedral under protest. Although he recognized the wisdom of Ansett's words he hated to think that he was missing out on any of the action and excitement.

The partisans woke up the next morning at the crack of dawn. Ansett cooked his men a hearty traditional English breakfast of bacon, eggs, sausages, mushrooms and tomatoes. When Ansett boasted with pride that the meat came from the farm one of the commandoes asked if the bacon and sausages were German-free. Ansett mockingly asked the soldier if he was a vegetarian. He assured the commando that a hint of German added a certain je ne sais quoi. The commando was not sure whether Ansett was joking or telling the truth. After breakfast, Ansett, Smith and Jones made sure that the explosives were set in the correct place and that the detonation chord and detonator worked. The other commandoes spent the time cleaning their weapons and rehearsing the plan so that everyone was sure of their role in the operation. There was a feeling of nervous anticipation and excitement in the air.

Ansett watched with eagle eyes as a platoon of German Army engineers made a final methodical sweep of the

Square equipped with mine detectors. Another section of soldiers used specially trained dogs to sniff for explosives. They paid particular attention to the flowerbeds that decorated the front of the Town Hall and the Cathedral and also to the small circle of soil that surrounded the base of the oak trees that were planted at regular intervals around the Square. He was also sure that another team of sappers would be searching the sewers that ran underneath the Square. Ansett grinned. The Huns were wasting their time: they would find nothing there; they were searching the wrong tunnels. Ansett looked at his watch. It was ten o'clock, exactly one hour before the Parade was due to take place and so far, no surprises, touch wood. He was watching from a small window that was located on the second floor of a spiral staircase in a turret on the left hand corner of the front side of the Cathedral. The ground floor door that led to the staircase was cunningly concealed in a utility room that contained brooms and mops and buckets. Ansett was confident that the Germans were not aware of the existence of the door. Never the less, his fully loaded Schmessier lay on the floor beside him within easy arms reach. It paid to expect the unexpected.

Ansett could not help smiling smugly as he observed that the Square could hardly be described as being overcrowded with spectators. There was a sprinkling of onlookers dotted here and there around the perimeter holding a mixture of German Swastika and British lightning bolt flags which hung limply on this windless day. They were probably the friends and relatives of the Blackshirts and St. George Legionnaires who were taking part in the Parade. The German Army soldiers and S.S. stromtroopers who were responsible for providing security for the Square easily outnumbered the Fascist spectators. So far it looked like everything was going smoothly and according to plan. When the bombs blew up they would inflict minimal civilian casualties and it appeared as if most of the spectators were Fascists anyway.

Major Alfredo Astray coughed into his fist. "Here he comes, Colonel," he warned.

Mendoza turned around. "Good morning, Obersturmbannführer," Mendoza said as he dipped his head in a bow.

"Good morning, Colonel Mendoza." Ulrich greeted Mendoza with a sparkling toothpaste advert smile as he joined him in the Town Hall foyer. "Nice day for it."

Mendoza raised his eyebrows with surprise at Ulrich's sang-froid and complete lack of nerves or concern. "A nice day for what, Norbert? A parade? I hate to tell you this, Obersturmbannführer, but the partisans are planning to rain on your parade."

"I know, Juan," Ulrich replied with a grin as he nonchalantly pulled on a pair of brown leather gloves.

"If they attack the Parade there will be a bloodbath," Mendoza warned.

Ulrich thought for a moment before he spoke. "Have you ever studied the Spartans, Colonel?"

"The Spartans?" Mendoza was confused. "No. Why do you ask?"

"Then allow me to tell you a story, Juan. Phillip II of Macedonia, Alexander the Great's father, wanted to conquer the whole of Greece and he sent a letter to Sparta in which he threatened: if I conquer Sparta I will burn it to the ground. The Spartans replied with one word. Do you know what that one word was, Colonel?" Ulrich smiled like a cat about to pounce on a mouse.

"No."

"If." Ulrich shook his head. "If you conquer Sparta. I agree that if the partisans attack the Parade there will be a bloodbath. However, the partisans will not attack the Parade."

"How can you know that, Ulrich?"

"Because I will stop them, Juan." Ulrich looked at his watch. It was nearly ten thirty. "Look out of the door."

Ansett sat up with a start. What the hell was going on? People were streaming into the Square from all directions and S.S. stormtroopers were shepherding the civilians into position behind the barricades that prevented access to the Square.

"Sir, I've come to ask you if you know where Alan is. It's ten thirty; he should be here by now," Sam asked as he climbed up the narrow turret stairs.

But Ansett did not reply. Sam glanced out of the small window. "Where have all of these people come from?" Sam asked with surprise. "The Square was virtually empty five minutes ago."

"I don't know, Sam, but there are a hell of a lot of them," Ansett answered with a confused frown.

"They have completely filled up the streets surrounding the Square and the crowd is now half a dozen people thick in some places." Sam shook his head with disbelief as he watched the S.S. soldiers distributing swastika and Union Jack flags to the spectators. "More people are coming in."

"The new comers aren't Fascists either, Sam. Many of them have dropped the flags onto the ground and have trampled them underfoot. These people aren't volunteers. They don't want to be here. These people are pressed men. The Huns have gathered these people from somewhere."

"But where have they come from, sir?"

Ansett's eyes lit up. "Look, Sam. They're all wearing their Sunday best. The Nazis have collected these people from church."

"Very clever, sir!" Sam said with genuine admiration.

"Elementary, my dear Watson!"

"But why have the Huns gathered them, sir? Are they embarrassed that there are so few spectators? Are they using them to thicken out the crowd?"

Ansett shook his head grimly. "I'm afraid that the reason is far more sinister than that, Sam: The Huns have surrounded the Square with civilians as a deterrent effect."

"The Huns think that we'll call off the mission if we think that the attack will cause too many civilian casualties?"

Ansett nodded sombrely.

"Well, are we?"

"Are we what?"

"Are we going to call it off?"

"Very clever, Norbert," Mendoza nodded his head with sincere praise. "You've killed two birds with one stone: you've created a crowd of spectators to watch the Parade and you've also created a buffer between your men and the partisans. Where did you find this rent-a-crowd?"

Ulrich smiled. "I ordered my men to flush out all of the people who live in the apartments and houses that surround the Square and bring them all here. And voila - instant crowd!" Ulrich spread both of his arms out wide. "If my men have carried out their orders properly every single civilian who lives within a fifty metre radius of this Square should now be part of this crowd."

"Very impressive, Obersturmbannführer," Mendoza said. "There's only one problem."

"What's that, Colonel?"

"You may not have enough."

"What do you mean?" Ulrich asked with a raised eyebrow.

"You may not have enough children in the crowd to deter a partisan attack."

Ulrich gazed out over the crowd and realised with a start that although there was a sprinkling of children in the crowd, most of the spectators were adults.

"When couples have a child or two they want to move out of the crowded city or town centre into the suburbs or the countryside where their rent or mortgage is cheaper and where houses are bigger and usually have a garden."

"I see …"

"I know this, Ulrich, because that's precisely what we did when Aurora was born. We moved out of Madrid into the countryside." Mendoza put his hand on Ulrich's shoulder. "I hope that I'm wrong, Ulrich, but I don't think that you have enough children in the crowd to deter a partisan attack."

Ulrich smiled grimly. "I hope that you're wrong as well, Juan, because as you said: if the partisans attack the Parade there will be a bloodbath."

"What are we going to do, sir?" Sam asked anxiously. "If we detonate the first bomb near the north east corner of the Square the explosion will kill or injure most of the people who are standing on the pavement within fifty yards of the explosion …"

"I know, Sam." Ansett closed his eyes and massaged his temples as he ran through all of the different options in his head.

"Sir! I don't believe this!" Sam stood up sharply. "Look what's happening now, sir!"

264

"What is it, Sam? Oh no!" Ansett put his hand up to his mouth with alarm.

"I hate to tell you this, Obersturmbannführer, but I told you so. I told you that I would protect the Parade, but you didn't believe me."

"By using children as hostages?" Ulrich asked.

Oberstleutnant Dahrendorf wagged his finger as he corrected Ulrich. "They are not 'hostages' my dear Ulrich: they are spectators. They are guests. They are special guests whom I have invited to attend the Parade."

Ulrich looked at Dahrendorf with an expression of complete and utter disbelief and incomprehension. "You forcibly kidnapped these school children from their homes and you have the nerve and audacity to claim that they came voluntarily?"

"My dear Obersturmbannführer," Dahrendorf chortled. "You could not be more mistaken: I have not kidnapped anyone, and certainly not these children. I asked the headmaster of St. John's last night if he would accept an invitation on behalf of his boarders to attend the Parade. He was happy to accept what he referred to as my 'generous invitation' and described it as an 'absolutely spiffing idea.' Mr Ashworth phoned the boarding houses last night and informed the various housemasters and mistresses of the plan. When my men arrived to collect them this morning the children couldn't climb onto the lorries quick enough. They were absolutely raring with enthusiasm to go to the Parade." Dahrendorf looked like the cat that had got the cream and looked enormously pleased with himself.

Ulrich watched with open-mouthed horror as approximately three hundred school children from St. John's eight boarding houses were shepherded to stand on either side of the rostrum where Reichkommissar

Schenk and Prime Minister Joyce would stand. Ulrich turned to look directly at Dahrendorf. "I hope you realise that this Parade may very well turn into their funeral."

Dahrendorf shrugged his shoulders dismissively. "That's for the Partisans to decide, not me. Let the deaths of these children rest on their conscience, because it certainly won't rest on mine."

Ansett raised his binoculars to his face and scanned the crowd of school children. He recognized almost all of the faces as he had taught virtually all of them in his twenty years as a teacher at St. John's. He realized with a sense of dreadful certainty and foreboding that Alan would be part of the crowd. No other reason could explain his non-appearance at the Cathedral. Ansett slowly lowered the binoculars to his chest as he ran through his options. If he detonated the bomb that the partisans had planted near the north east corner of the Square the explosion would kill and injure dozens, if not hundreds of children and also murder and maim many of the other civilians who were standing on the eastern side of the Square. On the other hand the explosion would create an extremely effective diversion and provide the perfect cover for the commando Kill Team to cross the Square and assassinate the Reichkommissar and Prime Minister Joyce. Ansett could hear the noise of the German Army Band playing as it started to leave the Castle. He looked at his watch. It was ten forty five; the band would arrive in the Square at five to eleven. Ansett was rapidly running out of time and options.

Alan swore in frustration and disgust at his predicament. He had been woken up by the house gong at eight thirty as normal on a Sunday morning and had joined the rest of Cromwell Boarding House at nine o'clock for breakfast in the dining room. At nine thirty he had taken part in the weekly ritual of writing a letter home to his parents and he had finished his letter by ten o'clock. The boarders were due to leave for their usual church service at a quarter past ten but Alan had planned to fake a migraine and so skive the service. Once he was certain that his fellow boarders had left for church Alan planned to sneak out of Cromwell and make his way to the Cathedral to take part in the murder and mayhem that was planned to start promptly at eleven. However, the Germans had arrived at ten o' clock and had completely scuppered Alan's plans. They had ' invited' the boarders to climb onto their lorries and the children had responded with enthusiasm and gusto. Alan had not been surprised that they had been as keen as mustard to attend the Parade: the boys would seize upon any opportunity not to go to church. Alan had been caught by surprise and did not have time to make his excuses to the new temporary housemaster Mr Harper, and so had no choice but to board the lorries with his fellow Cromwellians. Alan looked up at the rostrum to his left.

"Look up there, Davie," Alan pointed. "Lord Haw Haw himself is up on the rostrum. The dirty Blackshirt bastard!"

His younger brother grabbed Alan's arm with alarm. "Al, you must be careful," he warned. "Some one might hear you!"

Alan shrugged his shoulders dismissively and laughed. "I suppose that you're right, Davie. If we're close enough to smell his treacherous stink, then we're probably close enough for him and his Fascist friends and cronies to hear us." Alan's eyes suddenly lit up with a new idea. "Davie, I've just had a brainwave."

"What do you mean, Al?"

"Davie, you played in the School Cricket Team last summer, didn't you?"

"Yes, I did, Al. I was a bowler."

"I've always been a rotten bowler. I can throw far enough, but not accurately enough. But you have an accurate throwing arm, Davie?"

"Yes, Al. What's this all about?"

Alan turned to face his brother and placed both of his hands on Davie's shoulders. "Davie, are you still prepared to serve your King and country? To fight for the Cause?"

"Yes, I am, Alan. I'm prepared to fight for the Cause and die if necessary. Why?"

"Because, little brother, we might have to put your Cricket skills to the test."

"What are we going to do, sir?" Sam asked.

"I ... I don't know, Sam," Ansett answered hesitantly. "I need time to think about our options."

Sam looked at his watch. "Sir, it's ten to eleven. The band will arrive in the Square in five minutes. We don't have time to think through our options. We need to make a decision now." He was also keenly aware that Captain Smith and Second–Lieutenant Jones were down in the Crypt with their hands on the detonator: they needed to know if there was a change to the plan. Ansett appeared to have lost the plot and seemed dazed and indecisive. However, Sam was not going to alert Smith because the captain would have no choice but to relieve Ansett of his command and take over the operation. If this happened, regardless of the success or failure of the mission, Ansett's credibility and reputation would be ripped to shreds and he would never be given a position of command and responsibility again. "Sir, the problem is the children, isn't it?" Sam asked carefully.

"I killed thirteen innocent people at the Remembrance Day Massacre and I wounded another twenty four men, women and children," Ansett said in a monotone.

Sam shook his head and placed a sympathetic hand on Ansett's arm. "Sir, you didn't kill them: the Germans did."

Ansett slowly nodded. "I am responsible for their deaths, Sam and I am also responsible for the deaths of countless more at the St. George's Day Massacre." He turned and looked directly at Sam. "I will not be responsible for the deaths of anymore of our people."

Sam looked up as he heard the loud booming noise of the German Army Brass Band as it marched into the Square. He watched as the Luftwaffe platoon followed hot on its heels. It was five to eleven: they were out of time. "Sir, I have plan which will allow us to complete our mission and save the children at the same time."

Ansett nodded slowly. "Make it happen, Sam."

Alice and Aurora were walking quickly towards the sound of the music. Ulrich and Mendoza had both warned the girls to stay away from the Parade, as there was a very strong possibility that the partisans would attack. Of course the girls had both ignored the well-intentioned advice. Alice and Aurora were both determined to help with the mission despite the fact that they did not know what it was and had not been asked to participate. However, it was common sense to presume that the mission was an attempt to assassinate Reichkommissar Schenk and Prime Minister Joyce. Why else would the commandoes be here? They had certainly not flown all the way down south from Scotland in order to present the two men with flowers. Aurora also had an ulterior motive for joining the mission: she wanted to protect her father if possible, as she was sure that he had placed himself in harm's way. Alice also said that she wanted to help Aurora to protect her father. However, when Aurora asked Alice if her father was the only member of the enemy that she wanted to protect, Alice had blushed before she had answered 'of course.' She assured Aurora that being Ulrich's girlfriend was simply a matter of business to her: she had been given a mission to complete and she was performing it to the best of her ability. However, when Aurora had mischievously said: "Me thinks the lady doth protest too much," Alice had pretended not to have heard her. Regardless of what ever their personal reasons were, the girls were both looking for trouble: they had each hidden a Luger pistol in the small of their backs and a silencer attachment and a couple of magazines of 9 mm rounds in their underwear. They were tooled up and ready for action.

The girls had just walked onto Ely Road when they saw a familiar figure in the distance.

"Uh oh, here comes trouble," one of the Blackshirts said with a grin. "Sam?"

Sam turned around and swore. "Hello, sis. What are you doing here?"

"I might ask you the same thing, little brother. Up to no good, no doubt," Alice answered with a grin.

"But Major Ansett ordered you to stay away from here!"

" 'Ordered me?' " Alice shook her head. "Oh, I don't think so. I thought that it was more of a helpful hint."

"Or a friendly suggestion," Aurora added innocently.

Sam rolled his eyes in exasperation.

"Why are you all dressed up?" Aurora asked.

"We're in disguise," Corporal Colvin, the commander of the assault team, answered. "We're going to gate crash a Fascist fancy dress party."

"I see." Aurora quickly counted the four Blackshirts. "Where's Alan? It's not like him to miss out on a chance to cause mischief and mayhem."

Sam looked at Colvin before he answered. "Aurora, Alan is standing next to the rostrum with all of the other boarders."

"What?" Aurora's eyes bulged wide as she held her hand over her mouth with horrified disbelief.

"The Germans captured all of the boarders this morning and are holding them hostage. They think that the children will act as a deterrent which will prevent us from attacking them," Sam explained.

"And will it act as a deterrent?" Alice asked.

"Not if I can help it, sis," Sam replied with a Berserker's grin. "We can complete the mission and save the children, but I'll need your help to pull it off. Are you with me?"

Alice smiled. "Of course I am! Strength and honour, Sam! Aurora?"

"Strength and honour!"

"Strength and honour!" Sam repeated.

Colvin looked at his fellow commandoes who were smiling madly. "Strength and honour!" they all chorused.

The partisans stopped at the rear entrance to Blair's Garden Supply Store. Colvin took a quick look around before he knocked the rusty padlock off with the butt of his rifle. "Follow me," he ordered "and shut the door behind you." The guerrillas followed Colvin into the shop. "Gordon, guard the rear door. Duncan, guard the front door." The two commandoes nodded and walked away to take up their positions. Colvin entered the main area of the shop and stopped to face the remaining partisans. "Now, chaps listen carefully: Sam, I want you to find me as many bags of fertiliser or tree stump remover as you can. I want you to make sure that it contains one key ingredient: potassium nitrate. It's also known as saltpetre. Clear?"

"Clear, Corporal."

Colvin nodded. "Good lad. Off you go." Sam scurried off. "Now, ladies, follow me. We need to find the kitchen." Colvin turned around and headed back towards the rear of the shop. "Ah! The staff kitchen, just as I thought." Colvin entered the room. "Now, Aurora I want you to find me as many bags of sugar as you can. Alice, I want you to find me some cooking oil and also a roll of silver foil." Colvin was looking for something as he talked. "Eureka! There it is!" He exclaimed in triumph as he picked up a frying pan.

"I hate to ruin the party, Corporal," Alice said sarcastically, "but this is neither the time nor the place to start baking cakes."

Colvin chuckled. "We're not going to bake a cake, Alice. We're going to create a diversion that will distract the Huns and give the children a bona fide reason to leave the Square. We're going to make smoke bombs!"

Alice gave Colvin a look of complete and utter confusion.

"I've got the tree stump remover, Corporal," Sam announced as he handed over three 1 .5 kilogram bags of Crawford's Finest Tree Stump Remover.

"Good." Colvin opened the bag. "Alice, heat up the frying pan to medium heat, please."

Alice did as she was told. "Now, watch and learn, children: this is a useful trick to know. I'm going to mix three parts potassium nitrate to two parts sugar.

Aurora, please find as many metal baking trays as possible and lay some silver foil on all of them."

The partisans watched with fascination as Colvin patiently mixed the ingredients together until they melted and turned brown.

"It smells sweet," Aurora observed, "like caramel."

Colvin smiled. "You could probably eat it, although I wouldn't recommend it."

When the mixture was thoroughly melted together Colvin dropped some oil onto it. "Tray please, Aurora." He ladled out the mixture onto the silver foil covered tray where they sat like small caramel cakes. Colvin wiped his forehead with his sleeve. "We're going to cut it a bit fine." He looked at his watch. It was five past eleven. The band had stopped playing. It was now time for the speeches. Colvin started to repeat the procedure.

The partisans carried three caramel cake covered trays through to the main area of the shop and lined them up on the floor underneath an open window.

"Just in time, Corporal. I could do with a wee snack. You're a man of many talents." Duncan the commando said with genuine admiration.

"I haven't always been a soldier, you know," Colvin replied mysteriously. "What you're looking at, Duncan, is the product of a misspent youth. Now, gather round, chaps. Here's the plan ..." It was ten past eleven.

Alan watched as a plume of smoke started billowing out of the shop window.

"What the -?" Davie said incredulously.

"Get ready, Davie," Alan warned. "I hope that your throwing arm is in good shape because the attack is about to begin." He watched as a group of Blackshirts walked towards where he was standing.

"Mr Harper, the shop is on fire. Please escort the children away from danger back to their respective boarding houses," Aurora said.

Craig Harper, Cromwell's housemaster, looked at Aurora who was dressed in a League of British Girls uniform. The Blackshirt uniform gave her an air of authority and he did not think to question her right to give him orders. He quickly glanced at the huge column of smoke that was snaking high into the air above Blair's. The shop looked as if it was about to burst into flames any second. "Right you are, Aurora," Harper replied. "I'll go and tell the other house masters and mistresses that we're leaving. Alan," he shouted, "we're leaving. Tell the other house captains to walk at the back and act as the rear guard."

"Very good, sir." Alan turned to look at Aurora as Harper walked away. "I hope that you know what you're doing, Aurora."

"So do I," Aurora replied with a mischievous smile. "Are you ready?"

"I was born ready. Strength and honour!"

"Strength and honour!"

"Sir, Captain Smith wants to know when we'll be ready," Sam panted as he ran up the narrow turret spiral staircase.

Ansett took a quick look through his binoculars. The children had nearly all left the area beside the rostrum and were rapidly walking away from the north east side of the Square. Alice and the other partisans had also succeeded in shepherding the civilians away from the shop and spectators were busy leaving the southeast corner of the Square. The S.S. stormtroopers and the Blackshirts had not moved from their stand at ease position on the Parade Ground. Ansett smiled wolfishly and licked his lips. "Sam, in exactly five seconds it will be a quarter past eleven … five … four … three … two … one … mark. Do you concur?"

"Yes, sir." Sam looked at his watch that he had synchronised earlier with the rest of the partisans.

"Order Captain Smith to detonate the mines at exactly seventeen minutes past eleven. Clear?"

"Crystal clear, sir!" Sam smiled like a lunatic as he raced down the stairs.

"The partisans are going to attack the Parade, Oberstleutnant," Ulrich warned in a whisper as he stood beside Dahrendorf.

"They wouldn't dare: we're holding the children as hostages. They're our deterrence against attack. The children are our human shield," Dahrendorf replied confidently.

"You were holding the children as hostages, Dahrendorf," Ulrich corrected. "The children are leaving …"

"What?"

"Open your eyes, Dahrendorf," Ulrich hissed. "Your shield has been splintered and broken."

Dahrendorf craned his neck to look over the heads of the commanders of the foreign units that stood to his left and jolted backwards with surprise. The area beside the rostrum was empty. He spotted the smoke pouring out of the shop window and noticed the Blackshirts moving the spectators away from Blair's.

"The partisans are going to attack us. We need to move the Reichkommissar and the prime minister to a position of safety," Ulrich urged.

"When are they going to hit us?"

Ulrich glanced over the Square. "Now!"

Chapter Nineteen

The first mine detonated directly underneath the platoon of parading S.S. soldiers and sent a macabre mix of men, cobblestones and earth flying dozens of feet into the air. The second mine exploded a split second later beneath the platoon of Blackshirts. A bloody shower of dirt, stones and body parts cascaded down onto the Square.

The stormtroopers stationed on the roof of the Cathedral tower gawped with open mouthed horror as the Square erupted in a volcano of blood and bodies.

"Squad! One hundred metres, Square to the front, has anyone seen the enemy?" The S.S. sergeant bellowed at his shocked and confused soldiers.

"No, Scharführer!" The men responded automatically as their training kicked in and they began to watch for targets to shoot.

"These two explosions are only the start of the partisan attack," the sergeant warned. "They're trying to kill the Reichkommissar. The trouble is that we don't know where the guerrillas are. Where the bloody hell are you?"

"Look behind you!"

"Wha -?"

The sergeant and his men were cut down by a ferocious fusillade of machine gun fire before they had time to turn around. The partisan covering fire team had stealthily climbed the stairs to the top of the tower in the last few moments before the explosions and had burst through the door when the mines had detonated. The three commandoes stepped over the still smoking bodies of the dead Nazis and took up their former foes' positions. Two of the men positioned an MG 42 machine gun on the parapet as the fire team commander, Sergeant Thornton, raised a pair of binoculars to his face.

"Corporal Colvin and his men will be heading for the rostrum,"Thornton explained. "Fire team, two hundred metres, rostrum to your front, rapid fire!"

"Holy Mary, mother of God!" Dahrendorf swore as he crossed himself.

"Now do you believe me?" Ulrich asked. He was lying on his front with his left hand on top of his helmet and his right hand holding a Luger. The commanders of the other units were lying in a similar position on the rostrum. He looked across at Colonel Mendoza. The Spaniard was smiling and seemed to be enjoying himself. Mendoza caught Ulrich's eye and winked. "We need to get the Reichkommissar inside the Town Hall."

Dahrendorf nodded. "Right. But what about Joyce?"

"Bugger Joyce," Ulrich sneered. "Baby sitting Joyce is not our responsibility. He can be blown to kingdom come in the next explosion for all I care. Let the Blackshirts look after him. We look after our own. Agreed?"

"Agreed!"

"On the count of three we get up and grab him!"

"Davie! Are you ready? On my command I want you to throw two grenades at the Reichkommissar, all right?"

"But Al, I can't see him," Davie observed. "He must be lying down."

Alan quickly looked at the rostrum. "Damn! You're right, Davie. Schenk must be lying down." He shook his head in dismissal. "It doesn't matter: on my

277

command, throw your grenades at the front of the stage. Clear?"

"Clear!" Davie watched as his big brother extracted a Luger pistol from the small of his back. "Then what are you going to do?"

Alan flashed his teeth like a tiger. "I'm going to finish the job."

"One, two -!"

"Three!" Dahrendorf shouted as he stood up to run towards the Reichkommissar. He was immediately cut down by a fusillade of machine gun fire and collapsed to the ground in a bloody heap. Ulrich took cover as another burst of bullets stitched a neat line of holes in the wooden floorboards by his side. There were two sudden explosions as a pair of grenades detonated on the rostrum. Ulrich looked through the smoke as a schoolboy nimbly vaulted over the fence armed with a pistol. A dazed and confused Blackshirt colonel rose groggily to his feet to challenge him but the partisan sliced his hand across the man's neck and crushed his windpipe. An Italian officer raised his pistol but before he could fire the boy hit the tip of the man's nose with the heel of his hand, breaking the brittle cartilage and driving it straight into the Italian's brain like a razor sharp dagger. The man was dead before he hit the ground. Ulrich knew that he only had a matter of moments to act before the assassin reached him. He realised with sudden horror that he had dropped his Luger. He tried to search for his pistol, but he felt a sharp stab of pain. He swore under his breath. His arm must be broken. The boy reached Ulrich and turned him over.

"Norbert?"

"Hello, Alan," Ulrich replied croakily with a throat thickly crusted with cordite. "Fancy meeting you here."

"Where's Colonel Mendoza?"

"He was alive last time that I spoke to him. However, he might be dead now," Ulrich said matter of factly. "You need to be careful with grenades, Alan, you might kill someone if you're not careful."

"That's the general idea." Alan quickly looked around. "Where's Schenk?"

"He's over there," Ulrich gestured with his chin.

Alan walked over to Schenk and turned him over. The German looked as if he had been roasted like a pig on a spit. His uniform was toasted, tattered and torn. The grenades must have exploded at point blank range.

"Is he dead?" Ulrich asked.

Alan fired two rounds at point blank range into Schenk's forehead. "He is now," he replied coldly.

"Congratulations," Ulrich bowed. " He was a nasty piece of work."

"Thank you. Where's Joyce?"

"I don't know." Ulrich shrugged.

"Damn! I wanted Joyce, the dirty Blackshirt traitor." Alan punched his thigh with frustration. "Ulrich, close your eyes and play possum."

"What?"

"Pretend that you're dead," Alan hissed urgently.

Three pairs of combat boots pounded up the stairs. "My God, Alan, you've been busy!" Corporal Colvin gave a low whistle of appreciation. "I love your work. You make the St. Valentine's Day Massacre look like a Teddy Bear's Picnic!"

"Thank you, Corporal," Alan gave a bow. "You're too kind."

"Are they all dead?"

"Yes, including Schenk, but Joyce got away." Alan pointed at the bodies of three dead Blackshirts who lay sprawled in a heap by the main entrance to the Town

Hall. "His bodyguards must have been killed whilst trying to protect him."

"Damn!" Colvin shrugged his shoulders. "But it can't be helped: we'll catch up with him another time. Come on, let's go. The Nazis are getting restless."

Ansett lay in the prone position armed with an MG 42 at the right hand side of the main entrance to the Cathedral. Sam lay next to him feeding him a belt of machine gun bullets. Smith and Jones lay in an identical position on the left hand side of the door and the pair were armed with an identical weapon. Within the entrance lay the bodies of the stormtroopers who were supposed to be guarding the Cathedral. The Nazis had spectacularly failed to accomplish their mission and had he still been alive, the sergeant in command would have been severely reprimanded by his superior officer. As it was, he and his unfortunate soldiers had suffered the ultimate punishment for their lack of vigilance: death. The Germans had also rather thoughtfully provided the partisans with a pair of perfectly oiled and well looked after machine guns that their enemies were now using to deadly effect.

Colvin, Alan and the other two commandoes started running hell for leather towards the Cathedral. They were aided and abetted by Thornton's fire team on the Tower and by Ansett's fire team at the Cathedral. The two fire teams cleared a path for their comrades to run down straight through the devastated survivors of the two explosions. Anyone who so much as gave the partisans a dirty look was cut down before they could blink twice. Alan and the commandoes carved a route through the Square like Moses through the Red Sea and arrived at the Cathedral in less than half a minute.

Sam stood up and grabbed Alan's arm with concern. "Al, are you all right?"

Alan smiled through his blood, sweat and dirt covered face. "I'm all right, Sam, it's -"

"I know. It's not your blood!" Sam laughed and ruffled his best friend's hair.

"Come on, lads," Ansett said. "Let's get out of here. Sam, run upstairs and tell Sergeant Thornton that we're leaving. We'll provide covering fire until you get back."

"Yes, sir!" Sam disappeared like a streak of lightning.

"We killed Schenk, but we didn't get Joyce, sir. The bastard escaped." Alan's voice was heavy with disappointment.

"Well done on killing Schenk, Alan. That's a real feather in your cap," Ansett congratulated Alan with genuine gratitude and admiration. "And it doesn't matter about Joyce," he shook his head dismissively. "Schenk was the main target and Joyce was merely the icing on the cake. Anyway, if the Gods are smiling we may have a second chance to have another pop at him."

"What do you mean, sir?" Alan asked. "He'll be halfway to London by now."

"Not necessarily," Ansett shook his head. "He will have found out by now that there are major disturbances, demonstrations, riots and protests in towns and cities across the length and breadth of the Occupied South. The Resistance have launched attacks from Middlesborough in the north to Portsmouth in the south and from Plymouth in the west to Dover in the east."

"Is this it, sir? Is this Liberation Day?" Alan asked excitedly.

Ansett shook his head. "I'm afraid that it isn't, Alan. However, you could say that this is a dress rehearsal for L-Day."

"We're testing how long it takes for the Huns to react and finding out what steps they take to deal with the situation?"

"Precisely," Ansett answered with a smile. He felt proud that his young apprentice was able to understand the tactical situation so swiftly. "In view of the present some what precarious situation, Herr Joyce might think that the safest thing to do is to stay in Hereward until the security situation improves."

"But where will he stay, sir?" Alan asked.

"Well, where would you stay, Alan, if you were Joyce? Remember that he's a vain, self important and pompous swine; it would have to be a place that would be fit for a prime minister. And he will not suffer the humiliation and indignity of begging for shelter and protection from the Germans. He will want to stay somewhere that is quintessentially English and that is as comfortable as a five star hotel and as safe as a castle."

"The Keep at St. John's, sir!" Alan exclaimed triumphantly. "Although Hitler's room is not ready yet, I know for a fact that the guest rooms are complete. The Keep will not be officially handed over to the Huns until the all of the rooms are finished so technically speaking, the Keep is still English."

"Yes, Alan. Well done, you're learning fast."

"I had a good teacher, sir."

Ansett smiled at the compliment.

"But how will we get in, sir? It will be guarded more closely than the Sultan of Oman's harem!"

"Not only will we get in, Alan, but we will also get out-with Joyce."

"How?"

"I have a cunning plan …"

"Yes? What is it?" Sturmbannführer von Horn asked impatiently as he looked up from the map table. He was busy trying to organise the operation to hunt down the partisans who had carried out the attack on the Parade. Obersturmbannführer Ulrich had been wounded in the attack and had been evacuated to Hereward hospital and as a result von Horn had suddenly found himself in temporary command of the Triple S Brigade.

"There's an Askari major outside who wants to speak to you, sir," an S.S. corporal answered.

"Very well, Unterscharführer, show him in," von Horn said with irritation. He was painfully aware that he had a very narrow window of opportunity to capture the partisans and every minute that he wasted decreased his chances of catching them.

The S.S. corporal clicked his heels and left the room. He returned leading a Blackshirt major who marched into the room, halted smartly and flung out his arm in the universal Fascist salute.

"Hail Joyce!"

Von Horn returned the salute. "Heil Hitler! Now, what can I do for you, Major?"

The Major took off his peaked cap and ruffled his hair that was matted together with sweat and dirt. "Sturmbannführer, I don't have enough men to search for survivors of the explosions. I need to rescue the wounded as quickly as possible and get them to hospital. The problem is that many of my men are still buried underneath the rubble and I need more people to help dig them out."

"I'd love to help you out, Major, but I'm busy trying to organise an operation to capture the terrorists who carried out this atrocity. I need every man that I can lay my hands on. I'm sorry, but I simply can't spare the soldiers to help you dig out the dead and wounded."

"I apologise if I have not made myself clear, Sturmbannführer: I don't need soldiers, I need people. I understand that you have some prisoners in the cells underneath the Town Hall?"

"I would hardly describe them as cells, Major, they're more like storage rooms, but yes, we have about twenty political prisoners down stairs. Why?"

"Well, could I use them to help clear the rubble? I understand that you're going to execute them at some stage anyway, so they might as well do something useful for a change. There is also a certain irony that they will have to clean up the damage that their Jew loving Bolshevik friends have caused."

Von Horn thought for a spilt second before his face lit up with a smile. "Why not? As you English say, ' it's a capital idea.' I was planning to execute them in retaliation for this barbarous attack anyway. The dirty Communist swine might as well do something worthwhile with the rest of their soon to be short, miserable lives. If you would care to wait here, Major …?"

"Anderson, Peter Anderson," the Blackshirt major smiled as von Horn shook his hand.

"Pleased to meet you, Sturmbannführer von Horn."

Von Horn smiled. He was pleased that Anderson already knew his name. "If you would care to wait here, Major Anderson, I will give orders for the prisoners to be brought to you."

"Certainly, Sturmbannführer,"Anderson bowed. He smiled as the German returned to his map table.

"Aurora, I just want to emphasise that we're about to enter the lion's den; we're about to go deep cover," Alice said earnestly. "It is absolutely essential to remember that no matter how charming or chatty these Blackshirt bastards might be, these Fascists are not our friends, they are our enemies."

"I understand, Alice," Aurora replied with a faint hint of irritation in her voice. The girls were standing in front of the main gate to St. John's Academy.

Alice failed to heed the warning signs. "Because if we forget then we not only run the risk of jeopardising the success of the mission, we also run the risk of blowing our cover and revealing ourselves as partisans," Alice continued. "The future survival of the Hereward Resistance Unit rests on our shoulders."

"Look, Alice, I am painfully aware of the risks that we are running and the gravity of the situation," Aurora said with exasperation. "You seem to forget, that I've done this sort of thing before: this is not the first time that I've killed people that I've pretended to become friends with. I butchered all of my bodyguards in cold blood, remember?" Aurora asked angrily.

"You didn't 'butcher them,' Aurora. You killed them."

"Kill them or butcher them, what's the difference? Words are cheap. I walked up to them, I said 'good morning,' and then I shot them in the back of the head."

"They were enemy soldiers, Aurora, and in a war we kill the enemy and they try and kill us. It's not pretty, but that's the nature of the beast. It's what we do."

"They were not the ' enemy' to me, Alice!" Aurora thumped her fist on her chest with frustration and despair. "They were Spaniards! They were my fellow countrymen and I murdered them!"

"Barely two years ago these men were killing your ' fellow countrymen' in Spain, Aurora! They were busy killing Republicans, your Uncle Ramón's friends and comrades, in the streets of Madrid and Barcelona. They were Legiónaries, Aurora, they were professional soldiers. They knew the risks and they took their chances when they volunteered to accompany your father to Britain."

"But my father personally chose these men to become my bodyguards. He handpicked them because they were his best men and he trusted them to fight to the death to defend me. These Legiónaries would have sacrificed their lives without hesitation in order to protect me and how did I repay their trust? By murdering them as they ate at the table of my own house." Aurora's shoulders slumped and her eyes filled up with tears.

"We killed those men in order to fool your father into believing that we had been kidnapped, Aurora," Alice said forcefully. "The fear that we would be executed unless your father complied with the kidnappers' demands forced him to attempt to assassinate Hitler-"

"Except that the attempt failed!" Aurora interrupted. "The bomb attack didn't work and Hitler survived! It was all for nothing! I murdered my Legiónaries for nothing!"

Alice opened her mouth, but bit her tongue before she said 'but at least we tried.' She thought for a moment before she spoke. "Look, Aurora. If you don't feel up to it, if you don't think that you can do it, then we'll call off Operation Quebec. We'll put on our thinking caps and figure out a different way to accomplish the mission."

Aurora shook her head. "No, it's all right. I'm up for it. Let's push on."

Alice placed her hands on her friend's shoulders. "Are you sure?"

"Yes, I am." Aurora wiped away her tears with the back of her hand. "Let's crack on."

"All right. As long as you're crystal clear about the plan and happy about what we need to do."

"Yes, I am," Aurora answered with a weak smile.

"Bueno. Then let's get into character." Alice grinned mischievously. "Strength and honour!"

"Strength and honour!"

"Englanders, raus! Schnell! Schnell!" The S.S. guards poked and prodded the dazed and confused prisoners with the butts and barrels of their weapons. The captives emerged coughing and spluttering from the Town Hall into the Square and shielded their eyes against the glare of the noonday sun that shone through the smoke. Most of the hostages had spent many days in the subterranean gloom of the S.S. headquarters prison cells and were not used to natural sunlight. The Square was full of Fascists running hither and thither like angry ants whose nest had been kicked over by a giant. Bloody and broken bodies lay everywhere in heaps and on their own and the entire Square was covered in a thin layer of dismembered limbs and twisted pieces of military equipment. Fires were burning out of control in half a dozen places and thick, acrid smoke filled the air making it difficult to breathe and also hard to get an accurate picture of what was going on.

"What- what happened?" A female prisoner asked.

"No talking!"A stormtrooper barked as he butted the inquisitive woman in the back with his rifle.

"Terrorist attack," a Blackshirt guard answered.

"Oh … thank you," the woman replied as she rubbed her back and smiled surreptitiously at her fellow captives.

"Now listen in, Jew lovers!" A Blackshirt major shouted loudly. "You will be split into two groups: one group will stay here with me at this crater and the other group will follow my sergeant to the other crater. When you get to the crater you will place the wounded in one pile; the dead in another pile; military equipment in a third pile and clear away all of the rubble into a fourth pile. Do I make myself clear?"

The prisoners mumbled incoherently.

"Any questions?"

The prisoners averted their eyes and stared at the broken cobblestones that littered the Square.

"Good. Then let's get to work."

"Hail Joyce!" The two Blackshirts chorused as they thrust out their right arms. The man sitting on the chair smiled with genuine pleasure. It never failed to give him a thrill to hear those words. However, the scar on his cheek twisted the grin and made it appear mocking and uneven. He returned the salute with sincere appreciation. "Please forgive me for not standing up, ladies, but my legs are riddled with shrapnel from the explosion which makes it extremely painful for me to put any weight on them." The man's trouser legs had been cut off and his legs were swathed in bloody bandages from his ankles to his knees.

"We're just relieved to find that you are alive and well, my Leader," the older Blackshirt blurted out breathlessly. "It is a miracle that you survived and truly proves that God is with us."

"Gott mit uns, as our German comrades say," Joyce said with a lopsided smile as he looked at his attractive young admirers. "Now, I think that introductions are in order; you know my name, but I don't know yours. What are your names?"

"Alice Roberts."

"Aurora Mendoza." Both girls bowed slightly as they gave their names.

"I'm sorry, ladies. I didn't quite catch that. The explosion has made me somewhat deaf. Would you care to repeat your names?"

The girls did so and were too preoccupied to notice a Blackshirt captain standing behind them scribbling in a notebook. He nodded at Joyce when he had finished writing down the girls' names.

"And why are you here, ladies?" Joyce asked.

"I saw your car drive through the school gates and pull up at the Keep, my Leader, and so we came over to see if we could be of any assistance and help in any way," Alice explained.

Joyce nodded. "That's very public spirited of you, Miss Roberts."

"It's the least that we can do. If we can do anything to make your stay in Hereward more comfortable you have only to ask, my Leader. It would be our pleasure and our privilege," Alice said as she tucked a lock of blond hair behind her ear and smiled like a Hollywood starlet.

"It would be our honour," Aurora added as she batted her long brown eyelashes.

Captain Robert Garfield caught Joyce's eye and gave a knowing wink to his boss. It was good to know that the Leader was back on form and was up to his old tricks again. He doubted if Joyce's leg wounds would slow him down and throw him off his stride. With a bit of luck when Joyce was finished he would pass the girls on to his ever loyal and grateful bodyguards as per usual. The captain shrugged philosophically. He didn't mind getting sloppy seconds; after all, beggars couldn't be choosers. And after the recent events the bodyguard consisted of three fewer members that meant that each of the Blackshirts could spend more quality time with the talent.

Joyce licked his lips and felt a familiar tingle as his scar twitched. "Oh yes, Miss Roberts and Miss Mendoza; I am sure that my men and I will enjoy the hospitality that you Hereward ladies have to offer. Of that, I have no doubt."

"Do you think that it's worked? Do you think that they believe us?" Aurora asked anxiously.

Alice nodded. "We have them hook, line and sinker, Aurora," she replied confidently. The girls were busy in the kitchen making cups of tea for Joyce and his bodyguards. "If they don't believe that we're genuine Fascists then I'll give up my membership of the Cambridge University Amateur Dramatics Society."

"Bueno." Aurora smiled and let out a huge sigh of relief. "But I don't like the way that Joyce looked at us. And the way that he licked his lips?" Aurora shivered.

"I know what you mean." Alice placed a reassuring hand on her friend's shoulder. "He gives me the creeps as well. We'll need to watch him like a hawk."

"He was like the Big Bad Wolf looking at Little Red Riding Hood."

"Except that this time Little Red Riding Hood is hiding a machine gun under her cloak!"

Both of the girls laughed so much that they nearly knocked over the tray of teacups.

"Seriously though, Aurora. We will have to be extra careful around these Blackshirts, especially around Joyce's guard dog, Captain Garfield." Alice patted her holster.

"I wouldn't trust him as far as I could throw him," Aurora said with an involuntary shudder.

Alice nodded. She took out her Luger and made sure that it was fully loaded. "We must stick together, Aurora. We must always be vigilant and we must never relax our guard. We must never be caught on our own with even one of them. Agreed?"

"Agreed."

"Because if we are, then there's no telling what those evil Blackshirt bastards might be tempted to do."

The prisoners worked until their fingers were rubbed raw and their backs ached from lifting and carrying so many bodies. Their arms were caked from wrist to elbow in a thin layer of dust, dirt and blood and their hair was matted together with a noxious mixture of sweat and general gore. The hostages had not had anything to eat or drink since their meagre morning meal at 6 am in the Town Hall dungeons and it was now three o'clock in the afternoon. The captives' throats were parched dry and their stomachs rumbled with hunger like rolling thunder.

The Blackshirt major looked at the row of corpses that the prisoners had laid out in a line stretching away from the crater. He counted fifteen bodies; or more accurately, fifteen more or less complete corpses. The gravediggers had found too many arms and legs and not enough heads and torsos. It was as if a huge human spider had exploded. The blasts had completely destroyed the S.S. and Blackshirt platoons and there were no survivors. However, the prisoners working at the two craters had managed to salvage enough weapons to equip a small army. It appeared that metal and wood were hardier substances than flesh and bone.

The major watched as his second in command walked towards him.

"Sir, we've nearly finished clearing the craters. However, if we want to complete the clean up operation at dusk and not before, we'll have to slow down because if we keep working at this speed we'll finish whilst it's still daylight."

"You're right, Captain," the major nodded. "Stand the prisoners down and let them rest and recover. They've been working like slaves. Find some food and drink and feed them."

"From where, sir?" The captain asked. "All of the shops are shut on a Sunday."

The major thought for a moment before he replied. "Take a lorry with a couple of men and drive to the farm. Pick up enough food for ourselves and the prisoners and then return."

"Yes, sir." The captain saluted.

"And Captain?"

"Yes, sir?"

"I'd prefer chicken rather than pork for obvious reasons."

The captain smiled and left to gather his men.

When the Blackshirt major gave the order to cease work the prisoners collapsed to the ground with exhaustion. Most of them were too tired to engage in meaningful conversation and when they did communicate they did so using a mixture of grunts and monosyllabic words.

The inquisitive female prisoner who had asked the Blackshirt guard the question earlier swept her eyes over the blood soaked and bone strewn Square.

"What do you think happened here, Vera?" Her companion asked her.

"Partisan attack, Dolly. They set off two massive explosions which wiped out two platoons of Blackshirts and S.S."

"Good riddance to bad rubbish, I say," Dolly said with a hushed voice.

"The explosions also killed and wounded the St. George Legionnaires parading on the right of the Blackshirts and the French volunteers on the left." Vera looked at the long line of bodies that had been laid at the edge of the Square.

Dolly nodded. "The partisans have earned their pay today I reckon," she said with grim satisfaction.

"Did you notice that the Blackshirts didn't help their fellow wounded Fascists?" Vera asked with raised eyebrows. "Not one of them gave the survivors first aid or seemed particularly concerned whether or not they lived or died. Most of the wounded had died by the time that the ambulance crews got here."

"Why should the Blackshirts help the French survivors? Everyone knows that Joyce has made a deal with the Devil. Petain is only helping because he wants Joyce or Hitler to give him the Channel Islands. The Blackshirts are ultra Nationalists. They can hardly be thrilled at the prospect of handing over British territory to the French. One more Frenchie killed here in Britain means one less Frenchie to fight against later."

"But what about the Legionnaires? They're not French, they're British," Vera persisted.

Dolly shrugged her shoulders. "Who knows? Sibling rivalry? The Legionnaires are the flavour of the month at the moment. The Fascist Militia doesn't like all the attention and publicity their rivals are getting. Everyone's got their eye on them and everyone wants to find out how they perform against the Russkis. The Press and public consider them to be proper soldiers whilst the Blackshirts are their poorer country bumpkin cousins. Plus they're better paid, better dressed and better equipped than the Fascist Militia and the Blackshirts don't like it. They don't like it one little bit."

"Perhaps ..."

"Anyway, who cares? They're all dirty, stinking Fascists and as far as I'm concerned the only good Fascist is a dead Fascist. The partisans should feel

293

proud about a job well done," Dolly said with a triumphant smile.

"Fascists were not the only people that the partisans murdered today, Dolly," Vera said sombrely. "Did you notice the bodies of the children? Do you think that the partisans feel proud about murdering them?"

"The civilians weren't 'murdered,' Vera, they were killed. But the partisans didn't mean to kill them. It's a tragedy that they died, but their deaths were accidental. That's the difference between ourselves and the Germans: if we kill civilians then we do it by accident; we never do it on purpose, whereas the Huns deliberately murder civilians."

"All killing is murder."

"Well, what's the alternative, Vera? That we surrender? That we give up?" Dolly asked with increasing exasperation.

Vera thought for a moment before she replied. "How many of the enemy do you think the partisans killed today, Dolly?"

"Killed? I … I don't know. Fifty? One hundred?"

Vera nodded. "Let's say for the sake of argument that the partisans killed one hundred Fascists here today. I counted a dozen dead civilians, Dolly. Do you consider that to be a fair exchange? A dozen of our dead for a hundred of theirs?"

"I … I don't know. That's a bit cold hearted."

Vera shook her head. "Not at all. It's perfectly rational. As you know, the Germans consider one of their lives to be worth one hundred of ours and the Germans are very rational people. That's the current rate of exchange as far as executing hostages is concerned, isn't it? So if they have lost one hundred men today then, according to the going rate, they will have to execute ten thousand hostages in retaliation." Vera paused as she let the significance of that statement sink in. "If I was a betting woman I wouldn't put much money on our chances of surviving the weekend."

Dolly was too deep in thought to comment.

"Four children were also murdered today, Dolly, and one of them was a baby." A tear rolled down Vera's cheek. "And I'll tell you this for free, Dolly: I would not trade the life of that baby for one hundred dead Fascists, two hundred dead Fascists or a thousand dead Fascists. The number doesn't matter."

Dolly rallied. "But the partisans are fighting the Fascists in order to put a final stop to the murder of civilians! The only way to prevent the deaths of more children and babies is to defeat the Nazis once and for all. That's the only way to make peace, Vera!"

"The only way to make peace is by making more widows and orphans and by murdering more children and babies?" Vera shook her head sadly. "That makes absolutely no sense."

"I agree that it makes no sense, Vera, but that is the way of the world. That is the nature of war and we are fighting a war for our very survival. We have to be ruthless and we all have to make sacrifices."

"What kind of sacrifice would you make to win the war?"

"I have already made sacrifices, Vera," Dolly said stiffly. "You seem to have forgotten that James was killed last year when a U-boat sunk his ship in the Atlantic."

Vera bowed her head in apology. "I'm sorry, Dolly: I forgot that you'd already told me. Your husband was a sailor?"

Dolly nodded. "Yes, he was the captain of a destroyer, H.M.S. Apache. He was killed whilst escorting a convoy carrying wheat to Britain. He sacrificed his life delivering food to Britain so that we could eat," she said with her head held high.

"A professional fighting man. You must be very proud of him."

"I am. He was conscripted in 1918 and served his country for more than twenty years before he was killed."

"And you have a son as well?"

Dolly smiled. "Yes, I do. Ryan has just turned seventeen. It was his birthday earlier this month. He's the apple of my eye. He's all that I have left." Her eyes watered with emotion.

"Would you sacrifice Ryan's life to win the war?"

Dolly's face drained of all colour. "What?"

"Would you sacrifice Ryan's life to win the war?"

"But he's just a schoolboy!" Dolly protested.

"If God came down from heaven and said to you ' Dolly: I can win the war for Britain right now and end the bloodshed but I must sacrifice the life of your only son, Ryan, in order to do so.' Would you do it?"

"I … I don't know …"

Vera looked over at the four small bodies that had been laid in a line. "Now tell the parents of the murdered children that the sacrifice of their loved ones is a price worth paying to win the war."

Chapter Twenty

Captain Garfield slammed the phone down with so much force that he almost shattered the casing.

"Trouble, Captain?" Sergeant Swanmore asked unnecessarily. Garfield's face was beetroot red with murderous rage and fury. He was so angry that steam was practically coming out of his ears.

"You could say that, Sergeant," Garfield answered through tight, thin lips. "London's up in flames. The Reds are attacking all across the city and it's a case of all hands on deck. Headquarters can't spare the manpower to send reinforcements to escort us back to London."

"London can't spare a couple of armoured cars and a platoon of Blackshirts to escort us home?" Swanmore asked incredulously. "They do realise that it's the prime minister that we're talking about, the Leader himself, and not the minister of culture?" He said sarcastically.

Garfield nodded. "Yes, they do. But the Huns have commandeered every single armoured car within a fifty mile radius of London. You can't get your hands on one for love of money."

"It's unbelievable, sir," Swanmore shook his head with disbelief. "We've been abandoned. I never thought the day would come when a British soldier would refuse to go to the aid of a comrade. When does London think that they may be able to spare us the necessary men and equipment, sir?"

"Tomorrow lunch time, Sergeant. The Jerries have assured Headquarters that they will return their armoured cars to them by noon and then it will take a further two hours or so to drive up to Hereward."

"So we're spending the night here, sir?"

"Looks like it, Sergeant," Garfield nodded. "You'd better tell the men. Then we'll need to find enough bedding and enough food to feed the boys."

"Could be difficult on a Sunday, sir."

"I know, Sergeant." Garfield scratched his head. "But we need to find it from somewhere. We've lost half of our strength and the partisans are still on the loose. Every man will have to give 200% and you can't do that on an empty stomach. Feeding the boys is a top priority."

Alice coughed and put up her hand. "Sir, if I may?"

Garfield smiled with amusement. "You don't have to put up your hand to ask a question, Alice. You're not at school anymore."

Alice blushed bright red with embarrassment. "I'm sorry, Captain," she said bashfully. "Force of habit."

"It's all right, Alice. Don't be embarrassed. Old habits die hard. Now, what did you want to ask?"

"Sir, I can make a phone call and rustle up enough bedding and enough food to feed your men."

"Enough for all seven of us?" Garfield asked with raised eyebrows.

"I can find enough food to feed the five thousand, Captain," Alice boasted proudly.

"Where can you find all of this food at such short notice?"

"I could tell you, but then I'd have to kill you, sir." Garfield was momentarily taken back but then Alice flashed her most charming smile. "Our mysterious benefactors would like to remain anonymous, Captain. In these troublesome and turbulent times there are certain risks associated with being a supporter of the Fascist Party and our suppliers do not want to become a target for the terrorists. They support our cause, but they have no desire to become martyrs, sir."

298

"I understand perfectly well, Alice. I look forward to the day when Britons will be able to stand up tall and say loudly and proudly 'I am a Fascist' without fear of attack." Garfield puffed out his chest. "But in the meantime, it makes sense to take necessary precautions and avoid unnecessary risks. So please, make your phone call."

Captain Smith put down the phone. He had a massive grin on his face that stretched from ear to ear.

"What is it, Captain? Good news?"

"Excellent news, Iggy!" Smith replied and placed a hand on the old man's shoulder. "We've been presented with a golden opportunity to give the Fascists a bloody nose! Operation Quebec is cancelled, effective immediately; we are going to implement Operation Zelda."

"What do you need, Captain?" Paderewski asked.

"I need enough food to feed nine people for tonight's dinner and tomorrow's breakfast and lunch."

"May I suggest a selection of our finest bacon, sausages and pork for our unwelcome guests?"

"That goes without saying, Iggy; anything less would be considered a gross insult. With our secret ingredient, of course," Smith smiled wickedly.

"Of course," Paderewski bowed mockingly like a maître d'.

"Can we find enough pillows and blankets for nine people?"

Paderewski nodded. "We'll raid the nearest farms and houses on the outskirts of Frampton-on-the-Ouse, Captain. They're all deserted."

"Excellent. I love it when a plan comes together." Smith patted his Polish friend's shoulder with affection.

"When do you need it?"

"As soon as possible. I need to drop off the supplies with Alice and then tell the major about the change in plan."

"Verdamnt!" Sergeant Swanmore swore as he slammed down the telephone. "I swear: it's a bloody conspiracy!"

"What's the problem, Sergeant?" Alice asked.

"I phoned the German wing at Hereward Hospital and I asked them to send over a doctor to treat the Leader's wounds, but they explained that they were up to their eyeballs in casualties and they couldn't spare anyone. I then asked if they could send over an ambulance to pick up the Leader and take him to the hospital and they said that they couldn't do that either."

"Have you tried the civilian wing, Sergeant?" Alice suggested helpfully.

"I tried earlier, Miss Roberts, but I was unsuccessful."

"Please, Sergeant," Alice flashed her most dazzling smile, "call me Alice."

"All right ... Alice," Swanmore smiled. "Anyway, it was the same story: they explained that they could spare neither medical help nor transport." He took a deep breath. "As you can imagine, by this stage I was ready to shoot someone. I then tried the old 'Do you know who I am?' trick. I told them that I was Sergeant Swanmore, second-in-command of Prime Minister Joyce's personal bodyguard."

"What did they say?"

"The man asked 'do you know who I am?' I answered 'no,' and then he said 'good!' and hung up!"

Alice and Aurora covered their mouths with their hands in order to stifle their laughter.

Swanmore looked at them for a split second before he burst into a hysterical fit of laughter. He was followed a moment later by a pair of very relieved young women. Blackshirts were human and had a sense of humour after all.

Alice wiped away tears of laughter as she eventually calmed down. "I must congratulate you on your German, Sergeant."

"Please call me 'Charlie,' Alice. It's only fair."

"Are you sure that that is right and proper, Sergeant … I mean, Charlie? After all, we're both Blackshirts," Alice asked.

"Well, only call me Charlie in private, then."

"All right, Charlie. As I said earlier, you speak German like a native," Alice continued.

"That's because I am a native, Alice: I'm German."

"What? A German Blackshirt?"Alice said incredulously. Aurora instinctively placed her hand on her holster.

"Well, half German, actually. My mother was German."

" 'Was?' "Aurora asked.

Swanmore nodded. "Yes, she died two years ago."

Aurora bowed her head. "My commiserations, Charlie. I also lost my mother and so I understand your pain, suffering and sorrow."

"Thank you, Aurora," Swanmore dipped his head with gratitude. "I appreciate your kind words of sympathy. My father was a professional soldier and he fought from the beginning of the last War until the end. He was there at the Battle of Mons and he was there at the breakthrough in August 1918." Swanmore smiled with pride. "At the end of the war he took part in the occupation of the Rhineland. He met my mother in Cologne, they fell in love and I was born in 1920."

"What a beautiful story!" Aurora smiled. "Love conquers all and heals the wounds of the war!"

Swanmore grimaced. "Except that this story didn't have a happy ending, Aurora. From the moment that I was born my father was ostracised within the regiment. I was called a 'Rhineland Bastard,' and my father became an outcast, a pariah. His own friends and comrades wouldn't speak to him. Men whom he had served beside in the trenches, men whose lives he had saved and who had saved his would have nothing to do with him. They treated him like a leper."

"Why?" Aurora was absolutely bewildered.

"Because my mother was German." Swanmore punched a fist into his open palm. "Because my father was sleeping with the enemy. They called him a 'Hun loving traitor.' "

"Perhaps your father's friends had lost too many comrades in the war," Alice suggested gently.

"Perhaps …" Swanmore shrugged.

"What happened after that, Charlie?" Alice asked.

"My father had no choice but to leave the Army. He jumped before he was pushed. But there was massive unemployment after the war when the troops were demobilised. My father had been a professional soldier for all of his adult life. All he knew about was fighting and killing and now he had a wife and a newborn baby to look after. So he joined the Black and Tans and fought in Ireland against the rebels."

"What did he do when he returned to England?" Alice asked.

Swanmore shook his head. "He didn't: he was killed in an I.R.A. ambush."

"My God!" Aurora put her hand up to her mouth in horror. "How terrible!"

Swanmore smiled sadly and shrugged. "It was a long time ago. I was only a baby when he was killed. I don't remember a thing about him. All I have left is a photograph of him posing proudly in his Army uniform and the stories that my mother used to tell about him."

"Where did you live?" Alice asked.

"My mother's family were bakers so we opened up a bakery in Portsmouth. My mother pretended to be the Swiss-German widow of a British soldier who had been killed in the war. At least half of the cover story was true. I had a happy childhood: I went to the local primary school and I won a scholarship to Portsmouth Grammar School and I was studying German and English at Southampton University when war broke out. As soon as war was declared I volunteered for the R.A.F. but they turned me down; so did the Navy and the Army."

"But why?" Aurora asked incredulously. "At the risk of embarrassing you, Charlie, you are a prime example of what you British describe as a 'fine figure of a man.' " But it was Aurora that blushed.

"I don't understand, Charlie," Alice added. "I would've have thought that the Forces would be desperate to recruit German speakers, especially native ones."

"You would think so, wouldn't you?" Swanmore said with raised eyebrows. "Except that I wasn't dealing with rational thinking people: I was dealing with irrational racists and prejudiced bigots; I was dealing with Philistines and cavemen. They turned me down because I'm half German." He said bitterly.

"It's unbelievable!" Alice said incredulously.

"But I didn't give up. I was determined to serve my country as my father had done before me. I tried to join my local Home Guard unit and I was accepted."

"Hooray!" Alice cheered. "Well done, Charlie!"

"At last: some good news!" Aurora said with a smile.

"Everyone in my local unit welcomed me with open arms. I was well known in my neighbourhood as the son of Frau Swanmore, the Swiss baker. I was the local boy done good who had won a scholarship to Portsmouth Grammar School. I went to primary school with half of the men in my unit. I continued my studies at Southampton and drilled and trained once per week and every weekend." Swanmore smiled wistfully as he remembered those happy days. "But it was too good to last," his face clouded over. "British bureaucracy eventually caught up with me: a standard background check revealed that I was half German, not half Swiss as we had led everyone to believe ..." Swanmore swallowed heavily and took a deep breath. "I was drummed out of the Home Guard without ceremony and the neighbourhood turned on us: friends and neighbours who had known us for twenty years, customers whom my mum had extended credit to when they couldn't afford to buy bread during the Depression, they ... they cast the first stone. Young men whom I had sat beside in class smashed the windows of our shop; women whose children my mother had babysat looted the entire contents of the shop ... they burned the shop and our flat above it to the ground. We lost everything." Swanmore's voice trailed off.

"How did you escape?" Alice asked.

"I didn't. I was at university at the time."

Alice dreaded asking the next question. "And ... and your mother? Did she escape as well?"

"She was burned alive," Swanmore answered bluntly.

"My God! That's terrible ..." Aurora's bottom lip quivered and she blinked away tears.

"After the firebomb attack I was arrested in the middle of my lectures and deported to the Douglas Aliens Detention Camp on the Isle of Man."

"Surely they allowed you to visit the scene of your … your mother's death before they deported you?" Aurora asked.

Swanmore shook his head. "I wasn't even allowed to pack a suitcase. I was deported wearing the very clothes that I was wearing. My mother was buried in an unmarked grave in the grounds of the local Catholic Church that we used to attend. Many of the congregation threatened to boycott the church if that 'Nazi bitch' was buried there; however, the priest, Father McWilliams, stood his ground and insisted that as my mother had been one of his flock she deserved to be buried there as much as anyone."

"Good for him, Charlie! But the way that the British have treated you … it's absolutely monstrous!" Aurora bit her knuckles with anger.

"Did they ever find the killers?" Alice asked.

Swanmore shook his head sadly. "It could have been any one of half a dozen people who threw Molotov cocktails on that night and truth be told, I don't think that the local police tried particularly hard to solve the crime. I suspect that it was a case of having one less enemy alien to deal with in the future. They were probably grateful that the murderers had done the job for them."

Aurora shook her head in disgust.

"What was life like in the camp?" Alice asked as she tried to change the subject.

"It was boring, but it was bearable," Swanmore answered. "The guards treated us well and many of them were sympathetic to our plight and situation. Most of the detainees were German and Italian and most of them had lived in Britain for years and considered themselves to be British. Many of them were political refugees and many of them were also Jews. One man that I knew, Antonio Fattorini, had been born in Italy but had been a professional soldier in the British Army and had won the Victoria Cross fighting on the Western Front during the Great War. Despite his decoration, when he volunteered to join the Home Guard his request had been refused and instead he found himself locked up on the Isle of Man! How's that for British justice?"

"What happened when the Germans invaded?" Alice asked.

"We were evacuated to Scotland, but a U-boat sank our ship. Most of the passengers drowned, but I managed to swim ashore."

"Did you try and escape to Scotland?" Alice asked.

" 'Escape to Scotland?' " Swanmore looked at Alice as if she was soft in the head. "Why on earth would I do that? I wasn't going to risk life and limb trekking north to Scotland so that I could be put in another detention camp. No, the British have made it perfectly clear that they are not my people," he spat out the words with hatred. "The British turned their backs on me. I kept walking south until I made contact with my real people, the soldiers of the Wehrmacht, the German Army."

"Did you surrender?" Alice asked.

" 'Surrender?' Alice, have you not listened to a word that I've been saying for the last ten minutes? I joined them. I served as a guide during our advance north to the Scottish border. And there were many of us; I wasn't the only one. I joined the Fascist party and I was one of the founder members of the Militia. I became the very thing that the British have accused me of being since the very day that I was born: a German."

Swanmore looked at the girls defiantly as if daring them to question his motives and his actions.

Alice chose her next words carefully. "God knows that you've been treated unfairly, Charlie. I don't blame you for your decisions. You've been the victim of a gross injustice."

"I'm a man, more sinn'd against than sinning," Swanmore quoted eloquently.

The girls' ears suddenly pricked up like a pair of Golden Retrievers. "I didn't know that you were an admirer of the bard, Charlie?" Alice asked.

Swanmore smiled with amusement. "You seem surprised, Alice. You seem to forget that I studied German and English at Southampton University for two years before the Invasion. And God willing, when that Jew loving Bolshevik war mongerer Churchill finally sees sense and surrenders, I will complete my degree."

Alice was momentarily taken aback by how naturally Swanmore regurgitated the anti-Jewish Fascist propaganda. Or was it as 'natural' as it seemed? She casually glanced at Aurora who gave the barest of nods. Alice took a deep breath and nonchalantly stirred the spoon in her teacup. "Charlie, what's your favourite Shakespeare play?"

Swanmore looked at Alice and answered without a moment's hesitation, "Macbeth, the Scottish play. Why? What's yours?"

At that precise moment Captain Garfield entered the room. "Any luck with the hospital, Sergeant?" He asked as he took off his peaked officer's cap and peeled of his patent leather gloves.

Swanmore shook his head. "No joy, sir. They're too busy."

"Damn and blast!" Garfield slapped his gloves in his palm with frustration. "The prime minister will just have to wait until we get back to London tomorrow."

"I cannot believe that British doctors can refuse to treat the British prime minister because they are too busy."

"Me neither, Sergeant." Garfield shook his head with disgust. "O perfidious Albion!"

Alice stiffened. "You're a fan of Shakespeare, Captain?"

"I am a son of England, Alice, loyal and true. I would consider it to be damn right unpatriotic for an Englishman not to be able to quote at least a few verses penned by our greatest playwright." Garfield flashed his finest Errol Flynn grin. "I also studied English at Oxford before the war."

"I'm impressed, Captain." Alice smiled with admiration. "Tell me, sir, what's your favourite Shakespeare play?"

"Macbeth," Garfield answered immediately. " 'Is this a dagger I see before me?' " He said in his best Scottish accent. "I like the play because it's about a man who knows what he wants and is prepared to do whatever it takes in order to achieve his goal. It's a play about ambition and power. Macbeth is a man after my own heart; a sort of role model, if you will. What's your favourite Shakespeare play, Alice?"

"I like Macbeth as well, Captain, but for rather different reasons to yourself. The play is about a filthy, turn coat murderer and traitor who gets what he deserves. It's a play about revenge and divine retribution. Macbeth is the yang to my yin; he is the exact opposite of everything that I believe in and stand for: - loyalty, honour and friendship."

"And yet here you are, Alice: a Blackshirt and member of the Fascist Militia," Garfield said with a raised eyebrow. "I hate to question your morals and principles, Alice, but I'm sure that you're aware that if Churchill and the Reds take over England things will not go well for people like you and I. They consider us to be ' filthy, turn coat murderers and traitors' and we'll be strung up from the nearest lamp post before you can say 'gunpowder, treason and plot.' "

"I have my reasons for joining the Blackshirts, Captain Garfield," Alice said stiffly.

"Don't we all, Alice?" Garfield asked rhetorically. "But I wonder if we can live with them?"

"Major Ansett warned us that the Resistance had a man on the inside, Alice," Aurora said excitedly.

"Yes, he did, Aurora," Alice nodded, "But which one is it? Swanmore or Garfield? The major said that we had one man on the inside, not two." The girls were in the kitchen preparing dinner.

"Is it possible that two partisans have managed to infiltrate the Blackshirts and join Joyce's bodyguard?" Aurora asked.

Alice nodded thoughtfully. "Yes, it's possible; but surely they would have tried to get word to Edinburgh?"

"Maybe they did. Maybe Edinburgh knows about them," Aurora said hopefully.

"But why doesn't Captain Smith know that we have two men on the inside?"

"Well, Captain Smith and his team have been here for a week now."

"Yes, but we're in constant radio contact with Edinburgh. If headquarters have only found out recently that we have two men on the inside then they could easily have told the captain, but we've heard nothing about new spies."

The girls stood in silence as they considered their options.

"They both gave the same response," Alice said.

Aurora shook her head. "No, they didn't, Alice," she said firmly. "Swanmore did, but Garfield didn't, remember? He said 'MacBeth,' instead of 'MacBeth, the Scottish play' ".

Alice furrowed her brows as she wracked her memory. "You're right, Aurora. But maybe Garfield made a mistake. Perhaps he forgot the correct password?"

"Perhaps. Or maybe Garfield is a genuine Blackshirt," Aurora said. "I don't know about you, Alice, but the captain does not strike me as a particularly forgetful type of person. I'm sure that he's been appointed commander of Joyce's bodyguard because he a has a good memory."

"Excellent point, well made, Aurora." Alice looked at her watch. "It's seven o' clock already. It will be dusk soon and the Fascists will Stand to. We're cutting it a bit fine. However, I'm not willing to take action until we're absolutely sure who is with us and who is against us."

"But Swanmore absolutely hates the British, Alice. Look what happened to his family. His own friends and neighbours murdered his mother and he acted as a guide for the German invasion forces."

"He could have been ordered to help the Huns in order to establish a cover. God knows our people have been ordered to do worse," Alice said with a bitter taste in her mouth. "And how do we know that his mother was killed? That sob story might be part of his cover as well. Plus Garfield did give us the wrong password."

Aurroa opened her mouth to speak, but closed it again. She didn't know what to say.

"We need more time," Alice said.

"Sausages are a luxury that we have; bacon is a luxury that we have; time is a luxury that we don't have, Alice. Whatever we decide, one of these men will die tonight," Aurora said grimly.

"Then we'd better make sure that we make the correct decision."

"Captain Smith, the sun's setting," Ansett said. "We don't have much time. You know what to do."

Smith smiled. "Yes, sir." He turned around to face his men. "Sergeant Thornton, I want you to take the prisoners back to the farm and take care of them. After you've done that I want you to return to the Square."

"Very good, sir. Hail Joyce!" Thornton saluted. He turned to face the hostages. "Stop what you're doing, Jew lovers, and listen in! Load the bodies, damaged weapons and military equipment onto one lorry and the undamaged weapons onto the other lorry. Move!"

The prisoners completed the task with the Blackshirts barking at their heads and snapping at their heels like demented and deranged sheep dogs. "I'm not finished with you yet, you dirty Reds! Climb onto the front lorry, you Bolshevik bastards!" Thornton ordered harshly.

At that precise moment, two armoured personnel carriers trundled into the Square and came to a shuddering stop at the main entrance to the Town Hall. A squad of S.S. stormtroopers piled out of each vehicle. Their leader recognized the Blackshirt major and walked over with a smile.

"Good evening, Sturmbannführer von Horn," Major Ansett said pleasantly. "Good hunting?" the two men shook hands.

Von Horn shook his head. "No such luck, Major Anderson. The partisans have long since flown the nest." He removed his helmet and ruffled his hair that was matted together with dirt and sweat. "We won't catch them now that the sun is setting. I've called off the search. We'll resume the hunt tomorrow. How are things here?" He gestured with his chin.

"We've recovered all of the bodies," Ansett answered. "Unfortunately, there were no survivors; I'm afraid that all of my Blackshirts and all of your stormtroopers were killed."

"I didn't think that there would be any survivors," von Horn said sadly. He shrugged his shoulders. "C'est la guerre. Where are you taking the bodies?"

"To the cemetery."

Von Horn nodded. "And the prisoners?"

"I was going to take care of them for you."

Von Horn nodded. "That's very kind of you, Major. No doubt I will have to spend all of my waking hours in the foreseeable future hunting down these blasted partisans who have caused us so much trouble and grief. I simply do not have the time or the manpower to waste taking care of housekeeping. I know that there are only twenty of them and the going rate is one hundred of theirs for one of ours, but it can't be helped. We'll round up more hostages in due course. Twenty prisoners isn't enough, but it's a start."

"Permission to carry on, sir?"

"Permission granted. Carry on, Major Anderson."

"Hail Joyce!"

"Heil Hitler!"

"Where do you think they're taking us, Vera?" Dolly asked with concern.

"I don't know," Vera shook her head, "but it doesn't look good."

The two women were sitting in the back of the lorry that was carrying the undamaged weapons and military equipment. A Blackshirt sat at the rear of the lorry and was easily identifiable by the glow of his cigarette. Vera and Dolly sat in the front corner of the lorry where they were separated from the driver by a thin plywood partition. They were deep in the shadows where the Fascist couldn't see them. They could see the headlamps of the second lorry following behind them.

"We've passed the hospital and the cemetery. We're leaving town!" Dolly said with alarm.

"What? We can't be," Vera exclaimed with disbelief. "We're going to bury the dead Blackshirts in the cemetery. You must be mistaken."

"Well, we are leaving, Vera. Look, there's the 'Welcome to Hereward: the holiday town' sign."

"My God, you're right," Vera exclaimed with her hand on her mouth.

"What does this mean? Where are they taking us?" Panic was creeping into Dolly's voice.

"They're going to kill us and dump us in the forest with the other bodies," Vera said bluntly.

"No!"

Vera nodded slowly. "I'm afraid so, Dolly. I heard the major order the captain to ' take care of the prisoners' and that can only mean one thing. Look, we're leaving the main road. It won't be long now."

"Well, I meant what I said earlier, Vera; I won't go meekly like a lamb to the slaughter," Dolly said with fire in her voice. She stretched her right hand into her welly boot and took something out. It shone brightly as a shaft of moonlight reflected on its surface.

Vera smiled in the darkness as she ran her fingers along the cold, hard steel. "You sly old fox. I won't go out with a whimper either. If it's my time to die then I intend to go out with a bang." She extracted something from her bra and handed it over to her friend. Dolly ran her hands over the object's pineapple segmented surface.

"What about all of that 'turn the other cheek' pacifist nonsense that you were spouting earlier?" Dolly asked with a quizzically raised eyebrow.

Vera shrugged her shoulders. "I guess that when push comes to shove, I'm simply not ready to die yet. There's still plenty of life left in this old girl."

"That's more like it," Dolly smiled in the darkness and revealed a double row of wolf like teeth. "Are you ready?"

Vera nodded. "Yes, I am. God save the King!" The two women hugged briefly. "Excuse me, sir?" Vera shouted.

"Yes? What is it?" The Blackshirt replied.

"Could you spare me a cigarette?"

"Yes, of course." The Militiaman laid his Schmessier down on the floor so that he could search for his cigarettes in his breast pocket. Vera started making her way down the length of the lorry towards him. The vehicle sank in and out of potholes on the badly maintained track and she lurched from side to side.

"Here you go, love," the Blackshirt said as he handed the cigarette to Vera.

"Thank you, kind sir." Vera put the cigarette in her mouth.

The Fascist lit a match and held it to the cigarette. "Listen, love, there's something that I have to tell you-"He suddenly dropped the match as if he had burnt his fingers. "Wha -?" He slumped back to the bench and futilely tried to claw at the six-inch dagger that was buried up to the hilt in his neck.

"I'm sorry, but you left me with no choice." Vera unclipped the dying Blackshirt's webbing belt with shaking hands and put it on. " Dolly, help me."

314

"What the - ?" The driver of the second lorry said as the vehicle drove over a hard lump on the ground. "I know that the track is in need of repair, but I didn't think that the pot holes were that bad!"

"They're not, Gordon," Sergeant Thornton said. "Something's not right, something's wrong. I can feel it in my bones ..." The lights illuminated the rear of the leading lorry. "Where's Duncan? He's supposed to be sitting at the back." He said with a growing feeling of fear and foreboding.

"That wasn't a pothole! That was a - !"

The windscreen suddenly disintegrated under a hail of machinegun bullets. Thornton and Gordon were mortally wounded by the Schmessier rounds and then were killed outright when a grenade exploded in the cab.

"Driver! I have a machine gun pointed at the back of your head! Stop the lorry if you want to live!" Vera threatened through the flimsy plywood partition.

The driver swore and immediately pulled over.

"Everybody out!" Vera ordered. "Grab a weapon. Driver! Don't get out until I open your door! Dolly, pick a weapon from the pile, get out and go to the driver's door. I'll cover you. Don't do anything until I join you, all right?"

"All right, Vera!" Dolly nodded.

"Driver! Don't do anything stupid: I have a machine gun barrel pointed less than half an inch from your head. Understand?"

"Yes ... yes, I understand." The driver was absolutely terrified.

Vera climbed down from the rear and joined Dolly at the front of the lorry where she rapped on the driver's door. "Get out with your hands in the air!"

The driver gingerly climbed down from the cab with his hands stretched as high as they could reach.

"On your knees, Fascist scum!" Vera snarled. The Blackshirt complied immediately.

"Listen to me. There's been a terrible mistake!" The driver protested. "We're not Fascists-we're partisans!"

"Yes, and I'm the Queen of England." Vera fired a short burst and the Blackshirt was knocked onto his back. "Boring conversation anyway."

"Agreed," Dolly nodded. "But what now?"

"'What now?'" Vera shrugged her shoulders nonchalantly. "As our American cousins say: 'we get the hell out of Dodge.'"

"And then?"

"And then we find a deserted house or village where we can set up a base and then we tear up and down the country attacking Nazi and Blackshirt positions like Bonnie and Clyde."

"Sounds like a plan," Dolly smiled like a wolf. "Let's do it."

Chapter Twenty One

Captain Smith slowly put the phone down. His mouth hung open and his eyes bulged wide with shock and disbelief.

"Captain Smith, you look as if you've seen a ghost: what's the matter?" Ansett asked with concern.

"That ... that was Iggy at the farm," Smith answered as if he was in a trance. "Something ... something terrible has happened. Sergeant Thornton and the rest of the men are dead."

"What happened?" Ansett and the rest of the partisans stood as still as statues.

"Iggy heard machine gun fire and an explosion and called Stand To," Smith explained. "He sent out the Quick Reaction Force and they found the team. Thornton and Gordon were dead in the lorry and Duncan was lying underneath with a Blackshirt dagger buried in his neck. He'd also been run over ..."

"Good God!" Ansett exclaimed.

"They found Harry lying on the track. He'd been executed at point blank range."

"Christ!" Ansett shook his head with disgust. "And the prisoners?" Ansett asked.

Smith shrugged his shoulders. "Disappeared together with the first lorry and all of the weapons."

"Christ! There were about twenty weapons on that vehicle! And the second lorry?"

"A complete write-off," Smith shook his head grimly. "The grenade explosion completely destroyed the driver's cabin. Iggy used a tractor to drag it off the track. They've hidden it in one of the barns for the moment."

"My God," Second-Lieutenant Jones held his hand up to his mouth with horror. "What a bloody disaster. How did this happen?"

"I ordered Sergeant Thornton to tell the hostages that we were partisans when they reached the farm."

"He was too late," Smith said bluntly.

Captain Garfield returned from his inspection of the positions around the Keep that his men were guarding. He stood in front of the mirror and checked that his appearance was ship shape and Bristol fashion. He was about to report to the Leader, and it would not do if his uniform was anything other than perfect. No, it would not do at all.

Alice watched with interest as Garfield adjusted the medal that hung around his neck.

"Excuse me, Captain Garfield, but is that an Iron Cross?"

"It's an Iron Cross First Class actually, Alice," Garfield seemed to grow an extra inch taller in his jackboots.

"Are there many Blackshirts that have been awarded an Iron Cross First Class, Captain?" Aurora asked with interest.

Garfield shook his head. "Not that I'm aware of, Aurora. As far as I know, I'm the only one to have been awarded either an Iron Cross First or Second Class."

"I notice that you've been awarded the Military Cross as well, Captain," Alice said.

Garfield looked down at the white, purple and white medal ribbon on his tunic. "How very observant of you, Alice." He smiled with pleasant surprise. "How did you recognize it?"

"My father was awarded the same medal in the last war."

Garfield dipped his head in salute. "My compliments to your father, Alice. I'll wager that I'm the only person that has ever been awarded both the Military Cross and the Iron Cross First Class."

"How did you win the M.C. Captain?"

"I won it during the Battle of Arras in France," Garfield answered matter of factly.

Alice looked perplexed.

"You've never heard of it?" Garfield asked with raised eyebrows. He shrugged casually. "I'm not surprised. It was yet another British cock up that has been disguised and dressed up as a British victory," he sneered with derision. "Two divisions of 15,000 men and a combined force of 135 British and French tanks were supposed to launch a counter attack and cut off Rommel's 7th Panzer Division that was threatening Boulogne and Calais. That was what was supposed to happen." Garfield paused. "Do you know how many men actually attacked?"

Alice shook her head.

"Two battalions of 2,000 men!" Garfield held up two fingers. "Two battalions of the Durham Light Infantry instead of two divisions! 2,000 men instead of 15,000 men! Oh yes, I almost forgot: 75 British tanks attacked as well. The bloody French didn't bother turning up," he said bitterly. "They were probably too busy stuffing their fat French faces with fromage and baguettes and getting drunk on cheap gut rotting red vino." Garfield shook his head with disgust. "Eating is the only thing that there're good at, because they're certainly no good at fighting. The Frogs barely lasted six weeks before they surrendered."

"What happened?" Alice asked.

"I was in command of C Company of the 8th Battalion and despite the odds, we initially made good progress. We outfought the Jerry tanks but then we ran into Rommel's 88 mm anti-aircraft guns. They literally stopped us dead in our tracks. And then the Luftwaffe attacked. Talk about out of the frying pan and into the fire! Where was the R.A.F, you may well ask! Not over Arras, that's for sure!" Garfield shook his head with frustration. "The Stukas bombed the hell out of us and sent us on the run and then the Messerschmitts came along and strafed us as we retreated. Then the French finally decided to show up and grace us with their presence! They covered our retreat …" Garfield ran out of words as he ran out of breath. He was breathing heavily and his face was covered in sweat. "We lost over 100 men killed and over half of our tanks. And for what? So that we could sew 'Defence of Arras' as a Battle Honour onto our Regimental Colours?" Garfield snorted and shook his head with derision. "What a bloody waste of time, effort and lives."

"But I read that your attack knocked the Jerries' confidence so much that they halted their attack on Dunkirk." Alice tried to reassure Garfield that the sacrifice of his soldiers had not been made in vain.

Garfield shook his head with contempt. "Bah! You're a clever young woman, Alice; don't tell me that you've swallowed Churchill's propaganda? Hitler LET us escape to give us a second chance. He wanted to prove that he meant no harm towards the British Empire. He still hoped for a ceasefire and a negotiated peace treaty. Hitler has always admired our empire and means us no harm. In fact, he wants to rule Russia in the same manner and using the same methods as we use to rule India. Hitler has always hoped that Britain and Germany would become friends and allies and that we would eventually join him in his crusade against Communist Russia. And it looks like with the formation of the Legion of St. George, that is finally going to happen. So much for the 'Miracle of Dunkirk.'"

Alice and Aurora were too shocked to reply. They were appalled and flabbergasted that Garfield had dared to cast doubts and dispersions on the validity of the miracle of Dunkirk.

"It's not ... it's not just Dunkirk, Alice. Or Arras for that matter," Garfield began. "It's not just that our attack failed ... it's the fact that it was the only time that we attempted to counter attack and cut off the German spearhead. The only time that we actually tried to stop them and force them back! And it was like that ever since Belgium! I know, because I was there. Retreat, retreat, retreat, day after day, week after week!" Garfield ranted. "Do you know that we had over 305,000 men and 25,000 vehicles in France at the beginning of the war? That together with the French, we actually had more tanks than the Jerries? And we had 500 aeroplanes!" He shook his head with disbelief. "And we still managed to screw up! I did not see an R.A.F. plane for days at a time! But the Germans? They would bomb and strafe us at least half a dozen times a day!" Garfield hesitated as if he found it too painful to continue. "Instead of bravery, I saw cowardice; instead of efficiency, I saw incompetence; instead of discipline, I saw anarchy. Soldiers fought each other for a place on the boats leaving Dunkirk; officers abandoned their men and pushed to the front of the queue in their panic to escape; men swamped the boats carrying stretcher cases, capsized them and drowned the wounded." Garfield pinched his temples with his thumb and middle finger as if he was trying to force the horrific images from his head. "I would not have believed that British soldiers were capable of such despicable behaviour if I hadn't seen it with my own eyes."

"Is that why you joined the Blackshirts, Captain?" Alice asked gently, "as a reaction against what you'd witnessed?"

"Yes! Yes, it is, Alice!" Garfield's eyes blazed with the fiery fanaticism of the zealot. "When the Jerries invaded, I fought them all the way from the beaches until foot by foot, mile by mile, they pushed us all the way north towards Scotland. Ironically, I was captured near Durham, which is where I'm from. But the things that I saw … the way that the Jerries fought-magnificent! We were hopelessly outmatched, outclassed and outfought!" He looked out of the window as the sun began to set. "I had a Saul on the road to Damascus moment; an epiphany, if you will. I realised why the Germans have been sent here, Alice: God has sent them here to punish us for the error of our ways. Since the last war we have become cowardly, weak and divided. God has sent the Germans here to teach us, to show us the true path. Under their guidance and with their help we will become brave, strong and united again! We have so much to learn from these people! We will throw out Churchill and the old gang with their titles and their ranks; class will no longer divide us, blood will unite us! Britain will emerge from the ashes like a phoenix reborn and we will take our rightful place in the front rank of the brotherhood of Aryan nations in the crusade against communism! Hail Joyce!"

Alice looked at Garfield with astonishment. The captain was flushed and he was breathing heavily with the pride, passion and conviction of a convert.

"Hello, may I speak to Mr Branson, please?"

"Speaking."

"Mr Branson, do you recognize my voice?"

"No."Branson shook his head over the phone. "You'll have to give me a clue."

"It's Mr Smith. I came to see you the other day at your office."

"Ah, yes! Mr Smith!" Branson chuckled. "Now I remember you: you wanted to find out how the rationing system worked."

"That's right and I remember that you told me that you were an engineer in the last war."

"Yes, I served in the Sappers and you and I both served at the Somme."

Smith laughed. "Yes, the last of the Old Contemptibles. Do you still have engineering connections?"

"Yes, I do. Why do you ask?"

Smith explained what he wanted Branson to do.

"Consider it done, sir. God save the King!"

Corporal Colvin enjoyed cooking dinner for his fellow partisans that evening. He was very much aware that for many, if not all of them, this could very well prove to be their last supper. So he made an extra special effort to make dinner as delicious as possible. Colvin cooked sausages, bacon, mushrooms, tomatoes, fried eggs and toast that was washed down with strong tea and fresh full fat milk. All of the food was produced either on the Farm or on one of the satellite farms that the partisans had colonised on the outskirts of Frampton-on-the-Ouse. The guerrillas joked that they hoped that Colvin had served them the ' vegetarian' option, as they preferred to kill Germans rather than eat them.

After dinner the partisans prepared for Operation Zelda. They stripped, cleaned and lightly oiled the working parts of their weapons. The guerrillas emptied and reloaded all of their magazines making sure that all of their rounds were correctly aligned. If a magazine jammed in a fire fight it could prove fatal. They checked that the fuses on their grenades were all set for the correct time before they detonated. The partisans made sure that their daggers were close at hand and easily accessible for close quarter combat. They made sure that their webbing only contained equipment that was absolutely essential to the success of their mission: - magazines full of ammunition; grenades; a torch with a red filter; weapon cleaning kit and also a First Aid kit with a Field Dressing. The guerrillas made sure that their skeleton webbing did not rattle, creak or squeak when they walked, ran or jumped. They took off their jackboots and changed into black plimsolls. They needed to be able to move quickly and silently. The partisans applied black shoe polish to their faces, necks and hands in order to prevent their skin from shining in the pale moonlight. At last they finished their preparations: they were ready.

"Dinner is served!" Alice announced with a flourish and a smile as she entered the dining room. She placed a plate down on the table in front of Captain Garfield and another one in front of a second Fascist. Aurora followed, hot on her heels, and served the remaining two Blackshirts.

The Militiamen's eyes practically bulged from their sockets as they looked at the feast that the girls had prepared for them. The plates literally overflowed with a mountain of sausages, bacon, mushrooms, tomatoes, fried eggs and baked beans. Most of the Fascists had not eaten such a sumptuous and scrumptious meal since before the war began and a few of them had not eaten such a massive meal in their lives.

"Ladies, this is a feast fit for a king!" Garfield proclaimed. "Thank you very much," he said with sincere appreciation and gratitude.

"You're very welcome, Captain! Please tuck in, bon appetite!" Alice bowed.

"And so, without much further ado," Garfield smiled as he rubbed his hands together in gleeful anticipation.

"Captain Garfield, shall I take this up to the Leader?" Aurora asked as she held up a plate of food.

Garfield thought for a moment before he answered. "No, it's all right, Aurora. I'll take it up." He stood up and took the plate. "Thank you."

"Come in."

Garfield instinctively checked that his tie knot was tight before he opened the door and entered the room.

"Ah, dinner is served!" Joyce exclaimed with a smile. "At last, I'm absolutely starving! I could eat a whole Jew raw!"

Garfield laughed loyally.

"Captain Garfield, please put the food on that table over there and then help me to walk over."

"Certainly, my Leader." Garfield did as he was told and then wrapped an arm around Joyce's waist. Joyce stretched an arm around Garfield's shoulder and slowly stood up. Garfield helped to guide him towards the small dining table and lowered him down into a chair.

"Thank you, Captain," Joyce said.

"My pleasure, Prime Minister." Garfield bowed.

Joyce smiled as he felt a delicious tingle of pleasure shoot up his spine like an electric shock. No matter how many times he heard the title, it never failed to give him a thrill to be addressed as ' prime minister.' He tucked his napkin into his collar and picked up his knife and fork and waited until Garfield was half way out of the room. "And Captain?"

"Yes, my Leader?"

"After dinner I'd like to have the girls for desert. Please escort them up yourself with the necessary ... ah, equipment."

Garfield felt an icy hand squeeze his heart as his face drained of colour.

"Do you have a problem with my order, Captain?"

"No, Prime Minister." Garfield shook his head vehemently.

"Good. I'd hate to think that you're becoming squeamish in your old age, John. What's the point of ruling a country if you can't enjoy the simple pleasure of life such as wine, women and song? 'Heavy weighs the crown' and all that. The two young ladies down stairs are simply the perks of the job."

"Their names are Alice and Aurora," Garfield said through tightly gritted teeth.

Joyce chose to ignore Garfield's obvious reluctance to carry out the order. "You can have sloppy seconds and the boys can have the left overs as usual," Joyce said nonchalantly. "Don't say that I'm not good to you."

"As you command, my Leader," Garfield said formally. He bowed, clicked his heels together and thrust out his arm in the Fascist salute, "Hail Joyce!"

"Anyone else for seconds?" Alice asked with a cheery smile.

"Yes please, miss!" Three young Blackshirts chorused as they raised their arms in the air like schoolboys.

Garfield carefully placed his knife and fork side by side together on his plate.

Alice looked at the half eaten plate of food. "Have you lost your appetite, Captain?"

Garfield patted his stomach and smiled apologetically. "Not at all, Alice. It's just that I'm totally stuffed. That was absolutely delicious, but I couldn't eat another thing. Thank you."

Alice nodded. "My pleasure." She took Garfield's plate and picked up a second Fascist's as well. "More food coming right up, Tom, and there's more for you, Captain Garfield, if you change your mind."

"Thank you, Alice," Garfield said.

"Thank you, miss," Tom said as he watched Alice leave the dining room. The young militiaman stretched his arms and laced his fingers together behind his head. "I could get used to this very easily, sir."

"Forget it, Tom: she's out of your league," Garfield said with a sly grin.

Tom blushed a deep beetroot with embarrassment as Garfield read his mind. "Sir, I didn't mean-"

"Methinks the lady doth protest too much," Garfield interrupted.

Tom's cheeks burned even more as his companions dissolved into fits of laughter.

Aurora smiled and rolled her eyes as she gave Garfield a 'boys will be boys' look. She picked up the plates of the two remaining Fascists and disappeared into the kitchen.

"Garfield knows, Alice," she said grimly.

"I know, Aurora. He hardly touched his food. And did you see his face? He was sweating like a pig."

"And his hands were shaking so much that he could hardly hold his cutlery. So do we do it now?"

Alice looked at his watch. "Yes, they've been stuffing their fat Fascist faces for fifteen minutes now. The pills should start working at any moment."

"Are you sure about Swanmore?"

Alice slowly shook her head. "I'm not one hundred percent certain, but I'm prepared to give him the benefit of the doubt."

"All right," Aurora agreed reluctantly.

"Good. Are you ready?"

"Yes!" Aurora bared her teeth like a she wolf.

"Bueno. Then let's do this- Viva España!"

"God save the King!"

The girls entered the dining room carrying three hot plates of food. They placed them down in front of the three hungry Blackshirts who ooohed and aaahed as they rubbed their stomachs with appreciation.

"All right, lads: as soon as you've finished I want Richard and Connor to relieve Sergeant Swanmore and Will on top of the Keep so that they can eat, clear?"

"Yes, sir," the Fascists acknowledged between mouthfuls of baked beans and sausages.

"Tom, you'll stay here with me, all right?"

"Yes, sir." Tom was relieved that Garfield had not tried to embarrass him in front of Alice again.

"Now, lads, I'm going to pop upstairs and see how they're getting on." Garfield finished drinking his cup of tea. "I'll be back in ten minutes at five to eight and when I return I expect that you great greedy guts will have finished stuffing your fat faces." His men laughed as they continued doing just that. Garfield stood up with a groan. "My God, I've eaten so much that I can hardly move." He smiled as he saw Alice pick up his Schmessier to hand to him. "You handle that like a pro, Alice. Have you used one of these before?" His eyebrows rose with surprise as Aurora picked up another machine gun, cocked it and flicked off the safety catch in one practised fluid motion.

"Yes I have, Captain."

Garfield smiled. He was glad that Joyce would not be having the girls for desert after all.

"Charlie! Charlie! Come quickly, something terrible has happened!"

Swanmore pulled open the door to the roof. "What is it, Alice? What's the matter?" He asked with concern. Alice was covered in sweat and she was breathing heavily.

"One of the Blackshirts … went crazy … and opened fire …" she panted.

Swanmore grabbed her by the shoulders. "Captain Garfield?"

Alice shook her head. "I think that he's dead."

"Will! Follow me!" Swanmore ordered as he ran down the narrow spiral staircase as fast as his legs would carry him. He came to an abrupt stop when he reached the ground floor and waited for his fellow Fascist to catch up with him. Swanmore tucked his Schmessier tightly into his shoulder. "Will, cover me," he ordered. The other militiaman gulped heavily and took up position beside the door to the dining room. The sergeant slowly pushed open the door with the toe of his boot and cautiously entered the room. The dining room looked as if it had erupted in an explosion of food, blood and bodies. Sausages, bacon and baked beans lay everywhere. Swanmore did a double take as he counted the number of bodies. "Alice, I … I don't understand." He shook his head with confusion. "You said that a Blackshirt killed the captain, but all four of them are dead. So who killed them?"

"I did." Aurora opened fire and Will crumpled to the ground.

"Wha - ?" Swanmore collapsed as the machine gun butt hit him on the back of his head.

"Good night, Vienna," Alice said.

The girls tied Swanmore securely to a chair; blind folded him and left him facing a corner of the room. They still hadn't made up their mind which side he batted for and they were not prepared to take any chances. The partisans made sure that the front door to the Keep was bolted shut and then cautiously crept up the stairs to the fourth floor. They knocked on Joyce's door and when there was no answer they entered the room with their Schmessiers at the ready. The Leader lay on his bed snoring like a baby.

"Well, at least we know that the pills worked," Aurora said.

Alice nodded. "Come on. Let's tie him up."

After the girls had secured Joyce they collected his briefcase and returned down stairs to the dining room where they stripped the dead Militiamen of any equipment and uniforms that they could use for future operations. The guerrillas added the loot to the growing pile of weapons that they had already gathered. They also emptied the Blackshirt's pockets and put anything that looked interesting in Joyce's briefcase.

Alice looked at her watch with amazement. It was only nine o' clock. She could have sworn that it was later than that. Time seemed to have slowed down. Alice looked at Aurora and nodded. She picked up the phone and dialled the number.

"Hello? Yes … E.T.A. is as per plan. Thank you." Ansett put down the phone and smiled at his friends. "Gentlemen, Operation Zelda is good to go."

The girls found the alarm clock in the recently departed Captain Garfield's briefcase and set the alarm for two o' clock in the morning. They made the two sofas in the living room as comfortable as possible and settled down for a few hours' sleep.

Swanmore woke with a start. His head was throbbing and he had a sudden moment of panic when he found that he couldn't see. He calmed down when he realised that he was blind folded. He licked his lips and tasted a familiar metallic coppery flavour. It was his own blood. Swanmore tried to move, but he couldn't. He was tied fast to a chair. He flexed and unflexed his fingers and toes. He rotated his wrists and ankles. He stretched his arms and legs as far as his restraints would allow. He breathed a silent sigh of relief. Nothing seemed to be broken. Apart from his head, that is, which hurt as if a donkey had kicked it. However, if he could use his arms and legs that meant that he was still in the fight and he began to believe that if he kept his wits about him, he might survive to see the new dawn. Swanmore started to piece together the events of the day in order to figure out just what the hell was going on.

The sound of the phone ringing almost scared Alice out of her skin. She gingerly picked up the phone and carefully held the receiver to her ear. "Hello? ... I'm afraid that he can't come to the phone right now. Captain Garfield is inspecting the sentries' positions. Who are you? ... Ah, I see ... my name is Alice Roberts and I'm from the Hereward Blackshirt unit. Can I take a message? ... All right, Captain Johnson, we'll see you soon. Goodbye, sir." Alice put the phone down and stood rooted to the spot. "Well, that's thrown a spanner in the works."

"What is it, Alice?" Aurora asked as she placed a hand on her friend's shoulder. "You look as white as a sheet."

"That was Captain Johnson, the commander of one of Joyce's bodyguard units. They're on their way here from London as we speak."

"What?" Aurora's eyes widened with horrified surprise. "But they're not supposed to arrive here until tomorrow lunch time."

"They're running ahead of schedule."

"When are they due to get here?"

Alice looked at her watch. "In about half an hour: at three o' clock."

Swanmore listened carefully to the conversation. He sat with his head slumped on his chest with his eyes closed. He didn't want the girls to know that he had woken up.

Alice put the phone down and shook her head. "It's no use. They're not there. Major Ansett must have already left."

"What are we going to do?" Aurora asked.

"First, we double check that the front door is securely locked; second, we make sure that all of the weapons are close at hand and are made ready: we may soon have to repel intruders."

Aurora nodded. "What about Joyce?"

"What do you mean?"

"We can't afford to wait until the others turn up before we get him. If the Blackshirts get here before the major then all hell will break lose. When Major Ansett gets here it will be all hands on deck: we'll need everyone to fight off the Fascists and stop them from getting in. And if the Blackshirts manage to alert their German friends then it will probably be too late to grab Joyce; we'll be too busy trying to save ourselves. I think that we should get him now, Alice."

"But how are we going to do that, Aurora?" Alice asked. "There are only two of us and Joyce looks like a heavy bastard. How can we carry him down four flights of stairs? If we drag him and he bumps his head then we could do him a serious amount of injury. Edinburgh wants him alive, not dead."

"Use him," Aurora pointed.

"Swanmore? But we don't know if he's for us or against us."

"Well, there's only one way to find out: what he does in the next ten minutes will prove where his loyalties lie one way or another."

Alice swiftly made her mind up. "All right, Aurora. But we don't let him walk behind us, he always walks in front of us and we don't give him a weapon, we cover him at all times. Agreed?"

"Si, jefa."

"Bueno. And if he makes one false move, we kill him."

Ansett stopped at the door to the Crypt and turned around to face his team. "Listen in, men. From now on we are tactical: no talking, hand signals only."

"Hand signals only?" Sam was confused. "But how can we see them? It's pitch black in the tunnel."

"That's why we'll carry this." Ansett shined his red filtered torch on a piece of rope.

"What's that?" Sam asked. "A skipping rope? I hate to point this out, sir, but this is nether the time nor the place for fun and games."

"It's a communications cord, you numpty!" Alan punched his friend and gave him a dead arm.

"Ouch! I knew that." Sam said as he rubbed his arm.

"Pay attention, Laurel and Hardy," Ansett smiled indulgently. He was glad to see that that the boys had not lost their sense of humour. "I'll go first, then Captain Smith, Corporal Colvin, Steve, Alan, Sam and Second-Lieutenant Jones as rear guard. I want everyone to hold onto this comms cord in your left hand and carry your weapon in your right hand. One tug on the rope will mean stop; two tugs will mean go and three tugs will mean enemy. Clear?"

"Clear, sir," the partisans chorused.

"Good." Ansett nodded in the darkness. "Make ready, but keep your safety on."

Each guerrilla cocked his weapon, sending a round up the spout ready to fire. They double checked that their safety catches were on.

"According to the map, it's approximately eight hundred yards or half a mile from here to the Keep. It will probably take between ten and fifteen minutes walk in the pitch darkness to reach the castle." Ansett looked at his watch. "Prepare to synchronise watches. On my mark it will be two thirty ... three ... two ... one ... mark. If we leave now, we should get to the castle by a quarter to three. We go straight in, collect the girls, grab Joyce and get straight out again by three o' clock. If all goes according to plan, then we should be back here by a quarter past three."

"And if all does not go according to plan?" Alan asked.

"Then we kill Joyce, come back to the Cathedral, get on the lorry and drive like a bat out of hell back to the Farm. Clear?" Ansett answered.

"Crystal clear, sir," Alan said.

"Any more questions? Good. Is every one ready?"

"Yes, sir!"

"Then let's go! Strength and honour!"

"Strength and honour!"

"Charlie! Charlie! Wake up!" Alice shook Swanmore's shoulder.

"What's...what's going on?" Swanmore's voice was slurred.

"I'm sorry that I had to knock you out, Charlie, but I had to be sure whose side you're on," Alice apologised profusely.

"We need you to help us to carry Joyce downstairs," Aurora explained.

"Why? I don't understand."

"Because the enemy will be here any minute and we can't fight them off by ourselves. We need to get Joyce away before they arrive. So will you help us?" Alice asked.

Swanmore looked at the Luger that Alice was holding and the Schmessier that she wore slung on her shoulder. Aurora was identically armed. "I could never resist a damsel in distress," he replied with his best Errol Flynn smile. What choice did he have?

Swanmore looked at Joyce lying fast asleep on his bed. "Shouldn't we wake him?" he asked. "It would make it a whole lot easier to help him down the stairs."

Alice shook his head. "No. He's dosed up to his eyeballs with sleeping pills. We'll never wake him up. We'll have to carry him downstairs. Charlie, you grab him around his waist; Aurora and I will carry his legs."

"All right." Swanmore did as he was told and helped carry Joyce down four flights of stairs to the ground floor. When they finally reached the dining room they collapsed in an exhausted heap. Joyce was a big man and a ton weight.

Alice looked at her watch. "It's nearly a quarter to three. The major will be here any minute. Let's get ready to leave."

"Who's the major?" Swanmore asked.

"You'll find out soon enough," Alice answered cryptically.

"I look forward to it," Swanmore grinned.

Alice looked at Swanmore and thought for a moment before she walked over to the row of Blackshirt weapons and picked up a machine gun and half a dozen magazines. She presented the weapon and the ammunition to Swanmore with a smile. "You've demonstrated where your true loyalties lie, Charlie," she said confidently. "Welcome aboard."

"Thank you, Alice. What's the name of your ship?"

"H.M.S. Resistance, of course."

"Hello? Is anybody there?" a voice echoed down the corridor.

"They're here!" Alice yelled with delight. She looked at her watch again. "It's a quarter to three-they're bang on time!"

Swanmore's brow furrowed with confusion. "How did they get here? How did they get inside the Keep?"

"A tunnel leads form the Cathedral Crypt under the Square to the dungeons at the bottom of the Keep," Aurora explained.

"How very clever," Swanmore said with admiration.

"That's how they got in and that's how we're going to get out," Aurora said smugly.

"Wrong." Swanmore jumped outside the door and fired a burst of bullets down the corridor. "Get back, Reds!" He shouted.

"Charlie! What are you doing?" Alice's eyes were wide open with shock and incomprehension.

"Showing you where my true loyalties lie, Alice. Now, lower your weapons and put your hands up." He leaned out of the door. "Don't come any closer, Reds, or I'll kill the girls!" He shouted down the corridor.

"Charlie ... I don't understand," Alice protested.

"What do you find hard to understand, Alice? I'm loyal to Germany. They are my people now."

"But ... but you gave the correct password response: 'MacBeth, the Scottish play.' "

336

"You seem so surprised, Alice," Swanmore smirked with amusement. "You shouldn't be. After all, I did study English at Southampton and MacBeth actually is my favourite Shakespeare play. It was just a matter of good luck that it also happened to be your partisan password. Or more accurately: good luck for me, but bad luck for you."

"But that means that -"

"Yes," Swanmore interrupted, "It means that Garfield was your man on the inside and you killed him."

Alice's face drained of all colour and Aurora was violently sick on the carpet.

Chapter Twenty Two

"Right lads, the situation is that a Blackshirt has captured the girls and is holding them hostage. The corridor leading to the dining room is too narrow for more than one man at a time. That means that we can't carry out a frontal assault. However …" Ansett explained to Sam and Alan what he wanted them to do. The boys grinned like mad men and then took off back down stairs to the dungeons and the tunnel.

Ansett looked at his watch. It was ten to three. The next ten minutes would decide whether or not the girls lived or died and whether or not the mission succeeded or failed.

"But why? Why are you doing this?" Alice asked.

"The answer is blatantly obvious, Alice: if I stop you from kidnapping Joyce then I'll become a hero! I 'll be rewarded and I'll be promoted." He puffed out his chest like a robin. "I'll be awarded a medal. Maybe a Military Cross or perhaps even a V.C! And Joyce will owe me. He will owe me his life! He will be in my debt forever." Swanmore's eyes glazed over as he fantasized about the life of fame, fortune and glory that he would soon be enjoying. "There'll be no limit to what I can do! No man will dare to stand in the path of the hero who saved the Leader."

"But Charlie, you'll never be awarded the Military Cross, and certainly not the V.C," Alice explained. "Only the King can award those medals and the King is up in Edinburgh. Joyce and his small gang of Fascist cronies are the only people who will feel grateful towards you. The rest of the British people will regard you as a treacherous turncoat. You'll be remembered in the history books alongside other traitors and villains such as Prince John and Richard III."

"However, if you help us to capture Joyce then you'll become a hero, Charlie," Aurora continued. "You'll become famous as the man who kidnapped Joyce, the hated traitor, and brought him to Scotland to face justice. You will be rewarded and promoted ..."

"The King will probably pin the Military Cross on your chest in person." Alice added. "You'll be remembered in the History books as a true patriot like Robin Hood or Hereward the Wake. Your people will remember you as a hero for ever, Charlie."

Swanmore was momentarily lost for words. He was knocked off guard. Truth be told, he had not considered an alternative course of action. His only motivation had been to avenge the deaths of Captain Garfield and the rest of his men. Everything was happening too fast and events threatened to spin out of control. He needed to slow things down so that he could think and consider his next move. "They ... you're not my people, Alice."

"We're your father's people, Charlie. This is your chance to prove that they were wrong to treat you so badly and turn their backs on you. This is your chance to make your father feel proud of you. What would your father want you to do?"

Alan and Sam ran swiftly through the tunnel with only their red filter torches to guide them. They emerged puffing and panting at the base of the crater that had exploded underneath the S.S. stormtroopers, scrambled up the rubble strewn wall and launched themselves over the lip without pausing for breath. They ran silently through the sleeping streets of Hereward on their rubber plimsolls and only slowed down as they neared St. John's.

The boys took cover behind a wall as they peered around the corner at the main school gates. "Only two sentries, Al," Sam whispered as he counted the red glows of the lit cigarettes that the soldiers were smoking. "They're relaxed and off guard," he continued as he listened to them chatting happily.

"Good. They're going to pay the price for their lack of vigilance," Alan said grimly.

"Silencers. I'll take the one on the left, you take the one on the right, Sam."

"All right." The partisans slung their machine guns on their shoulders, extracted a Luger from their holsters and screwed on a silencer attachment. They cocked their weapons, raised their pistols to the ready position and flicked off their safety catches. "Ready."

"Let's go." The guerrillas steadily and stealthily approached the enemy position in the pitch-blackness. A cloud suddenly parted and a bright shaft of moonlight shined on the two assassins.

"What the hell -!"

Sam and Alan both fired a double tap and the Blackshirt sentries fell to the ground. The boys grabbed them under their armpits, dragged them into the depths of their sentry boxes and dumped them in a crumpled heap.

"Fascist Militia, Al. They make me sick." Sam spat on the bodies with disgust.

"If the Blackshirts change guard at three o' clock then they'll find their dead friends and we'll be in big trouble, Sam," Alan said.

"I agree, Al: we need to find out when they change guard or the game's up."

"And how are we going to find out?"

"Leave it to me, Al," Sam smiled wickedly. "I have a cunning plan."

"My father would want me to stay loyal. To stay true." Swanmore spoke as if he was in a daze.

"Then join us, Charlie! Come over to our side!" Alice urged.

"I can't, Alice. Even if I wanted to- it's too late."

"It's never too late, Charlie," Aurora joined in. "Everyone deserves a second chance. Everyone deserves redemption."

The boys ran through the grounds of the school until they sighted the Keep. They skirted around the edge of the fortification making sure that they had cover from view as well as cover from fire from any sentry that might be positioned at the top of the castle. At last they spotted what they were looking for.

"But … but they killed my mother!" Swanmore snarled angrily. "The British, her … her friends and neighbours burnt her alive as she slept in her own bed!" Tears ran freely down the sergeant's face.

"I … I know, Charlie," Alice said in her most soothing voice. "Your neighbours, the British people committed a terrible crime and they should be punished; but the best way that they can begin to make up for it, the best way that they can seek your forgiveness is by apologising and by asking you to join them again, by asking you not to turn your back on them, on your people, on your country in its hour of need. The best way that you can seek revenge is by forcing them to welcome you as a British hero."

"You will become famous, Charlie, as the man who kidnapped Joyce, " Aurora added.

"People will tell stories about you to their children and to their grandchildren for generations to come."

"You will join the ranks of other great British heroes such as Wellington, Nelson and Wolfe!"

Swanmore lowered his Schmessier a few inches. "I need time to think."

Alan spotted what they were searching for first. "Bingo," he whispered, "cover me." He cautiously crossed the cobblestones and carefully avoided banging into one of the half a dozen metal rubbish bins that blocked his path. He carefully turned the door handle. It was locked. "Blast!" He swore under his breath.

"Here, Al. Let me have a go," Sam offered as he joined his friend's side.

Alan stepped aside as Sam lowered a leather rucksack from his shoulders. He unclipped the clasp and took out a collection of skeleton keys.

"Where on earth did you get those, Sam?" Alan asked with fascinated surprise.

"From Corporal Colvin. Before the war he was more often on the side of Professor Moriarty than on the side of Sherlock Holmes," Sam answered with a grin as he fiddled with the door lock.

"Hey, presto!" He slowly swung the door open. "Age before beauty."

"Pearls before swine," Alan smiled as he entered the Keep with his pistol drawn.

"I've killed many partisans in the past year, Alice," Swanmore admitted sombrely. "I doubt if Edinburgh would be willing to forgive and forget the deaths of her men."

Alice shook her head. "None of that will matter, Charlie; if you help us to capture Joyce then the slate will be swept clean. Edinburgh will not care what you did before the kidnapping. If anyone questions you then you can always explain that it was part of your cover story. It was regrettable, but necessary in order to establish your credibility as a Blackshirt and enable you to infiltrate your way into Joyce's personal bodyguard."

"You will be a new man, Charlie," Aurora said. "You will be reborn like Saul on the road to Damascus."

"And if you didn't want to, I'm sure that you wouldn't have to venture south of the border again. I'm certain that Edinburgh would be grateful to have your services training new recruits in the Highlands," Alice continued.

Swanmore shook his head firmly. "That would never do. I'm a fighting man. It would drive me crazy to be stuck in an office. All I've ever wanted, is to be a soldier like my father was before me." He pushed out his chest. "I would rather shoot myself in the head than be a pen pusher or a bean counter."

Alice surreptitiously looked at Aurora and smiled. It was working-Swanmore was turning.

Alan slowly but surely crept through the kitchen with Sam covering his back a few paces behind him. He hoped that the endless hours spent training at the pistol range developing and improving his marksman skills were about to bear fruit. Alice and Aurora's lives depended on it.

"How are you going to explain what happened here, Alice?" Swanmore asked.

Alice's eyes lit up with hope. "Will captured us, but then you over powered him, killed him and freed us."

"Will it work?"

Alice nodded. "It will," she answered confidently. "The major will believe anything that I tell him, especially if you and Aurora back me up."

"What about Garfield?" Swanmore asked.

Alice shrugged her shoulders dismissively. "Garfield was a dirty, stinking Blackshirt traitor, plain and simple. You were our inside man and revealed your identity to us today. The major doesn't know who our spy is."

Swanmore slowly nodded his head with sincere admiration. "It might just work, Alice. I'm glad to see that you're not just a pretty face."

"Thank you." Alice smiled. She felt a warm glow of satisfaction in her stomach. They had done it. They had won Swanmore over.

"On the other hand, it might not work." Swanmore's face suddenly darkened. "After all, I only have to wait for Captain Johnson and his team to get here and then I'll be able to return to London in time for breakfast and medals."

"Charlie, wait!"

There were two explosions in the distance. "What the -?" Swanmore turned around as Alan burst through the kitchen door and shot the startled sergeant twice in the chest. Alan walked up to him and calmly gave him a double tap to the forehead. Sam swept the room with his Luger and then popped his head outside into the corridor. "All clear!" He shouted.

Major Ansett entered the dining room in an instant. "Is everyone all right?" Alice and Aurora gave their brother and boyfriend a massive bear hug.

"We are now," Alice said gratefully.

"Who's he?" Ansett pointed at Swanmore's still smoking corpse.

Aurora shrugged her shoulders nonchalantly. "No one important. Just another traitor."

Ansett nodded.

"Sir, we've got trouble," Sam announced. "The Huns have discovered the dead sentries at the school gates."

"Some of your handiwork, no doubt?" Ansett asked with a quizzically raised eyebrow.

"Naturally," Sam smiled cold-heartedly.

"That's my boy!" Ansett ruffled his hair affectionately. "Then it's time to leave. I'll lead with Captain Smith following. Steve, Alan and Sam will carry Joyce. Alice and Aurora will carry any captured weapons and equipment with Corporal Colvin as rear guard. Clear?"

"Clear, sir!" The partisans chorused.

"Then let's go."

Aurora and Alice stopped to look at Swanmore for the last time. His wide unseeing eyes stared at the ceiling.

"Do you think that he would've joined us, Alice?" Aurora asked.

"I don't know," Alice said sadly. "And we'll never find out now." She gently placed her hand on her friend's shoulder. "Come on, Aurora: we've got a traitor to kidnap and a war to win!"

Captain Johnson jumped off his seat when he heard and saw the two explosions. "Partisan attack! Pull over, Adam," he ordered. The driver pulled over and Johnson piled out. He waved the armoured car and the lorry that was following his car to stop.

A head popped out of the top of the armoured vehicle.

"Chris, we've got trouble ahead. I think that the Reds are attacking the building where the Leader is staying." Johnson explained. A Blackshirt sergeant appeared beside him. "Sergeant Plows, get your men off the lorry and into file behind the armoured car. Chris, your vehicle will lead and we'll follow you straight through the school gates to the Keep. When we get there I want you to take up position in front of the main entrance. Sergeant Plows, when we reach the Keep I want your men to take cover in extended line with one section to the left of the armoured car and one section to the right. Clear?"

"Clear, sir!"

"Good. Then let's go. Hail Joyce!"

"Hail Joyce!"

"An armoured Blackshirt unit has arrived to escort Joyce back to London, Captain Smith," Ansett announced as he looked through the window. "They'll be able to knock down the Keep's front door with a single blast of their cannon. We can't afford to let them get into the castle. It will take us about fifteen minutes to carry Joyce through the tunnel and if they catch up with us whilst we're doing that then there'll be a massacre."

"Corporal Colvin, Steve and I can remain behind, sir," Jones offered. "We can hold them off whilst you escape. Once we've dealt with the Blackshirts we'll catch you up."

Smith looked at Jones and nodded. "Sir," he said to Ansett, "it's the only way."

"I know," Ansett said grimly, "but I don't like it. However, I don't see what other choice we have. Captain Smith, you and the boys will carry Joyce; Alice and Aurora, you will be the rear guard. Girls, you may well have to fight: only carry what you feel you can comfortably. Leave behind the rest of the weapons and the equipment." Ansett turned to face the Stay Behind party. "Second-Lieutenant Jones, do you think that you can hold off the Fascists for fifteen minutes until a quarter past three for me?"

"We'll hold them until hell freezes over if necessary, sir," Jones replied confidently.

"Good. Then best of luck to you, gentlemen."

"Thank you, sir. God save the King!" Both men saluted and shook hands.

"Blackshirts, sir," Plows announced.

"Christ!" Johnson swore. "How many?"

"Two, sir. Blown to bits with hand grenades."

"What a mess," Johnson said as he looked at the mangled and bloody bodies. "All right, lads. Make ready and safeties off," he ordered. "Prepare to assault the position. Follow me."

The armoured car led the way down the cobble stone drive towards the Keep with the Fascists following behind in file.

"Fifteen minutes, sir?" Corporal Colvin's eyes bulged wide open with barely controlled fear. "Once that armoured car starts firing, we'll be lucky to last fifteen seconds."

"Then we'll just have to stop the armoured car from firing in the first place, won't we, Corporal?" Jones said with a mischievous smile.

"And how are we going to manage that, sir?"

"By using smoke and mirrors, Corporal."

Johnson banged on the brass knocker with growing impatience.

"Perhaps they're not in, sir?" Adam Chester, Johnson's driver suggested hopefully.

"It's three o'clock in the morning, Adam," Johnson said frostily. "I'm quite sure that they're in."

"Maybe they're heavy sleepers?"

"You're not helping, Private Chester," Johnson said through gritted teeth.

"Sorry, sir."

"Captain Garfield had a full bodyguard detail of eight men with him. There should be four men on guard at any one time and either Captain Garfield or Sergeant Swanmore should be on duty."

"But some of Captain Garfield's men were killed in the partisan attack yesterday, sir," Chester reminded his captain.

"You're quite correct, Adam. I'd forgotten that they'd suffered casualties," Johnson conceded. "However, at least some of Garfield's bodyguard should be awake and alert."

"Yes, sir."

Johnson rapped on the doorknocker again. "I swear to God, if no one opens the door within the next ten seconds I will huff and I will puff and I will blow the door down with the armoured car's cannon!"

At that precise moment a window opened above Johnson's head. "Halt! Who goes there?"

"Friend! "

"Advance one and be recognized!" The guard ordered. Johnson and Chester stepped away from the door and allowed the sentry to shine a torch on their faces and uniform.

"Captain Johnson with Private Chester. We've come to escort the Leader back to London."

"Very good, sir!"

"Who are you? I don't recognise you. You're not a member of Captain Garfield's unit."

"My name's Corporal Colvin. I'm from the Cambridge Fascist Militia. My unit arrived last night as reinforcements for Captain Garfield's team."

Johnson nodded. "Very well. Where's Captain Garfield, Corporal?"

"Asleep, sir."

"Well, for God's sake, wake him up, Corporal!" Johnson was becoming more and more agitated. "I want to collect the Leader and take him back to London before dawn. And let me in! It's three o' clock in the morning and I'm freezing my balls off out here! My men need food and a hot drink."

"I'll be down in a jiffy, sir." Colvin disappeared from the window and arrived at the front door. He opened the door a few inches. "Identification check, sir. Please pass over your Pay Book and your I.D. tags."

"Are you sure that this is strictly necessary, Corporal?" Johnson asked tersely. "My men and I have travelled for many hours through hostile territory to get here and I'm not in the mood to play cops and robbers."

"I'm afraid that it is necessary, sir," Colvin replied politely, but firmly. "Captain Garfield's standing orders. We can't afford to take any chances, sir. After all, you could be partisans disguised as Blackshirts for all we know."

"Fair enough, Corporal," Johnson conceded grudgingly. He did as he was asked and handed over the papers. After a cursory examination he was granted permission to enter the Keep. "About bloody time,"he grumbled under his breath.

Johnson never saw the blow that felled him. "Timber!" Jones said with a smile. Chester followed his master through the main entrance and was promptly knocked out as well. Jones stood over his captives like a big game hunter admiring his kills. "That's bought us at least another five minutes and possibly more. It will take that long for the Fascists to figure out what's happened and decide what they should do next." Jones looked at his watch: it was five minutes past three.

"How long has Captain Johnson been inside, sir?" Sergeant Plows asked.

Second-Lieutenant Chris Lucas looked at the luminous dials of his watch. "Only a few minutes, Sergeant."

"How much longer are we going to give him, sir?"

Lucas looked down from the turret of the armoured car. "What do you mean, Sergeant?" he asked with furrowed brows. "I'm afraid that I don't understand your question."

Plows stepped closer to the vehicle so that none of the other Blackshirts could over hear their conversation. "What I mean, sir, is that something's not right. I feel exactly the same as I did before the Reds jumped us at Cable Street-something's wrong."

"Listen, Sergeant," Lucas said with the voice of reason, "I have no doubt that Captain Garfield is giving Captain Johnson a situation report as we speak and they are probably discussing the best method to carry out a casualty evacuation of the Leader. After all, I understand that he has been wounded. I'm sure that everything is perfectly in order, Sergeant Plows," Lucas smiled condescendingly.

"I'm afraid that I don't share your confidence, sir," Plows said with persistence. "Something stinks. I can feel it in my bones."

Lucas thought for a moment before he spoke. "I tell you what, Sergeant. In order to allay your fears and put your suspicions to rest, at ten past three you can go to the Keep and find out what is causing the hold up. I can't say fairer than that, Sergeant. What do you say?"

Plow's teeth flashed white in the darkness. "Sounds like a plan, sir."

Jones rested his thumb on his safety catch as he watched the solitary figure emerge from the darkness. He looked at his watch and smiled. "Ten past three. Right on cue." When the lone Blackshirt reached the Keep, Jones abruptly pulled the door open and pointed his pistol straight at Plow's nose. "Listen very carefully, Sergeant; I will say this only once."

"Yes - yes, sir," the startled Plows replied.

"I want you to park your lorry with the tail gate facing the door right here." Jones used his hands to indicate where he wanted the vehicle to be positioned.

"I ... I'll have to clear these instructions with my superior officer, sir."

Jones shook his head. "You don't have time, Sergeant. I'll give you exactly three minutes to get your lorry into position. I will execute one hostage for every minute that you are late. I'll work my way through Captain Garfield and his bodyguard, then Private Chester and Captain Johnson and then finally your beloved Leader himself. I'm sure that you don't want Joyce's death on your conscience, do you?"

"No ... no, sir," Plows stuttered.

"I thought so," Jones nodded. "I want you to drive the vehicle yourself. Stay in the cab with your hands on the wheel and don't get out. Clear?"

"Yes, sir."

"Needless to say, you'll be unarmed. If I find that you're hiding a weapon then I'll kill you without hesitation. Do you understand, Sergeant?"

"Yes, sir."

"Good." Jones looked at his watch. "It's almost twelve minutes past three. You have until a quarter past three to get your lorry into position. Move!"

"Now, Sergeant Plows, you know fine well that it's government policy not to negotiate with terrorists," Lucas quoted the official Fascist Party line.

"But, sir," Plows protested, "if we don't follow their orders the Reds will execute the hostages!"

"We can't give in to Bolshevik terrorists, Sergeant." Lucas said stubbornly. He was absolutely determined to stick to his guns. "If we give in to them once then they'll do it again and again and they'll be no stopping them."

351

Plows looked at his watch with alarm. "Sir, we're rapidly running out of time," he warned. "It's almost a quarter past three. You may be prepared to gamble with Captain Johnson's life, but I'm not." Plows started to walk towards the lorry.

"Sergeant Plows!" Lucas barked as he blocked Plow's path. "I'm in command here, I call the shots and I make the decisions! We don't negotiate with terrorists and that's final. We're going to assault the enemy position and rescue the hostages."

"But sir - !"

"That's enough, Sergeant!" Lucas snarled as he pointed his revolver at Plow's face. "You will stand down! That's a direct order and I will execute you if you continue to disobey and defy me! The only way that those dirty Jew lovers will get their stinking hands on my lorry is over my dead body - !"

A rapid burst of machine gun fire made the two men instinctively duck and take cover behind the armoured car. The Keep door opened and a voice shouted, "You're late, Sergeant!" Plows watched with open-mouthed horror as a body was unceremoniously dumped outside the door like a sack of potatoes. A red mist of rage and raw hatred descended like a veil over his eyes.

"Now wait a minute, Sergeant;" Lucas protested. "How was I to know that - ?"

Two shots cut Lucas off before he could finish his sentence. The officer fell to the ground with a look of utter shock and surprise on his pale face.

"Would anyone else care to disagree with my decision to hand the lorry over to the Reds?" Plows asked as smoke coiled out of the barrel of his revolver.

None of the other Blackshirts so much as blinked.

"I didn't think so," Plows said as he stepped over Lucas' dead body. "Having two weapons pointed in my face in one evening is quite enough."

Plows tried to use his side mirrors to watch as the partisans loaded something onto the back of the lorry. However, it was a complete waste of time as it was pitch black and the angle was so awkward that it would have been virtually impossible to see even in broad daylight.

Presently a face appeared at his window. "Listen in, Sergeant. We've loaded all of the wounded onto your lorry. Some of the injured men are mine and some of them are yours, but they are all wearing Blackshirt uniforms. I want you to drive to a certain address where you will be met by the Resistance. The guerrillas will be able to see you, but you won't be able to see them. Once they've removed our wounded they will contact me here at the Keep and I will release all of the hostages apart from Joyce."

"How do I know that you'll keep your end of the deal?" Plows asked.

"You don't," Jones answered bluntly. "However, I give you my word as an officer and a gentleman that as soon as my comrades inform me that my wounded are in safe hands the prisoners will be set free."

Plows nodded. "That's good enough for me, sir. And what of my wounded?"

"The partisans will leave them with you to do with as you will."

"Thank you, sir."

Jones bowed graciously. "If you play me true tonight them there's a good chance that you and the rest of your men will live to see another day. However, if you play me false then I promise you that you and all your men will be dead by sunrise. Do I make myself clear?"

"Crystal clear, sir."

"Oh yes. One more thing."

"Yes, sir?"

"Before you drive away I want you to order the crew of your armoured car to disembark and join the rest of the platoon. The armoured car is not to follow you."

"Yes, sir." Plows walked away to give his men their instructions. When he returned Jones told him where he was to rendezvous with the partisans.

Plows had been standing with his hands on top of his head for half an hour before he turned around. He was momentarily blinded by the glare of his lorry's headlights and cursed as he lost his night vision. He slowly lowered his arms and looked at his watch. The sergeant had left the Keep at three twenty five and he had arrived at the burnt out ruins of "The Laughing Cavalier" pub next to Ely railway station at five to four. It was now twenty past four.

The sergeant walked to the rear of the lorry and lowered the tailgate. He took a torch from a pouch on his webbing belt and shined it into the back of the vehicle. Plows counted six Blackshirts. He shook his head. They might have been alive when the partisans had loaded them into the lorry, but they were now very much dead. There was still absolutely no sign of the Resistance.

By the time that Plows realised that the guerrillas were not coming, both Ansett and Jones had arrived safe and sound back at the Farm. Jones had pulled out his team as soon as the Blackshirt sergeant had driven away from the Keep. It had taken the commandoes less than ten minutes to run through the tunnel under the Square to the Crypt and rendezvous with Ansett in the Bishop's house. After an emotional, if brief reunion, the partisans had piled onto their lorry and had driven in the pitch-blackness back to Headquarters. The returning heroes were greeted with an avalanche of manly handshakes, rib crushing bear hugs and tear stained wet kisses of congratulations and relief at a job well done. Ansett was pleased to discover that the guerrillas that had remained at the Farm had followed his instructions to the letter and had positioned the beacons accurately. The bonfires were lit at a quarter past four, the Lysander landed at half past four and after the partisans had unloaded the supplies and loaded Joyce, the biplane took off at exactly a quarter to five. The pilot landed back in Edinburgh in time for his porridge.

At half past four, Plows finally realised that the guerrillas were not coming and drove back to Hereward. The sergeant told the armoured car crew to remount their vehicle and he ordered one section of Blackshirts to search for an alternative entrance to the castle. Much to Plows's surprise, his men soon reported back that they had discovered an open door that led to the kitchen. The sergeant cautiously led his Militiamen into the Keep and found Private Chester and Captain Johnson lying semiconscious in the dining room, trussed up like chickens. Plows checked the two men for injuries and was relieved to discover that, apart from feeling groggy and disorientated, Chester and Johnson appeared to be none the worse for wear. The partisan captain had, indeed, kept his word to spare the hostages. By the time that Plows had arrived at the Keep, Joyce had already left English soil and was flying on his way up north to Scotland.

Joyce nearly had a heart attack when he woke up and realised that instead of being safely tucked up in bed in Buckingham Palace, he was chained to a bed in Edinburgh Castle. He spent two weeks recuperating and recovering until he was fit and well enough to stand trial. He was tried on three counts of high treason:-

1. William Joyce, on the 18th of September 1939, and on other days between that day and the 27th September 1940, being a person owing allegiance to our Lord the King, and while the German Realm against our King was carrying on a war, did traitorously adhere to the King's enemies in Germany, by broadcasting propaganda.

2. William Joyce, on the 26th of September, 1940, and on other days between that day and the 27th September, 1940, being a person owing allegiance to our Lord the King, and while a war was being carried on by the German Realm against our King, did traitorously adhere to the King's enemies in Germany, by purporting to become a naturalized subject of Germany.

3. William Joyce, on the 27th of September, 1940, and on other days between that day and the 28th September, 1941, being a person owing allegiance to our Lord the King, and while a war was being carried on by the German Realm against our King, did traitorously adhere to the King's enemies in Germany, by serving in the puppet Government of National Unity.

Joyce was found guilty on all three counts and was executed on the 5th of November 1941. His body was cremated and his ashes were scattered in the Firth of Forth.

Remember, remember the fifth of November,
Gunpowder, treason and plot.
I see no reason why gunpowder treason
Should ever be forgot.

The message that the British Government in Edinburgh sent was very clear: the only fitting punishment for traitors was death.

THE END.